VOLUME THE FIRST

THE JANE AUSTEN LIBRARY

The Jane Austen Library has been established
to make available rare or otherwise
unavailable editions of the novelist's work and
of the most important biographical and
critical studies. In particular, the Library will
include the authoritative texts of the juvenilia
and other smaller works and unfinished
manuscripts originally prepared by
Dr R W Chapman and issued by The Clarendon
Press. All the volumes in the Library will
carry a new Preface by Brian Southam and a
Series Foreword by Lord David Cecil.

THE JANE AUSTEN LIBRARY

VOLUME THE FIRST

Jane Austen

Edited by R. W. Chapman

SCHOCKEN BOOKS
NEW YORK

First American edition published by
Schocken Books 1985
10 9 8 7 6 5 4 3 2 1   85 86 87 88
Copyright © Publisher's Preface and Foreword
The Athlone Press 1984
All rights reserved
Published by agreement with
The Athlone Press Limited, London

Library of Congress Cataloging in Publication Data
Austen, Jane, 1775-1817.
Volume the first.
(The Jane Austen Library; v. 2)
1. Children's writings, English. I. Chapman,
R. W. (Robert William), 1881-1960. II. Title.
III. Series.
PR4032.C58 1984 823'.7 84-5535

This reprint has been authorized by the
Oxford University Press. Reprinted from the Clarendon Press
edition 1925 by permission of the Oxford University Press.

Manufactured in Great Britain
ISBN 0-8052-3937-5

CONTENTS

FOREWORD
by Lord David Cecil

Jane Austen does not seem to have taken either her works or herself over seriously. Certainly she showed no signs that they would be of interest to posterity. Yet now, after 150 years, she is one of the most popular of our classical novelists; moreover interest in her novels has begun to extend into interest in her. People want to know as much about her as they can, both as a writer and as a woman. The purpose of this Library is to do something to satisfy this want.

To take the writer first: the Library will include those of her writings that were not published in her lifetime; the skits and sketches she wrote as a child, already revealing her unique characteristic humour and turn of phrase; her

one unpublished novel *Lady Susan;* the
two books that she never finished *The
Watsons, Sanditon;* also the last chapters of *Persuasion* in their first, afterwards
discarded, form. All these in their different ways tell us much about her methods
of work and her judgement as to when
she thought she had succeeded and
failed.

Next the woman. In this section we will
find descriptions of her by people who
knew her, in particular her nephews and
nieces; she was the most delightful and
loved of aunts. There will also be accounts of places she knew well, like
Bath and Lyme Regis, and her relation
to them.

The final section will consist of selected
biographical and critical studies of her
and her work by authorities in the subject.

The Library as a whole should expand
and enrich our picture of Jane Austen,
woman and novelist. A homogeneous

picture; for the more we learn about her the more we discover that unlike many authors, the novelist and woman are of a piece. Knowledge of one throws light on knowledge of the other; and increases our delight in them both.

PREFACE
by Brian Southam

Volume the First is a manuscript notebook collecting some of Jane Austen's
earliest childhood writings, probably
dating from about 1787, when she was a
girl of 12, up to about June 1793 (as 'Ode
to Pity' is dated).

These pieces are not originals but tran-
scriptions which Jane Austen made later,
when she was compiling a record of her
early work for the convenience of reading aloud to the family and her close
friends. The intimate, *family* nature of
these little literary and personal jokes is
indicated in Dr Chapman's Preface,
where he records the words written
inside the cover of the notebook by
Cassandra, recollecting—doubtless for

the sake of later generations—that 'a few of the trifles in this Vol: were written expressly for' the 'amusement' of her brother Charles.

Trifles indeed they are. But it is in this mood of lightness and youthful gaiety that we catch a glimpse of Jane Austen's sense of fun, the sharpness of her wit and the unerring accuracy and deadly skill with which she impaled and parodied contemporary styles of fiction, drama and verse. Here, we can see the literary excursions of an observant and essentially critical genius, the other face to the creative genius, which came to maturity in the six novels.

PREFACE

In *my edition*[1] *of the* Memoir *of Jane Austen by her nephew James Edward Austen-Leigh I gave in an introduction the following account of her most youthful writings.*[2]

'*Jane Austen is believed to have left three volumes of* Juvenilia. *One of these, the second, is the property of Mrs. Sanders, grand-daughter of Sir Francis Austen, by whose authority it was published, as* Love and Freindship, *in* 1922.[3] *The third volume, which I have seen, is dated* 1792. *It contains a short skit, and the opening chapters of a tale.*[4] *The first volume, which seems not to have been traced, was perhaps the source of the dramatic fragment printed in the* Memoir.[5]

'*A collection is also extant, written in a later generation, of pieces "from Miss Austen's*

---

[1] Oxford, 1926. [2] She was born on Dec. 16th, 1775.
[3] Chatto and Windus.
[4] *Evelyn* and *Kitty or the Bower.* See *Life and Letters* (by W. and R. A. Austen-Leigh, 1913), pp. 55–6.
[5] Chapter III (p. 45 of my edition).

*writings". One of these is dedicated to Jane Anna
Elizabeth Austen (afterwards Mrs. Ben Lefroy) in
the year of her birth, by her "very affectionate
aunt"; another to "Mr. Francis William Austen,
Midshipman on board his Majesty's ship the
Perseverance"; a third to Miss Austen (i.e. Cassandra).'[1]*

*The first volume has now been found, and
has been acquired by the Friends of the
Bodleian. It is a notebook measuring $8 \times 6\frac{1}{4}$
inches, bound in marbled boards, with a
leather back, and entitled on the front cover*

VOLUME THE FIRST

*It contains 92 leaves, the first two unnum-
bered, the rest paged 1–180. The watermarks
are undated, and the only dates in the manuscript are 'June 2^d 1793' (p. 173) and, at
the end, 'End of the first Volume June 3^d
1793'. But further indications of date are
supplied by the dedication to 'Miss Cooper',
who became Jane Williams in December
1792, and by the dedications to Francis*

---

[1] For further details see *Life and Letters*, p. 57.

Austen, 'Midshipman on board his Majesty's Ship the Perseverance'; for Francis left the Perseverance *in November* 1791.[1] *The author is nowhere named. The handwriting, which in most of the book is somewhat large and not completely formed, becomes smaller and more mature towards the end, and in the concluding pages is not unlike the hand which wrote* THE WATSONS *not earlier than* 1803.

Inside the front cover is written in pencil —doubtless in Jane Austen's hand (certainly not in that of her sister Cassandra):

For my Brother Charles

Just below is pasted a scrap of paper on which Cassandra has written:

For
my Brother Charles
I think I recollect that a few of the trifles in this Vol: were written expressly for his amusement
C. E. A.

[1] This date comes from a memorandum in the Admiral's hand, communicated to me by his grandson.

The discovery of the lost volume confirms the conjecture that it was the source of the dramatic fragment (THE MYSTERY) printed in the MEMOIR. It was the source also of the collection mentioned above.

The dates given in the Second Volume[1] are June 13th, 1790 (to LOVE AND FREIND-SHIP), and Nov. 26th, 1791 (to the HISTORY OF ENGLAND). The only date in the Third Volume recorded in the LIFE AND LETTERS is August 1792. The dates, therefore, show that these volumes were not written in chronological order, though that may be approximately the order of their contents. The three volumes clearly form a collected edition of the author's works up to June 1793, and must have been transcribed from lost originals.

The text does not show much sign of revision, but certain passages have been expunged. These have been deciphered, and

---

[1] I rely on *Love and Freindship* as printed.

are printed within brackets. Other corrections are ignored.

It will always be disputed whether such effusions as these ought to be published; and it may be that we have enough already of Jane Austen's early scraps. The author of the MEMOIR thought a very brief specimen sufficient. But perhaps the question is hardly worth discussion. For if such manuscripts find their way into great libraries, their publication can hardly be prevented. The only sure way to prevent it is the way of destruction, which no one dare take.

R. W. C.

VOLUME THE FIRST

To Miss Lloyd

MY DEAR MARTHA

As a small testimony of the gratitude I feel for your late generosity to me in finishing my muslin Cloak, I beg leave to offer you this little production of your sincere Freind

THE AUTHOR

FREDERIC & ELFRIDA

A NOVEL

CHAPTER THE FIRST

THE Uncle of Elfrida was the Father of Frederic; in other words, they were first cousins by the Father's side.

Being both born in one day & both brought up at one school, it was not wonderfull that they should look on each other with something more than bare politeness. They loved with mutual sincerity but were both determined not to transgress the rules of Propriety by owning their attachment, either to the object beloved, or to any one else.

They were exceedingly handsome and so much alike, that it was not every one who knew them apart. Nay even their most intimate freinds had nothing to distinguish them by, but the shape of the face, the
                                    colour

colour of the Eye, the length of the Nose & the difference of the complexion.

Elfrida had an intimate freind to whom, being on a visit to an Aunt, she wrote the following Letter.

TO MISS DRUMMOND

DEAR CHARLOTTE

I should be obliged to you, if you would buy me, during your stay with Mrs Williamson, a new & fashionable Bonnet, to suit the complexion of your

E. FALKNOR

Charlotte, whose character was a willingness to oblige every one, when she returned into the Country, brought her Freind the wished-for Bonnet, & so ended this little adventure, much to the satisfaction of all parties.

On her return to Crankhumdunberry (of which sweet village her father was Rector) Charlotte was received with the greatest Joy by Frederic & Elfrida, who, after pressing

her

her alternately to their Bosoms, proposed to her to take a walk in a Grove of Poplars which led from the Parsonage to a verdant Lawn enamelled with a variety of variegated flowers & watered by a purling Stream, brought from the Valley of Tempé by a passage under ground.

In this Grove they had scarcely remained above 9 hours, when they were suddenly agreably surprized by hearing a most delightfull voice warble the following stanza.

SONG

That Damon was in love with me
I once thought & beleiv'd
But now that he is not I see,
I fear I was deceiv'd.

═══

No sooner were the lines finished than they beheld by a turning in the Grove 2 elegant young women leaning on each other's arm, who immediately on perceiving them, took a different path & disappeared from their sight.

CHAPTER

CHAPTER THE SECOND

As Elfrida & her companions, had seen enough
of them to know that they were neither the
2 Miss Greens, nor Mrs Jackson and her
Daughter, they could not help expressing
their surprise at their appearance; till at
length recollecting, that a new family had
lately taken a House not far from the Grove,
they hastened home, determined to lose no
time in forming an acquaintance with 2 such
amiable & worthy Girls, of which family they
rightly imagined them to be a part.

Agreable to such a determination, they
went that very evening to pay their respects
to Mrs Fitzroy & her two Daughters. On
being shewn into an elegant dressing room,
ornamented with festoons of artificial flowers,
they were struck with the engaging Exterior
& beautifull outside of Jezalinda the eldest
of the young Ladies; but e'er they had been
many minutes seated, the Wit & Charms
which shone resplendent in the conversation
of

of the amiable Rebecca, enchanted them so much that they all with one accord jumped up and exclaimed.

"Lovely & too charming Fair one, notwithstanding your forbidding Squint, your greazy tresses & your swelling Back, which are more frightfull than imagination can paint or pen describe, I cannot refrain from expressing my raptures, at the engaging Qualities of your Mind, which so amply atone for the Horror, with which your first appearance must ever inspire the unwary visitor."

"Your sentiments so nobly expressed on the different excellencies of Indian & English Muslins, & the judicious preference you give the former, have excited in me an admiration of which I can alone give an adequate idea, by assuring you it is nearly equal to what I feel for myself."

Then making a profound Curtesy to the amiable & abashed Rebecca, they left the room & hurried home.

From this period, the intimacy between

c   the

the Families of Fitzroy, Drummond, and Falknor, daily increased till at length it grew to such a pitch, that they did not scruple to kick one another out of the window on the slightest provocation.

During this happy state of Harmony, the eldest Miss Fitzroy ran off with the Coachman & the amiable Rebecca was asked in marriage by Captain Roger of Buckinghamshire.

Mrs Fitzroy did not approve of the match on account of the tender years of the young couple, Rebecca being but 36 & Captain Roger little more than 63. To remedy this objection, it was agreed that they should wait a little while till they were a good deal older.

CHAPTER THE THIRD

In the mean time the parents of Frederic proposed to those of Elfrida, an union between them, which being accepted with pleasure, the wedding cloathes were bought & nothing

nothing remained to be settled but the naming of the Day.

As to the lovely Charlotte, being importuned with eagerness to pay another visit to her Aunt, she determined to accept the invitation & in consequence of it walked to Mrs Fitzroys to take leave of the amiable Rebecca, whom she found surrounded by Patches, Powder, Pomatum & Paint with which she was vainly endeavouring to remedy the natural plainness of her face.

"I am come my amiable Rebecca, to take my leave of you for the fortnight I am destined to spend with my aunt. Beleive me this separation is painfull to me, but it is as necessary as the labour which now engages you."

"Why to tell you the truth my Love, replied Rebecca, I have lately taken it into my head to think (perhaps with little reason) that my complexion is by no means equal to the rest of my face & have therefore taken, as you see, to white & red paint which I would scorn to use on any other occasion as I hate art."

Charlotte

Charlotte, who perfectly understood the meaning of her freind's speech, was too good-temper'd & obliging to refuse her, what she knew she wished,—a compliment; & they parted the best freinds in the world.

With a heavy heart & streaming Eyes did she ascend the lovely vehicle[1] which bore her from her freinds & home; but greived as she was, she little thought in what a strange & different manner she should return to it.

On her entrance into the city of London which was the place of Mrs Williamson's abode, the postilion, whose stupidity was amazing, declared & declared even without the least shame or Compunction, that having never been informed he was totally ignorant of what part of the Town, he was to drive to.

Charlotte, whose nature we have before intimated, was an earnest desire to oblige every one, with the greatest Condescension & Goodhumour informed him that he was to drive to Portland Place, which he accordingly

[1] a post-chaise.

did

did & Charlotte soon found herself in the arms of a fond Aunt.

Scarcely were they seated as usual, in the most affectionate manner in one chair, than the Door suddenly opened & an aged gentleman with a sallow face & old pink Coat, partly by intention & partly thro' weakness was at the feet of the lovely Charlotte, declaring his attachment to her & beseeching her pity in the most moving manner.

Not being able to resolve to make any one miserable, she consented to become his wife; where upon the Gentleman left the room & all was quiet.

Their quiet however continued but a short time, for on a second opening of the door a young & Handsome Gentleman with a new blue coat, entered & intreated from the lovely Charlotte, permission to pay to her, his addresses.

There was a something in the appearance of the second Stranger, that influenced Charlotte in his favour, to the full as much as the
appearance

appearance of the first: she could not account for it, but so it was.

Having therefore agreable to that & the natural turn of her mind to make every one happy, promised to become his Wife the next morning, he took his leave & the two Ladies sat down to Supper on a young Leveret, a brace of Partridges, a leash of Pheasants & a Dozen of Pigeons.

CHAPTER THE FOURTH

It was not till the next morning that Charlotte recollected the double engagement she had entered into; but when she did, the reflection of her past folly, operated so strongly on her mind, that she resolved to be guilty of a greater, & to that end threw herself into a deep stream which ran thro' her Aunt's pleasure Grounds in Portland Place.

She floated to Crankhumdunberry where she was picked up & buried; the following epitaph, composed by Frederic Elfrida & Rebecca, was placed on her tomb.

EPITAPH

EPITAPH

Here lies our friend who having promis-ed
That unto two she would be marri-ed
Threw her sweet Body & her lovely face
Into the Stream that runs thro' Portland Place.

———

These sweet lines, as pathetic as beautifull were never read by any one who passed that way, without a shower of tears, which if they should fail of exciting in you, Reader, your mind must be unworthy to peruse them.

Having performed the last sad office to their departed freind, Frederic & Elfrida together with Captain Roger & Rebecca returned to Mrs Fitzroy's at whose feet they threw themselves with one accord & addressed her in the following Manner.

"Madam"

"When the sweet Captain Roger first addressed the amiable Rebecca, you alone objected to their union on account of the tender years of the Parties. That plea can be no more, seven days being now expired, together with

with the lovely Charlotte, since the Captain first spoke to you on the subject."

"Consent then Madam to their union & as a reward, this smelling Bottle which I enclose in my right hand, shall be yours & yours forever; I never will claim it again. But if you refuse to join their hands in 3 days time, this dagger which I enclose in my left shall be steeped in your hearts blood."

"Speak then Madam & decide their fate & yours."

Such gentle & sweet persuasion could not fail of having the desired effect. The answer they received, was this.

"My dear young freinds"

"The arguments you have used are too just & too eloquent to be withstood; Rebecca in 3 days time, you shall be united to the Captain."

This speech, than which nothing could be more satisfactory, was received with Joy by all; & peace being once more restored on all sides, Captain Roger intreated Rebecca to favour

favour them with a Song, in compliance with which request having first assured them that she had a terrible cold, she sung as follows.

SONG

When Corydon went to the fair
  He bought a red ribbon for Bess,
With which she encircled her hair
  & made herself look very fess.

―――
―――

CHAPTER THE FIFTH

―――
―――

AT the end of 3 days Captain Roger and Rebecca were united and immediately after the Ceremony set off in the Stage Waggon for the Captains seat in Buckinghamshire.

The parents of Elfrida, alltho' they earnestly wished to see her married to Frederic before they died, yet knowing the delicate frame of her mind could ill bear the least exertion & rightly judging that naming her wedding day would be too great a one, forebore to press her on the subject.

Weeks & Fortnights flew away without

D   gaining

gaining the least ground; the Cloathes grew out of fashion & at length Capt: Roger & his Lady arrived, to pay a visit to their Mother & introduce to her their beautifull Daughter of eighteen.

Elfrida, who had found her former acquaintance were growing too old & too ugly to be any longer agreable, was rejoiced to hear of the arrival of so pretty a girl as Eleanor with whom she determined to form the strictest freindship.

But the Happiness she had expected from an acquaintance with Eleanor, she soon found was not to be received, for she had not only the mortification of finding herself treated by her as little less than an old woman, but had actually the horror of perceiving a growing passion in the Bosom of Frederic for the Daughter of the amiable Rebecca.

The instant she had the first idea of such an attachment, she flew to Frederic & in a manner truly heroick, spluttered out to him her intention of being married the next Day.

To one in his predicament who possessed
less

less personal Courage than Frederic was master of, such a speech would have been Death; but he not being the least terrified boldly replied.

"Damme Elfrida *you* may be married to-morrow but *I* wont."

This answer distressed her too much for her delicate Constitution. She accordingly fainted & was in such a hurry to have a succession of fainting fits, that she had scarcely patience enough to recover from one before she fell into another.

Tho', in any threatening Danger to his Life or Liberty, Frederic was as bold as brass yet in other respects his heart was as soft as cotton & immediately on hearing of the dangerous way Elfrida was in, he flew to her & finding her better than he had been taught to expect, was united to her Forever—.

FINIS

JACK

JACK & ALICE

A NOVEL

Is respectfully inscribed to Francis William Austen Esqr Midshipman on board his Majesty's Ship the Perseverance by his obedient humble Servant The Author

---

CHAPTER THE FIRST

MR JOHNSON was once upon a time about 53; in a twelvemonth afterwards he was 54, which so much delighted him that he was determined to celebrate his next Birthday by giving a Masquerade to his Children & Freinds. Accordingly on the Day he attained his 55th year tickets were dispatched to all his Neighbours to that purpose. His acquaintance indeed in that part of the World were not very numerous as they consisted only of Lady Williams, Mr & Mrs Jones, Charles Adams

Adams & the 3 Miss Simpsons, who composed the neighbourhood of Pammydiddle & formed the Masquerade.

Before I proceed to give an account of the Evening, it will be proper to describe to my reader, the persons and Characters of the party introduced to his acquaintance.

Mr & Mrs Jones were both rather tall & very passionate, but were in other respects, goodtempered, wellbehaved People. Charles Adams was an amiable, accomplished & bewitching young Man, of so dazzling a Beauty that none but Eagles could look him in the Face.

Miss Simpson was pleasing in her person, in her Manners & in her Disposition; an unbounded ambition was her only fault. Her second sister Sukey was Envious, Spitefull & Malicious. Her person was short, fat & disagreable. Cecilia (the youngest) was perfectly handsome but too affected to be pleasing.

In Lady Williams every virtue met. She was a widow with a handsome Jointure & the remains of a very handsome face. Tho'
                                    Benevolent

Benevolent & Candid, she was Generous & sincere; Tho' Pious & Good, she was Religious & amiable, & Tho' Elegant & Agreable, she was Polished & Entertaining.

The Johnsons were a family of Love, & though a little addicted to the Bottle & the Dice, had many good Qualities.

Such was the party assembled in the elegant Drawing Room of Johnson Court, amongst which the pleasing figure of a Sultana was the most remarkable of the female Masks. Of the Males a Mask representing the Sun, was the most universally admired. The Beams that darted from his Eyes were like those of that glorious Luminary tho' infinitely superior. So strong were they that no one dared venture within half a mile of them; he had therefore the best part of the Room to himself, its size not amounting to more than 3 quarters of a mile in length & half a one in breadth. The Gentleman at last finding the feirceness of his beams to be very inconvenient to the concourse by obliging them to croud together in one corner of the

room

room, half shut his eyes by which means, the Company discovered him to be Charles Adams in his plain green Coat, without any mask at all.

When their astonishment was a little sub-sided their attention was attracted by 2 Domino's who advanced in a horrible Pas-sion; they were both very tall, but seemed in other respects to have many good quali-ties. "These said the witty Charles, these are Mr & Mrs Jones" and so indeed they were.

No one could imagine who was the Sultana! Till at length on her addressing a beautifull Flora who was reclining in a studied attitude on a couch, with "Oh Cecilia, I wish I was really what I pretend to be", she was dis-covered by the never failing genius of Charles Adams, to be the elegant but ambitious Caro-line Simpson, & the person to whom she addressed herself, he rightly imagined to be her lovely but affected sister Cecilia.

The Company now advanced to a Gaming Table where sat 3 Dominos (each with a bottle

bottle in their hand) deeply engaged: but a
female in the character of Virtue fled with
hasty footsteps from the shocking scene,
whilst a little fat woman representing Envy,
sate alternately on the foreheads of the 3
Gamesters. Charles Adams was still as bright
as ever; he soon discovered the party at play
to be the 3 Johnsons, Envy to be Sukey
Simpson & Virtue to be Lady Williams.

The Masks were then all removed & the
Company retired to another room, to par-
take of an elegant & wellmanaged Entertainment, after which the Bottle being pretty
briskly pushed about by the 3 Johnsons, the
whole party not excepting even Virtue were
carried home, Dead Drunk.

CHAPTER THE SECOND

FOR three months did the Masquerade afford
ample subject for conversation to the inhabitants of Pammydiddle; but no character
at it was so fully expatiated on as Charles
Adams

Adams. The singularity of his appearance, the beams which darted from his eyes, the brightness of his Wit, & the whole *tout ensemble* of his person had subdued the hearts of so many of the young Ladies, that of the six present at the Masquerade but five had returned uncaptivated. Alice Johnson was the unhappy sixth whose heart had not been able to withstand the power of his Charms. But as it may appear strange to my Readers, that so much worth & Excellence as he possessed should have conquered only hers, it will be necessary to inform them that the Miss Simpsons were defended from his Power by Ambition, Envy, & Selfadmiration.

Every wish of Caroline was centered in a titled Husband; whilst in Sukey such superior excellence could only raise her Envy not her Love, & Cecilia was too tenderly attached to herself to be pleased with any one besides. As for Lady Williams and Mrs Jones, the former of them was too sensible, to fall in love with one so much her Junior & and the latter, tho' very tall & very

E   passionate

passionate was too fond of her Husband to think of such a thing.

Yet in spite of every endeavour on the part of Miss Johnson to discover any attachment to her in him, the cold & indifferent heart of Charles Adams still to all appearance, preserved its native freedom; polite to all but partial to none, he still remained the lovely, the lively, but insensible Charles Adams.

One evening, Alice finding herself somewhat heated by wine (no very uncommon case) determined to seek a relief for her disordered Head & Love-sick Heart in the Conversation of the intelligent Lady Williams.

She found her Ladyship at home as was in general the Case, for she was not fond of going out, & like the great Sir Charles Grandison scorned to deny herself when at Home, as she looked on that fashionable method of shutting out disagreable Visitors, as little less than downright Bigamy.

In spite of the wine she had been drinking,
poor

poor Alice was uncommonly out of spirits; she could think of nothing but Charles Adams, she could talk of nothing but him, & in short spoke so openly that Lady Williams soon discovered the unreturned affection she bore him, which excited her Pity & Compassion so strongly that she addressed her in the following Manner.

"I perceive but too plainly my dear Miss Johnson, that your Heart has not been able to withstand the fascinating Charms of this young Man & I pity you sincerely. Is it a first Love?"

"It is."

"I am still more greived to hear *that*; I am myself a sad example of the Miseries, in general attendant on a first Love & I am determined for the future to avoid the like Misfortune. I wish it may not be too late for you to do the same; if it is not endeavour my dear Girl to secure yourself from so great a Danger. A second attachment is seldom attended with any serious consequences; against *that* therefore I have nothing to say.

Preserve

Preserve yourself from a first Love & you need not fear a second."

"You mentioned Madam something of your having yourself been a sufferer by the misfortune you are so good as to wish me to avoid. Will you favour me with your Life & Adventures?"

"Willingly my Love."

CHAPTER THE THIRD

"My Father was a gentleman of considerable Fortune in Berkshire; myself & a few more his only Children. I was but six years old when I had the misfortune of losing my Mother & being at that time young & Tender, my father instead of sending me to School, procured an able handed Governess to superintend my Education at Home. My Brothers were placed at Schools suitable to their Ages & my Sisters being all younger than myself, remained still under the Care of their Nurse.

Miss Dickins was an excellent Governess. She

She instructed me in the Paths of Virtue; under her tuition I daily became more amiable, & might perhaps by this time have nearly attained perfection, had not my worthy Preceptoress been torn from my arms, e'er I had attained my seventeenth year. I never shall forget her last words. 'My dear Kitty she said Good nightt'ye.' I never saw her afterwards" continued Lady Williams wiping her eyes, "She eloped with the Butler the same night".

"I was invited the following year by a distant relation of my Father's to spend the Winter with her in town. Mrs. Watkins was a Lady of Fashion, Family & fortune; she was in general esteemed a pretty Woman, but I never thought her very handsome, for my part. She had too high a forehead, Her eyes were too small & she had too much colour."

"How can *that* be?" interrupted Miss Johnson reddening with anger; "Do you think that any one can have too much colour?"

"Indeed

"Indeed I do, & I'll tell you why I do my dear Alice; when a person has too great a degree of red in their Complexion, it gives their face in my opinion, too red a look."

"But can a face my Lady have too red a look?"

"Certainly my dear Miss Johnson & I'll tell you why. When a face has too red a look it does not appear to so much advantage as it would were it paler."

"Pray Ma'am proceed in your story."

"Well, as I said before, I was invited by this Lady to spend some weeks with her in town. Many Gentlemen thought her Handsome but in my opinion, Her forehead was too high, her eyes too small & she had too much colour."

"In that Madam as I said before your Ladyship must have been mistaken. Mrs. Watkins could not have too much colour since no one can have too much.'

"Excuse me my Love if I do not agree with you in that particular. Let me explain myself clearly; my idea of the case is this.
                                    When

When a Woman has too great a proportion of red in her Cheeks, she must have too much colour.'

"But Madam I deny that it is possible for any one to have too great a proportion of red in their Cheeks.'

"What my Love not if they have too much colour?"

Miss Johnson was now out of all patience, the more so perhaps as Lady Williams still remained so inflexibly cool. It must be remembered however that her Ladyship had in one respect by far the advantage of Alice; I mean in not being drunk, for heated with wine & raised by Passion, she could have little command of her Temper.

The Dispute at length grew so hot on the part of Alice that "From Words she almost came to Blows" When Mr Johnson luckily entered & with some difficulty forced her away from Lady Williams, Mrs Watkins & her red cheeks.

CHAPTER

CHAPTER THE FOURTH

My Readers may perhaps imagine that after such a fracas, no intimacy could longer subsist between the Johnsons and Lady Williams, but in that they are mistaken for her Ladyship was too sensible to be angry at a conduct which she could not help perceiving to be the natural consequence of inebriety & Alice had too sincere a respect for Lady Williams & too great a relish for her Claret, not to make every concession in her power.

A few days after their reconciliation Lady Williams called on Miss Johnson to propose a walk in a Citron Grove which led from her Ladyship's pigstye to Charles Adams's Horsepond. Alice was too sensible of Lady Williams's kindness in proposing such a walk & too much pleased with the prospect of seeing at the end of it, a Horsepond of Charles's, not to accept it with visible delight. They had not proceeded far before she was roused from the reflection of the happiness

happiness she was going to enjoy, by Lady Williams's thus addressing her.

"I have as yet forborn my dear Alice to continue the narrative of my Life from an unwillingness of recalling to your Memory a scene which (since it reflects on you rather disgrace than credit) had better be forgot than remembered."

Alice had already begun to colour up & was beginning to speak, when her Ladyship perceiving her displeasure, continued thus.

"I am afraid my dear Girl that I have offended you by what I have just said; I assure you I do not mean to distress you by a retrospection of what cannot now be helped; considering all things I do not think you so much to blame as many People do; for when a person is in Liquor, there is no answering for what they may do [a woman (?) in such a situation is particularly off her guard because her head is not strong enough to support intoxication."][1]

"Madam, this is not to be borne; I insist—"

---

[1] Erased in MS.

"My

"My dear Girl dont vex yourself about the matter; I assure you I have entirely forgiven every thing respecting it; indeed I was not angry at the time, because as I saw all along, you were nearly dead drunk. I knew you could not help saying the strange things you did. But I see I distress you; so I will change the subject & desire it may never again be mentioned; remember it is all forgot—I will now pursue my story; but I must insist upon not giving you any description of Mrs Watkins: it would only be reviving old stories & as you never saw her, it can be nothing to you, if her forehead *was* too high, her eyes *were* too small, or if she *had* too much colour."

"Again! Lady Williams: this is too much"——

So provoked was poor Alice at this renewal of the old story, that I know not what might have been the consequence of it, had not their attention been engaged by another object. A lovely young Woman lying apparently in great pain beneath a Citron tree,

was

was an object too interesting not to attract their notice. Forgetting their own dispute they both with simpathizing tenderness advanced towards her & accosted her in these terms.

"You seem fair Nymph to be labouring under some misfortune which we shall be happy to releive if you will inform us what it is. Will you favour us with your Life & adventures?"

"Willingly Ladies, if you will be so kind as to be seated." They took their places & she thus began.

CHAPTER THE FIFTH

"I AM a native of North Wales & my Father is one of the most capital Taylors in it. Having a numerous family, he was easily prevailed on by a sister of my Mother's who is a widow in good circumstances & keeps an alehouse in the next Village to ours, to let her take me & breed me up at her own expence. Accordingly I have lived with her for the

the last 8 years of my Life, during which time she provided me with some of the first rate Masters, who taught me all the accomplishments requisite for one of my sex and rank. Under their instructions I learned Dancing, Music, Drawing & various Languages, by which means I became more accomplished than any other Taylor's Daughter in Wales. Never was there a happier creature than I was, till within the last half year—but I should have told you before that the principal Estate in our Neighbourhood belongs to Charles Adams, the owner of the brick House, you see yonder."

"Charles Adams!" exclaimed the astonished Alice; "are you acquainted with Charles Adams?"

"To my sorrow madam I am. He came about half a year ago to receive the rents of the Estate I have just mentioned. At that time I first saw him; as you seem ma'am acquainted with him, I need not describe to you how charming he is. I could not resist his attractions;"——

"Ah!

"Ah! who can," said Alice with a deep sigh.

"My aunt being in terms of the greatest intimacy with his cook, determined, at my request, to try whether she could discover, by means of her freind if there were any chance of his returning my affection. For this purpose she went one evening to drink tea with Mrs Susan, who in the course of Conversation mentioned the goodness of her Place & the Goodness of her Master; upon which my Aunt began pumping her with so much dexterity that in a short time Susan owned, that she did not think her Master would ever marry, 'for (said she) he has often & often declared to me that his wife, whoever she might be, must possess, Youth, Beauty, Birth, Wit, Merit, & Money. I have many a time (she continued) endeavoured to reason him out of his resolution & to convince him of the improbability of his ever meeting with such a Lady; but my arguments have had no effect & he continues as firm in his determination as ever.' You may
imagine

imagine Ladies my distress on hearing this;
for I was fearfull that tho' possessed of
Youth, Beauty, Wit & Merit, & tho' the
probable Heiress of my Aunts House &
business, he might think me deficient in
Rank, & in being so, unworthy of his hand."

"However I was determined to make a
bold push & therefore wrote him a very kind
letter, offering him with great tenderness my
hand & heart. To this I received an angry &
peremptory refusal, but thinking it might be
rather the effect of his modesty than any
thing else, I pressed him again on the subject. But he never answered any more of
my Letters & very soon afterwards left the
Country. As soon as I heard of his departure
I wrote to him here, informing him that I
should shortly do myself the honour of
waiting on him at Pammydiddle, to which
I received no answer; therefore choosing to
take Silence for Consent, I left Wales, unknown to my Aunt, & arrived here after a
tedious Journey this Morning. On enquiring
for his House I was directed thro' this Wood,

to

to the one you there see. With a heart elated by the expected happiness of beholding him I entered it & had proceeded thus far in my progress thro' it, when I found myself suddenly seized by the leg & on examining the cause of it, found that I was caught in one of the steel traps so common in gentlemen's grounds."

"Ah cried Lady Williams, how fortunate we are to meet with you; since we might otherwise perhaps have shared the like misfortune."

"It is indeed happy for you Ladies, that I should have been a short time before you. I screamed as you may easily imagine till the woods resounded again & till one of the inhuman Wretch's servants came to my assistance & released me from my dreadfull prison, but not before one of my legs was entirely broken."

CHAPTER

CHAPTER THE SIXTH

AT this melancholy recital the fair eyes of Lady Williams, were suffused in tears & Alice could not help exclaiming,

"Oh! cruel Charles to wound the hearts & legs of all the fair."

Lady Williams now interposed & observed that the young Lady's leg ought to be set without farther delay. After examining the fracture therefore, she immediately began & performed the operation with great skill which was the more wonderfull on account of her having never performed such a one before. Lucy, then arose from the ground & finding that she could walk with the greatest ease, accompanied them to Lady Williams's House at her Ladyship's particular request.

The perfect form, the beautifull face, & elegant manners of Lucy so won on the affections of Alice that when they parted, which was not till after Supper, she assured her that except her Father, Brother, Uncles, Aunts

Aunts, Cousins & other relations, Lady Williams, Charles Adams & a few dozen more of particular freinds, she loved her better than almost any other person in the world.

Such a flattering assurance of her regard would justly have given much pleasure to the object of it, had she not plainly perceived that the amiable Alice had partaken too freely of Lady Williams's claret.

Her Ladyship (whose discernment was great) read in the intelligent countenance of Lucy her thoughts on the subject & as soon as Miss Johnson had taken her leave, thus addressed her.

"When you are more intimately acquainted with my Alice you will not be surprised, Lucy, to see the dear Creature drink a little too much; for such things happen every day. She has many rare & charming qualities, but Sobriety is not one of them. The whole Family are indeed a sad drunken set. I am sorry to say too that I never knew three such thorough Gamesters as they are, more particularly Alice. But she is a

G   charming

charming girl. I fancy not one of the sweetest
tempers in the world; to be sure I have seen
her in such passions! However she is a sweet
young Woman. I am sure you'll like her. I
scarcely know any one so amiable.—Oh!
that you could but have seen her the other
Evening! How she raved! & on such a trifle
too! She is indeed a most pleasing Girl! I
shall always love her!"

"She appears by your ladyship's account
to have many good qualities", replied Lucy.
"Oh! a thousand," answered Lady Williams;
tho' I am very partial to her, and perhaps
am blinded by my affection, to her real
defects."

CHAPTER THE SEVENTH

THE next morning brought the three Miss
Simpsons to wait on Lady Williams, who
received them with the utmost politeness &
introduced to their acquaintance Lucy, with
whom the eldest was so much pleased that at
parting

parting she declared her sole *ambition* was to have her accompany them the next morning to Bath, whither they were going for some weeks.

"Lucy, said Lady Williams, is quite at her own disposal & if she chooses to accept so kind an invitation, I hope she will not hesitate, from any motives of delicacy on my account. I know not indeed how I shall ever be able to part with her. She never was at Bath & I should think that it would be a most agreable Jaunt to her. Speak my Love, continued she, turning to Lucy, what say you to accompanying these Ladies? I shall be miserable without you—t'will be a most pleasant tour to you—I hope you'll go; if you do I am sure t'will be the Death of me—pray be persuaded"——

Lucy begged leave to decline the honour of accompanying them, with many expressions of gratitude for the extream politeness of Miss Simpson in inviting her.

Miss Simpson appeared much disappointed by her refusal. Lady Williams insisted

on

on her going—declared that she would never forgive her if she did not, and that she should never survive it if she did, & in short used such persuasive arguments that it was at length resolved she was to go. The Miss Simpsons called for her at ten o'clock the next morning & Lady Williams had soon the satisfaction of receiving from her young freind, the pleasing intelligence of their safe arrival in Bath.

It may now be proper to return to the Hero of this Novel, the brother of Alice, of whom I beleive I have scarcely ever had occasion to speak; which may perhaps be partly oweing to his unfortunate propensity to Liquor, which so compleatly deprived him of the use of those faculties Nature had endowed him with, that he never did anything worth mentioning. His Death happened a short time after Lucy's departure & was the natural Consequence of this pernicious practice. By his decease, his sister became the sole inheritress of a very large fortune, which as it gave her fresh Hopes of rendering

rendering herself acceptable as a wife to Charles Adams could not fail of being most pleasing to her—& as the effect was Joyfull the Cause could scarcely be lamented.

Finding the violence of her attachment to him daily augment, she at length disclosed it to her Father & desired him to propose a union between them to Charles. Her father consented & set out one morning to open the affair to the young Man. Mr Johnson being a man of few words his part was soon performed & the answer he received was as follows—

"Sir, I may perhaps be expected to appeared [*sic*] pleased at & gratefull for the offer you have made me: but let me tell you that I consider it as an affront. I look upon myself to be Sir a perfect Beauty—where would you see a finer figure or a more charming face. Then, sir I imagine my Manners & Address to be of the most polished kind; there is a certain elegance, a peculiar sweetness in them that I never saw equalled & cannot describe—. Partiality aside, I am certainly

certainly more accomplished in every Language, every Science, every Art and every thing than any other person in Europe. My temper is even, my virtues innumerable, my self unparalelled. Since such Sir is my character, what do you mean by wishing me to marry your Daughter? Let me give you a short sketch of yourself & of her. I look upon you Sir to be a very good sort of Man in the main; a drunken old Dog to be sure, but that's nothing to me. Your Daughter Sir, is neither sufficiently beautifull, sufficiently amiable, sufficiently witty, nor sufficiently rich for me—. I expect nothing more in my wife than my wife will find in me—Perfection. These Sir, are my sentiments & I honour myself for having such. One freind I have & glory in having but one—. She is at present preparing my Dinner, but if you choose to see her, she shall come & she will inform you that these have ever been my sentiments."

Mr Johnson was satisfied: & expressing himself to be much obliged to Mr Adams

for

for the characters he had favoured him
with of himself & his Daughter, took his
leave.

The unfortunate Alice on receiving from
her father the sad account of the ill success
his visit had been attended with, could
scarcely support the disappointment. She
flew to her Bottle & it was soon forgot.

CHAPTER THE EIGHTTH

WHILE these affairs were transacting at
Pammydiddle, Lucy was conquering ever
[*sic*] Heart at Bath. A fortnight's residence
there had nearly effaced from her remembrance the captivating form of Charles. The
recollection of what her Heart had formerly
suffered by his charms & her Leg by his trap,
enabled her to forget him with tolerable
Ease, which was what she determined to
do; & for that purpose dedicated five
minutes in every day to the employment of
driving him from her remembrance.

Her

Her second Letter to Lady Williams contained the pleasing intelligence of her having accomplished her undertaking to her entire satisfaction; she mentioned in it also an offer of marriage she had received from the Duke of —— an elderly Man of noble fortune whose ill health was the chief inducement of his Journey to Bath. "I am distressed (she continued) to know whether I mean to accept him or not. There are a thousand advantages to be derived from a marriage with the Duke, for besides those more inferior ones of Rank & Fortune it will procure me a home, which of all other things is what I most desire. Your Ladyship's kind wish of my always remaining with you, is noble & generous but I cannot think of becoming so great a burden on one I so much love & esteem. That one should receive obligations only from those we despise, is a sentiment instilled into my mind by my worthy aunt, in my early years, & cannot in my opinion be too strictly adhered to. The excellent woman of whom I now speak, is I hear too much

much incensed by my imprudent departure from Wales, to receive me again—. I most earnestly wish to leave the Ladies I am now with. Miss Simpson is indeed (setting aside ambition) very amiable, but her 2^d Sister the envious & malevolent Sukey is too disagreable to live with. I have reason to think that the admiration I have met with in the circles of the great at this Place, has raised her Hatred & Envy; for often has she threatened, & sometimes endeavoured to cut my throat. —Your Ladyship will therefore allow that I am not wrong in wishing to leave Bath, & in wishing to have a home to receive me, when I do. I shall expect with impatience your advice concerning the Duke & am your most obliged

&c. Lucy."

Lady Williams sent her, her opinion on the subject in the following Manner.

"Why do you hesitate my dearest Lucy, a moment with respect to the Duke? I have enquired into his Character & find him to be

H   an

an unprincipaled, illiterate Man. Never shall
my Lucy be united to such a one! He has
a princely fortune, which is every day en-
creasing. How nobly will you spend it! what
credit will you give him in the eyes of all!
How much will he be respected on his Wife's
account! But why my dearest Lucy, why
will you not at once decide this affair by
returning to me & never leaving me again?
Altho' I admire your noble sentiments with
respect to obligations, yet, let me beg that
they may not prevent your making me
happy. It will to be sure be a great expence
to me, to have you always with me—I shall
not be able to support it—but what is that in
comparison with the happiness I shall enjoy
in your society? 'twill ruin me I know—
you will not therefore surely, withstand
these arguments, or refuse to return to yours
most affectionately &c. &c.

C. WILLIAMS"

CHAPTER

CHAPTER THE NINTH

WHAT might have been the effect of her Ladyship's advice, had it ever been received by Lucy, is uncertain, as it reached Bath a few Hours after she had breathed her last. She fell a sacrifice to the Envy & Malice of Sukey who jealous of her superior charms took her by poison from an admiring World at the age of seventeen.

Thus fell the amiable & lovely Lucy whose Life had been marked by no crime, and stained by no blemish but her imprudent departure from her Aunts, & whose death was sincerely lamented by every one who knew her. Among the most afflicted of her freinds were Lady Williams, Miss Johnson & the Duke; the 2 first of whom had a most sincere regard for her, more particularly Alice, who had spent a whole evening in her company & had never thought of her since. His Grace's affliction may likewise be easily accounted for, since he lost one for whom he had

had experienced during the last ten days, a tender affection & sincere regard. He mourned her loss with unshaken constancy for the next fortnight at the end of which time, he gratified the ambition of Caroline Simpson by raising her to the rank of a Dutchess. Thus was she at length rendered compleatly happy in the gratification of her favourite passion. Her sister the perfidious Sukey, was likewise shortly after exalted in a manner she truly deserved, & by her actions appeared to have always desired. Her barbarous Murder was discovered & in spite of every interceding freind she was speedily raised to the Gallows—. The beautifull but affected Cecilia was too sensible of her own superior charms, not to imagine that if Caroline could engage a Duke, she might without censure aspire to the affections of some Prince—& knowing that those of her native Country were cheifly engaged, she left England & I have since heard is at present the favourite Sultana of the great Mogul—.

In

In the mean time the inhabitants of Pammydiddle were in a state of the greatest astonishment & Wonder, a report being circulated of the intended marriage of Charles Adams. The Lady's name was still a secret. Mr & Mrs Jones imagined it to be, Miss Johnson; but *she* knew better; all *her* fears were centered in his Cook, when to the astonishment of every one, he was publicly united to Lady Williams—

FINIS

EDGAR

EDGAR & EMMA

A TALE

CHAPTER THE FIRST

"I CANNOT imagine," said Sir Godfrey to his Lady, "why we continue in such deplorable Lodgings as these, in a paltry Market-town, while we have 3 good Houses of our own situated in some of the finest parts of England, & perfectly ready to receive us!"

"I'm sure Sir Godfrey," replied Lady Marlow, "it has been much against my inclination that we have staid here so long; or why we should ever have come at all indeed, has been to me a wonder, as none of our Houses have been in the least want of repair."

"Nay my dear," answered Sir Godfrey, "you are the last person who ought to be displeased with what was always meant as

a

a compliment to you; for you cannot but be sensible of the very great inconvenience your Daughters & I have been put to, during the 2 years we have remained crowded in these Lodgings in order to give you pleasure."

"My dear," replied Lady Marlow, "How can you stand & tell such lies, when you very well know that it was merely to oblige the Girls & you, that I left a most commodious House situated in a most delightfull Country & surrounded by a most agreable Neighbourhood, to live 2 years cramped up in Lodgings three pair of Stairs high, in a smokey & unwholesome town, which has given me a continual fever & almost thrown me into a Consumption."

As, after a few more speeches on both sides, they could not determine which was the most to blame, they prudently laid aside the debate, & having packed up their Cloathes & paid their rent, they set out the next morning with their 2 Daughters for their seat in Sussex.

Sir Godfrey & Lady Marlow were indeed
very

very sensible people & tho' (as in this instance) like many other sensible People, they sometimes did a foolish thing, yet in general their actions were guided by Prudence & regulated by discretion.

After a Journey of two Days & a half they arrived at Marlhurst in good health & high spirits; so overjoyed were they all to inhabit again a place, they had left with mutual regret for two years, that they ordered the bells to be rung & distributed ninepence among the Ringers.

CHAPTER THE SECOND

THE news of their arrival being quickly spread throughout the Country, brought them in a few Days visits of congratulation from every family in it.

Amongst the rest came the inhabitants of Willmot Lodge a beautifull Villa not far from Marlhurst. Mr Willmot was the representative of a very ancient Family & possessed besides

besides his paternal Estate, a considerable share in a Lead mine & a ticket in the Lottery. His Lady was an agreable Woman. Their Children were too numerous to be particularly described; it is sufficient to say that in general they were virtuously inclined & not given to any wicked ways. Their family being too large to accompany them in every visit, they took nine with them alternately. When their Coach stopped at Sir Godfrey's door, the Miss Marlow's Hearts throbbed in the eager expectation of once more beholding a family so dear to them. Emma the youngest (who was more particularly interested in their arrival, being attached to their eldest Son) continued at her Dressing-room window in anxious Hopes of seeing young Edgar descend from the Carriage.

Mr & Mrs Willmot with their three eldest Daughters first appeared,—Emma began to tremble. Robert, Richard, Ralph, & Rodolphus followed—Emma turned pale. Their two youngest Girls were lifted from the

Coach

Coach—Emma sunk breathless on a Sopha. A footman came to announce to her the arrival of Company; her heart was too full to contain its afflictions. A confidante was necessary—In Thomas she hoped to experience a faithfull one—for one she must have & Thomas was the only one at Hand. To him she unbosomed herself without restraint & after owning her passion for young Willmot, requested his advice in what manner she should conduct herself in the melancholy Disappointment under which she laboured.

Thomas, who would gladly have been excused from listening to her complaint, begged leave to decline giving any advice concerning it, which much against her will, she was obliged to comply with.

Having dispatched him therefore with many injunctions of secrecy, she descended with a heavy heart into the Parlour, where she found the good Party seated in a social Manner round a blazing fire.

CHAPTER

CHAPTER THE THIRD

EMMA had continued in the Parlour some time before she could summon up sufficient courage to ask Mrs Willmot after the rest of her family; & when she did, it was in so low, so faltering a voice that no one knew she spoke. Dejected by the ill success of her first attempt she made no other, till on Mrs Willmot's desiring one of the little Girls to ring the bell for their Carriage, she stepped across the room & seizing the string said in a resolute manner.

"Mrs Willmot, you do not stir from this House till you let me know how all the rest of your family do, particularly your eldest son."

They were all greatly surprised by such an unexpected address & the more so, on account of the manner in which it was spoken; but Emma, who would not be again disappointed, requesting an answer, Mrs Willmot made the following eloquent oration.

"Our

"Our children are all extremely well but at present most of them from home. Amy is with my sister Clayton. Sam at Eton. David with his Uncle John. Jem & Will at Winchester. Kitty at Queen's Square. Ned with his Grandmother. Hetty & Patty in a Convent at Brussells. Edgar at college, Peter at Nurse, & all the rest (except the nine here) at home."

It was with difficulty that Emma could refrain from tears on hearing of the absence of Edgar; she remained however tolerably composed till the Willmot's were gone when having no check to the overflowings of her greif, she gave free vent to them, & retiring to her own room, continued in tears the remainder of her Life.

FINIS

HENRY

HENRY AND ELIZA

A NOVEL

Is humbly dedicated to Miss Cooper by her obedient Humble Servant

THE AUTHOR

═══

As Sir George and Lady Harcourt were superintending the Labours of their Hay-makers, rewarding the industry of some by smiles of approbation, & punishing the idle-ness of others, by a cudgel, they perceived lying closely concealed beneath the thick foliage of a Haycock, a beautifull little Girl not more than 3 months old.

Touched with the enchanting Graces of her face & delighted with the infantine tho' sprightly answers she returned to their many questions, they resolved to take her home &, having no Children of their own, to educate her with care & cost.

Being good People themselves, their first & principal care was to incite in her a Love

of

of Virtue & a Hatred of Vice, in which they
so well succeeded (Eliza having a natural
turn that way herself) that when she grew
up, she was the delight of all who knew her.

Beloved by Lady Harcourt, adored by
Sir George & admired by all the World, she
lived in a continued course of uninterrupted
Happiness, till she had attained her eigh-
teenth year, when happening one day to be
detected in stealing a banknote of 50£, she
was turned out of doors by her inhuman
Benefactors. Such a transition to one who
did not possess so noble & exalted a mind as
Eliza, would have been Death, but she,
happy in the conscious knowledge of her own
Excellence, amused herself, as she sate beneath a tree with making & singing the following Lines.

SONG

Though misfortune my footsteps may ever attend
  I hope I shall never have need of a Freind
as an innocent Heart I will ever preserve
  and will never from Virtue's dear boundaries
    swerve.

                    Having

Having amused herself some hours, with this song & her own pleasing reflections, she arose & took the road to M. a small market town of which place her most intimate freind kept the red Lion.

To this freind she immediately went, to whom having recounted her late misfortune, she communicated her wish of getting into some family in the capacity of Humble Companion.

Mrs Willson, who was the most amiable creature on earth, was no sooner acquainted with her Desire, than she sate down in the Bar & wrote the following Letter to the Dutchess of F, the woman whom of all others, she most Esteemed.

———

"To the Dutchess of F."

———

Receive into your Family, at my request a young woman of unexceptionable Character, who is so good as to choose your Society in preference

preference to going to Service. Hasten, &
take her from the arms of your
SARAH WILSON."

The Dutchess, whose freindship for Mrs
Wilson would have carried her any lengths,
was overjoyed at such an opportunity of
obliging her & accordingly sate out immediately on the receipt of her letter for the red
Lion, which she reached the same Evening.
The Dutchess of F. was about 45 & a half;
Her passions were strong, her freindships
firm & her Enmities, unconquerable. She was
a widow & had only one Daughter who was
on the point of marriage with a young Man of
considerable fortune.

The Dutchess no sooner beheld our Heroine
than throwing her arms around her neck, she
declared herself so much pleased with her,
that she was resolved they never more should
part. Eliza was delighted with such a pro-
testation of freindship, & after taking a most
affecting leave of her dear Mrs Wilson, accompanied her grace the next morning to her
seat in Surry.

With

With every expression of regard did the Dutchess introduce her to Lady Hariet, who was so much pleased with her appearance that she besought her, to consider her as her Sister, which Eliza with the greatest Condescension promised to do.

Mr Cecil, the Lover of Lady Harriet, being often with the family was often with Eliza. A mutual Love took place & Cecil having declared his first, prevailed on Eliza to consent to a private union, which was easy to be effected, as the dutchess's chaplain being very much in love with Eliza himself, would they were certain do anything to oblige her.

The Dutchess & Lady Harriet being engaged one evening to an assembly, they took the opportunity of their absence & were united by the enamoured Chaplain.

When the Ladies returned, their amazement was great at finding instead of Eliza the following Note.

"MADAM

We are married & gone.

HENRY & ELIZA CECIL."

K   Her

Her Grace as soon as she had read the letter, which sufficiently explained the whole affair, flew into the most violent passion & after having spent an agreable half hour, in calling them by all the shocking Names her rage could suggest to her, sent out after them 300 armed Men, with orders not to return without their Bodies, dead or alive; intending that if they should be brought to her in the latter condition to have them put to Death in some torturelike manner, after a few years Confinement.

In the mean time Cecil & Eliza continued their flight to the Continent, which they judged to be more secure than their native Land, from the dreadfull effects of the Dutchess's vengeance, which they had so much reason to apprehend.

In France they remained 3 years, during which time they became the parents of two Boys, & at the end of it Eliza became a widow without any thing to support either her or her Children. They had lived since their Marriage at the rate of 18,000£ a year,

of

of which Mr Cecil's estate being rather less than the twentieth part, they had been able to save but a trifle, having lived to the utmost extent of their Income.

Eliza, being perfectly conscious of the derangement in their affairs, immediately on her Husband's death set sail for England, in a man of War of 55 Guns, which they had built in their more prosperous Days. But no sooner had she stepped on Shore at Dover, with a Child in each hand, than she was seized by the officers of the Dutchess, & conducted by them to a snug little Newgate of their Lady's, which she had erected for the reception of her own private Prisoners.

No sooner had Eliza entered her Dungeon than the first thought which occurred to her, was how to get out of it again.

She went to the Door; but it was locked. She looked at the Window; but it was barred with iron; disappointed in both her expectations, she dispaired of effecting her Escape, when she fortunately perceived in a Corner of her Cell, a small saw & Ladder of ropes.

With

With the saw she instantly went to work &
in a few weeks had displaced every Bar but
one to which she fastened the Ladder.

A difficulty then occurred which for some
time she knew not how to obviate. Her
Children were too small to get down the Ladder by themselves, nor would it be possible
for her to take them in her arms, when *she*
did. At last she determined to fling down
all her Cloathes, of which she had a large
Quantity, & then having given them strict
Charge not to hurt themselves, threw her
Children after them. She herself with ease
discended by the Ladder, at the bottom of
which she had the pleasure of finding her
little boys in perfect Health & fast asleep.

Her wardrobe she now saw a fatal necessity of selling, both for the preservation of
her Children & herself. With tears in her
eyes, she parted with these last reliques of
her former Glory, & with the money she got
for them, bought others more usefull, some
playthings for her Boys and a gold Watch
for herself.

But

But scarcely was she provided with the above-mentioned necessaries, than she began to find herself rather hungry, & had reason to think, by their biting off two of her fingers, that her Children were much in the same situation.

To remedy these unavoidable misfortunes, she determined to return to her old friends, Sir George & Lady Harcourt, whose generosity she had so often experienced & hoped to experience as often again.

She had about 40 miles to travel before she could reach their hospitable Mansion, of which having walked 30 without stopping, she found herself at the Entrance of a Town, where often in happier times, she had accompanied Sir George & Lady Harcourt to regale themselves with a cold collation at one of the Inns.

The reflections that her adventures since the last time she had partaken of these happy *Junketings*, afforded her, occupied her mind, for some time, as she sate on the steps at the door of a Gentleman's house. As soon

as

as these reflections were ended, she arose &
determined to take her station at the very
inn, she remembered with so much delight,
from the Company of which, as they went in
& out, she hoped to receive some Charitable
Gratuity.

She had but just taken her post at the
Innyard before a Carriage drove out of it,
& on turning the Corner at which she was
stationed, stopped to give the Postilion an
opportunity of admiring the beauty of the
prospect. Eliza then advanced to the carriage & was going to request their Charity,
when on fixing her Eyes on the Lady, within
it, she exclaimed,

"Lady Harcourt!"

To which the lady replied,

"Eliza!"

"Yes Madam it is the wretched Eliza herself."

Sir George, who was also in the Carriage,
but too much amazed to speak, was pro-
ceeding to demand an explanation from
Eliza of the Situation she was then in,
                                    when

when Lady Harcourt in transports of Joy, exclaimed.

"Sir George, Sir George, she is not only Eliza our adopted Daughter, but our real Child."

"Our real Child! What Lady Harcourt, do you mean? You know you never even was with child. Explain yourself, I beseech you."

"You must remember Sir George, that when you sailed for America, you left me breeding."

"I do, I do, go on dear Polly."

"Four months after you were gone, I was delivered of this Girl, but dreading your just resentment at her not proving the Boy you wished, I took her to a Haycock & laid her down. A few weeks afterwards, you returned, & fortunately for me, made no enquiries on the subject. Satisfied within myself of the welfare of my Child, I soon forgot I had one, insomuch that when, we shortly after found her in the very Haycock, I had placed her, I had no more idea of her being my own, than you had, & nothing I will

will venture to say would have recalled the circumstance to my remembrance, but my thus accidentally hearing her voice, which now strikes me as being the very counterpart of my own Child's."

"The rational & convincing Account you have given of the whole affair, said Sir George, leaves no doubt of her being our Daughter & as such I freely forgive the robbery she was guilty of."

A mutual Reconciliation then took place, & Eliza, ascending the Carriage with her two Children returned to that home from which she had been absent nearly four years.

No sooner was she reinstated in her accustomed power at Harcourt Hall, than she raised an Army, with which she entirely demolished the Dutchess's Newgate, snug as it was, and by that act, gained the Blessings of thousands, & the Applause of her own Heart.

FINIS

THE

THE ADVENTURES OF

MR HARLEY

a short, but interesting Tale, is with all imaginable Respect inscribed to Mr Francis William Austen Midshipman on board his Majestys Ship the Perseverance by his Obedient Servant   THE AUTHOR.

MR HARLEY was one of many Children. Destined by his father for the Church & by his Mother for the Sea, desirous of pleasing both, he prevailed on Sir John to obtain for him a Chaplaincy on board a Man of War. He accordingly, cut his Hair and sailed.

In half a year he returned & set off in the Stage Coach for Hogsworth Green, the seat of Emma. His fellow travellers were, A man without a Hat, Another with two, An old maid & a young Wife.

This last appeared about 17 with fine dark Eyes & an elegant Shape; in short Mr Harley soon found out, that she was his Emma & recollected he had married her a few weeks before he left England.

FINIS

L   SIR

SIR WILLIAM MOUNTAGUE

an unfinished performance
is humbly dedicated to Charles John
Austen Esqre, by his most obedient humble
Servant
THE AUTHOR

SIR WILLIAM MOUNTAGUE was the son of Sir
Henry Mountague, who was the son of Sir
John Mountague, a descendant of Sir Chris-
topher Mountague, who was the nephew of
Sir Edward Mountague, whose ancestor was
Sir James Mountague a near relation of Sir
Robert Mountague, who inherited the Title
& Estate from Sir Frederic Mountague.

Sir William was about 17 when his Father
died, & left him a handsome fortune, an
ancient House & a Park well stocked with
Deer. Sir William had not been long in the
possession of his Estate before he fell in Love
with the 3 Miss Cliftons of Kilhoobery Park.
These young Ladies were all equally young,
equally handsome, equally rich & equally
amiable—Sir William was equally in Love
with

with them all, & knowing not which to prefer, he left the Country & took Lodgings in
a small Village near Dover.

In this retreat, to which he had retired in
the hope of finding a shelter from the Pangs
of Love, he became enamoured of a young
Widow of Quality, who came for change of
air to the same Village, after the death of
a Husband, whom she had always tenderly
loved & now sincerely lamented.

Lady Percival was young, accomplished
& lovely. Sir William adored her & she
consented to become his Wife. Vehemently
pressed by Sir William to name the Day in
which he might conduct her to the Altar, she
at length fixed on the following Monday,
which was the first of September. Sir William was a Shot & could not support the idea
of losing such a Day, even for such a Cause.
He begged her to delay the Wedding a short
time. Lady Percival was enraged & returned
to London the next Morning.

Sir William was sorry to lose her, but as
he knew that he should have been much
more

more greived by the Loss of the 1st of September, his Sorrow was not without a mixture of Happiness, & his Affliction was considerably lessened by his Joy.

After staying at the Village a few weeks longer, he left it & went to a freind's House in Surry. Mr Brudenell was a sensible Man, & had a beautifull Neice with whom Sir William soon fell in love. But Miss Arundel was cruel; she preferred a Mr Stanhope: Sir William shot Mr Stanhope: the lady had then no reason to refuse him; she accepted him, & they were to be married on the 27th of October. But on the 25th Sir William received a visit from Emma Stanhope the sister of the unfortunate Victim of his rage. She begged some recompence, some atonement for the cruel Murder of her Brother. Sir William bade her name her price. She fixed on $\frac{S}{14}$. Sir William offered her himself & Fortune. They went to London the next day & were there privately married. For a fortnight Sir William was compleatly happy, but chancing one day to see a charming young Woman

Woman entering a Chariot in Brook Street, he became again most violently in love. On enquiring the name of this fair Unknown, he found that she was the Sister of his old freind Lady Percival, at which he was much rejoiced, as he hoped to have, by his acquaintance with her Ladyship, free access to Miss Wentworth. . . . .

FINIS

To

To Charles John Austen Esqre

SIR,

Your generous patronage of the unfinished tale,
I have already taken the Liberty of dedicating to
you, encourages me to dedicate to you a second, as
unfinished as the first.

I am Sir with every expression
of regard for you & yr noble
Family, your most obed^{t}
&c. &c. . . .
THE AUTHOR

MEMOIRS OF MR CLIFFORD

AN UNFINISHED TALE

MR CLIFFORD lived at Bath; & having never
seen London, set off one monday morning
determined to feast his eyes with a sight of
that great Metropolis. He travelled in his
Coach & Four, for he was a very rich young
Man & kept a great many Carriages of which
I do not recollect half. I can only remember
that

that he had a Coach, a Chariot, a Chaise, a Landeau, a Landeaulet, a Phaeton, a Gig, a Whisky, an italian Chair, a Buggy, a Curricle & a wheelbarrow. He had likewise an amazing fine stud of Horses. To my knowledge he had six Greys, 4 Bays, eight Blacks & a poney.

In his Coach & 4 Bays Mr Clifford sate forward about 5 o'clock on Monday Morning the 1st of May for London. He always travelled remarkably expeditiously & contrived therefore to get to Devizes from Bath, which is no less than nineteen miles, the first Day. To be sure he did not get in till eleven at night & pretty tight work it was as you may imagine.

However when he was once got to Devizes he was determined to comfort himself with a good hot Supper and therefore ordered a wnole Egg to be boiled for him & his Servants. The next morning he pursued his Journey & in the course of 3 days hard labour reached Overton, where he was seized with a dangerous fever the Consequence of too violent Excercise.

Five

Five months did our Hero remain in this celebrated City under the care of its no less celebrated Physician, who at length compleatly cured him of his troublesome Disease.

As Mr Clifford still continued very weak, his first Day's Journey carried him only to Dean Gate, where he remained a few Days & found himself much benefited by the change of Air.

In easy Stages he proceeded to Basingstoke. One day Carrying him to Clarkengreen, the next to Worting, the 3d to the bottom of Basingstoke Hill, & the fourth, to Mr Robins's. . . .

FINIS

THE

THE BEAUTIFULL CASSANDRA

A NOVEL IN TWELVE CHAPTERS

dedicated by permission to Miss Austen.

Dedication.

MADAM

You are a Phoenix. Your taste is refined, your Sentiments are noble, & your Virtues innumerable. Your Person is lovely, your Figure, elegant, & your Form, majestic. Your Manners are polished, your Conversation is rational & your appearance singular. If therefore the following Tale will afford one moment's amusement to you, every wish will be gratified of

> Your most obedient
> humble servant
> THE AUTHOR

CHAPTER THE FIRST

CASSANDRA was the Daughter & the only Daughter of a celebrated Milliner in Bond Street. Her father was of noble Birth, being the near relation of the Dutchess of —— 's Butler.

M   CHAPTER

CHAPTER THE 2ᵈ

WHEN Cassandra had attained her 16ᵗʰ year,
she was lovely & amiable & chancing to fall
in love with an elegant Bonnet, her Mother
had just compleated bespoke by the Coun-
tess of —— she placed it on her gentle Head
& walked from her Mother's shop to make
her Fortune.

CHAPTER THE 3ᵈ

THE first person she met, was the Viscount
of —— a young Man, no less celebrated for
his Accomplishments & Virtues, than for his
Elegance & Beauty. She curtseyed & walked
on.

CHAPTER THE 4ᵗʰ

SHE then proceeded to a Pastry-cooks where
she devoured six ices, refused to pay for
them

them, knocked down the Pastry Cook &
walked away.

CHAPTER THE 5th

SHE next ascended a Hackney Coach &
ordered it to Hampstead, where she was no
sooner arrived than she ordered the Coachman to turn round & drive her back again.

CHAPTER THE 6th

BEING returned to the same spot of the same
Street she had sate out from, the Coachman
demanded his Pay.

CHAPTER THE 7th

SHE searched her pockets over again &
again; but every search was unsuccessfull.
No money could she find. The man grew
peremptory. She placed her bonnet on his
head & ran away.

CHAPTER

CHAPTER THE 8th

THRO' many a street she then proceeded &
met in none the least Adventure till on turning a Corner of Bloomsbury Square, she met
Maria.

CHAPTER THE 9th

CASSANDRA started & Maria seemed surprised; they trembled, blushed, turned pale
& passed each other in a mutual silence.

CHAPTER THE 10th

CASSANDRA was next accosted by her friend
the Widow, who squeezing out her little Head
thro' her less window, asked her how she
did? Cassandra curtseyed & went on.

CHAPTER

CHAPTER THE 11th

A QUARTER of a mile brought her to her paternal roof in Bond Street from which she had now been absent nearly 7 hours.

CHAPTER THE 12th

SHE entered it & was pressed to her Mother's bosom by that worthy Woman. Cassandra smiled & whispered to herself "This is a day well spent."

FINIS

AMELIA

AMELIA WEBSTER

an interesting & well written Tale
is dedicated by Permission
to
Mrs Austen
by
Her humble Servant
THE AUTHOR

Letter the first

TO MISS WEBSTER

MY DEAR AMELIA

You will rejoice to hear of the return of
my amiable Brother from abroad. He arrived on thursday, & never did I see a finer
form, save that of your sincere freind

MATILDA HERVEY

Letter the 2d

TO H. BEVERLEY ESQre

DEAR BEVERLEY

I arrived here last thursday & met with
a hearty reception from my Father, Mother
&

& Sisters. The latter are both fine Girls—
particularly Maud, who I think would suit
you as a Wife well enough. What say you
to this? She will have two thousand Pounds
& as much more as you can get. If you don't
marry her you will mortally offend

GEORGE HERVEY

Letter the 3ᵈ

TO MISS HERVEY

DEAR MAUD

Beleive me I'm happy to hear of your
Brother's arrival. I have a thousand things
to tell you, but my paper will only permit
me to add that I am yʳ affecᵗ Freind

AMELIA WEBSTER

Letter the 4ᵗʰ

TO MISS S. HERVEY

DEAR SALLY

I have found a very convenient old hollow
oak to put our Letters in; for you know we
have

have long maintained a private Correspondence. It is about a mile from my House
& seven from yours. You may perhaps imagine that I might have made choice of a tree
which would have divided the Distance more
equally—I was sensible of this at the time,
but as I considered that the walk would be
of benefit to you in your weak & uncertain
state of Health, I preferred it to one nearer
your House, & am y^r faithfull

BENJAMIN BAR

*Letter the 5*th

TO MISS HERVEY

DEAR MAUD

I write now to inform you that I did not
stop at your house in my way to Bath last
Monday.—I have many things to inform you
of besides; but my Paper reminds me of concluding; & beleive me y^{rs} ever &c.

AMELIA WEBSTER

Letter

*Letter the 6*th

MADAM   Saturday

An humble Admirer now addresses you. I saw you lovely Fair one as you passed on Monday last, before our House in your way to Bath. I saw you thro' a telescope, & was so struck by your Charms that from that time to this I have not tasted human food.

GEORGE HERVEY

*Letter the 7*th

As I was this morning at Breakfast the Newspaper was brought me, & in the list of Marriages I read the following.

"George Hervey Esqre to Miss Amelia Webster"

"Henry Beverley Esqre to Miss Hervey"

&

"Benjamin Bar Esqre to Miss Sarah Hervey".

yours, TOM

FINIS

N   THE

THE VISIT

A COMEDY IN 2 ACTS

Dedication

To the Revd James Austen

SIR,

The following Drama, which I humbly recommend to your Protection & Patronage, tho' inferior to those celebrated Comedies called "The School for Jealousy" & "The travelled Man", will I hope afford some amusement to so respectable a *Curate* as yourself; which was the end in veiw when it was first composed by your Humble Servant the Author.

Dramatis Personae

Sir Arthur Hampton	Lady Hampton
Lord Fitzgerald	Miss Fitzgerald
Stanly	Sophy Hampton
Willoughby, Sir Arthur's nephew	Cloe Willoughby

The scens are laid in Lord Fitzgerald's House.

ACT

ACT THE FIRST

Scene the first, a Parlour

enter LORD FITZGERALD & STANLY

STANLY. Cousin your servant.

FITZGERALD. Stanly, good morning to you. I hope you slept well last night.

STANLY. Remarkably well, I thank you.

FITZGERALD. I am afraid you found your Bed too short. It was bought in my Grandmother's time, who was herself a very short woman & made a point of suiting all her Beds to her own length, as she never wished to have any company in the House, on account of an unfortunate impediment in her speech, which she was sensible of being very disagreable to her inmates.

STANLY. Make no more excuses dear Fitzgerald.

FITZGERALD. I will not distress you by too much civility—I only beg you will consider yourself as much at home as in your Father's house. Remember, "The more free, the more Wellcome."

[*exit* FITZGERALD

STANLY

STANLY. Amiable Youth!

"Your virtues could he imitate
How happy would be Stanly's fate!"

[*exit* STANLY

Scene the 2ᵈ

STANLY & MISS FITZGERALD, *discovered*.

STANLY. What Company is it you expect to dine with you to Day, Cousin?

MISS F. Sir Arthur & Lady Hampton; their Daughter, Nephew & Neice.

STANLY. Miss Hampton & her Cousin are both Handsome, are they not?

MISS F. Miss Willoughby is extreamly so. Miss Hampton is a fine Girl, but not equal to her.

STANLY. Is not your Brother attached to the Latter?

MISS F. He admires her I know, but I beleive nothing more. Indeed I have heard him say that she was the most beautifull, pleasing, & amiable Girl in the world, & that of all others he should prefer her for his Wife. But it never went any farther I'm certain.

STANLY

STANLY. And yet my Cousin never says a thing he does not mean.

MISS F. Never. From his Cradle he has always been a strict adherent to Truth [He never told a Lie but once, & that was merely to oblige me. Indeed I may truly say there never was such a Brother!][1]

> [*exeunt Severally*

End of the First Act.

ACT THE SECOND

Scene the first. The Drawing Room.

Chairs set round in a row. LORD FITZGERALD, MISS FITZGERALD & STANLY *seated.*

Enter a Servant.

SERVANT. Sir Arthur & Lady Hampton. Miss Hampton, Mr & Miss Willoughby.

> [*exit* SERVANT

Enter the Company.

MISS F. I hope I have the pleasure of seeing

[1] Erased in MS.

your

your Ladyship well. Sir Arthur, your servant. Yrs Mr Willoughby. Dear Sophy, Dear Cloe,—

[*They pay their Compliments alternately.*

MISS F. Pray be seated.

[*They sit*

Bless me! there ought to be 8 Chairs & there are but 6. However, if your Ladyship will but take Sir Arthur in your Lap, & Sophy my Brother in hers, I beleive we shall do pretty well.

LADY H. Oh! with pleasure. . . .

SOPHY. I beg his Lordship would be seated.

MISS F. I am really shocked at crouding you in such a manner, but my Grandmother (who bought all the furniture of this room) as she had never a very large Party, did not think it necessary to buy more Chairs than were sufficient for her own family and two of her particular freinds.

SOPHY. I beg you will make no apologies. Your Brother is very light.

STANLY

STANLY, *aside*) What a cherub is Cloe!

CLOE, *aside*) What a seraph is Stanly!

Enter a Servant.

SERVANT. Dinner is on table.

[*They all rise.*

MISS F. Lady Hampton, Miss Hampton, Miss Willoughby.

STANLY *hands* CLOE, LORD FITZGERALD, SOPHY, WILLOUGHBY, MISS FITZGERALD, *and* SIR ARTHUR, LADY HAMPTON.

[*Exeunt.*

Scene the 2ᵈ

The Dining Parlour.

MISS FITZGERALD *at top.* LORD FITZGERALD *at bottom. Company ranged on each side. Servants waiting.*

CLOE. I shall trouble Mr Stanly for a Little of the fried Cowheel & Onion.

STANLY. Oh Madam, there is a secret pleasure in helping so amiable a Lady —.

LADY H. I assure you my Lord, Sir Arthur

never

never touches wine; but Sophy will toss off a bumper I am sure to oblige your Lordship.

LORD F. Elder wine or Mead, Miss Hampton?

SOPHY. If it is equal to you Sir, I should prefer some warm ale with a toast and nutmeg.

LORD F. Two glasses of warmed ale with a toast and nutmeg.

MISS F. I am afraid Mr Willoughby you take no care of yourself. I fear you dont meet with any thing to your liking.

WILLOUGHBY. Oh! Madam, I can want for nothing while there are red herrings on table.

LORD F. Sir Arthur taste that Tripe. I think you will not find it amiss.

LADY H. Sir Arthur never eats Tripe; tis too savoury for him you know my Lord.

MISS F. Take away the Liver & Crow & bring in the suet pudding.

(*a short Pause.*)

MISS F. Sir Arthur shant I send you a bit of pudding?

LADY

LADY H. Sir Arthur never eats suet pudding Ma'am. It is too high a Dish for him.

MISS F. Will no one allow me the honour of helping them? Then John take away the Pudding, & bring the Wine.

[SERVANTS *take away the things and bring in the Bottles & Glasses.*

LORD F. I wish we had any Desert to offer you. But my Grandmother in her Lifetime, destroyed the Hothouse in order to build a receptacle for the Turkies with it's materials; & we have never been able to raise another tolerable one.

LADY H. I beg you will make no apologies my Lord.

WILLOUGHBY. Come Girls, let us circulate the Bottle.

SOPHY. A very good notion Cousin; & I will second it with all my Heart. Stanly you dont drink.

STANLY. Madam, I am drinking draughts of Love from Cloe's eyes.

SOPHY. That's poor nourishment truly. Come, drink to her better acquaintance.

[MISS FITZGERALD *goes to a Closet & brings out a bottle*

MISS F. This, Ladies & Gentlemen is some of my dear Grandmother's own manufacture. She excelled in Gooseberry Wine. Pray taste it Lady Hampton?

LADY H. How refreshing it is!

MISS F. I should think with your Ladyship's permission, that Sir Arthur might taste a little of it.

LADY H. Not for Worlds. Sir Arthur never drinks any thing so high.

LORD F. And now my amiable Sophia condescend to marry me.

[*He takes her hand & leads her to the front*

STANLY. Oh! Cloe could I but hope you would make me blessed—

CLOE. I will.

[*They advance.*

MISS

MISS F. Since you Willoughby are the only one left, I cannot refuse your earnest solicitations—There is my Hand.

LADY H. And may you all be Happy!

FINIS

THE

THE MYSTERY

AN UNFINISHED COMEDY

Dedication

To the Revd George Austen

S_IR_

I humbly solicit your Patronage to the following Comedy, which tho' an unfinished one, is I flatter myself as *complete* a *Mystery* as any of its kind.

> I am Sir your most Hum^le
> Servant
> T_HE_ A_UTHOR_

THE MYSTERY

A COMEDY

Dramatis Personae

MEN	WOMEN
Colonel Elliott	Fanny Elliott
Sir Edward Spangle	Mrs Humbug
Old Humbug	and
Young Humbug	Daphne
and	
Corydon	

A_CT_

ACT THE FIRST

Scene the 1st

A Garden.

Enter CORYDON.

CORY.) But Hush! I am interrupted.

[*Exit* CORYDON

Enter OLD HUMBUG *& his* SON, *talking.*

OLD HUM:) It is for that reason I wish you to
follow my advice. Are you convinced of its
propriety ?

YOUNG HUM:) I am Sir, and will certainly act
in the manner you have pointed out to me.

OLD HUM:) Then let us return to the House.

[*Exeunt*

Scene the 2d

A Parlour in HUMBUG'S *House.*

MRS HUMBUG *&* FANNY, *discovered at work.*

MRS HUM:) You understand me my Love ?

FANNY) Perfectly ma'am. Pray continue
your narration.

MRS HUM:) Alas! it is nearly concluded,

for

for I have nothing more to say on the Subject.

FANNY) Ah! here's Daphne.

Enter DAPHNE.

DAPHNE) My dear Mrs Humbug how d'ye do? Oh! Fanny t'is all over.

FANNY) Is it indeed!

MRS HUM:) I'm very sorry to hear it.

FANNY) Then t'was to no purpose that I. . . .

DAPHNE) None upon Earth.

MRS HUM:) And what is to become of? . . .

DAPHNE) Oh! thats all settled. (*whispers* MRS HUMBUG)

FANNY) And how is it determined?

DAPHNE) I'll tell you. (*whispers* FANNY)

MRS HUM:) And is he to? . . .

DAPHNE) I'll tell you all I know of the matter.

(*whispers* MRS HUMBUG *&* FANNY)

FANNY) Well! now I know everything about it, I'll go [and dress]¹ away.

MRS HUM:⎫
DAPHNE ⎬ And so will I.

[*Exeunt*

¹ *Erased in MS.*

Scene

Scene the 3ᵈ

The Curtain rises and discovers SIR ED-
WARD SPANGLE *reclined in an elegant Attitude on a Sofa, fast asleep.*

Enter COLONEL ELLIOTT.

COLONEL) My Daughter is not here I see . . .
there lies Sir Edward . . . Shall I tell him the
secret ? . . . No, he'll certainly blab it. . . .
But he is asleep and wont hear me. . . . So
I'll e'en venture.

[*Goes up to* SIR EDWARD, *whispers him, &*
Exit

End of the 1ˢᵗ Act.

FINIS

To

To Edward Austen Esqre

The following unfinished Novel
is respectfully inscribed
by
His obedient hum^le serv^t
THE AUTHOR

THE THREE SISTERS

A NOVEL

Letter 1st

MISS STANHOPE TO M^rs ...

MY DEAR FANNY

I am the happiest creature in the World,
for I have received an offer of marriage from
Mr Watts. It is the first I have ever had & I
hardly know how to value it enough. How
I will triumph over the Duttons! I do not
intend to accept it, at least I beleive not, but
as I am not quite certain I gave him an
equivocal answer & left him. And now my
dear

dear Fanny I want your Advice whether I should accept his offer or not, but that you may be able to judge of his merits & the situation of affairs I will give you an account of them. He is quite an old Man, about two & thirty, very plain, *so* plain that I cannot bear to look at him. He is extremely disagreable & I hate him more than any body else in the world. He has a large fortune & will make great Settlements on me; but then he is very healthy. In short I do not know what to do. If I refuse him he as good as told me that he should offer himself to Sophia and if *she* refused him to Georgiana, & I could not bear to have either of them married before me. If I accept him I know I shall be miserable all the rest of my Life, for he is very ill tempered & peevish extremely jealous, & so stingy that there is no living in the house with him. He told me he should mention the affair to Mama, but I insisted upon it that he did not for very likely she would make me marry him whether I would or no; however probably

P   he

he *has* before now, for he never does anything he is desired to do. I believe I shall
have him. It will be such a triumph to be
married before Sophy, Georgiana & the
Duttons; And he promised to have a new
Carriage on the occasion, but we almost
quarrelled about the colour, for I insisted
upon its being blue spotted with silver, & he
declared it should be a plain Chocolate; & to
provoke me more said it should be just as
low as his old one. I wont have him I declare. He said he should come again tomorrow & take my final answer, so I beleive I
must get him while I can. I know the Duttons will envy me & I shall be able to chaprone Sophy & Georgiana to all the Winter
Balls. But then what will be the use of that
when very likely he wont let me go myself,
for I know he hates dancing & [has a great
idea of Womens never going from home]¹
what he hates himself he has no idea of any
other person's liking; & besides he talks a
great deal of Women's always staying at

¹ Erased in MS.

home

home & such stuff. I beleive I shant have him; I would refuse him at once if I were certain that neither of my Sisters would accept him, & that if they did not, he would not offer to the Duttons. I cannot run such a risk, so, if he will promise to have the Carriage ordered as I like, I will have him, if not he may ride in it by himself for me. I hope you like my determination; I can think of nothing better;

And am your ever Affec^{te}

MARY STANHOPE

FROM THE SAME TO THE SAME

DEAR FANNY

I had but just sealed my last letter to you when my Mother came up & told me she wanted to speak to me on a very particular subject.

"Ah! I know what you mean; (said I) That old fool Mr Watts has told you all about it, tho' I bid him not. However you shant force me to have him if I don't like it."

"I am not going to force you Child, but only want

want to know what your resolution is with regard to his Proposals, & to insist upon your making up your mind one way or t'other, that if *you* dont accept him *Sophy* may."

"Indeed (replied I hastily) Sophy need not trouble herself for I shall certainly marry him myself."

"If that is your resolution" (said my Mother) why should you be afraid of my forcing your inclinations?"

"Why, because I have not settled whether I shall have him or not."

"You are the strangest Girl in the World Mary. What you say one moment, you unsay the next. Do tell me once for all, whether you intend to marry Mr Watts or not?"

"Law Mama how can I tell you what I dont know myself?"

"Then I desire you will know, & quickly too, for Mr Watts says he wont be kept in suspense."

"That depends upon me."

"No it does not, for if you do not give him your final answer tomorrow when he drinks

Tea

Tea with us, he intends to pay his Addresses to Sophy."

"Then I shall tell all the World that he behaved very ill to me."

"What good will that do? Mr Watts has been too long abused by all the World to mind it now."

"I wish I had a Father or a Brother because then they should fight him."

"They would be cunning if they did, for Mr Watts would run away first; & therefore you must & shall resolve either to accept or refuse him before tomorrow evening."

"But why if I don't have him, must he offer to my Sisters?"

"Why! because he wishes to be allied to the Family & because they are as pretty as you are."

"But will Sophy marry him Mama if he offers to her?"

"Most likely, Why should not she? If however she does not choose it, then Georgiana must, for I am determined not to let such an opportunity escape of settling one

of

of my Daughters so advantageously. So, make the most of your time; I leave you to settle the Matter with yourself." And then she went away. The only thing I can think of my dear Fanny is to ask Sophy & Georgiana whether they would have him were he to make proposals to them, & if they say they would not I am resolved to refuse him too, for I hate him more than you can imagine. As for the Duttons if he marries one of *them* I shall still have the triumph of having refused him first. So, adeiu my dear Friend—

Y^{rs} ever M.S.

MISS GEORGIANA STANHOPE TO MISS X X X

MY DEAR ANNE   Wednesday

Sophy & I have just been practising a little deceit on our eldest Sister, to which we are not perfectly reconciled, & yet the circumstances were such that if any thing will excuse it, they must. Our neighbour Mr Watts has made proposals to Mary: Proposals which she knew not how to receive,

for

for tho' she has a particular Dislike to him
(in which she is not singular) yet she would
willingly marry him sooner than risk his
offering to Sophy or me which in case of a
refusal from herself, he told her he should do,
for you must know the poor Girl considers
our marrying before her as one of the greatest
misfortunes that can possibly befall her, & to
prevent it would willingly ensure herself ever-
lasting Misery by a Marriage with Mr Watts.
An hour ago she came to us to sound our inclinations respecting the affair which were
to determine hers. A little before she came
my Mother had given us an account of it,
telling us that she certainly would not let
him go farther than our own family for a
Wife. "And therefore (said she) If Mary
wont have him Sophy must, & if Sophy wont
Georgiana *shall*". Poor Georgiana!—We
neither of us attempted to alter my Mother's
resolution, which I am sorry to say is generally more strictly kept than rationally
formed. As soon as she was gone however
I broke silence to assure Sophy that if Mary
should

should refuse Mr Watts I should not expect her to sacrifice *her* happiness by becoming his Wife from a motive of Generosity to me, which I was afraid her Good nature & sisterly affection might induce her to do.

"Let us flatter ourselves (replied She) that Mary will not refuse him. Yet how can I hope that my Sister may accept a Man who cannot make her happy."

"*He* cannot it is true but his Fortune, his Name, his House, his Carriage will and I have no doubt but that Mary will marry him; indeed why should she not? He is not more than two & thirty; a very proper age for a Man to marry at; He is rather plain to be sure, but then what is Beauty in a Man; if he has but a genteel figure & a sensible looking Face it is quite sufficient."

"This is all very true Georgiana but Mr Watts's figure is unfortunately extremely vulgar & his Countenance is very heavy."

"And then as to his temper; it has been reckoned bad, but may not the World be deceived in their Judgement of it. There is

an

an open Frankness in his Disposition which becomes a Man; They say he is stingy; We'll call that Prudence. They say he is suspicious. *That* proceeds from a warmth of Heart always excusable in Youth, & in short I see no reason why he should not make a very good Husband, or why Mary should not be very happy with him."

Sophy laughed; I continued,

"However whether Mary accepts him or not I am resolved. My determination is made. I never would marry Mr Watts were Beggary the only alternative. So deficient in every respect! Hideous in his person and without one good Quality to make amends for it. His fortune to be sure is good. Yet not so very large! Three thousand a year. What is three thousand a year? It is but six times as much as my Mother's income. It will not tempt me."

"Yet it will be a noble fortune for Mary" said Sophy laughing again.

"For Mary! Yes indeed it will give me pleasure to see *her* in such affluence.'

Q   Thus

Thus I ran on to the great Entertainment of my Sister till Mary came into the room to appearance in great agitation. She sate down. We made room for her at the fire. She seemed at a loss how to begin & at last said in some confusion

"Pray Sophy have you any mind to be married?"

"To be married! None in the least. But why do you ask me? Are you acquainted with any one who means to make me proposals?"

"I—no, how should I? But mayn't I ask a common question?"

"Not a very *common* one Mary surely." (said I). She paused & after some moments silence went on—

"How should you like to marry Mr Watts Sophy?"

I winked at Sophy & replied for her. "Who is there but must rejoice to marry a man of three thousand a year [who keeps a post-chaise & pair, with silver Harness, a boot before & a window to look out at behind?"][1]

[1] *Erased in MS.*

"Very

"Very true (she replied) That's very true. So you would have him if he would offer, Georgiana, & would *you* Sophy?"

Sophy did not like the idea of telling a lie & deceiving her Sister; she prevented the first & saved half her conscience by equivocation.

"I should certainly act just as Georgiana would do."

"Well then said Mary with triumph in her Eyes, *I* have had an offer from Mr Watts."

We were of course very much surprised; "Oh! do not accept him said I, and then perhaps he may have me."

In short my scheme took & Mary is resolved to do *that* to prevent our supposed happiness which she would not have done to ensure it in reality. Yet after all my Heart cannot acquit me & Sophy is even more scrupulous. Quiet our Minds my dear Anne by writing & telling us you approve our conduct. Consider it well over. Mary will have real pleasure in being a married Woman, & able to chaprone us, which she certainly shall do, for I think myself
bound

bound to contribute as much as possible to her happiness in a State I have made her choose. They will probably have a new Carriage, which will be paradise to her, & if we can prevail on Mr. W. to set up his Phaeton she will be too happy. These things however would be no consolation to Sophy or me for domestic Misery. Remember all this & do not condemn us.

Friday.

Last night Mr Watts by appointment drank tea with us. As soon as his Carriage stopped at the Door, Mary went to the Window.

"Would you beleive it Sophy (said she) the old Fool wants to have his new Chaise just the colour of the old one, & hung as low too. But it shant—I *will* carry my point. And if he wont let it be as high as the Duttons, & blue spotted with silver, I wont have him. Yes I will too. Here he comes. I know he'll be rude; I know he'll be illtempered & wont say one civil thing to me! nor behave

at

at all like a Lover." She then sate down &
Mr Watts entered.

"Ladies your most obedient." We paid
our Compliments & he seated himself.

"Fine weather Ladies." Then turning to
Mary, "Well Miss Stanhope I hope you have
at last settled the Matter in your own mind;
& will be so good as to let me know whether
you will *condescend* to marry me or not".

"I think Sir (said Mary) You might have
asked in a genteeler way than that. I do not
know whether I *shall* have you if you behave
so odd."

"Mary!" (said my Mother) "Well Mama
if he will be so cross. . . . ."

"Hush, hush, Mary, you shall not be rude
to Mr Watts."

"Pray Madam do not lay any restraint
on Miss Stanhope by obliging her to be civil.
If she does not choose to accept my hand,
I can offer it else where, for as I am by no
means guided by a particular preference to
you above your Sisters it is equally the same
to me which I marry of the three." Was
there

there ever such a Wretch! Sophy reddened with anger, & I felt *so* spiteful!

"Well then (said Mary in a peevish Accent) I *will* have you if I *must*."

"I should have thought Miss Stanhope that when such Settlements are offered as I have offered to you there can be no great violence done to the inclinations in accepting of them."

Mary mumbled out something, which I who sate close to her could just distinguish to be "What's the use of a great Jointure if Men live forever?" And then audibly "Remember the pinmoney; two hundred a year."

"A hundred and seventy-five Madam."

"Two hundred indeed Sir" said my Mother.

"And Remember I am to have a new Carriage hung as high as the Duttons', & blue spotted with silver; and I shall expect a new saddle horse, a suit of fine lace, and an infinite number of the most valuable Jewels. Diamonds such as never were seen, [Pearls
as

as large as those of the Princess Badroul-
badour in the 4th Volume of the Arabian
Nights and Rubies, Emeralds, Toppazes,
Sapphires, Amythists, Turkeystones, Agate,
Beads, Bugles & Garnets][1] and Pearls,
Rubies, Emeralds and Beads out of number.
You must set up your Phaeton which must
be cream coloured with a wreath of silver
flowers round it, You must buy 4 of the
finest Bays in the Kingdom & you must drive
me in it every day. This is not all; You must
entirely new furnish your House after my
Taste, You must hire two more Footmen to
attend me, two Women to wait on me, must
always let me do just as I please & make a
very good husband."

Here she stopped, I beleive rather out of
breath.

"This is all very reasonable Mr Watts for
my Daughter to expect."

"And it is very reasonable Mrs Stanhope
that your daughter should be disappointed."
He was going on but Mary interrupted him

[1] *Erased in MS.*

"You

"You must build me an elegant Greenhouse & stock it with plants. You must let me spend every Winter in Bath, every Spring in Town, Every Summer in taking some Tour, & every Autumn at a Watering Place, and if we are at home the rest of the year (Sophy & I laughed) You must do nothing but give Balls & Masquerades. You must build a room on purpose & a Theatre to act Plays in. The first Play we have shall be *Which is the Man*, and I will do Lady Bell Bloomer."

"And pray Miss Stanhope (said Mr Watts) What am I to expect from you in return for all this."

"Expect? why you may expect to have me pleased."

"It would be odd if I did not. Your expectations Madam are too high for me, & I must apply to Miss Sophy who perhaps may not have raised her's so much."

"You are mistaken Sir in supposing so, (said Sophy) for tho' they may not be exactly in the same Line, yet my expectations are to the full as high as my Sister's; for I expect

my

my Husband to be good tempered & Chear-
ful; to consult my Happiness in all his Actions,
& to love me with Constancy & Sincerity."

Mr Watts stared. "These are very odd
Ideas truly young Lady. You had better
discard them before you marry, or you will
be obliged to do it afterwards."

My Mother in the meantime was lecturing
Mary who was sensible that she had gone
too far, & when Mr Watts was just turning
towards me in order I beleive to address me,
she spoke to him in a voice half humble, half
sulky.

"You are mistaken Mr Watts if you think
I was in earnest when I said I expected so
much. However I must have a new Chaise."

"Yes Sir, you must allow that Mary has a
right to expect that."

"Mrs Stanhope, I *mean* & have always
meant to have a new one on my Marriage.
But it shall be the colour of my present one."

"I think Mr Watts you should pay my
Girl the compliment of consulting her Taste
on such Matters."

Mr

Mr Watts would not agree to this, & for some time insisted upon its being a Chocolate colour, while Mary was as eager for having it blue with silver Spots. At length however Sophy proposed that to please Mr W. it should be a dark brown & to please Mary it should be hung rather high & have a silver Border. This was at length agreed to, tho' reluctantly on both sides, as each had intended to carry their point entire. We then proceeded to other Matters, & it was settled that they should be married as soon as the Writings could be completed. Mary was very eager for a Special Licence & Mr Watts talked of Banns. A common Licence was at last agreed on. Mary is to have all the Family Jewels which are very inconsiderable I beleive & Mr W. promised to buy her a Saddle horse; but in return she is not to expect to go to Town or any other public place for these three Years. She is to have neither Greenhouse, Theatre or Phaeton; to be contented with one Maid without an additional Footman. It engrossed the whole Evening

Evening to settle these affairs; Mr W. supped with us & did not go till twelve. As soon as he was gone Mary exclaimed "Thank Heaven! he's off at last; how I do hate him!" It was in vain that Mama represented to her the impropriety she was guilty of in disliking him who was to be her Husband, for she persisted in declaring her aversion to him & hoping she might never see him again. What a Wedding will this be! Adeiu my dear Anne. Y^r faithfully Sincere

GEORGIANA STANHOPE

FROM THE SAME TO THE SAME

DEAR ANNE   Saturday

Mary eager to have every one know of her approaching Wedding & more particularly desirous of triumphing as she called it over the Duttons, desired us to walk with her this Morning to Stoneham. As we had nothing else to do we readily agreed, & had as pleasant a walk as we could have with Mary whose conversation entirely consisted in abusing the Man she is so soon to marry & in in longing for a blue Chaise spotted with Silver. When we reached the Duttons we found the two Girls in the dressing-room with a very handsome Young Man, who was of course introduced to us. He is the son of Sir Henry Brudenell of Leicestershire—[Not related to the Family & ... even but distantly connected with it. His Sister is married to John Dutton's Wife's Brother. When you have puzzled over this account a little you will understand it.][1] Mr Brudenell is the handsomest Man I ever saw in my Life; we are all three very much pleased with him. Mary, who from the moment of our reaching the Dressing-room had been swelling with the knowledge of her own importance & with the Desire of making it known, could not remain long silent on the Subject after we were seated, & soon addressing herself to Kitty said,

"Dont you think it will be necessary to have all the Jewels new set?"

"Necessary for what?"

[1] *Erased in MS.*

"For

"For What! Why for my appearance."

"I beg your pardon but I really do not understand you. What Jewels do you speak of, & where is your appearance to be made?"

"At the next Ball to be sure after I am married."

You may imagine their Surprise. They were at first incredulous, but on our joining in the Story they at last beleived it. "And who is it to" was of course the first Question. Mary pretended Bashfulness, & answered in Confusion her Eyes cast down "to Mr Watts". This also required Confirmation from us, for that anyone who had the Beauty & fortune (tho' small yet a provision) of Mary would willingly marry Mr Watts, could by them scarcely be credited. The subject being now fairly introduced and she found herself the object of every one's attention in company, she lost all her confusion & became perfectly unreserved & communicative.

"I wonder you should never have heard of it before for in general things of this Nature

Nature are very well known in the Neighbourhood."

"I assure you said Jemima I never had the least suspicion of such an affair. Has it been in agitation long?"

"Oh! Yes, ever since Wednesday."

They all smiled particularly Mr Brudenell.

"You must know Mr Watts is very much in love with me, so that it is quite a match of affection on his side."

"Not on his only, I suppose" said Kitty.

"Oh! when there is so much Love on one side there is no occasion for it on the other. However I do not much dislike him tho' he is very plain to be sure."

Mr Brudenell stared, the Miss Duttons laughed & Sophy & I were heartily ashamed of our Sister. She went on.

"We are to have a new Postchaise & very likely may set up our Phaeton."

This we knew to be false but the poor Girl was pleased at the idea of persuading the company that such a thing was to be & I would

would not deprive her of so harmless an Enjoyment. She continued.

"Mr Watts is to present me with the family Jewels which I fancy are very considerable." I could not help whispering Sophy "I fancy not". "These Jewels are what I suppose must be new set before they can be worn. I shall not wear them till the first Ball I go to after my Marriage. If Mrs Dutton should not go to it, I hope you will let me chaprone you; I shall certainly take Sophy & Georgiana."

"You are very good (said Kitty) & since you are inclined to undertake the Care of young Ladies, I should advise you to prevail on Mrs Edgecumbe to let you chaprone her six Daughters which with your two Sisters and ourselves will make your Entrée very respectable."

Kitty made us all smile except Mary who did not understand her Meaning & coolly said that she should not like to chaprone so many. Sophy & I now endeavoured to change the conversation but succeeded only for a

few

few Minutes, for Mary took care to bring back their attention to her & her approaching Wedding. I was sorry for my Sister's sake to see that Mr Brudenell seemed to take pleasure in listening to her account of it, & even encouraged her by his Questions & Remarks, for it was evident that his only Aim was to laugh at her. I am afraid he found her very ridiculous. He kept his Countenance extremely well, yet it was easy to see that it was with difficulty he kept it. At length however he seemed fatigued & Disgusted with her ridiculous Conversation, as he turned from her to us, & spoke but little to her for about half an hour before we left Stoneham. As soon as we were out of the House we all joined in praising the Person & Manners of Mr Brudenell.

We found Mr Watts at home.

"So, Miss Stanhope (said he) you see I am come a courting in a true Lover like Manner."

"Well you need not have *told* me that. I knew why you came very well."

Sophy & I then left the room, imagining of
course

course that we must be in the way, if a Scene
of Courtship were to begin. We were surprised at being followed almost immediately
by Mary.

"And is your Courting so soon over?"
said Sophy.

"Courting! (replied Mary) we have been
quarrelling. Watts is such a Fool! I hope
I shall never see him again."

"I am afraid you will, (said I) as he dines
here today. But what has been your dispute?"

"Why only because I told him that I had
seen a Man much handsomer than he was
this Morning, he flew into a great Passion &
called me a Vixen, so I only stayed to tell him
I thought him a Blackguard & came away."

"Short & sweet; (said Sophy) but pray
Mary how will this be made up?"

"He ought to ask my pardon; but if he
did, I would not forgive him."

"His Submission then would not be very
useful."

When we were dressed we returned to the

s   Parlour

Parlour where Mama & Mr Watts were in close Conversation. It seems that he had been complaining to her of her Daughter's behaviour, & she had persuaded him to think no more of it. He therefore met Mary with all his accustomed Civility, & except one touch at the Phaeton & another at the Greenhouse, the Evening went off with great Harmony & Cordiality. Watts is going to Town to hasten the preparations for the Wedding.

I am your affec^{te} Freind G.S.

To

To Miss Jane Anna Elizabeth Austen

MY DEAR NEÏCE

Though you are at this period not many degrees removed from Infancy, Yet trusting that you will in time be older, and that through the care of your excellent Parents, You will one day or another be able to read written hand, I dedicate to You the following Miscellanious Morsels, convinced that if you seriously attend to them, You will derive from them very important Instructions, with regard to your Conduct in Life.—If such My hopes should hereafter be realized, never shall I regret the Days and Nights that have been spent in composing these Treatises for your Benefit. I am my dear Neice

Your very Affectionate
Aunt.

THE AUTHOR

June 2ᵈ
1793

[A FRAGMENT

written to inculcate the practise of Virtue

WE all know that many are unfortunate in their progress through the world, but we do

s 2

not

not know all that are so. To seek them out to study their wants, & to leave them unsupplied is the duty, and ought to be the Business of Man. But few have time, fewer still have inclination, and no one has either the one or the other for such employments. Who amidst those that perspire away their Evenings in crouded assemblies can have leisure to bestow a thought on such as sweat under the fatigue of their daily Labour.][1]

A BEAUTIFUL DESCRIPTION OF THE DIFFERENT EFFECTS OF SENSIBILITY ON DIFFERENT MINDS.

I AM but just returned from Melissa's Bedside, & in my Life tho' it has been a pretty long one, & I have during the course of it been at many Bedsides, I never saw so affecting an object as she exhibits. She lies wrapped in a book muslin bedgown, a chambray gauze shift, and a french net nightcap. Sir William is constantly at her bedside. The only repose he takes is on the Sopha in the

---

[1] *Erased in MS.*

Drawing

Drawing room, where for five minutes every
fortnight he remains in an imperfect Slum-
ber, starting up every Moment & exclaiming
"Oh! Melissa, Ah! Melissa," then sinking
down again, raises his left arm and scratches
his head. Poor Mrs Burnaby is beyond measure afflicted. She sighs every now & then,
that is about once a week; while the melancholy Charles says every Moment "Melissa
how are you?" The lovely Sisters are much
to be pitied. Julia is ever lamenting the
situation of her freind, while lying behind
her pillow & supporting her head—Maria
more mild in her greif talks of going to Town
next week, & Anna is always recurring to
the pleasures we once enjoyed when Melissa
was well.—I am usually at the fire cooking
some little delicacy for the unhappy invalid
—Perhaps hashing up the remains of an old
Duck, toasting some cheese or making a
Curry which are the favourite dishes of our
poor friend. In these situations we were this
morning surprised by receiving a visit from
Dr Dowkins: "I am come to see Melissa,"
                                        said

said he. "How is She?" "Very weak indeed,
said the fainting Melissa. "Very weak, replied the punning Doctor, aye indeed it is
more than a very *week* since you have taken
to your bed—How is your appetite?" "Bad,
very bad, said Julia." "That *is* very bad—
replied he. Are her spirits good, Madam?"
"So poorly Sir that we are obliged to
strengthen her with cordials every Minute."
—"Well then she receives *Spirits* from your
being with her. Does she sleep?" "Scarcely
ever."—"And Ever Scarcely I suppose when
she does. Poor thing! Does she think of
dieing? "She has not strength to think at
all. "Nay then she cannot think to have
Strength."

THE GENEROUS CURATE

a moral Tale, setting forth the
Advantages of being Generous and a Curate.

In a part little known of the County of
Warwick, a very worthy Clergyman lately
resided. The income of his living which
amounted to about two hundred pound, &
the

the interest of his Wife's fortune which was
nothing at all, was entirely sufficient for the
Wants & Wishes of a Family who neither
wanted or wished for anything beyond what
their income afforded them. Mr Williams
had been in possession of his living above
twenty Years, when this history commences,
& his Marriage which had taken place soon
after his presentation to it, had made him
the father of six very fine Children. The
eldest had been placed at the Royal Academy
for Seamen at Portsmouth when about thir-
teen years old, and from thence had been
discharged on board of one of the Vessels of
a small fleet destined for Newfoundland,
where his promising & amiable disposition
had procured him many freinds among the
Natives, & from whence he regularly sent
home a large Newfoundland Dog every
Month to his family. The second, who was
also a Son had been adopted by a neighbour-
ing Clergyman with the intention of educat-
ing him at his own expence, which would
have been a very desirable Circumstance had
the

the Gentleman's fortune been equal to his generosity, but as he had nothing to support himself and a very large family but a Curacy of fifty pound a year, Young Williams knew nothing more at the age of 18 than what a twopenny Dame's School in the village could teach him. His Character however was perfectly amiable though his genius might be cramped, and he was addicted to no vice, or ever guilty of any fault beyond what his age and situation rendered perfectly excusable. He had indeed sometimes been detected in flinging Stones at a Duck or putting brickbats into his Benefactor's bed; but these innocent efforts of wit were considered by that good Man rather as the effects of a lively imagination, than of anything bad in his Nature, and if any punishment were decreed for the offence it was in general no greater than that the Culprit should pick up the Stones or take the brickbats away.—

FINIS

To

To Miss Austen, the following Ode to Pity is
dedicated, from a thorough knowledge of her piti-
ful Nature, by her obed[t] hum[le] Serv[t]

THE AUTHOR

ODE TO PITY

1

Ever musing I delight to tread
    The Paths of honour and the Myrtle
      Grove
Whilst the pale Moon her beams doth shed
      On disappointed Love.
While Philomel on airy hawthorn Bush
    Sings sweet & Melancholy, And the thrush
Converses with the Dove.

2

Gently brawling down the turnpike road,
    Sweetly noisy falls the Silent Stream—
The Moon emerges from behind a Cloud
    And darts upon the Myrtle Grove her
      beam.

Ah!

Ah! then what Lovely Scenes appear,
    The hut, the Cot, the Grot, & Chapel queer,
And eke the Abbey too a mouldering heap,
    Conceal'd by aged pines her head doth rear
And quite invisible doth take a peep.

END OF THE FIRST VOLUME

June 3d 1793

CONTENTS

The Analysis of Defense:
The Ego and the Mechanisms of
Defense Revisited

The Analysis of Defense:
The Ego and the
Mechanisms of Defense
Revisited

Joseph Sandler
with
Anna Freud

International Universities Press, Inc.
New York   New York

Library of Congress Cataloging in Publication Data

Sandler, Joseph.
   The analysis of defense.

   Bibliography: p.
   Includes index.
   1. Freud, Anna, 1895-   . Ich und die Abwehhr-mechanismen. 2. Ego (Psychology) 3. Defense mechanisms (Psychology) I. Freud, Anna, 1895-   . II. Title.
BF173.F6183S26   1984   154.2′2   84-12980
ISBN 0-8236-0496-9

Contents

v

Part III
Examples of Two Types of Defense

Part IV
Defense Motivated by Fear of the
Strength of the Instincts
Illustrated by the Phenomena of Puberty

Preface

Following a number of meetings of the Index Research
Group at the Hampstead Clinic, London, at which various problems relating to defense mechanisms were discussed, it became apparent that it would be of the
greatest value to look again at Anna Freud's classic work,
The Ego and the Mechanisms of Defense. Fortunately
Miss Freud was able and willing to join with the research
group in undertaking a series of discussions over the
period of a year in 1972–73. I took the chair at these
meetings, and in a way acted as spokesman for the group,
so that for the most part the discussions take the form
of a dialogue between Anna Freud and myself. Staff
members, senior students, and occasional visitors attended the discussions, which were tape recorded and
later transcribed. The verbatim transcripts were subsequently edited, and the "discussion" format of the in-
terchanges was retained. The result was a series of papers
published in *The Bulletin of the Hampstead Clinic* from
1980 onward. This book contains the essential material

in those papers, edited slightly to remove redundant material.

Miss Freud read the bulk of the edited transcripts before publication in the *Bulletin*, and made a few amendments. Unfortunately she became seriously ill and died just before the final chapters were to be submitted to her. The discussions, in which she participated so actively, took place over a period during which she celebrated her seventy-sixth birthday, and will remain as a tribute to her remarkable intellectual powers and clarity of expression. The content of her remarks has taken our understanding of the mechanisms of defense many steps forward, and has served to place *The Ego and the Mechanisms of Defense* in a truer and clearer perspective.

Psychoanalysis has developed and expanded very much since 1936, the year Anna Freud's book was published in German by the *Internationaler Psychoanalytischer Verlag*. The English edition, translated by Cecil Baines, appeared in the International Psycho-Analytical Library (The Hogarth Press and the Institute of Psycho-Analysis, London) in 1937, and a revised English edition, containing minor changes only, was published in 1966. In the United States both English language editions were published by International Universities Press.

Before our discussions got under way, Anna Freud commented on the translation of the book into English. "The English is not mine," she said, "because at the time the book was written I did not yet write in English, and the book had to be translated. I never corrected the translation later, nor did I make it more personal, so in certain respects the German version is very much closer to the original meaning than the English one." We were able to take up questions of the appropriateness of the translation at various points in the discussions.

The organization of this volume follows that of Anna Freud's book, and the titles of the parts and chapters are the same as hers. Each chapter is introduced by a summary of the corresponding chapter in *The Ego and the Mechanisms of Defense*, and reports of the various sessions devoted to discussion of issues arising from that chapter then follow. To some extent the material has been rearranged for this book to bring related remarks together and to avoid the discontinuity that inevitably affects this sort of discussion. The numbers given in parentheses throughout the text are the appropriate page numbers of the 1937 and 1966 editions respectively. The quotations in the text are taken from the 1966 American edition.

Many acknowledgments are due to those who have helped bring this volume into being. The Index Committee at the time consisted of Maria Berger, Marion Burgner, Rose Edgcumbe, Alex Holder, Ann Hurry, Hansi Kennedy, and myself (as Chairman). Trudi Dembovitz and Doreen Ross were responsible for transcribing the discussions, and we are extremely grateful to them for their painstaking and accurate work. Alex Holder, editor of *The Bulletin of the Hampstead Clinic*, was most helpful in seeing the original transcripts through to publication, and a great debt is owed to him and to his able assistant, Barbara Sullivan. The following participated to greater or lesser degree in the discussions and provided, both by their contributions and their presence, a most supportive background to the meetings: Maria

Berger, Lucy Biven, Dorothy Burlingham, Donald
Campbell, Arthur Couch, Rose Edgcumbe, Irmi Elkan,
Robert Evans, W. Ernst Freud, Ralph Greenson, Ilse
Hellman, Alex Holder, Ann Hurry, Hansi Kennedy,
Tom Lopez, Molly Mason, Renate Putzel, Sara Rosenfeld, Mahmoud Sanai, Lore Schacht, Marjorie Sprince,
Vann Spruiell, Robert L. Tyson, and Clifford Yorke.
The editing and preparation of the material for this
book has been carried out at the Sigmund Freud Center
for Study and Research in Psychoanalysis at the Hebrew
University of Jerusalem, and it gives me great pleasure
to acknowledge the excellent help of Meir Perlow, Research Fellow at the Center, and the constant support
of the Center's administrator, Hannah Groumi, whose
intelligence, skill, and limitless capacity for work steered
this manuscript through to completion. Michele Morow-
itz's dedication to the difficult typing and editing of the
final manuscript deserves very special mention. Finally,
many thanks are due to Anne-Marie Sandler and Rivka
Eifermann for reading and commenting on the manuscript during the editing process.
The Hampstead Clinic has at times received financial
support from the following: the American Philanthropic
Foundation, Philadelphia; the Gustave M. Berne Foundation, New York; Lionel Blitsten Memorial, Inc., Chicago; the G. G. Bunzl Fund; the H. Daroff Foundation,
New York; the Division Fund, Chicago; the Herman A.
and Amelia S. Ehrmann Foundation, New York; the
Field Foundation, New York; the Foundation for Research in Psychoanalysis, Beverly Hills, California; the
Foundation for Research in Psychiatry, New Haven,
Conn.; the Freud Centenary Fund, London; Grant

Foundation Inc., New York City; the Estate of Flora
Haas, New York; the Lita Hazen Charitable Fund, Philadelphia; the A. and M. Lasker Foundation, New York;
the Anne Pollock Lederer Research Institute, Chicago;
the Leslie Foundation, Chicago; the John D. and Cath-
erine T. MacArthur Foundation, Chicago; the Andrew
Mellon Foundation, later Paul Mellon; the Walter E.
Meyer Research Institute of Law, New Haven, Conn.;
the National Institute of Mental Health, Bethesda, Md.;
the New-Land Foundation, New York; the Overbrook
Fund, New York; the Psychoanalytic Research and De-
velopment Fund, New York; the William Rosenwald
Family Fund, Inc., New York; the William Sachs Foun-
dation, New York; the J. and M. Scheider Foundation,
New York; the Philip M. Stern Foundation, Washington,
D.C.; the W. Clement and Jessie V. Stone Foundation,
Chicago; the Taconic Foundation, New York; the Leslie
Tuchman Fund, New York; the Wolfson Foundation,
London; and a number of private donors.

Finally, special thanks are due to the Foundation for
Research in Psychoanalysis in Los Angeles, and to the
Sturman Center for Human Development of the Hebrew
University of Jerusalem for financial assistance at various
points in the preparation of the manuscript.

Joseph Sandler
Jerusalem, December 1983

Part I

Theory of the Mechanisms of Defense

CHAPTER 1

The Ego as the Seat of Observation

Anna Freud begins the first chapter of her book by pointing out that psychoanalysis had, in the past, concentrated on studying the content of what was deeply repressed. Emphasis was placed on processes occurring in the depths of the mind, and it was thought to be nonpsychoanalytic, until the twenties (with the publication of *Group Psychology and the Analysis of the Ego* and *Beyond the Pleasure Principle*), to study adjustment to the external world and similar ideas. There may have been some historical justification for the older view, for psychoanalysis was, as Anna Freud put it, "pre-eminently a psychology of the unconscious or, as we should say today, of the id" (4,4). However, she goes on to say that such a definition "immediately loses all claim to accuracy when we apply it to psychoanalytic therapy. From the beginning analysis, as a therapeutic method, was con-

3

cerned with the ego and its aberrations: the investigation of the id and of its mode of operation was always only a means to an end. And the end was invariably the same: the correction of these abnormalities and the restoration of the ego to its integrity" (4,4).

Anna Freud then points out that one might now define the task of analysis as being to gain as much knowledge as possible of id, ego, and superego, as well as their relations to one another and to the external world. Further, the analytic task is "in relation to the ego, to explore its contents, its boundaries, and its functions, and to trace the history of its dependence on the outside world, the id, and the superego; and, in relation to the id, to give an account of the instincts, i.e., of the id contents, and to follow them through the transformations which they undergo" (5,5).

In this chapter Anna Freud remarks that our knowledge of the id or of the system Unconscious is gained from derivatives which enter the systems Preconscious and Conscious. If the id is quiescent, then it will not intrude upon the ego, it will not create tension, and we cannot observe it. Even the superego, normally much more conscious, will not be perceived if it is at one with the ego. It becomes distinct only when it is at odds with the ego, as when it arouses guilt feelings. From this Anna Freud concludes that "the proper field for our observation is always the ego" (6,6). When the relation of id to ego is a peaceful one, the ego permits the id access to motility and satisfaction, and might put its energies at the id's disposal. The instinctual impulse can be clearly observed. However, the territory of the ego provides an "alien atmosphere" (7,7) for the impulse, which normally follows the primary process and the pleasure principle in the id. In the ego the instinctual impulse has to conform to reality and to the standards of the superego. This may bring an end to the good relations between the id and the ego, and the impulses will then, Anna Freud says, make "hostile incursions" (7,7) into the territory of the ego, which counterattacks, using appropriate defenses. Now what is seen is a combination of id impulse and ego defenses, and it is the work of the analyst to dissect the picture into its components.

The ego knows nothing of its own defensive measures, and the observer can reconstruct the operation of the defenses only by their outcome. For example, successful repression leads to the noticeable absence of certain material. Similarly, the ego is unaware of what goes on in the creation of a reaction formation. Anna Freud notes that important knowledge has been gained by studying the way in which id impulses are dealt with by the ego. They may break through, as in neurosis, and we can then study the processes well. Similarly, reaction formations in the process of breakdown, in which the impulse as well as the defense can at times be seen to co-exist within the ego, can provide fruitful material for analytic study.

The Discussion

Joseph Sandler: Miss Freud, I should like to introduce the discussion by asking what we should consider to be the instinctual or id "unit" that is worked on and transformed by the ego. You speak of the *impulse*, but it is not clear here whether the term refers to drive energy, to some unknowable urge, or to an unconscious wish that contains mental content. Is it sufficient, from a psychological point of view, for us to speak of the instinctual wish, and to treat this as a psychologically irreducible unit? If we do this, then we would think of the wish, after a certain point in development has been passed, as involving self- and object representations, and we could also see the aim of the instinctual wish as being represented to the ego. So while on the one hand we might speak of the id as the source of instinctual drives, on the other we might perhaps better refer to the instinctual wish as the psychologically meaningful id element. Would that be correct?

Anna Freud: Yes, what you say about the drive impulse and the wish is quite correct. What I had in mind when I wrote the book was what we would now call the wish, as well as the other psychological ways in which derivatives of the drive can appear in consciousness. It is perhaps not quite easy for those who read the book today to grasp the atmosphere in which it was written. One might well ask, when one reads the first chapter, Why does the further content of the book need something which is almost an apology? But you should remember that these were the years when the introduction of the ego as such into psychoanalytic discussion or into the literature was suspect to most analysts. From my side I put forward ideas about the ego's relationship to the unconscious id. From Heinz Hartmann's side came ideas relating to the conflict-free area of the ego. And these two came more or less together before the Vienna Society. There was quite a big body of opinion very much hostile to any attempt to deal with the ego or with ego activity as such. This was never the case in my father's writings, but it was very much so in the minds of the other analysts. I remember Helene Deutsch, who was at the time half in America, saying that I will finish myself with analysts forever with that book because I dealt with the ego and not with the id. Of course, this is not true because I dealt with the relations between the two. What I want to convey is the atmosphere at the time, and that was really what I battled with in the first chapter of my book. I was saying, "Look at it, the ego has always been included in the analytic work, the whole analytic work is undertaken for its sake." It is all very difficult for us to imagine now.

Joseph Sandler: As theoretical conceptions have always followed technique in the development of psychoanalysis, it would be helpful if you could comment on what has been called *defense analysis*. It has always seemed to me that the term might be rather misleading, because from a technical point of view our emphasis is more on the analysis of resistances than on particular defenses. We only interpret defenses in the context of whatever is being defended against. And what was the status of the analysis of resistances at the time you wrote the book? There are still important differences between analysts in this regard.

Anna Freud: Defense analysis did not exist as a technical term at that time. I seem to remember that the term was introduced by Berta Bornstein in the area of child analysis. At that time we talked of analyzing the defenses first. What I tried to bring out in a later chapter of my book is that I think the way to arrive at the understanding of the defenses is to watch for their appearance as resistances in analysis. Of course this was always present in our technique, but it was not discussed, nor was it recognized for what it was.

Joseph Sandler: Perhaps the analysis of resistances or of specific defenses was regarded as part of the art of analysis. By interpreting the patient's conflict or anxiety the patient could feel easier about releasing repressed material.

Anna Freud: Yes, that was very much our technique, but we relied greatly on free association bringing up the resistances. At that time there was much more insistence on free association than there is now, because it was really the task of the patient to free associate. Nowadays, for many analysts, to ask the patient to undertake free association represents an undue interference with his rights as a citizen, with his right to say what he wants to say, and to retain what he does not want to say. But at that time an analyst was entitled to give up a patient if he did not agree to free associate.

Joseph Sandler: There are many analysts who take the view that, at all costs, one must not do anything which guides or leads the patient.

Anna Freud: Yes, the idea is "let him do what he wants." But in the past we thought that without free association one would never get at the unconscious.

Maria Berger: I should like to ask whether in the days preceding the emphasis on the ego and on the defenses one dealt with the patient's resistance differently. In other words, is not one of the messages in your book to treat resistance as a manifestation of defenses and to interpret them? Perhaps before that resistances were considered as something bad which got in the way of the analytic work.

Anna Freud: That may have been the case at the very beginning, but certainly it has not been so for many years. In regard to resistance one has to differentiate between the conscious withholding of material and a withholding that is determined by the patient's defenses. This difference is enormous. If a patient says to the analyst, as many patients now do, "Of course I can't tell you anything about my sex life, that's much too embarrassing," many analysts would accept it now and say to themselves, "perhaps next year." Whereas in the past one would have said, "All right, but don't expect me to help you until you tell me about it, because we will not be doing the analysis until you do." A patient may say nowadays, "Of course I can't mention money, that's very embarrassing."

Joseph Sandler: Or thoughts about the analyst . . .

Anna Freud: . . . because that would be rude, or thoughts about something outside the analysis—that would be indiscreet. In the past one would say to the patient, "Well, of course, don't if you don't want to, but then the analytic method that I explained to you won't work because it is built on your saying what is in your mind."

Joseph Sandler: Perhaps there would be a case for saying, "Well, if you can't talk about this there must be a good reason, and perhaps we should look at the reason."

Anna Freud: But he might just say, "Yes, it makes me feel very embarrassed." I remember a woman patient to whom I pointed out that she always became very vague whenever any mention of money was called for. She was withholding consciously, and she told me, "Well, you aren't my Tax Inspector." Nowadays the attitude toward free association is perhaps different because the analyst, I suppose, hopes that what free association will not bring in will be brought in by the transference. Only the transference is also subject to free association.

Joseph Sandler: If we have a patient who says, "I can't say what I thought about you when I came in, I'm too embarrassed," would it not be a mistake to have a head-on confrontation about free association? Might it not be better to say something like, "Why should you be so embarrassed? Do you have any idea why you are so embarrassed?" Is it worth trying to get associations to the resistance?

Anna Freud: It is not resistance in this case. Conscious withholding is never resistance. I would say something quite different to the patient. I would say, "It's a very good sign that you told me so soon that you can't talk about it, because that means that you will mention it very soon." The real withholding is not to mention it at all. In the past we did not use the word "resistance" for conscious withholding, which is more an unwillingness to cooperate.

Joseph Sandler: I think that the concept must have been extended, especially with children.

Anna Freud: With children there is no contract with the child. This makes an enormous difference.

Ilse Hellman: I agree that there is an enormous difference, yet analyzing the reasons for conscious withholding leads to an understanding of the resistance which led to the withholding. For example, I can quote a patient who had no sexual life at all for a long time. She was afraid of it. Then she had her first affair, and for a long time I heard nothing about this at all. When I mentioned this fact, it led to nothing further. She said that she was not going to talk about it. When I tried to analyze what was underlying her determination not to talk about the affair she snapped at me, saying, "It's not your business to know anything that is good and happy. It is all quite straightforward." Then she brought indications of a transference fantasy that I ruined good things and would ruin the happy things in her life. So here there was conscious withholding. She had decided not to talk, but beneath this was an unconscious fantasy in the transference that I was a malevolent and destructive person, and therefore she had to keep good things hidden from me. Here we have a combination of conscious and unconscious aspects.

Anna Freud: There is, of course, another distinction which is important, and which we should take into account. There is a difference between the case of the patient who simply withholds, and that of the patient who attempts to tell something to the analyst but finds it difficult or impossible. In the latter case, the treatment alliance or the willingness to do free association is there as an obligation that the patient finds impossible to fulfill for some reason. That is, of course, very analyzable. But if this last component is missing, the whole method is turned into something different.

Marjorie Sprince: I should like to ask whether what has been said about conscious withholding applies only to those children or adults who have more or less reached the oedipal stage or have passed it. I am thinking of cases who intend to speak when they come but are unable to speak once they have arrived at the session. When they do speak, and often when they are silent, I have the feeling that they are communicating something which enhances my understanding. The withholding may be related to envy or to anal conflicts, but while the ability to speak is certainly under control what seems important is that they cannot let themselves speak. I have the impression that the withholding really reflects preoedipal pathology.

Anna Freud: Certainly, because withholding, just like silence in analysis, can have many meanings. It can have an anal cause, or an aggressive one. But that is not what is meant in this discussion. Perhaps conscious withholding is not a good phrase—willful withholding might be better. What I mean is that there is a disregard of free association or of the analytic contract. There is an opting out of the obligation to speak the truth and to say what is in one's mind. After all, that is all we want from our patients. We want them to come to the hour, to speak the truth, and to say what is in their minds. This does not concern children because they have never subscribed to an agreement to do this, and one does not make use of free association.

Sara Rosenfeld: I am rather bothered by the idea that if we insist on free association we may be bypassing the reality that so many thoughts and images cross the patient's mind that even if he wants to comply with the rule of free association he cannot. He scans his impressions, thoughts, ideas, and images and selects his associations from that.

Joseph Sandler: This seems to me to be very important. The whole question of free association deserves to be looked at much more carefully, because it does involve selection on the part of the patient, and a certain understanding by the patient of what is appropriate and what is not in terms of the working alliance or the expectations of the analyst. Such expectations are very important. There are some analysts who don't give any instructions or explanations to the patient at the beginning of the analysis, and I think this is a serious mistake. I have had patients who have had previous analyses who were surprised to hear that the random intrusive thought which they regard as a trivial thought about the analyst might be the most important thing of all to say. We do, in a sense, teach the patient that if he has a thought about the analyst it should be given priority over other thoughts. Because the patient sees that the analyst is interested in the patient's relationship to him there will be a certain bias in the patient's selection of material for free association. But if I understand you correctly, Miss Freud, it is a question of the goodwill and conscious intent of the patient.

Anna Freud: Because, after all, it is the inability to carry out that conscious intent which shows us the resistances due to the defenses. If the intent is not there, we cannot see the resistance. That is my main point. Of course, many patients, especially at the beginning of an analysis, say, "There is so much more in my mind than I can say." My answer to that is, "That is quite natural. Never mind it, just take what is uppermost."

Joseph Sandler: My impression is that if patients keep on saying that, it is usually a reflection of resistance. If they say too often that there are so many things which they want to say, in the end it turns out that they have, quite frequently, said nothing. But we come now to the concept of the treatment alliance, which we have tended to see as representing the sum total of all the factors which oppose the resistances. Naturally the amount of treatment alliance fluctuates, and when the resistance is greater than the treatment alliance, presumably we get a breakdown of the analysis or a conscious withholding, or something of that sort.

Anna Freud: It is interesting that at the time I wrote the book the phrase did not exist, but actually the alliance existed in a much more noticeable form.

Joseph Sandler: Miss Freud, you have made it clear that you deal in your book with concepts relating to processes we cannot directly observe. We use the data of observation, particularly when conflict occurs, to reconstruct the functioning of the id and the superego, and for theoretical purposes it becomes convenient to speak of a conflict between the ego and the id on the one hand, and the id and the superego on the other. However, although it is useful to speak, for example, of conflict between ego and id, in a sense the conflict is always in the ego because of the arousal of a threat of something unpleasant occurring. Would that be correct?

Anna Freud: The point I wanted to emphasize is that if the ego and the id are in agreement nothing is seen, and the analyst has a chance of realizing what is going on in the patient only at moments of disagreement. I think that what you are hinting at is that the ego is always the central point for noticing the conflict. I have treated it in the book as it might be seen from the outside. I say only that the two institutions pursue different aims.

Joseph Sandler: You make the point very clearly that the ego will go along with the id if it can, and I assume the same is true of ego and superego. However, would conflict not then be conflict between two tendencies of the ego, for example a tendency to satisfy instinctual wishes on the one hand and a wish to conform to superego ideals on the other? This is then essentially a conflict within the ego.

Anna Freud: It really depends on whether one is looking from the outside or from within the ego.

Joseph Sandler: You refer in the first chapter of your book to a state of calm and satisfaction prevailing in the id, a consequence of which is that there is no occasion for any instinctual impulse to invade the ego in search of gratification, with resulting tension and unpleasure in the ego (5,5). Presumably the states of calm and satisfaction would not be states of the person's feelings as far as the id is concerned, but states of the energy or drive. What about the calm and satisfaction of the ego? What of the well-being of the ego? When, as you say at the end of the chapter, "peace reigns once more in the psyche" (10,10), is there a state of calm, safety, and well-being in the ego?

Alex Holder: One might ask whether in fact it ever exists in the id. Is there ever calm and quiet in the id?

Anna Freud: It is a hypothetical state in which nothing moves, no wish strives after satisfaction.

Alex Holder: I can't imagine such a state. In the id something is always struggling.

Anna Freud: Except in the moment of gratification. I want to stress that I am speaking of a hypothetical state.

Joseph Sandler: The baby asleep at the breast would be a model for this.

Anna Freud: Or the adult asleep after successful intercourse. Even wishes stop sometimes, don't they?

Joseph Sandler: I think that the notion of a "steady state" is for the psyche, just as for the body, a hypothetical baseline which is probably never exactly attained, but is an idea needed in order to assess fluctuations from the baseline.

Anna Freud: In the chapter I have made only very gross distinctions, but we should remember that a certain level of drive intensity has to be reached for the ego to take notice of the drive. You will remember my father's comments about those states in which fantasies recede but are not blotted out. It is simply that they have not got enough energy to be disturbing. It is a question of threshold. The ego is satisfied if it can appease the forces that impinge on it from above, from below, and from outside.

Joseph Sandler: This might be a convenient point to ask about the distinction between those forces which act on the ego and the feelings within the ego. For so many years in psychoanalysis the word "tension" has been used to describe both a *state* of energic tension and a *feeling* of unpleasurable tension. The two were equated because obviously they often go together. This book extended Freud's idea about anxiety arising from the outside world, and introduced the notion of defense against unpleasure or threat arising from outside. In many places in the book there is a reference to the ego being at peace with the id, with the instincts. Are we concerned here with something conceived of purely in energic terms, or are we considering something which can be thought of in terms of feelings within the ego? After all, one can look at anxiety from the point of view of the energy involved or one can look at it from the side of the feeling state of anxiety. We know that for many years the energic and feeling aspects were put together in psychoanalytic writings, so that to cathect or invest someone with libido was to invest them or their representation with energy, but it also meant to love, so the two meanings were brought together. Is it not worth making a distinction between the feeling aspect and the energic aspect?

Anna Freud: The two go hand in hand, and we can see the relation if we look at anxiety, which shows both sides—that is, an energic side and a feeling side. However, I think that they are best described by speaking of the presence or absence of anxiety. Naturally we include under "anxiety" many shades of emotion that might be called something else—a lack of the feeling of intactness or of the feeling of safety. But if I can bring the discussion back to the chapter, what was really meant was that whatever an analyst sees, he sees in terms of the ego in its relationship to all the other aspects. And I make a plea for not neglecting the ego as that part of the patient who presents to the analyst what goes on inside him. What was said does not mean much more than that.

Joseph Sandler: Of course there is also the question of

defense "against" versus defense "toward." Do we defend in order to gain or maintain a good feeling of security or safety, or do we defend against anxiety, against pain, against intrusive wishes or painful reality, and so on? Connected with this is a question arising from the comment referring to the relation between the ego and the id. The relevant remark in the book is, "In favorable cases the ego does not object to the intruder but puts its own energies at the other's disposal and confines itself to perceiving; it notes the onset of the instinctual impulse, the heightening of tension and the feelings of unpleasure by which this is accompanied and, finally, the relief from tension when gratification is experienced. . . . The ego, if it assents to the impulse, does not enter into the picture at all" (6–7,6). Are there not difficulties in conceiving of the ego assenting to the impulse? Would it not be better to speak of the ego as collaborator?

Anna Freud: What I meant is that even if the ego is a collaborator, it imposes on the drive derivative its own method of functioning. I think that is what you have in mind.

Joseph Sandler: That is exactly what I am thinking of. It seems to me to be extremely important that if we think of the ego going along with the id we think of it as shaping and directing, as well as looking for the best way of satisfying the instinctual wish.

Anna Freud: Yes, it thereby imposes on the id its method of functioning. It slows down the instinctual wish, it interposes thought before the action. We see a very different method of working.

Joseph Sandler: And, of course, instinctual impulses do not develop *in vacuo*. They develop hand in hand with what we conceive of as the ego. One thinks naturally of oedipal wishes, where the ego plays such a major part.

Anna Freud: Of course the whole psychological content is added to the drives. The term "collaborator" is a very good one here.

Joseph Sandler: You point out, Miss Freud, that the proper field for our observations is always the ego, and comment that "the instinctual impulses continue to pursue their aims with their own peculiar tenacity and energy, and they make hostile incursions into the ego, in the hope of overthrowing it by a surprise attack. The ego on its side becomes suspicious; it proceeds to counterattack and to invade the territory of the id. Its purpose is to put the instincts permanently out of action by means of appropriate defensive measures, designed to secure its own boundaries" (7–8,7). The references to "hostile incursions into the ego," to "the hope of overthrowing it," are rather graphic ways of saying "realizing their own aims" or "getting their own way" as far as the ego is concerned.

Anna Freud: Yes, from the point of view of the id it is a matter of "whatever way the ego wants it, I'll have my satisfaction."

Joseph Sandler: And then one could say the ego, becoming suspicious, counterattacks, invading the territory of the id. This leads to the ego's deployment of repression and other defenses in order to protect itself. Presumably the instinctual wish would proceed a certain way into the ego (prior to the structural theory one would say that it proceeded into the Preconscious) and would then be sampled. As the wish contains representations, these would arouse an anxiety signal of some sort and defenses might then be initiated to prevent its finding expression, so-called discharge. What I am leading up to is that the ego must constantly be aware of the impulses intruding into it, and assessing them as well as the anxiety or other signals aroused by the instinctual wishes. It must make a judgment about whether it can proceed to be a collaborator, or whether it has to put the wish "out of action." Would this be another way of putting the paragraph quoted?

Anna Freud: Yes.

Joseph Sandler: I think that this point is worth clarifying. I remember that not so long ago a distinguished visiting analyst maintained that if the instinctual wish is defended against, if it is repressed, then the ego is neither consciously nor unconsciously aware of the wish. I remember arguing at the time that the repression would have to be continuously reapplied each time the wish reasserted itself. He rejected this vehemently, and asserted that successful repression is like a solid barrier being set up. I think that this is a sort of displacement of the idea of consciousness to the structural concept of the ego. In your reference, Miss Freud, in the chapter to the ego securing its own boundaries, guarding against a surprise attack, there must be the assumption that the ego has to be able to become aware—unconsciously—when this surprise attack starts, so that it can put its defenses into action.

Anna Freud: Yes, but if the barrier were a reaction formation, I think it would be a more constant barrier. If the barrier were repression not secured by something additional, there would have to be a constant vigil on the part of the ego.

Joseph Sandler: People who have reaction formations sometimes make slips of the tongue which show that the impulse defended against can evade the barrier. This in turn suggests that it is somehow not applied in sufficient time when the impulse arises.

Anna Freud: I think that the ego (if we can personify it this way) relies on the reaction formation in order to defend itself. We can see this in regard to aggression and pity, or anality and overcleanliness.

Joseph Sandler: And can the reaction formation become autonomous in this way? Surely there must be an arousal of a signal, even a little one, when the impulse proceeds?

Anna Freud: Heinz Hartmann would say that it can become automatic.

Joseph Sandler: But this would mean only that the process would occur automatically, and I still think that there must be an awareness of the impulse to evoke the response.

Anna Freud: Hartmann and I discussed it at the time, in 1936 and 1937. There must be a momentary awareness.

Joseph Sandler: An unconscious awareness?

Anna Freud: It could even be a conscious momentary awareness. One can sometimes see it with patients in the various forms of what we call "the return of the repressed." Of course, some rigid characters do not show such breakthroughs.

Ilse Hellman: Is there not a difference between reaction formation and repression, in that satisfaction is gained in an opposite way through the reaction formation, as when the sadist is changed into a nurse or doctor who gets satisfaction from his work, while repression is not maintained by a satisfying experience?

Joseph Sandler: Nevertheless the idea of a barrier which can be static obscures an important dynamic point. One would not lose anything and would gain a lot by saying that, in its deeper parts, so to speak, the ego will scan any impulse coming up, will assess it and put a counterforce against it if it does represent a danger. If it is a well-known danger, the ego may automatically take an opposite stance, as in a reaction formation, but the process of scanning and sampling has, in my view, to occur over and over again, even though it may proceed extremely quickly. There might be a minute anxiety signal which each time initiates the defense. I have difficulty with the idea that defenses may be set up and crystallized so that they can work on their own. Something must initiate their operation. The important thing is, it seems to me, that there is a process following a threat, and that the ego can then go into action immediately. The process aspect is important.

Anna Freud: What speaks for your version is that in the analytic technique we count on the defense being part of the process and not a fossilized structure. Otherwise we could probably not undo it, and we see that, as the analysis proceeds, it becomes more of a process.

Joseph Sandler: And the phrase "designed to secure its own boundaries" would be quite consistent with this, inasmuch as the ego may be said to wait for the attack, to identify the attacker's credentials, so to speak; it may then decide to repel the invader, or at least to ward him off. And though the invader may not get further than a step inside the boundary, he has to make the move inside in some way, in order to be recognized.

Anna Freud: I am reminded by this discussion of the work of Wilhelm Reich on character armor. This armor is evidently a stabilizing defensive system.

Joseph Sandler: I think that we have to stop now.

Anna Freud: I feel as if I have been trying to justify my own past!

CHAPTER 2

The Application of Analytic Technique to the Study of the Psychic Institutions

In this chapter Anna Freud makes an important distinction between analysis of the id and that of the ego, and considers in some detail the technical implications of the differences between the two. She begins by pointing out that the preanalytic use of hypnosis aimed at discovering the unconscious (the id), the ego having been put out of action. What was discovered by hypnosis was then shown to the ego, resulting in a symptomatic cure while the ego was still under the influence of the hypnotist. But the ego later revolted against its new knowledge, and the therapeutic success did not last. On the other hand, in free association the patient's ego is not eliminated, but is required to stand aside so that the derivatives of the id can reach consciousness more easily. The patient is requested to translate ideas into words, but not to allow these ideas to take control of the motor apparatus, which has been put out of action by adherence to the analytic rule. So the patient's impulses are encouraged to express themselves, but are at the same time not permitted direct gratification.

Anna Freud goes on to say that it is impossible for the patient to relax his guard so much that his associations can come into consciousness without modification. For a while id derivatives do force their way into consciousness, but then the ego intervenes, making use of its defense mechanisms. It "counterattacks" and puts up resistances. Now the defensive measures taken by the ego against the id become the object of the analyst's attention. However, whereas in analyzing the id the analyst is helped by the tendency of id derivatives to come to the surface, he gets no such help in analyzing the ego's defensive processes. As a result, ego analysis is less satisfactory than id analysis, as the defenses can be reconstructed only from the effect they have on the patient's associations. The type of defense mechanism employed can be recognized indirectly from the nature of the change involved (e.g., omission, reversal). The analyst then has the task of undoing the work of the defenses and, through showing the patient what has happened, of reestablishing "the severed connections." The work can then turn again to id analysis. We should speak of psychoanalysis only if we focus at one time on the id and at another on the ego, working with the conflicts which arise as a result of the patient's trying to follow the fundamental rule.

Anna Freud points to the similarity between the processes of dreaming and free association. In dreaming, latent dream thoughts are converted into manifest dream content, and the distortions correspond to those which can be seen in free association when the patient is in resistance. Thus dream interpretation helps the analyst not only to discover latent dream thoughts (id content) but also to see which mechanisms have been used by the censor to defend against awareness of the unconscious.

Symbols, which are "constant and universally valid relations between particular id contents and specific word or thing representations" (16,16), can be used to advantage to understand the id, but they do not tell us anything about the history of the ego of the person. Similarly, slips (parapraxes) can be useful as chance demonstrations of unconscious processes.

Transference interpretation is "the most powerful instrument" of the analyst (18,18). "By transference," writes Anna Freud, "we mean all those impulses experienced by the patient in his relation with the analyst which are not newly created by the objective analytic situation but have their source in early—indeed, the very earliest—object relations and are now merely revived under the influence of the repetition compulsion" (18,18).

Here again Anna Freud distinguishes between id and ego. In the transference of libidinal impulses the patient is disturbed in his relationship with the analyst and resists these emotions. The impulses concerned originate in old "affective constellations" and can only be understood in the context of childhood. They give information about the past, and interpretation of such id impulses is felt as a relief by the patient. *But the repetition compulsion applies equally to past defenses, so that the patient also transfers old defensive distortions of the instinctual impulses.* Occasionally only the specific defense may be transferred, and the patient cannot expose the underlying impulse, however much the analyst insists on the basic rule. At this point, says Anna Freud, the analyst must focus on the mechanisms of defense, moving his attention from id to ego. If the path followed by the drive in its defensive transformations can be traced, knowledge is gained both of the patient's instinctual life and of his ego development. The transference of defense is responsible for the majority of technical difficulties in analysis, for the patient does not feel the defense to be alien to him. It is "ego syntonic," and he makes use of rationalization to hide the fact that the transference is inappropriate and that the ego "is wholly opposed to the work of analysis" (22,21).

Anna Freud comments that under the conditions of the analytic situation the id has a relatively greater influence than the ego, and the "analyst lacks opportunities of observing the patient's whole ego in action"; with the intensification of the transference the patient "begins to act out in the behavior of his daily life both the instinctual impulses and the defensive reactions . . ." (24,23). This is *acting* in the transference, and to the extent that the analyst can become aware of it, he can obtain insight into the relative functioning of id and ego outside the analytic situation. However, the analyst gains little from such acting, and tries to restrict it by appropriate interpretations and prohibitions.

We are warned in this chapter against one-sidedness in our technique—we should no longer see the role of the ego as simply resisting that which comes from the id. Because large parts of the ego are unconscious, they must be brought to consciousness just as the id derivatives must. This analysis of the ego is a substantial part of our analytic work, and in this connection it is important to study the vicissitudes and transformations of the id impulses, rather than to translate them directly. If the id elements in the transference are concentrated upon too much, the patient may produce an overwhelming amount of id material, behaving in an infantile way so that the ego will tend to act instead of analyzing.

The Discussion

Session one

Anna Freud: I re-read Chapter 2 for today. I was quite surprised.

Joseph Sandler: I was again intrigued by the fact that one can think of the ego in terms of depth, in terms of distance from consciousness, the deeper strata of the ego being seen as being the location of earlier modes of functioning. It does seem to be worth noting, Miss Freud, that the "deeper" functions of the ego were regarded by you as those which relate to an earlier time in the life of the child.

I should now like to go straight to a point on which I would very much like to hear your comments, one relating to the role of the unconscious ego. If I am correct, with the introduction of the structural theory the replacement of the dynamic system Unconscious by the id represented an attempt to deal with problems that had been confronting Freud in regard to the topographical model. The system Preconscious, at least since 1915, had been seen as an organization that could make use of repression (that is, could defend both on its border with the system Unconscious and on the border between the Preconscious and the Conscious systems). In a way, it seems natural now that the overburdened topographical model had to be reorganized into the structural model. But one consequence of this is that the use of the word "unconscious" in a descriptive sense (to include the contents of what was the Preconscious system), as well as in reference to a dynamic system (the Unconscious, but not the Preconscious) leads to complications for an analyst who moves from one frame of reference to another, from the structural to the topographical and back again. In fact, Miss Freud, in this chapter you have moved from the one frame of reference to the other; and it seems natural to do this. What bothers me a little is that you have said so much in terms of the id and its derivatives without mention of the unconscious ego. For example, latent dream thoughts are equated with id content (16,16). I have a problem here. Is the concept of the id, as you saw it at that time, something which included part of the functioning of the system Preconscious in the topographical model? Should we not really be speaking of the id in collaboration with some aspect of the unconscious ego, which might in turn be defended against? In your chapter you have written very clearly about ego versus id; but is there not an intervening area, so to speak, of the "deeper" ego where, for example, latent dream thoughts are formed? Presumably these would then be defended against as they approached the surface. If we think of the analytic situation in terms of the topographical model, we could regard transference derivatives of the past as perhaps being defended against *again* at the border between the Preconscious and the Conscious systems. In structural terms, would we not have to say that the derivative can be defended against when it is within the ego but getting too close to consciousness? It becomes too great a threat, arouses an anxiety signal and defense. The distinction between ego and id seems to me a little too clear-cut in this chapter, although I think I understand why you put it the way you did.

Anna Freud: I know what you mean. Different from the people who found the structural theory existing when they entered psychoanalysis and saw the topographical scheme as a thing of the past, I grew up with the topographical scheme, and had a gradual transition to the structural in my own psychoanalytic development. I must say that in my writing I never made the sharp distinction between the two that later writers made, but according to my own convenience I used the one or the other frame of reference. I definitely belong to the people who feel free to fall back on the topographical aspects whenever convenient, and to leave them aside and to speak purely structurally when that is convenient. I agree that what I describe here as id content is, if one takes it very sharply and seriously, preconscious, and one would say, therefore, that it is ego content.

Joseph Sandler: One can see that you are happier when you speak, for example in relation to parapraxes, of the vigilance of the ego being relaxed or diverted and of an unconscious impulse being suddenly reinforced. This leaves the question open since the term "unconscious" is really used descriptively, and we can be referring to an unconscious derivative which involves the ego, even though it may come from the id.

Anna Freud: Yes, it has the *quality* of being "unconscious."

Joseph Sandler: If I may, I should like to pursue my point a little further. When Freud introduced the idea in 1900 (and again in 1915) that the censorship can operate at both ends of the system Preconscious, we have the background to saying, in regard to the structural model, that censorship and defense can take place across the whole range of the unconscious ego, that censorship of an impulse can occur at any point on the way to the surface. So something may be allowed through, into the ego, and not be immediately defended against. Alternatively, it may be defended against in a primitive (that is, "deeper") way, giving rise to a derivative which may, as it approaches consciousness or action, be seen as a threat. Then further defenses might be applied. Would you agree with this formulation?

Anna Freud: Yes. You know, perhaps it is partly covered by the old distinction between primary repression and secondary repression. Primary repression relates to the idea that what is repressed has never reached the Preconscious. By the way, this bad habit of mine of living between the two frames of reference—the topographical and the structural—is much to be recommended because it simplifies thinking enormously and simplifies description when necessary.

Joseph Sandler: I am sure that this is absolutely right, as long as one distinguishes between the dynamic Unconscious and what is descriptively unconscious!

Anna Freud: Yes.

Joseph Sandler: We gained a great deal, but also lost something, it seems, with the introduction of the structural theory.

Anna Freud: And therefore, you know, I tried to keep what has been lost by reverting whenever I feel it necessary to the former, because we got along quite well with the former model for a long time.

Joseph Sandler: It is very useful to have made explicit the notion that defense can occur at any point on the path of the impulse toward consciousness. We could say, I suppose, that even when something has entered consciousness it can be defended against. This can be an after-expulsion, for example.

Anna Freud: To personify the idea of the ego for the moment, it seems to me that the ego doesn't mind where the content comes from that is objected to. What the ego minds is the content becoming conscious.

Joseph Sandler: I am glad that we can agree that one of

the main functions of the ego, even after the introduction of the structural theory, can be regarded as the task of protecting consciousness. This is very often forgotten.

Anna Freud: Yes. It is very interesting to look at the losses in psychoanalytic theory that occur under the name of progress. It is important to see that with every step forward we lose some very useful things.

Sara Rosenfeld: I have always had a problem with primary repression, and more so today when you made the point, Miss Freud, referring to content which has never become preconscious. Can you expand on it?

Alex Holder: Freud uses the terms *Urverdrängung*, which is primal repression, and *primäre Verdrängung*, referring to primary repression as opposed to secondary repression, that is, "repression proper." I am not sure that the primal and primary repression are the same. There are inconsistencies.

Anna Freud: It seems to me that there is really no difference, and that what you described is something which happens in development when the division between id and ego occurs. Certain elements of the id were never taken over. They remained where they were, which means that we are not dealing with a mechanism, but rather a failure, I would say, in regard to absorbing these contents during the process of higher development. They remain on a lower level of primitive functioning. I think this is the only distinction. Whereas other contents, later on, developed to higher levels, and if they are then unwelcome, they are rejected, and that's repression proper.

Maria Berger: Then it would appear that the primary repression is not a mechanism in the way we usually understand it.

Anna Freud: I think that is so. If we look at it from the point of view of the rejected content we can say that it has not been let in, yet at the same time it has not been thrown out. It has been edged into a corner, not assimilated. I think that is the original meaning.

Robert Evans: I think that Freud made a point of saying that without primal repression we would not have a sufficient "pull" from below, so it would appear to be essential for the theory of secondary repression.

Anna Freud: Yes, the idea was that these impulses which had been subject to primary repression created an underworld of their own. They did not enter the secondary process at all, not having words to represent them. They did not qualify for the surface, but now they invite others from the surface to join them.

Maria Berger: Would it be right to say that with the development of speech these very primitive wishes or impulses later acquire a different status, so that they then can be subjected to repression proper? I can think, for example, of very early biting, cannibalistic wishes, for which there are no words. As the child grows, impulses like this are translated into words and thoughts so that they find ways to become conscious and can then be repressed.

Joseph Sandler: This sounds like something which parallels the idea of the backward pull of the fixation points in regression. But I find this much more difficult to understand than the idea that fixation points exert such a backward pull. Why should material which has been subject to primary repression exert a pull in a direction away from consciousness? Why should we think of such a pull away from consciousness when there is a whole movement on the other hand toward expression on the surface in one form or another?

Anna Freud: I would not compare the backward pull to regression. This is a very different concept, although it does mean a tendency to return to an earlier form of satisfaction. But if we assume that there is a synthetic function, which means the unification of psychic material, one can see what goes on in two ways. There is first a constant upward move from the Unconscious, from the id, from the impulses (whichever way you want to put it) but there is also a counterpull in the opposite direction. Because of the synthetic tendency, it is as if the impulse says, "If I can't rise up perhaps you will come to me." This happens in sleep, where the whole of our functioning sinks down to the lower level, and I suppose there is a unification between what is in the system Unconscious, and the rest of what is unconscious, together with what is conscious.

Joseph Sandler: Yes, but dreams show the move in the

other direction during sleep. They show the tendency for the "return of the repressed" in a disguised form.

Anna Freud: They also show how the upper layers make use of the lower layers to acquire energy.

Joseph Sandler: Well, perhaps we can put a mark against this topic so that we can return to it at a later point.

Anna Freud: A fixation point!

Joseph Sandler: Miss Freud, turning now to the contrast between id analysis and ego analysis in the book, we can assume that you have put it as a contrast of extremes in order to make a comparison between the two approaches. In practice we do not first do a period of id analysis, then a period of ego analysis, and then a period of id analysis again, but rather we have constantly to be ready to do both.

Anna Freud: Yes.

Joseph Sandler: I also found interesting the point that you made about the transference of libidinal impulses. I think that you would now say instinctual impulses, to include aggressive wishes.

Anna Freud: Yes, of course.

Joseph Sandler: In this chapter you make the suggestion, in the section on transference of libidinal impulses (18,18), that a transferred impulse can come to the surface and then be found to be ego alien. You say of the patient, "Generally he is quite willing to cooperate with us in our interpretation, for he himself feels that the transferred affective impulse is an intrusive foreign body. By putting it back into its place in the past we release him from an impulse in the present which is alien to his ego, thus enabling him to carry on the work of analysis" (19,19). Could you say a little more about this, Miss Freud? You give a picture of someone admitting to a sexual or aggressive thought about the analyst, and then, being conscious of it, feeling a distaste for it. You indicate that the process of free association allows the id derivatives to have relatively free access to consciousness. I found this a little puzzling because it seems to me that it is relatively rare for derivatives to come up in an ego alien or ego dystonic way. My own experience is that by the time they reach consciousness, the defenses have worked on them and they have been modified so that they are ego syntonic. Did you put it the way you did for purposes of exposition only? I wonder whether you would now take more account of the role of the defenses, in particular of rationalization, in making transferred instinctual impulses acceptable to the ego in free association.

Anna Freud: I suppose what I was thinking of at the time was the contrast between the way in which, let us say, an hysterical patient might transfer a passionate wish to be loved onto the analyst, even though the observing ego might say, "Well, this is neither my father, nor my husband, nor my son. This is my analyst. I've come here to be cured, why do I suddenly feel like this?" At least we would like the patient to think this. What I was thinking of was how much transferences happen when the observing ego is intact, and the transferred impulse appears in consciousness with a force which is not yet overwhelming. Later it can acquire a new force, in which the observing ego is not there anymore, and I refer to this as "acting" in the transference—in German it was *agieren*. But let us take the case in which the ego is still observing and the impulse arrives undisguised. Then the patient certainly feels relief when he can say, "Oh, that's why." He understands that it does not belong here, but belonged in the past. But it is certainly true that it rarely comes that way. Usually, by the time it arrives in consciousness, it has already been altered by the customary defenses.

Joseph Sandler: On the other hand, we are familiar with the patient who is horrified at his thoughts and is honest enough to report having had an "unacceptable" thought which was something that had broken through into consciousness. But, of course, this does not happen so often.

Anna Freud: It seems more usual for a thought to come up in this form when it is a purely aggressive one. The patient may then think, "I have no reason to hate or to revenge myself to that extent. Why am I suddenly hating like this?" The libidinal impulse is often more overwhelming, and the observing ego may be lost. Of course, in an account of the sort which I give in my book, each little section in each chapter is there in order to show one possibility in an extreme form.

Joseph Sandler: How difficult it must have been at that time to write such a book!

Anna Freud: Yes, but you know, even at that time people used to complain at my trying to give a very clear, extreme picture. For instance, I remember Otto Fenichel saying that I always stopped talking about things when they began to be really interesting. Which meant that I stopped before giving the details, because I felt that they might harm the clarity of the picture I wanted to give.

Joseph Sandler: I remember something you said years ago, Miss Freud. It was that one should not look too closely and in too much detail at what you have written when you have tried to put things simply.

Anna Freud: And when I now re-read what I wrote in the chapter I realize what I had wanted to do there. I really wanted to show certain things very clearly. And to do that one had to exclude many of the details.

Joseph Sandler: I think this is a function of scientific development in general. Of necessity the theory has to be an oversimplification. Later, when the theory is no longer adequate, we get further scientific development.

Miss Freud, I was very taken by your reference to the affects (19,19). I wonder if you would care to say something about the relation of the instinctual drives, as you saw them then, to the passionate emotions such as love, hate, jealousy, panic, and so on. You speak of the "old affective constellation," but we tend now to link affects with the ego.

Anna Freud: Yes. At that time I took the position which my father described in "Instincts and Their Vicissitudes": that the affects were not drive derivatives, but rather adjuncts, things accompanying the drive derivatives. At the same time we did not conceive of any independent life of the affects. It was Landauer, I think, who tried first (not very successfully) to deal with this; so it was left as it was. In the German, it was *Affektbetrag*—the quantity of affect—which would be added to the drive derivatives. I used it in that sense in my discussion.

I could perhaps at this point say something connected with the idea of transference of defense. Of course, many of the things I said in the chapter we are discussing were common knowledge at the time I wrote it, but the idea of the transference of defense was *not* common knowledge. It was really a new aspect. My idea was that the resistance in analysis is so extremely valuable for us because it makes use of the defense for specific purposes. This was for some reason not generally recognized at the time.

Joseph Sandler: The point about transference of defense and analysis of resistances was surely a crucial turning point in psychoanalytic thinking. I would like to ask you if you now think that there is a case for distinguishing between transference of defense, where it is the early defense which is now repeated, and defense against transference, where a later defense might be employed against an earlier impulse. There might be two separate things here. The child may repeat, in relation to the object, a defensive maneuver of an early age, or he may now become anxious because he is beginning to transfer certain infantile feelings to the analyst, and makes use of one of his favorite defenses, which might come from a later age. In the chapter you refer specifically to the repetition of the previous defensive technique of the ego as it gets brought up from the past, repeating itself in the present in relation to the analytic situation.

Anna Freud: Yes, anything can be used in the defense against transference. But what I point to in the book is the use of the analysis of defense to discover the ingrained defensive methods of the ego.

Joseph Sandler: Would it be carrying it too far to refer in this connection to ego regression to fixation points of the ego? I do not want to develop this line of thought, except to say that I believe that there can be functional fixations of the ego which can be revived, and that this includes defense mechanisms which may have been given up, but which can be returned to.

Anna Freud: I quite agree, but I would call them something else. They are old modes of functioning, and we can fall back on them. I think that the idea of a functional regression of the ego is there in the literature. Certainly my father wrote of various forms of regression, including what you speak of as a functional regression. What he calls formal regression is what you call functional regression.

Joseph Sandler: In the section on transference of libidinal impulses you speak, Miss Freud, of "old affective constellations, such as the oedipus and the castration complex" (19,19), and of course we can assume that a part of these constellations will be the instinctual wishes which are defended against because they arouse anxiety or guilt. These are wishes which have been formed in the child, let us say, at the age of four or five. Would we not have to say that the ego has played a very definite part in the formation of these wishes? We know of the ego's role in the creation of wishful fantasies, of how it is involved in perception of the object, and we are familiar with all the different ways in which the ego contributes to object relationships, in addition to the contribution of the drives. We know that castration fears, which had a large contribution from the ego, can be repressed. In these affective constellations we have wishes which were at one time ego syntonic, which were a product of both id and ego. These wishes were then repressed, and we can see them revived again. What is their status in terms of our theory? I know that I have asked this question before, but I feel that it is important enough to return to again. Having been repressed, say, at the age of five or six, such combined id-ego derivatives of instinctual drives are now again subjected to repression, and being repressed, one would have to say they are relegated to the id. With the topographical model one would have said that they were repressed into the dynamic Unconscious. When we deal with the revival of such "affective constellations" as the oedipus complex, are we not dealing with the revival of wishes which represented the ego having worked in collaboration with the id, with joint id-ego work from an earlier age? Of course, when these wishes are revived later, there may be an anxiety signal or a guilt signal, and defenses may be applied. I think that we have a real problem in trying to put this into terms of id and ego, for we are dealing with complicated wishes toward parents, not simply blind, simple, or unelaborated instinctual wishes. We are dealing with wishes which may show the influence of past defenses, for example the defense of turning an active wish into a passive one. Let us say that the oedipal boy developed, for purposes of defense and concealed gratification, the fantasy of being seduced because he could not tolerate the wish to approach the mother sexually in an active way. What may come up later in the child as an unconscious wish, which might have to be defended against, is the wish to be seduced, because although ego syntonic earlier on, later it became ego dystonic. Are we not speaking here of a combined id-ego movement of an infantile sort which arouses anxiety in what we would call the more mature part of the ego, causing new defensive action to be taken in the present? It seems to me that it is more correct to put it like this than to say that the oedipal wish has been relegated to the id and that the ego has been pitted against it. For our theory of defense, quite a lot hinges on this, I believe.

Anna Freud: When you speak of the unconscious wish having been added to and transformed by ego elements, this is what used to be referred to as a "complex." Why have we retained this very convenient term only for the oedipus and castration complexes? But I wonder whether it isn't simpler here to speak in terms of what is conscious and what is unconscious. The conscious attitude of the patient to the analyst may be, let us say, a hopeful, trusting one—"You will help me to get rid of my internal conflicts." But suddenly the analyst becomes instead a threat, making things worse, depriving the patient of what he cherishes, interfering with his pleasures, and so on. This comes from the past. The analyst has been given the past role of, let us say, a castrating father, or a threatening mother, or whatever figure we want to name. Isn't the main item in the situation the fact that the past has put itself in the place of the present? The patient's fear was not always unconscious but it has been removed, forgotten, or repressed. For a long time it played no part in the patient's conscious life, but the analytic situation invited it to spread itself. We do not need to translate it into any theoretical framework.

Joseph Sandler: I don't think that we are in difficulties if we follow the formula you have given us. We are dealing with something which is, descriptively speaking, unconscious, and if we take the point which you make in your book—that the deeper layers of the ego are the earlier layers—then we have no difficulty with this. What it means is that there is an unconscious tendency in the ego, with the id pushing right behind that tendency, so to speak. It is an unconscious tendency of the ego to give an instinctual impulse a particular form, but as this approaches consciousness there may be an anxiety signal. It may, particularly in the analytic situation, approach more closely to consciousness than usual. We may then, as analysts, see further defenses evoked. So a defense can be initiated, it seems to me, against a combined id-ego movement which is unconscious and which comes from early childhood, but which is "consciousness dystonic" in a sense, rather than ego dystonic (in the structural sense of "ego"). Or we could say that it is dystonic for the later developmental levels of the ego.

Anna Freud: It is *present* dystonic.

Joseph Sandler: And this involves the more mature levels of the ego.

Anna Freud: Because the contrast here is not so much between conscious and unconscious, but between past and present. The question for the patient is: "Why do I behave in the present—or why am I forced to behave and feel in the present—in a manner which is appropriate only to a past situation?"

Joseph Sandler: The clinical importance of this seems tremendous, Miss Freud. We can see in analysis that what people defend against are impulses which at one time were ego syntonic. These impulses move toward the surface, up to a certain point, but then, in the present, they give rise to anxiety, they arouse conflict, and defenses are mobilized.

Anna Freud: A patient of mine was never able to express hostile impulses in his analysis, except in a very circumscribed way, by falling asleep, by coming late, by not functioning, as I would put it. Apart from this he could not show his hostile impulses. But on one occasion he went into a very bad state, and in that state a fantasy rushed into his mind. He came to his analytic hour with the idea that he could live only if I died, which was, of course, the thought that was always behind the hostility that was unconsciously expressed in very different ways. Now this was the death wish against his mother, against a very difficult mother, and it was a wish he was never able to tolerate in consciousness. At the age of three or four or five, probably linked with the birth of the next siblings, such a wish might have been near consciousness, but there was no sign in the analysis that the patient had ever been conscious of a wish to kill his mother. What was clear in the analysis is that from time to time, from very early on, he had a wish to commit suicide, which was the killing wish turned against himself. Now what would you say? What has come up there?

Joseph Sandler: I would say that this was a childhood wish which shows the hallmarks of secondary process, of cause and effect. I would also say that it must therefore have been preconscious at the very least, and that it was then defended against. I would think that the turning of aggression against himself represented the conscious derivative of the wishful fantasy elaborated preconsciously.

Anna Freud: I also had the feeling that, probably in his adolescence, and in a milder form, he formed the idea that he could become a real man only if freed from the influence of his mother, if she became ill or died. But while such a thought may have been near consciousness at one time, it was never ego syntonic.

Joseph Sandler: Well, perhaps it could have been ego syntonic at a deeper level of the ego, and dystonic at the higher level.

Anna Freud: Perhaps one should rather say that it was never consciousness syntonic. And, just for the record, I want to say that what is translated here as "institutions" was *Instanzen* in German. One would now say agencies of the mind, not institutions. I never corrected the translation.

Session two

Joseph Sandler: You say in this chapter, Miss Freud, that analysts have been criticized on the basis that "they may have a good knowledge of a patient's unconscious but are bad judges of his ego" (23–24,23). It seems to me that nowadays the situation is often the reverse. Many analysts seem to have lost the skill needed to understand unconscious latent content, and this seems to have been replaced, in some quarters, by a preoccupation with ego psychology. Perhaps the pendulum has swung in the other direction.

Anna Freud: It has not quite swung that way in the Kleinian handling of the patient, because when you listen to the accounts of Kleinian analysts there is a great deal of information about unconscious fantasies, and it is only sometimes, at the very end of the account, that we get a glimpse of the patient's ego functions, his ego achievements. These are added as a sort of afterthought.

Joseph Sandler: I was thinking of our own closer colleagues in whom emphasis on mechanisms, on ego functioning, on conflict-free functions, as well as on the defenses, may have led to a lack of interest in the interpretation of unconscious content.

Anna Freud: What I wanted to make clear in my book was that either preference is wrong. It is as if one were to say that one liked the right side of a person better than his left side. These are only parts of the person, and there should be no preference.

Joseph Sandler: I suppose that at the time you wrote there was much more emphasis on interpreting everything—works of art, stories, myths, and so on. Anything could be interpreted.

Anna Freud: Any *content.*

Joseph Sandler: You say that "the interpretation of 'acting' in the transference affords us some valuable insight," but that "the therapeutic gain is generally small" (24,23). A little later you remark that the form of transference we call acting out "is even more difficult for the analyst to deal with than the transference of the various modes of defense" (25,24). You go on to say that it is natural that the analyst should "try to restrict it as far as possible by means of the analytic interpretations which he gives and the nonanalytic prohibitions which he imposes" (25,24). I think that we all understand your point well, as an aim in analysis is to get the patient to verbalize, yet I am struck by two things. One is that Freud said that transference is itself a form of acting out. Presumably he was referring to gross transferences, like falling in love with the analyst, and the resulting attempts of the patient to change the analytic situation into a nonanalytic one, but I think that we need some clarification of this. And to what extent do you think, Miss Freud, that the prohibitions that used to be put onto the patient in regard to acting out should still be imposed?

Anna Freud: Well, prohibitions in analysis have very much gone out of fashion. This is not always to the benefit of the patient. Of course, the use of the word "prohibition" can easily be misunderstood. What I meant was rather restrictions—attempts to restrict the material to what can be handled within the analytic hour.

Joseph Sandler: In the German edition you used the word *einzuschränken*, which I think means limiting, confining, or restricting.

Anna Freud: Yes. There were many attempts made at that time to impose restrictions. For instance, the patient was told not to make major decisions during analysis, because these decisions could so easily be based on feelings, emotions, and impulses that had not been dealt with. But what can be said against this at the present time is that analyses used to be much shorter, so it was easier to put off decisions until the end of the analysis. Now, when analyses are so long, one can't stop living.

Joseph Sandler: I know that I tend to say to patients that any major decisions should be discussed at length in the analysis, and I imagine many people use a formula of this sort. But I also know that there are some analysts who give the patient no instructions at all and simply take everything as material to be interpreted. There also seems to be a tendency nowadays to regard a limited amount of acting out as being a useful way for the patient to bring material. I want to ask, Miss Freud, whether enactments which are really slips, such as the patient knocking something over in the consulting room, or forgetting to pay his bill, would come into the general category of acting out.

Anna Freud: I would not call these things acting out.

Joseph Sandler: Would you then restrict the concept to enactments toward objects outside the analysis?

Anna Freud: There are some obvious examples. If, shall we say, in the resistance against the transference which occurs at the beginning of analysis, the patient immediately forms an outside relationship to counterbalance the beginning relationship to the analyst, that would be a definite piece of acting out.

Joseph Sandler: It has a defensive element in it as well, then?

Anna Freud: Defending against the transference, yes. We always see acting out when the patient is in resistance.

Ilse Hellman: I see the degree of acting out as a measure

of the patient's incapacity to contain his impulses in thoughts and fantasies, and then to verbalize them. This is important technically. We would, for example, not contribute to the heightening of a tense situation that the patient could not contain, and that we could not deal with simply by restriction or prohibition. And, on the other hand, from the patient's acting out we can get a picture of the capacity of his ego to deal with certain impulses.

Joseph Sandler: I was thinking of the patient in resistance who reports that he has impulsively bought something he does not need, for, let us say, a small sum. This has meaning, and arises in a particular context in his associations and we then understand what the resistance is about. But if such a patient comes to his session and says he has spent all his savings buying something bigger, which he also does not need, we are more likely to call it acting out because he did not first bring his self-damaging wish into the analysis. Obviously there is a question of degree in what we call acting out, and this cannot be dealt with by a definition. If I understood Miss Freud correctly, she was referring to relatively gross forms of enactment which we would normally expect to arise as feelings, thoughts, wishes, and fantasies toward the analyst in the transference. Instead they lead the patient into an outside involvement in a way which has implications for his real life.

Anna Freud: There is another point which I had very much in mind at the time I wrote this book. Let us say that an impulse is aroused in the patient due to the analytic work. It can be either an aggressive or a libidinal impulse. Further, this particular patient cannot contain it, keep it in the analysis, verbalize it, and keep it unsatisfied, which is the state in which we want to analyze it. Instead he acts on it in his outside life. By the time we get it into the analysis the impulse has run its course, has satisfied itself, and we get it cold instead of getting it hot. This was really the main point about trying to limit acting in the transference. I remember that I wrote this section very much under the influence of my work with a patient who could not contain her impulses at all. This led to a number of acting out relationships outside the analysis, but although these could be followed perfectly afterward, by the time they emerged in the analysis they had already lost either their libidinal or aggressive cathexis, or the anxiety attached to them.

Ilse Hellman: But wouldn't this then be a matter of working through? Because, by analyzing it cold, as you put it, there is still some change and insight brought about which would influence the repetition of such acting out activity.

Anna Freud: My feeling is that with the real acting out patient the repetition of the acting out is not much influenced. I remember that the particular piece of acting out I was thinking of happened eight times, I think. The gain in knowledge for the analyst is quite considerable, but the therapeutic result and the gain in insight for the patient is purely intellectual. It is as if you are running after the patient, but are not with him at the height of the event.

Joseph Sandler: I think that in order to get this into perspective we have to think of the time that you wrote about this, Miss Freud, and the point that you were making in contrasting "acting" with other types of transference, adding what we would now call acting out in the transference to the two other forms of transference you describe. Of course, when we start to apply definitions strictly, we get into difficulties, because there are certain patients in whom new material can show itself through some action outside the session rather than through verbalization in the analysis. The action may be a relatively minor one, which is then reported, and can be worked on. There must be many patients for whom the impulse is brought into the session neither cold nor hot, but sufficiently lukewarm to be usefully analyzed.

We come now to a rather different point. You say a little further on: "Analytic theory has ceased to hold that the concept of the ego is identical with that of the system of perceptual consciousness; that is to say, we have realized that large portions of the ego institutions are themselves unconscious and require the help of analysis in order to become conscious. The result is that analysis of the ego has assumed a much greater importance in our eyes. Anything which comes into the analysis from the side of the ego is just as good material as an id derivative. We have no right to regard it as simply an interruption to the analysis of the id" (26,25). In this context you show us that we can reconstruct the defense mechanisms used by the patient from the form of the material which he brings to the analysis. It occurs to me that if we distinguish between subjective experiential content which is kept out of consciousness and defense mechanisms which are unconscious in quite a different sense, then we could say that our interpretation of the defense mechanisms is really a creating of new mental representations for the patient in analysis of the mechanisms he is using. This last is quite different from something which was once conscious, from which attention was withdrawn, counterforces applied, and which might become conscious again. If we interpret mechanisms, we interpret machinery of the ego, so to speak, and can give the patient, perhaps for the first time, a representation of the mechanisms he has used. I wonder if you would care to comment on this.

Anna Freud: Yes, I quite agree. I want to say that from the id we get help in the analytic process, because what is in the id strives to become conscious, even if consciousness does not like it (I deliberately personify here). We get no such help from the ego mechanisms. They would like to stay in the dark, because when they are uncovered, anxiety is aroused. They were employed to avoid this anxiety, and so the ego sees no direct advantage in making them conscious. The defenses work in the dark, and work automatically, and once they are brought into consciousness and the patient understands what he has been doing, they cease to work with the same efficiency. The patient says, "Yes, I see that I used to do that before, and it was so comfortable, but it's much more difficult to do it now that I know that I am doing it." At least, that is what the hope was at the time I wrote the book.

Joseph Sandler: You sound as if you are not quite so optimistic about it now.

Anna Freud: Well, it doesn't always work. Some people go on employing the same mechanisms. I always say that they don't employ them with the same pleasure. Perhaps we should say that "the intention is," rather than "the hope was."

Joseph Sandler: One has the hope, of course, that the process of working through enables people to become their own policemen in regard to the defenses they employ.

Maria Berger: I would like to raise a point in connection with something we touched on last time. When you spoke about the oedipus complex being repressed, together with the defensive measures used at the time, I found myself at a loss to understand about the repression that the defenses underwent. Can defense be repressed?

Anna Freud: No.

Maria Berger: But what happened to the defense? It was in the dark, but did one get at it in the analysis one way or another?

Anna Freud: Yes, but when you ask whether it was repressed, the answer is no. It is automatic, and goes on without a contribution from consciousness and, as Dr. Sandler said, "What one does is to connect it with experience and consciousness."

Joseph Sandler: I should like to make two comments. First, we can speak of the content, which has undergone transformation, being repressed. This does not mean that the defense has been repressed, and I understand Miss Freud's comments about the oedipus complex in this way. Second, it occurs to me that if one looks upon the defenses as organized substructures, one can say that they may be used or not as necessary. The use of a defense can be revived, the defense having been unused for a while during the course of development. And one hopes that, following analysis, certain of the patient's defenses can be put aside, because they come to arouse in turn a new sort of signal anxiety, a sort of "analytic guilt," so that one does not want to use them. But this is rather a giving up of a use than a repression of content away from conscious experience.

Anna Freud: You could say that it involves an avoidance of unpleasure or anxiety, which then becomes automatic.

Joseph Sandler: If we return to something we discussed earlier, we can say that in all these discussions what we are really dealing with are the vicissitudes of wishes. The function of the defense mechanism is to modify the *content* of the wish, that is, the mental representational content, so that something which is unconsciously experienced as part of the self-representation, for example, would in the mechanism of projection be attributed to an object representation. The content of experience would then change, and the wish would be felt not as a wish but as an aggressive act or intention coming back at the subject from someone else. The new content would be a disguised wish fulfillment which, by virtue of the change brought about by the defense, is allowed to come into consciousness or to find expression in action. Would that be a correct statement? We could add that specific mechanisms such as projection might be used by some individuals rather than by others with a different constitution and history.

Anna Freud: I only wonder if we can take it for granted that the defense is always directed against the impulse or wish. One could also say that the defense is really directed against the anxiety or unpleasure aroused by the wish.

Joseph Sandler: Yes, but does not the ego defend against the anxiety by operating against the content of the wish?

Anna Freud: If we take one of the simplest examples, that of a pre-stage of defense, we know that the little child, when he has done something wrong, habitually says things like "the cat has done it," or "the other child has done it." This is an immediate throwing out of the activity from the self and attributing the forbidden wish or action to someone else. Well, what would you call that defense? Is it a projection or an externalization?

Joseph Sandler: It would be a defense of either sort if the child were unconscious of what he was doing. But if, in this particular case, what we see is downright lying, I do not think that we should speak of a mechanism of defense.

Anna Freud: It is an immediate warding off of a feeling of responsibility, of guilt, of a punishable action.

Ilse Hellman: We saw this with the little puddles our eighteen-month-old children made at the Hampstead Nursery. They used to point at the dog. We could call these conscious maneuvers pre-stages of defense, as you have done, Miss Freud. Perhaps the child believes them after a little while, and then we might say that we have defenses proper, but at the time it is an attempt to evade responsibility.

Lucy Biven: Isn't it also an attempt not to be the person Mummy would not love? It is not just "don't punish me," not simply lying to avoid punishment.

Anna Freud: It is an attempt to say, "I am a good girl."

Joseph Sandler: Miss Freud, you say in this chapter, "But of course anything which comes from the ego is also a resistance in every sense of the word: a force directed against the emerging of the unconscious and so against the work of the analyst" (26,25). I wonder if you would comment on that remark.

Anna Freud: At the very beginning of the book I compared analytic technique with hypnosis, with the idea of showing how easily we could gain knowledge of the unconscious if the ego were only out of the way, and we could have direct access to what was unconscious. So long as the ego is there, it will interrupt our view of the id. Now, unlike the hypnotic method, free association represents an imperfect attempt to achieve the same result, by asking the ego to put itself out of action. Of course, this can only succeed to a certain extent, but wherever the ego comes into contact with action, it comes in as an interference. Yet this interference is as useful to what we call analysis as the analysis of the id itself.

Ilse Hellman: This leaves out those aspects of the ego which are so specially necessary for self-observation.

Anna Freud: Of course I am not referring to the time when the ego allies itself with the analyst's effort, becomes an observer, a reporter, or when the patient plays analyst himself. Apart from that, the activity of the ego is a hindrance.

Joseph Sandler: If the ego did not function it would be traumatically overwhelmed by impulses, wishes, and the content of experience, so it needs to keep things under control. It occurs to me that part of the control can be to give acceptable form to unconscious wishes, so that in that sense the very censorship of the ego can also function to allow things to come to the surface. So the censorship could be regarded as something positive, although it is directed against the direct expression of instinctual wishes. The ego needs to keep them controlled in some way. It is like the press office of a politician which releases information. We know that it is highly biased information, that it is tendentious and meant to give a particular impression, but nevertheless we can gain some information from it by reading between the lines, and some information is better than none.

Anna Freud: Yes, I would only say that in these circumstances we learn very little about ego activity. Our aim is to learn as much about the ego as we learn about the id, and we only learn where the ego comes in as interference. Otherwise it is very difficult to say what is id and what is ego.

Joseph Sandler: We might refer back to the statement you have made about the ego having an innate disposition against the drives, an idea which has been questioned by some people.

Anna Freud: Many people have questioned it. They ask how I could say that. But my feeling was always that this is what the ego was meant to do from the beginning. That is why it was set up at all, to control, to impede the id.

Joseph Sandler: This would fit with the notion that there is always a level of resistance in our work with patients, and that this level fluctuates but never disappears. There is always some degree of resistance because of the need for the individual to maintain his sanity.

Anna Freud: We even get a bit worried if there is a complete absence of resistance in the patient, and a sudden flow from the unconscious. This often means a breakthrough that is not at all welcome.

Joseph Sandler: I think of the analytic student in analysis who uses that form of resistance which is to show, apparently, no resistance. If we see that, and the analysand is not breaking down, then one wonders what he is hiding.

Toward the end of the chapter (28,27), Miss Freud, you refer to the behavior of the ego as an infantile ego, under the domination of the repetition compulsion. I suppose that you might have said in your text that the ego behaves in an infantile way because of the repetition compulsion.

Anna Freud: What I take up here is the overwhelming urge to repeat; but looked at from its other side one could say that it is a regression.

Joseph Sandler: Would you say that the repetition compulsion, then, as an urge to repeat, applies equally to the ego in all aspects of its functioning; that given the chance, the ego would give up its high level of functioning and repeat its more primitive modes of functioning? I think this does happen, but the term "repetition compulsion" is not usually applied in this way.

Anna Freud: The concept was first applied to the drives, but I think that now, if we were to think it over, we would apply it equally to the urge to repeat early modes of functioning.

Joseph Sandler: Perhaps we could say it applies to the whole constellation of drives and ego, to all earlier aspects of the apparatus and its functioning.

Anna Freud: I would think so. I have not really thought it through.

Joseph Sandler: This may be well worth looking at again because it has interesting implications. Of course, the question of the repetition compulsion being truly a compulsion is always questioned, and I do not know whether there is a problem of translation here. It is more a *tendency* to repeat.

Anna Freud: It is called *Wiederholungszwang* in German. It really refers to an urge, a compulsion in the sense of an urge. For example, in the hysteric we can also see a compulsion to identify, although we do not usually call it that. In German the word has a technical as well as an ordinary meaning. I suppose a better translation that "compulsion" would be "force," because *Zwang* really is a force to do something. One is forced, compelled, which is not really the same as "compulsion" in the technical, clinical, psychiatric sense.

Robert L. Tyson: I felt that the way you used it in relation to the defenses implied that the patient is limited in his repertoire because he is compelled to repeat the past in regard to this particular aspect of his ego functioning. He has not been able to develop some other means of coping with the dangerous impulses, because he is compelled to use earlier methods.

Joseph Sandler: So when you speak, Miss Freud, of transference phenomena, which are repetitions of the past, saying that they have two parts—the libidinal or aggressive elements belonging to the id, and the defense mechanisms which we attribute to the ego—the way in which you use repetition compulsion there would apply equally to the defense.

Anna Freud: I think so.

Joseph Sandler: Right at the end of the chapter you say, "If we must give up free association, make but a sparing use of the interpretation of symbols, and begin to interpret the transference only at an advanced stage in the treatment, three important avenues to the discovery of id contents and ego activities are closed to us" (29,27). Then comes the question which is dealt with in the following chapter. How, in child analysis, can we make good these technical deficiencies? I want to ask about your comment that we should make sparing use of the interpretation of symbols. This injunction applies equally to child and adult patients.

Anna Freud: What it meant at that time was a turning against the Kleinian technique, which consisted almost exclusively of the translation of symbols. The child played and the analyst translated. I remember Ernest Jones reporting what his little daughter, who was in a Kleinian analysis, said at the time about analysis: "While children play, women talk." In my own teaching of the technique of child analysis, I warned consistently against that sort of translation. In the last paragraph of this chapter there is also a warning against interpreting transference too early, and this was also directed against the Kleinian technique, in which, from the first hour onward, whatever the child did was taken as transference, and was explained to the child in those terms. This was never our technique.

Joseph Sandler: It is very good that you have explained this, Miss Freud, because many of us now would question the point about interpreting the transference only at an advanced stage in the treatment. It is important that we know the context in which you wrote this paragraph. I am sure we would all agree now that sometimes it is necessary to interpret the transference early. I do not know what your feelings are about this at the moment, but you are very familiar with the issue.

Anna Freud: There are differences from case to case, but after all the child does not immediately form a transference. It takes some time until what the child feels toward the parents as his main objects comes into the transference, and by then we are at a more advanced stage of treatment. But, as you know, whatever we do, it is quite different from the technique of not waiting for transference, but rather of forcing everything into the transference, which is interpreted immediately.

Ilse Hellman: There is some confusion about this whole issue. When we think of the child's feelings about starting the session, we might comment immediately to the child that he is frightened of the analyst, whom he does not know. Some people would call this a transference interpretation, while we would see it simply as the verbalization of the child's anxiety about treatment.

Joseph Sandler: When some supervisors (foolishly) say

to students, "Don't interpret the transference for six months," or something similar, an injunction like that is quite harmful if the student understands it as "Don't mention the patient's feelings about you for six months." The advice would be quite wrong, because the patient might feel about the analyst as he might feel about going to the dentist, and it might be necessary for the analyst in the first session to interpret the patient's anxieties.

Anna Freud: Well, you know, we might modify it and say, "Don't interpret transference before it *is* transference." These beginning reactions are not transference, but are the natural reactions of a child meeting a stranger in a frightening situation, being forced to do something new or urged to something that he does not want to do. That is not yet transference.

CHAPTER 3

The Ego's Defensive Operations Considered as an Object of Analysis

This chapter begins with a recapitulation of the view that it is the analyst's work to "bring into consciousness that which is unconscious, no matter to which psychic institution it belongs." And, as Anna Freud puts it in a famous statement, "when he sets about the work of enlightenment, he takes his stand at a point equidistant from the id, the ego, and the superego" (30,28).

As far as the id is concerned, the work of analysis reinforces the id's tendency to express itself on the surface. But the situation is different with the ego and the superego. The aim of the analyst and of the patient's ego are at variance with one another. Although the analyst and the patient's ego work together during the analysis in the process of self-observation, the ego is biased, distorting and rejecting certain facts. Moreover, the ego's unconscious operations are themselves the object of analysis, and naturally it resists the process of making them conscious.

Anna Freud points out that "in analysis all the material which assists us to analyse the ego makes its appearance in the form of resistance to the analysis of the id" (32,30). While there are other sources of resistance (transference resistance and the working of the repetition compulsion) it is important to analyze the ego resistances in order to make conscious the unconscious defenses of the ego, which show themselves as a strengthening of defensive measures and as hostility to the analyst.

The ego defends itself not only against instinctual impulses and their derivatives, but also against the affects associated with such impulses (e.g., love, longing, jealousy, mortification, pain, and mourning). The fate of an affect is not necessarily the same as that of the ideational content of the instinctual demand, but a knowledge of the way the patient defends himself against his instinctual impulses will tell us about the defenses he will probably use toward his own unwelcome affects.

Anna Freud now refers to Wilhelm Reich's idea of character armor (*Charakterpanzerung*). This reflects attitudes (in particular, bodily attitudes and character traits) that are residues of past defenses which have become, in the course of time, separated from the original conflict situation. The analysis of character armor is difficult, and such traits should be concentrated on in the analysis only when the analyst cannot detect a current conflict involving ego, drive, and affect. In general, the analysis of resistance should be applied to all resistances and not only to character resistances. Analysis shows that neurotic symptoms involve defense mechanisms and compromises in which specific methods of defense are used unvaryingly. There is a special relation between particular neuroses and certain mechanisms of defense. We can see the operation of such defenses on the patient's free associations, and can therefore gain an understanding of his symptoms from the form of his resistances. Thus the resistances of the hysteric and of the obsessional patient are quite different.

Next the case of a young girl who had symptoms of acute anxiety is described. She avoided making references to her symptoms during the analysis. When the analyst commented on this the patient became contemptuous, and the analyst felt at a loss. Later it was seen that the resistance was not a transference reaction in the true sense, but reflected the patient's vehemently critical attitude toward herself whenever she experienced affects of tenderness, longing, or anxiety. The interpretation of the content of the anxiety had no result until the patient's method of defending herself (based on identification with her critical father) had been analyzed.

The parallel between a patient's defense against his drives and against his affects, and that between his symptoms and his resistance, is of great technical relevance. This is especially so in child analysis, where the analyst cannot use free association and must resort to other methods. But the child's play is not completely equivalent to free association, and it is by turning to the analysis of the way in which the child's affects have been transformed that we may learn more of the ego's activities. Thus in child analysis the analysis of defenses against affects is of particular importance. It gives the analyst clues to the child's attitude toward his instincts and to the nature of his symptom formation. Anna Freud illustrates this by reference to a little boy who defended himself against castration anxiety by dressing up as a soldier and being aggressive. He reversed the affect of anxiety by turning it into its opposite. He was also obsessional, indicating that he did the same sort of "turning around" in his instinctual life. Anna Freud then gives two further examples to illustrate the parallel between defenses against affects and those against instinctual impulses. She concludes the chapter by pointing out that the analysis of defensive changes in regard to affects corresponds to the resolution of ego resistances (as they are found in free association). The more we can bring ego resistances and defenses against affects into consciousness the nearer we shall get to an understanding of the patient's id.

The Discussion

Session one

Joseph Sandler: I should like to begin by referring to the question of unconsciousness discussed in this chapter. You say there, Miss Freud, that "it is the task of the analyst to bring into consciousness that which is unconscious, no matter to what psychic institution it belongs. He directs his attention equally and objectively to the unconscious elements in all three institutions" (30,28). We have a problem, I think, of different sorts of unconsciousness, and of what it is that one makes conscious through interpretation. It seems that we should really spell out a distinction between, for example, making conscious again a memory or an image which has been repressed, and making the patient aware of a mechanism which he is using. He may never have been conscious of that mechanism. One might compare it to the engine of a motor car. The driver may never have seen that piece of machinery, but in order to understand the functioning of the car—particularly if something has gone wrong—one might give him a representation of it. This is very different from releasing a repressed memory. Would you go along with such a distinction, Miss Freud? I suppose that we could also say in this context that there are two sorts of interpretation which can be given.

Anna Freud: There are. There are also two sorts of unconsciousness, and descriptively speaking, both things you have described are unconscious, but one is repressed content, and the other is an automatic process which we try to lift into consciousness. Naturally there is a great difference between the two, and the analytic work is different. It is received in a different way by the patient. It is, of course, a topic I stress in this chapter, but from a descriptive point of view the task is the same.

Joseph Sandler: The analyst verbalizes and brings to the surface something that the individual has not been conscious of before. Phrases like "brought to the surface" and "lift into consciousness" refer, of course, to both processes you mentioned. However, in this chapter you put stress on something which involves spelling out for the patient what he is actually doing, so that he becomes aware of it perhaps for the first time. Although people do not like the word, in a sense one "educates" the patient about his defense mechanisms.

Anna Freud: One demonstrates his defense mechanisms to him. The analyst shows him something he knows in his unconscious (in the descriptive sense of the word).

Joseph Sandler: I don't think that one can say that the patient is unconsciously aware of the defense mechanisms he uses.

Anna Freud: There is one important similarity between the two processes, of interpreting defense mechanisms and of bringing content to the surface. Both are resisted by the ego for the same reasons. The one because the defense is undone and anxiety aroused when the analyst lifts a repressed content to the surface, and the second because an anxiety or other affect which has been warded off now has to be experienced. That is where the similarity lies.

Joseph Sandler: If we go to the second paragraph in Chapter 3, Miss Freud, you say that "the id impulses have of themselves no inclination to remain unconscious. They naturally tend upward and are perpetually striving to make their way into consciousness" (30,29). You go on to say that the analyst's work follows the same direction as this upward tendency and reinforces it. From the point of view of the repressed elements in the id the analyst is helping them in their move toward the surface. There is something about this which puzzles me. Why is it that a repressed wish, or perhaps an instinctual wish in general, obtains gratification if it can find its way to consciousness?

Anna Freud: It doesn't find it, but it looks for it. This is really the way in which the id is deceived during analysis. The upward move to the surface is a striving toward gratification. The analytic work attempts to catch it before gratification is achieved. Of course the mere fact of the impulse being verbalized gives a slight amount of satisfaction, but this is certainly not what the id intended. I think this is what the psychoanalytic method is based on.

Joseph Sandler: Could you elaborate on this a little, Miss Freud? We speak of the wish reaching consciousness, and sometimes of gaining access to motility. In the analytic situation, of course, motility is hindered. The patient lies on the couch and, like the person who is asleep, cannot discharge the wish in a physical way. If I understand it correctly, you would say that at the moment of the person becoming conscious of the wish he would experience some slight gratification, some wish fulfillment. Do you mean that he would, for example, experience a wish fulfilling fantasy?

Anna Freud: We know that the most effective discharge of an impulse is through the action which leads to gratification. But there are, after all, lesser modes of discharge with reduced amounts of gratification—for example, discharge into words. Discharge into fantasy which can be put into words is what we analysts prefer, but as analysts we also see discharge through acting out. Acting out really means that what has come to the surface has escaped the analyst's grasp, has gone into action, whether the analyst wanted it to go there or not. If we can catch it before it goes into action, then we have really done what we wanted to do.

Joseph Sandler: If we think for the moment not of an instinctual impulse, but of a need like hunger, the person who becomes aware that he is hungry will often feel more hungry as a result of that awareness. Would that not also apply, say, to a sexual wish? If a person has a sexual impulse and becomes aware of it, can we really say that discharge takes place at that moment? Are you not in fact referring here to a derivative of the impulse, to a wishful fantasy, into which a modicum of satisfaction has already been embroidered? I refer to something which is a wish fulfillment in a partial form. If we use the phrase "id impulse reaching the surface" are we not speaking too broadly?

Anna Freud: What I have written refers to the impulse or its derivative, but I have certain examples in mind. I remember hearing an analyst describe his work with a case of latent homosexuality, and he could show that he had been successful in reaching the wish behind the attitude that made for the latent homosexuality. But his patient actually became homosexual. The analyst didn't seem to mind, but he should have minded, because he should have caught the homosexual wish before it went into action. Otherwise, you know, the patient may like it so much that the analyst may never catch it again.

Joseph Sandler: What happens if this patient really had a strong homosexual disposition and the heterosexuality was a defensive facade? What right have we to bring our morality and sexual preferences into the situation? May not the satisfactory progress of the analysis result in the person becoming an overt homosexual, following analysis of the defenses?

Anna Freud: It is not our morality that made him defend against the homosexual wish. It is *his* morality. It is *his* conflict about his wish to be homosexual. It is only at the very moment that the impulse which he has repressed becomes conscious again that he is swamped by it, because the conscious impulse now has more force. One could ask, "What about a murderous wish?" Think of the patient who has displayed only a very loving attitude toward his mother, but behind it is the wish to kill her. Naturally, you as his analyst would want to uncover that, but is it an analytic success if he then kills his mother? You might say, "Well, if he wants to be a murderer it is his affair." Only he doesn't want to be a murderer —otherwise he would never have developed his neurosis.

Joseph Sandler: If one has a patient that one suspects might be dangerous, who might actually murder his mother, I think one would tread very warily and perhaps abandon strict analytic work. In fact, I don't know of any instance in which the analyst has gone on with a patient in such circumstances. I don't imagine that you would have gone on analyzing a patient in whom you felt there was risk that he might discharge his aggressive wishes in action as violent as this. We must all have experience of cases in which we felt that analysis was not really indicated any longer, and have then taken it easy, soft-pedaled, been supportive and interpreted only selectively because of the fear of the wish being turned into action. I suppose that this relates to the question of selection of cases for analysis. I don't know if you agree.

Anna Freud: I agree in one way, because the ordinary sort of patient, the neurotic patient, has actually built up his whole character on the basis of repressed wishes. The analysis puts pressure on that character and usually the patient will be able to deal with what is coming up again. Perhaps I should not have chosen the example of the murderer, but if such an aggressive impulse does come up, and you do not catch it in the analysis, it can go into action. While the patient may not murder his mother or his wife, he may wound them or offend them, to an extent that through acting out he destroys a relationship which he never meant to destroy.

Joseph Sandler: Are we not speaking of two completely different things here? First there is the failure of the analyst to interpret and to verbalize something, so that instead of this being contained as a thought or idea, the patient acts out or enacts the impulse. This puts the patient and the environment at risk in some way. But the other case is that of the patient who has tendencies which are truly related to fixation points to which he may have regressively retreated. So he has tendencies which we would call perverse, and has built up a layer of defenses against these. When he becomes able to tolerate such impulses in his awareness, he might say, "Why should I not enjoy myself in this perverse way instead of being completely asexual?" I have a patient who was completely sexually inhibited before he started analysis but regarded himself as heterosexual. He had no heterosexual relations during analysis but has now had some homosexual experiences which he accepts and enjoys. He feels that this is an improvement, and I also think it is. Perhaps one day he will get around to heterosexuality, because possibly he has a basically heterosexual disposition, but I doubt it. This could all be considered acting out, but I do not see it as acting out in my patient.

Anna Freud: You know, it depends very much on external circumstances, because the whole idea of acting out an impulse which has come up from the unconscious is connected with our view of the potential harm the patient can do himself if he decides to act on the impulse. If he acts out, and that lands him in prison, or smashes his career, then we certainly haven't done him any good, and he has not done himself any good. If it is harmless, and (as we hope) transitory, then that is another matter. This may be true for the homosexual. Under certain conditions he could harm himself very much, and under other conditions not at all. But I really speak here from the point of view of the impulse itself. If it could speak it would say, "I would never have come up if I hadn't hoped that I could break into action." And what I wanted to point out in this chapter, and nothing else, is that there is nothing in the unconscious defense mechanism (perhaps I should say "not-conscious" defense mechanism) similar to this. The not-conscious mechanism has no reason to become conscious.

Joseph Sandler: When you say that the analyst's attitude to the impulse depends on the way he sees it in terms of danger to the patient, how would this affect the analyst's work?

Anna Freud: It would make him more eager to catch the material before it goes over into action.

Joseph Sandler: So with certain material one is much more on the alert in regard to acting out than with other impulses.

Anna Freud: Yes. After all, what comes up may be a suicide wish. If this goes into action, you have lost the patient, and the patient has lost his life or his health. If you catch it in time, it is extremely useful. I think that much of analytic technique in the past was built on the analyst's skill in this regard.

Joseph Sandler: I am reminded of the way in which one may warn the patient about a tendency to act in some particular way, after a bit of analytic work has been done. I am not thinking here so much of acting out an instinctual wish, but more of negative therapeutic reactions based on guilt. One might say to the patient, "Now you feel very pleased with yourself, but you know what has happened in the past," warning the patient that he might be tempted to do something self-damaging because of guilt feelings following his pleasure in gaining a piece of insight. This can be a very convincing confirmation for the patient if he actually does something one has predicted he might do. The next time he might not, because he is on his guard.

Lucy Biven: Surely the whole idea of not acting out is in order to facilitate the process of working through?

Joseph Sandler: Do you mean that working through involves thinking and verbalizing, and that it is better to have the material brought into the analysis than transformed into action which may bypass the patient's insight?

Lucy Biven: It also involves feelings. It is important that the patient feel what is verbalized by the analyst.

Donald Campbell: What about impulsive children, where an interpretation seems to be a sanction for action?

Anna Freud: Nothing we have been saying refers to child analysis, because the child has made no contract that he will not act on whatever is discussed. Many interpretations with children really do act as permission. The child thinks that if you can talk about it so quietly, it can't be so bad.

Joseph Sandler: Does this not also refer to adults? A lot of our work with our patients is showing that the super-ego is criticizing the patient more severely than it might.

Anna Freud: Only with adults. The patient, through his

illness, is given evidence of the action of his superego, of his defensive organization, of his power of repression, of his condemnation of certain things in himself. The child is usually not given evidence of this kind.

Marjorie Sprince: It seems to me that what we are really saying is that as analysts we have to decide which impulses are acceptable and which are not. And then, as Miss Freud says, we have to catch them as they come up. I am often troubled by the idea that the analyst has to decide in this way—for example, in connection with homosexuality —rather than the patient's deciding. It seems to me that the analyst's job is to bring the patient's own wishes to the surface. Isn't it a problem of how far the analyst takes on a superego attitude?

Anna Freud: No, I think you have misunderstood the situation. We are not selective, and the analytic work in regard to bringing impulses to the surface is the same no matter what the impulse. But the analyst cannot help being more on the alert when he feels that the patient might endanger either his own life or the life of others, and that he, the analyst, would then really be responsible for what the patient does to himself or to others. It is an attitude in the analyst. It doesn't change the procedure but it sharpens the alertness of the analyst.

Joseph Sandler: I'm glad, Miss Freud, that you are being so frank and direct in this, because so often we hear public statements about the "purity" of the analytic process, with the analyst seeming to function almost as an interpreting machine. Of course, it isn't like that at all.

If the homosexual patient we have been discussing was tempted, say, to seduce little children, one might say something to him like, "Look, you had better be careful, because people are caught doing this. You involve some-one else, and can do that person harm. I think we should talk more about it." We might not say that in regard to another wish. As Miss Freud says, there is a certain responsibility felt by the analyst in regard to what the patient does, although this raises many difficulties. The analyst would be less than human if he didn't feel such a responsibility. To think that our job is only to translate what the patient says in an automatic or "objective" way, without being concerned at all about what the patient does, is a big mistake.

Anna Freud: Yes. One has only to try out these thoughts in regard to the suicidal impulse of a patient. If you feel that what is coming up might easily lead to his carrying out his suicidal impulse, you certainly would not inter-pret it with the same quiet attitude as you would another impulse.

Joseph Sandler: We come now, Miss Freud, to the ques-tion of the distinction between defense against drives and defense against affect. In my own mind I always see defense as being defense against affect, in the sense that if it were not for the unpleasant affect, one would not defend. But the distinction to which you refer lies in regard to what is worked on in the defense; that is, the ideational content that is transformed on the one hand, and the affect that is avoided or reduced on the other. It isn't altogether clear whether there are two sorts of defense, or two motives for defense, or some other difference.

Anna Freud: Well, if I think back to the climate in which this was written, I remember well that at the time defense against affect was not really talked about. As you have said before, affect was considered as an accompaniment to the drive or as a drive derivative, and it was more or less taken for granted that the defense was directed against the drive and not the affect. What I had in mind here was something slightly different. I meant that every individual has a limited number of defenses at his disposal, and that he may use them against the drive or against the affect, but (and this takes us over to child analysis) the defense against the affect is much easier to demonstrate to the patient. If we start from the defense against the affect, we get an inkling of what defenses the patient uses against the drive. Then we usually have a fairly good knowledge of what the patient should feel at a certain moment, of what is appropriate for him. I mean that when something bad happens, the patient should not begin to giggle, as so many patients do; or have a sudden feeling of elation when he is deeply disappointed. I think of a patient who, whenever a girl he loved told him the affair was over, became elated when he should have been depressed. It wasn't that he was glad to be rid of her; it simply was not the affect that one would have expected. We all know from child analysis that if the child shows the wrong affect at the wrong moment, this is a very helpful thing, a useful guide to the defenses. This then leads one to the defenses against the drive derivative. When I wrote what I did, I took it much more from that point of view.

Joseph Sandler: It is very clear how you have used this point as a bridge from adult to child analysis. In this connection, you are saying that we can see defensive operations working on the child's mood and on his feelings in the same way we see them working on ideational content. But there is another level in which all defense is ultimately defense against the signal of trauma, against anxiety or against any other unpleasant affect or the affect signal.

Anna Freud: I agree, but I also took it from another point of view. If one notices that the appropriate affect isn't there, and one starts with the defense against the affect, which has nothing to do with the drive, it still leads one to the battle against the drive.

Joseph Sandler: I cannot tell you how delighted I am to hear you make these points, Miss Freud. So many analysts have been hindered for a very long time in trying to deal with the psychoanalytic theory of affect because they have assumed that all affects were to be considered drive derivatives. But is it not obvious that some affects arise because of the influence of the external world? We have really been speaking about defenses which involve the manipulation of affect, as opposed to defenses involving manipulations of ideational content and ideational representation. Knowledge of one context in which defenses are used gives us clues to the defenses used in another context, but this doesn't mean that the first context is a derivative of the second.

Anna Freud: Yes.

Maria Berger: It seems to me that we are dealing with two issues. One is the question of what the motive for defense is, and it has been said that it is basically to avoid unpleasant feelings, to avoid anxiety. But the other issue has to do with what it is that we manipulate in the defensive process. What do we act on when we defend? For instance, when one sees examples of reversal of affect, one sees the patient dealing with the painful situation by altering the affect. In other defenses one manipulates not only the affect, but the drive expression, as in reaction formation. I wonder whether this was not what you had in mind, Miss Freud, because on the one hand we have the question of what prompts the defense, and on the other what actually happens in the defensive process itself.

Anna Freud: Quite right. You know, it is difficult to discuss one piece of a chapter except in relation to the next piece. What I tried to establish here is a unity between defense against the drive, defense against the affects (wherever they come from), and resistance in analysis. Resistance in analysis is, of course, resistance against the unpleasure that is aroused by the analytic process. And if it is true that the three can all reflect the same defensive process, one can start from any one of the three and throw light on the other two.

Joseph Sandler: Perhaps with adults one can add another area in which we see defense. I mean the area of dreams, where the defenses used tend to be those that are generally used by the patient. If he tends to project his feelings onto others in his general life, he will tend to externalize aspects of his own self onto other figures in dreams. If he tends to use displacement, he will show more displacement in his dreams. I think that one can pick up an indication of the patient's repertoire of defenses from the way in which his dream work has gone on. Perhaps with adults there are a number of paths one can take toward an understanding of the defenses, whereas with children we are much more limited.

Anna Freud: With the dreams there is an added complication. What we see in the dreams are those defense mechanisms that have a very strong relationship with the primary process. And that makes it not quite the same.

Joseph Sandler: I am sure that it is correct that one has more condensation, displacement, reversal, and equation of opposites in dreams. But I do have the impression that one can also see, perhaps particularly in the revision of the dream and in the recounting of the dream, the defense mechanisms that are characteristic of the patient.

Anna Freud: I think you are right about the recounting of the dream, which means producing the last version, but I am not so sure about the dream itself. I would be more doubtful about that.

Joseph Sandler: It is time for us to move on to the dis-

cussion of the permanent defense phenomena. Miss
Freud, you have drawn attention here to Wilhelm
Reich's views (35,33). What I understand from what you
say is that certain modes of functioning which were originally defensive have, in a sense, become autonomous.
They don't depend any longer on the particular impulse
defended against in the present, and have become part
of what we would call the person's "style." Incidentally,
when Heinz Hartmann developed his idea of secondary
autonomy and change of function in relation to such
things as skills (he spoke of "apparatuses"), he did not
take the step of speaking of the secondary autonomy of
symptoms and of character traits. We know that there
are symptoms which are not necessarily solutions of conflict at the moment, but have crystallized, just as Reich's
character traits have become "fixed." I suppose that one
could speak of a secondary autonomy both of symptoms
and of character traits, and in analysis we would have to
look at symptoms of this sort differently from the way
in which we look at recent symptoms or those which
develop during the analysis, which may be compromises
of a neurotic sort. It seems to me that you have drawn
attention to something which has not yet been sufficiently studied.

Anna Freud: I would like to add to this that there was
quite a battle at the time over this idea of Wilhelm Reich,
who was then a very good analyst. His ideas had caught
on, and although I agreed with Reich in many instances,
I fought against his maintaining over and over again that
the "fixed" defensive attitude in a patient was really
transference. If it was it would mean that the attitude

was aroused at that particular moment by the analytic situation. I used to say, "But the patient does that wherever he is, outside the home, with his children, with his parents, with his colleagues. It has nothing to do with what is aroused in the analytic situation." And therefore I felt that the character trait had to be reached in a completely different way. It is not material for the analysis, unless something happens which revives it. I probably would not have discussed things in this particular way in the book if there hadn't been such a lively battle at the time.

I remember Reich used as an example the submissive patient, the patient who agreed with whatever the analyst said. Well, Reich said that there is a passive feminine transference to the analyst, and he analyzed it as such. But is it not a passive feminine character attitude which has been built up over a long time, and which is now displayed toward everybody, not just the people who aroused it in the first place? It seemed to me that there was an enormously important difference here.

Joseph Sandler: It is one which is still vital for us now when we think of the differences we have with some of our colleagues about transference.

Anna Freud: Yes, some people hold the view that whatever the patient says or does is transference.

Joseph Sandler: We have, of course, the question of what we choose to take up in the analysis. Is there a case for interpreting a character attitude as transference, when it comes up in the analysis, even though we know that it also comes up everywhere else, as you described? The patient also brings his character to the analysis. Or should we interpret it in some other way? Some people might argue that the only effective analytic way is to take the transference aspects as if the attitude involved the analyst only.

Anna Freud: I would call this "forcing it into the transference," because the way to reach it in the transference is to show how it is inappropriate in all situations.

Joseph Sandler: There are big differences between individual analysts in this regard. For example, there is the difference between those who will say to a child "you are angry" and those who will say "you are angry with me," if something has happened to annoy the child in the session. It has become almost automatic for some analysts to add the "with me," to pull the material into the transference. And I think they would say that they are "leading" rather than "forcing" it into the transference. There is perhaps something to be discussed here in terms of technique. We know that with certain patients, particularly those with narcissistic character disorders, the material they report has very much to do with their character and appears to have little to do with the transference, at least at the beginning. The analyst may be set up by the patient as a good, listening figure, and one has to do one's interpretive work about the way the patient interacts with other people. If one waits for a transference neurosis it may never come, because the patient may like coming to the analysis, may keep the analyst as a "good" figure. He may defend successfully against the development of other sorts of transference. I think that sometimes one has to go along with the patient for quite a long time, showing him the mechanisms he has been using, leaving oneself out until the patient is well and truly in analysis. My experience is that taking up all the material in terms of transference early in the analysis may put certain patients into resistance and may lead to a breakdown of the analysis.

Anna Freud: Because it extends the transference to a phenomenon that the patient has no need to feel. The original idea about transference is that it is something the patient feels that is going on in him, not something that is dragged in by the analyst.

Ilse Hellman: I am not quite clear about this, because we may see that the mechanism is there in the analysis, and if our aim is to analyze character traits, we go from what we experience in the analysis to its origin in the past, to the point where the particular defense or character trait has come into being. In terms of reaching the goal of analyzing a character trait, one would have to start with what one can reach in the analytic situation.

Anna Freud: But there is a great difference between something awakened by the analytic situation and something carried into it, as it might be carried into any other relationship.

Ilse Hellman: What has to be done in the analytic work doesn't seem to be all that different.

Anna Freud: The patient's reaction to it is *very* different. I think that all we can do is bring home to the patient where the fixed character attitude is. We oppose it to the expected attitude. We have to do that, whatever happens. Then the patient can see what he carries into the analysis.

Joseph Sandler: Perhaps the point you are making, Miss Freud, is that one would not refrain from interpreting the attitude in regard to oneself even though it is a fixed character trait, although one would also show how general it is. So for the patient who is overly submissive one might say, "I am very struck by the fact that you have agreed with everything I have said since the beginning of this analysis." This might be better than saying, "I am struck by the fact that you agree with what everybody says to you."

Anna Freud: I would say, "How curious that you agree even when it is quite obvious that you disagree, when I would expect you to disagree." There is a different technique of interpretation here.

Joseph Sandler: Of course, showing the patient that he has taken up a particular attitude in the analysis does not mean that it is transference in the original sense.

Anna Freud: You have no idea how difficult it was to differentiate these things in the past. Reich was very insistent on seeing it all as transference.

Joseph Sandler: This is a facet of psychoanalytic history

very different from what we are used to. I must confess I had the impression that there was much more explaining and relatively less transference interpretation than one sees nowadays.

Anna Freud: The whole question is whether transference is in the patient's mind or in the analyst's. And one should interpret what is in the patient's. That is the great difference.

Session two

Joseph Sandler: Last time we discussed a number of issues arising from Chapter 3, but we did not finish our consideration of the chapter. There are some points about symptom formation that are intriguing. You say, Miss Freud, when speaking of symptom formation, that "the part played by the ego in the formation of those compromises which we call symptoms consists in the unvarying use of a special method of defense, when confronted with a particular instinctual demand, and the repetition of exactly the same procedure every time that demand recurs in its stereotyped form" (36,34).

Presumably the procedure you refer to is the use of the defense mechanisms. You go on to point to the connection between particular modes of defense and types of illness. Perhaps it is worth commenting that we also traditionally link the different neuroses to the fixation points to which the individual has returned. Certainly we emphasize this less nowadays in regard to psychotics, but it is still an important part of our clinical theory that the obsessional, for example, regresses to anal fixation points. But linked with these fixation points are also particular types of defense. We may ask whether the person persisted in the use of specific defense mechanisms (doing and undoing, for example) before the regressive revival on the side of the drives, which then had to be dealt with by the symptoms of the neurosis; or whether there is also a regressive *revival* of the particular defense mechanisms involved in the neurosis. I have the impression that such mechanisms as reaction formation and undoing may be built into the character of those predisposed to obsessional neurosis. In this connection one has to think of the patient who may show drive regression to the anal phase but does not develop an obsessional neurosis. Instead he may develop some other "anal" symptom. From what you say it is the defense mechanisms which turn the regressively revived instinctual wishes into the obsessional neurosis.

Anna Freud: Yes. But you introduce another subject into the discussion, which is not really touched on in the chapter. What you ask about is a very much later consideration concerning regression within the ego. At the time I wrote the book it played no part at all in our thinking, because the whole concept of regression was limited to the side of the drives. And with ego regression we get regression in the use of defense mechanisms.

Joseph Sandler: I have a general question. It relates to the problem of whether the ego unconsciously takes part in forming the symptom, or whether we have to consider the ego as standing aside while the symptom bypasses it. My own inclination is to say that the ego colludes, or participates, in the formation of neurotic symptoms. This is not the traditional view, which regards the instinctual wish as making a path through the ego in the formation of the symptom.

Anna Freud: The ego takes part, and the whole creation of the symptom is a compromise. If it were not like this the whole idea of the symptom as a compromise formation would not make sense. The ego is involved in demanding a compromise, and takes part in bringing it about. And the ego brings it about by contributing or offering the defense mechanism. This is a major part of symptom formation.

Joseph Sandler: If we think of the symptom as a derivative that in certain cases can have a symbolic meaning, then I would imagine that the symptom work parallels the dream work. We could then speak of the manifest content of the symptom, and assume that it involves compromise formation, wish fulfillment, defense, and so on.

Anna Freud: But this would never come about unless the ego actively participates.

Joseph Sandler: You make the point, Miss Freud, that the formation of symptoms relieves the ego of the task of mastering its conflict because it has found a solution. Do you mean the *conscious* ego?

Anna Freud: What I had in mind is that the ongoing battle really ends with the formation of the symptom, because then the symptom exists, if it is permanent, as a solution offered once and for all. Nothing further needs to be done about it, except that the person now suffers from the symptom, and has further reactions, which depend on the particular symptom. But the conflict is solved. It is a bad solution, but it's a solution. In analyzing children as we do, we very often get them at the stage before a solution—the formation of a symptom—has been found. We get them while the battle is still raging, and that is so very different from adult neurotics. It is perhaps a difference that we don't discuss sufficiently. We often see in our diagnostic evaluations of children that the child hasn't found the solution yet. The ego doesn't yet know what it will make of the conflict, which might still end up in an obsessional neurosis, in delinquent acts, or in a depression or a suicide attempt. We don't know because the process hasn't yet been brought to a solution. I think that is what I really had in mind.

Joseph Sandler: I think we ought also to note that not all neurotic symptoms have to be seen as compromise formations. Certain psychosomatic symptoms, or the symptoms of such affective disorders as depression, need not be concealed forms of an instinctual wish finding gratification in the shape of a compromise with the defense or with the punishment, as was classically thought to occur.

There is a point about the response to affect I should like to raise, Miss Freud. In this chapter you refer to the young girl who came to see you because of states of acute anxiety. At one point you say, "The more powerfully the affect forced itself upon her, the more vehemently and scathingly did she ridicule herself. The analyst became the recipient of these defensive reactions only secondarily, because she was encouraging the demands of the patient's anxiety to be worked over in consciousness" (39,36). You then say that it was impossible to bring the unconscious content into consciousness until you had made the patient aware of the way she defended herself against her feelings by contemptuously disparaging herself. Later you show how you elucidated her resistance in the transference. Was the method the patient used to defend herself taken up and shown to her in relation to you as a person, as the patient's customary attitude to herself ?

Anna Freud: Well, it comes to the analyst's notice because suddenly the analyst becomes the innocent victim of the patient's attacks. But it isn't the transference of an object relationship. What she displays toward the analyst is an attitude toward herself, and it reveals itself in what we might call a form of transference. But if it did not reveal itself in the transference, the analyst would notice after some acquaintance with the patient that this particular attitude appears at inappropriate moments. One could say to the patient, "Why are you so angry with yourself ?" Just as later on one could say, "Why are you so angry with me?" Then we could show the patient her way of warding off unwelcome feelings. I have a patient now where I see something like this. Whenever she has feelings of, let us say, guilt or tenderness, which also make her unhappy, she becomes extremely tough in her feelings. And she does exactly the same thing in relation to me. If I side with her feelings, she becomes tough with me. But that is secondary. It isn't her anger with me, it is her anger with her feelings. This brings us to a useful distinction, because here what we have is a pseudotransference.

Joseph Sandler: You have made a useful distinction for us, Miss Freud. Again we see that the patient can be involved with the analyst without it being a real transference. We have a reflection of an habitual mode of reacting, which at a particular time involves the analyst. I suppose that the question which nags at me is whether one would take this up in relation to oneself as analyst, or whether one would put it in general terms to the patient. What you call pseudotransference may perhaps be dealt with in a useful way by saying to the patient, "You know, when you feel tender toward me, you have to be tough," or, the other way around, "When you disparage yourself now, I think you do so in reaction to a tender feeling toward me," rather than "This is what you do whenever you feel tender."

Anna Freud: I know that it is a current idea that only material which comes into the transference, and is shown as a transference phenomenon, can be helpful to the patient. I don't quite believe it. I don't see that there is a great difference between the analyst putting it in terms of the patient's relation to herself or in other terms. So long as you get hold of it the impression on the patient is very much the same. It does not matter whether you say, "Now I know whenever you are angry with me such and such is really the case," or whether you say, "Whenever you are so self-abusive it is because of so and so."

I do not see the difference as being so glaring as people do nowadays.

Sara Rosenfeld: Would you say that the use of the mechanism of externalization, involving the analyst, is what we are talking about?

Anna Freud: No, I wouldn't. I don't think that it is an externalization. The analyst sides with the feelings and therefore becomes an ally of what is warded off. And that is why the anger switches over toward the analyst.

Joseph Sandler: I think we have here again a multiple use of the term transference that is very confusing. When we use it in a general sense, we use it as a synonym for "relationship," something quite different from the intensification of feeling focusing on the person of the analyst, a revival of the past in the analytic situation. In transference, the patient sees what is happening as something new in the present, but it is something specific to the analytic situation. We often say transference instead of relationship, and when we speak of interpreting in the transference, we often mean interpreting in the relationship, opposing this to interpreting the defense. I am not sure that such an opposition is a valid one, because the analyst can be drawn into the working of the defense without it being transference in the narrower sense of the term. There is a significant difference between analysts in their approach to this particular problem. Some more than others want to draw the patient into a heightened awareness of feelings toward the analyst in the analytic situation, even though the patient may be reacting to the analyst in an habitual way, particularly at the beginning of the analysis. The argument would be, I think, that the threshold for perception and awareness of later, "truer" transference phenomena would be heightened.

Anna Freud: It would probably be the argument, but I think that it would be much the same whether you start with the attitude of the patient toward herself, and then seeing the same happening to the analyst, or whether you start with the analyst and then show her that she does the same to herself. I think that one has to do both.

Maria Berger: I have a question about your patient, Miss Freud. You explain that her attitude toward herself is based on her identification with her father. Could there have been great anger with him behind this, which might be what was transferred in what you described as her outburst?

Rose Edgcumbe: This is relevant to the question of interpreting in the transference. We have to ask whether in the analysis one takes up a transference of a relationship to part of the patient's self, or something which was originally a relationship to an object. This connects with whether the analyst is simply trying to show the patient the defense involved in the conflict within herself, or whether he is interpreting a repetition of the original relationship. I think this links with the point Dr. Sandler was trying to make.

Anna Freud: The idea is that, after all, one takes the

whole thing in small steps. As long as the patient has the habitual reaction of decrying all tender feelings, the analyst will not get any further. Once you arrive at the patient's feelings behind the defense, you will also arrive at the history of the feelings. But that is a later step.

Joseph Sandler: With this we get into the area of so-called "mutative" interpretations, which led to the tendency (in England certainly) to put everything in transference terms. It led to the idea that no comment should be made to the patient without bringing in the analyst.

Anna Freud: It reminds me of the patient who says to the analyst, "You can never say anything without bringing yourself into it."

Joseph Sandler: We have all heard this as a complaint from patients. And of course, the patient may have a real cause for grievance.

Anna Freud: That's right.

Joseph Sandler: Toward the end of the chapter you speak, Miss Freud, of the defense mechanism of reversal, which you call "a kind of reaction formation against the affect" (44,40). I'm sure that when you wrote this book you didn't expect every word to be pondered over, and the text to be dissected so minutely, but I do want to ask about the idea of defending by reversing the affect. It sounds as if one takes the affect itself and stands it on its head. If I understand you correctly, what you are saying is that one replaces the affect with its opposite, which is, of course, like the reaction formation. But it is not the affect that is being reversed, but a new and opposite experience that is being created.

Anna Freud: If someone says to you that whenever he feels sad he laughs it off, would you say that he creates a new experience?

Joseph Sandler: Yes, I would. Otherwise it would sound as if he were taking the sadness and transmuting it into laughter.

Anna Freud: It's a very fine theoretical distinction. We speak about transforming anxiety, but it is not strictly meant that way. What is meant is that the opposite appears on the surface.

Joseph Sandler: I am glad to hear you say this because there are still those who believe that we can see the affect as an energy that can be transformed, and that by producing the opposite we are using the same energy. Clinically, when we speak of the child who is sad but appears to be happy, I think we would say that he is producing his happiness in order to mask his sadness, to prevent himself from experiencing it.

Maria Berger: There is the complication that some children replace one affect with another, while others cover up their feeling of anger or sadness with a layer of a different affect. How do we know which is which?

Joseph Sandler: I suppose that this relates to the problem of interpreting the child's affects, which is so important in our work. Perhaps we do not train people well enough to "read" affects in patients. Can we say that the Kleinian concept of manic defense is really reversal of affect in the sense in which you use it, Miss Freud?

Anna Freud: Yes.

Joseph Sandler: Of course, the idea of manic defense is used very widely, to include overactivity aimed at warding off anxiety. This may differ somewhat from reversal of affect.

Anna Freud: Yes.

Joseph Sandler: We come closer now to the actual mechanisms of defense, Miss Freud, which we will discuss in much greater detail next time. I should like to start by commenting that in the past we have found it practically impossible to give an unambiguous definition of defense. Of course we distinguish between defense mechanisms and defensive measures (or maneuvers), which seem to be more complicated processes. But the mechanisms we call defenses are not necessarily simple units. Some of them are quite complicated, involving several steps. Yet, from an historical point of view the defenses have emerged as mechanisms of particular clinical significance which could be identified by particular characteristics. This seems to have been sufficient for them to be singled out as mechanisms of defense. Where we had difficulty in our discussions in the past was in deciding how one could say, for other than historical reasons, that something should be called a defense mechanism as opposed to a defensive maneuver. For example, it is clear that a reaction formation is a particular constellation with a certain coherence, and we can identify it. At the same time we know there is no reaction formation without there being at the same time an identification with an attitude of the parent or of some other authority figure. This would be an attitude which is opposed to the impulse or to the affect concerned. So identification is one component of the reaction formation, but the reaction formation is nevertheless identifiable as something with its own characteristics. Why do we label that compound reaction as a mechanism of defense, whereas such things as clowning or joking might be categorized as defensive maneuvers or measures and not defense mechanisms proper?

Anna Freud: I suppose you are right that the reason is historical. But there is a close connection between the defense mechanism and the neurosis proper, whereas what we call defensive maneuvers are nearer to the normal and nearer also to character formation. We cannot really link them specifically with any of the major neuroses. I think that the distinction is made from the side of pathology.

Joseph Sandler: You mean that if we are to distinguish neuroses in terms of particular patterns of defenses used, the units involved would be the defense mechanisms, whereas the defensive measures would not be parts of, say, an obsessional neurosis or hysteria.

Anna Freud: I don't remember when the distinction between defense mechanisms and defensive maneuvers was introduced. I don't think it existed in German at all.

Maria Berger: You introduced it, Miss Freud, some years ago.

Anna Freud: I think that it is the defense mechanisms that have clinical importance.

Joseph Sandler: I remember we came to the conclusion that in teaching technique one needs to demonstrate the major defense mechanisms to students very carefully, because they are consistently used by patients and we can identify them. But we have a certain amount of difficulty when we come to what one might call the minor defenses. Here we find that we have increased our list of mechanisms of defense to a point where we have far too many, and differences become difficult to see. You know how subtle the distinction is between reversal of roles, identification with the aggressor, turning passive into active, and so on. Identification with the aggressor is clear, but reversal of roles comes close to it, yet isn't quite the same.

Anna Freud: It is only identification with the aggressor which is a newcomer to the aristocracy.

Joseph Sandler: To Freud's list.

Anna Freud: Yes.

Joseph Sandler: One wonders whether it is appropriate to keep on adding to the list.

Anna Freud: It is good to know them all, list or not.

Joseph Sandler: Of course we know now that practically everything can be used for the purposes of defense, and this makes the situation even more difficult.

Anna Freud: Take, for example, falling asleep. Falling asleep is certainly not a defense mechanism, but it can be used to defend against aggression, to ward it off. For the person who is using it at a particular time it is defensive, but it's not a general defensive measure, let alone a defense mechanism.

Joseph Sandler: We still have the problem of where to draw the line between the mechanism and the measure, and I think we can't do this except on an historical and clinical basis. The major defenses were, of course, first described by Freud, and some were added by you, Miss Freud. Since then we have had the difficult task of trying to decide whether to include new ones, which were not mentioned by you, or whether we should consider them automatically as defensive measures. As you point out, we can have an infinite number of defensive measures.

Anna Freud: I would say that whatever serves a particular individual for the purpose of warding off either id content or affect (or whatever the ego doesn't want to accept) would be defensive. If it is personal to the individual, or to a few selected individuals, we can call it a defensive measure. If it is general in the sense that it is always tied to specific clinical states, which could not exist without it, we put it in another, more important category. You have mentioned clowning, which is certainly important as a defensive measure, and you could name character types that are based on it, but can you name illnesses that are based on it?

Joseph Sandler: Now that we recognize so much more the existence of narcissistic disorders, it seems to me that something like clowning could be considered to be specifically defensive, directed toward restoring self-esteem. Would we still consider it to be something that is part of a person's character, or would we have to give it the status of a defense mechanism?

Anna Freud: It is important to know where these things belong, and you are quite right that probably the narcissistic states and the disturbances of narcissism are linked to this specific defense. But whether you want to call it a mechanism or a measure doesn't really matter. When I explain the difference between defense mechanism and defensive measures, I compare the defenses to weapons which exist only as weapons, things such as guns and spears, and so on. There are other things you use for a weapon only at a certain moment. There is a young man before the courts at present, accused of killing his mother with a frying pan. Now is the frying pan a weapon or a measure? It's something that is really there for another purpose and is used only for the moment as a weapon. Isn't that the best way of making the distinction? This means that repression or projection would always be defense mechanisms, but clowning or many other activities would be picked up only for momentary use; they are defensive measures.

Joseph Sandler: Last time, when we were speaking of the clinical units of defense, Miss Freud, you said that the mechanisms used were what characterized each type of neurosis. But isn't repression, for example, something we need to use normally? If we didn't we would be overwhelmed by the return of what is normally unconscious and would become quite psychotic.

Anna Freud: That wouldn't alter the fact that repression always serves the purpose of keeping something out of the ego, or rather out of consciousness: a protective device.

Joseph Sandler: Perhaps we can end today by referring again to the distinction you made, Miss Freud. You referred to the mechanisms as ready-made tools developed for protection of the ego, used specifically for that purpose, in normality or in pathology. Defensive measures might be any form of activity, which might well be normal ways of expressing a whole variety of things, which can also be used for purposes of defense. Would that then be your point?

Anna Freud: Yes.

CHAPTER 4

The Mechanisms of
Defense

Freud originally used the term "defense" for the ego's
struggle against unpleasant ideas or affects. Later the
term "repression" was used instead, but in 1926 he returned to the use of "defense" as the general term, while
"repression" was used to designate the specific measure
that was originally called "defense."

Anna Freud suggests in this chapter that we inquire
into other specific modes of defense, and refers again to
Freud's suggestion that there may be a special connection between forms of defense and particular illnesses,
commenting that Freud has shown us that regression as
well as reaction formation, isolation, and "undoing" occur
in obsessional neurosis.

Anna Freud then reminds us of Freud's description
of introjection (or identification) and projection as defensive mechanisms at work in neurosis. Freud described

the processes of turning against the self and reversal, and sees these "vicissitudes of instinct" as also reflecting mechanisms of defense. She points out that "every vicissitude to which the instincts are liable has its origin in some ego activity" (47,44).

Nine methods of defense had been described previously (regression, repression, reaction formation, isolation, undoing, projection, introjection, turning against the self, and reversal). To these must be added a tenth—sublimation or the displacement of instinctual aims. The ego "has these ten different methods at its disposal in its conflicts with instinctual representatives and affects"; she goes on to say that it is the task of the analyst "to discover how far these methods prove effective in the processes of ego resistance and symptom formation" (47,44). Anna Freud then describes a case in which a girl, tortured by penis envy and jealousy which resulted in hostility to the mother, dealt with her ambivalence by displacing one side of her ambivalent feelings onto another female object. This proved inadequate, and the little girl then turned her hatred on her self. This too proved insufficient, and she then made use of projection, convinced that the female objects she had hated now hated and persecuted *her*. But these three defense mechanisms did not suffice to solve her conflicts, and although her guilt feelings were relieved by feelings of persecution, she remained tormented.

By contrast, in hysteria a problem such as that arising from hatred of the mother due to penis envy is solved by repression. The aggressive impulses may be changed into bodily symptoms in some cases, and in others a phobia may develop. In obsessional neurosis, however, hatred of the mother and penis envy are first repressed, and this is reinforced by reaction formations. Aggression may become excessive tenderness, and envy and jealousy may change into unselfishness and thoughtfulness toward others. Obsessional rituals protect the love objects from any outbreak of aggression, and the person's own sexuality is controlled by a strict moral code.

Conflicts mastered in an hysterical or obsessional way are more pathological than in the first patient considered. Part of the person's affective life has been removed. The little girl loses her relationship to her mother and to her own femininity, and much energy is used in maintaining the repression. The child who solves her conflicts by repression alone is at peace, but may suffer in a secondary way because of the neurosis. Repression relieves the ego of the task of mastering its conflicts.

Anna Freud points out that in practice repression is usually combined with other techniques of defense. She cites the case of a patient with a repressed wish to bite off her father's penis. The patient replaced this idea with a disinclination to eat, which was accompanied by feelings of disgust. The parts of the patient's instinctual life represented by the oral wish had been dealt with, but the wish to rob her father remained until it was later repudiated by her superego. The urge to rob was changed into "a peculiar kind of contentedness and unassumingness" (53,49). This resulted in a substratum of hysteria on which was imposed a specific ego modification.

Repression has a special place in relation to the other methods of defense, in that it is effective in a way in which the other methods of defense are not. It represents a "permanent institution demanding a constant expenditure of energy" (53,49–50), whereas the other mechanisms have to be employed again and again whenever the instinctual urge arises. Repression is also one of the most dangerous mechanisms of defense. Through it, whole areas of instinctual and affective life become dissociated, and the integrity of the personality may be destroyed. But the other defense mechanisms may also produce serious consequences, resulting in all sorts of transformations and distortions of the ego.

Anna Freud now refers to Freud's suggestion that there may be differences between defenses according to the age at which they first develop. Thus the child needs to have achieved a differentiation between ego and id in order to employ repression. In the same way, projection and introjection depend on a differentiation of self from the external world. Sublimation requires the existence of superego values, and it follows that repression and sublimation cannot be used until relatively late. Regression, reversal, or turning against the self seem to be independent of the stage of development. It may well be that they are the earliest defense mechanisms used by the ego.

On the other hand we have the problem that the earliest neurotic symptoms in children are hysterical, and these are certainly connected with repression. Similarly, genuine masochistic phenomena, based on the turning of a drive toward the self, are rarely met with in earliest childhood. It is clear, says Anna Freud, that the attempt to classify defense mechanisms is very difficult, and it might be best to study in detail those situations which evoke the defensive reactions.

The Discussion

Session one

Joseph Sandler: Miss Freud, last time we began to discuss defense mechanisms, and now I would like to turn to your reference in this chapter to Freud's view that introjection (or identification) and projection are defenses that are important "neurotic mechanisms." We may add sublimation to identification, introjection, and projection and comment that all such mechanisms also play a part in normal development. For example, introjection has been seen as the mental counterpart of oral "taking in," an essential element in building up the child's inner world. It seems that we have a whole group of mechanisms that may at times be used for defensive purposes, but need not always function as defense mechanisms.

Anna Freud: Introjection and projection are nearer to the id than are other defense mechanisms. When they are close to the primary process they are not defensive. But such mechanisms may make another appearance when used by the ego for defensive purposes.

Joseph Sandler: When you speak of introjection and projection as being primary process mechanisms, are you not really speaking of condensation and displacement?

Anna Freud: That's very near to it. But although we can give the processes other names, they are very much the same. So displacement on the primary process level is projection on the ego level. The person who develops first primary and then secondary process is still the same person, and the earliest defense mechanisms of the ego are based on primary processes. The experience gained by the individual from his primary processes is used by him in the elaboration of the defense mechanisms. Of course later defenses are much more sophisticated, and much more under the influence of the ego. But if we look at the very early stages of development we can see how close the little child's projections are to primary process functioning. We know how insecure the boundaries are in the small child, and it is much easier for him to say "I haven't done it, you have done it" than later on, when the boundaries are more efficient.

Joseph Sandler: It is often said that the earliest defense mechanisms are introjection and projection. But for these mechanisms to be effective as defenses, mustn't a very definite boundary exist between self and not-self ? Introjection is often described as a defense against loss of an object, and projection as a defense against feelings the child doesn't like and wants to remove from his own self-representation. Can we call such processes defenses before boundaries exist?

Anna Freud: If you project something and it is still felt to be yourself, it is an unnecessary exercise. You haven't gained anything.

Joseph Sandler: We come again to the question of whether the list you have given in this chapter should be regarded as definitive. I wonder why, for example, you had not included displacement as a defense. We know that displacement is part of primary process, but we know also that it has a defensive function when used by the ego. It can protect the person from, for example, a conflict of ambivalence. In fact you describe it in regard to the patient who "displaced outward one side of her ambivalent feeling" (48,45). Did you have any special reason for not including displacement in the list of defense mechanisms?

Anna Freud: I suppose it was partly because displacement is so clearly a primary process mechanism. When you ask whether the list is definitive, I would say of course it is not. It seemed the best I could do at that time. I remember that I was very reluctant to say there were nine mechanisms, because I had the feeling that if I said there were nine there might by then be ten. One should never count these things.

Joseph Sandler: I should think we've probably got twenty by now.

Anna Freud: Yes.

Maria Berger: I was rather surprised, Miss Freud, to find that identification with the aggressor was not included in your list.

Anna Freud: I didn't list it here because I thought only of the recognized defense mechanisms, and I felt modest about this new one. I didn't think it had a claim to be introduced yet.

Maria Berger: I should like to ask about introjection,

because you have used it interchangeably with identification. Do you differentiate between the two?

Anna Freud: You know, at the time there was a great deal of discussion about the difference between identification and introjection. Someone came up with the idea that introjection really meant the mental counterpart of physical "taking in." I hadn't at that time become accustomed to using the two terms for different processes.

Joseph Sandler: I think that the situation must have been complicated by the way the term "ego" was used. Of course we now see that it is necessary to differentiate the self-representation from the ego as a structure. In your book there are times when you use "ego" where I think that you quite clearly mean "self." This double meaning must have caused a lot of problems at the time. So many complications arose in the past because the word "ego" was used for oneself as an object.

Anna Freud: And of course there is no word for the noun "self" in German.

Joseph Sandler: The French have tried to introduce *le soi*, but it doesn't seem to have worked very well. I think that in other languages the English word "self" tends to be used where there isn't an appropriate word.

Sara Rosenfeld: At some point in the book there is a reference to introjection enriching the ego, and I wonder whether we ought not to distinguish more precisely between the defensive aspects of introjection and its ego-building aspects.

Joseph Sandler: This problem too is connected with the need to distinguish between the ego as a structure and the self-representation. One can say that identifications can change the self-representation. But learning has a very strong component of identification in it, so one can say also that identification enriches the ego as a structure. Whether introjection can be distinguished similarly, I don't know. Of course, it was also used in a different sense to refer to the internalization of the parents to form the superego. There is here a double meaning of the term. It refers on the one hand to very early "taking in" and on the other to superego formation when the child is about five. Students of psychoanalysis have pondered for years the reference in Freud to the ego as the precipitate of abandoned object cathexes. What does this famous phrase mean?

Anna Freud: What is meant is very simply that every abandoned object relationship leaves its residue in the self, or the person, or the ego, and enriches it thereby.

Tom Lopez: When we speak of abandoned object cathexes, this does not actually mean that the person goes away, does it? Is it not that certain ways of relating are abandoned?

Anna Freud: No, it doesn't mean that the person is really lost, but rather that the object cathexis is withdrawn and replaced by an identification. It is very important that the object libido can be changed back into narcissistic libido, that the libido can then take the self as an object.

Joseph Sandler: If we use the model of libido and its transformation and displacement, would we not then say that the building up of secondary narcissism is an essential part of development? It involves a withdrawal of investment from the object and an attachment of the affection felt for the object to the self-representation. Identification would then be a major vehicle for secondary narcissism. If one copies an admired aspect of the object, then some of the admiration, affection, and esteem for the object can be transferred to the self, adding to secondary narcissism. It goes hand in hand with identification.

Anna Freud: Yes, that's right.

Joseph Sandler: I wonder how you saw the specific defense mechanisms, Miss Freud. You mention regression as a defense, and again we have a mechanism which is at times a defense, and at times not. Presumably this double aspect can apply to all the mechanisms. You have often referred to children regressing toward the end of the schoolday, and I suppose we would not call this regression a defense. In fact, one might conjecture that we have constantly to do a certain amount of work to prevent ourselves from regressing at any time, and when we get tired we can't do that work as well, so we give in to the pull toward childhood modes of behavior.

Anna Freud: We know how children regress to more and

more infantile modes of behavior in the period just before they go to sleep.

Alex Holder: I have always had problems with the concept of regression as a defense. It seems to me, Miss Freud, that you refer here to libidinal regression, rather than to regression as a defense on the side of the ego. I think that regression, as usually described, takes place outside the ego. What I mean is that after the ego defends against some unacceptable impulse, instinctual drive regression may follow and earlier drive contents be revived. The ego has then to deal with a regressively revived derivative which tries to force its way through again. I have always thought that the ego does not *actively* institute the regression, as it does, for instance, in the case of repression or reaction formation. Rather, regression is something that happens *in consequence of* the ego's defending against an impulse. This makes me question whether it is a defense at all.

Anna Freud: I remember it being said that regression is the most efficient way for the whole personality to adapt to an intolerably difficult situation. I don't know whether it occurs outside the ego, so to speak, or whether the ego institutes it actively. But certainly the return to a lower form of functioning is a way of avoiding intolerable stress.

Joseph Sandler: Perhaps we can say that it is a way of *attempting* to avoid something intolerable, by reverting to a mode of functioning characteristic of an earlier time when such conflicts didn't exist. But this can get the individual in trouble because, as you have often pointed out, a new conflict may arise as a result of the regression, in particular a conflict with a superego which hasn't regressed. I am reminded of a patient of mine who became increasingly angry with his mother-in-law after she came to stay, but was not aware of his anger. His repressed angry wishes revived childhood sadistic impulses which had been relatively dormant. The patient then had a greater conflict because of his revived sadistic wishes. His anger with his mother-in-law had aroused, quite unconsciously, the wish to kill and maim her. Regression then reinforced a neurotic conflict, but I don't think that the regression was a defense in this case.

Anna Freud: What you describe is more a revival than a regression. I wouldn't call it regression. I think that the new experience touches off the earlier one, revives it, brings the emotions of the past into the present.

Joseph Sandler: Would you then not say that the child who is angry, who then loses control and resorts more and more to throwing things around and making a mess as he gets angrier and angrier, is showing a regression?

Anna Freud: I would call it an overwhelming of the ego's controls by the strength of the emotion.

Joseph Sandler: This raises the interesting point of whether the instinctual drives, which may be seen as regressively revived, are normally active but kept in control. Or are they dormant but reactivated? Or do both processes occur? It seems to me that we do need to distinguish between, on the one hand, something which is active but is being successfully defended against all the time, being held back under pressure or being diverted in some way, and on the other something which is there in a relatively latent form only, but which can become stronger when it is revived (in terms of the energy theory, I suppose one would say recathected).

Anna Freud: What about the crime of passion, when somebody kills someone else in a rage? How would you define it? The person does not need to be someone who is usually given to rages, or who knows about his murderous impulses. On the other hand, we know that these murderous impulses are there, are present in everybody, but are kept under repression and are controlled. But at some point passion may overwhelm the individual, and the ego's control is lost. I think that it is essentially a quantitative matter, and what we see is that for the moment the affect and the impulse are stronger than any of the restraints which usually keep them in check.

Joseph Sandler: I wonder if you could comment on the clinical significance of the difference between children in whom there is a weakness of control on the part of the ego, so that infantile modes of expression are allowed through, and cases in which there is a reinforcement due to regression or to a sudden stimulation of an infantile wish.

Anna Freud: We know both situations. The result is the same, because the balance is disturbed. The balance can be disturbed on the one side or on the other. It can be disturbed because the impulse becomes overwhelming for some reason, or because the ego becomes unduly weakened. The reasons are different, but the effect is the same.

Joseph Sandler: Could you say something, Miss Freud, about the question of superego regression? We usually say that the superego doesn't regress, yet we speak of more archaic forms of superego functioning returning; or we say that the superego has become more sadistic because of regression.

Anna Freud: One usually doesn't call this regression, but rather a dissolving of the superego—as in the saying that the superego is that part of the mental apparatus which is soluble in alcohol.

Joseph Sandler: I was thinking of the change in the superego which we see in melancholia, in the self-reproaching type of depression.

Anna Freud: It becomes more cruel. You could very well call it a regression.

Robert Evans: Could you say something about regression of the ego? It is said that it follows different laws, but I have never really got that straight in my mind.

Anna Freud: This is a subject we have discussed a lot. The ego follows quite different laws as far as regression is concerned. Regression is really a different concept here, but we use the same name. The earlier idea was that in regression the libido returned to fixation points, to earlier stations where some libido had been left behind. This notion cannot, of course, be used for the ego. With the ego what we see is a regression merely to earlier stages, but without the idea that it is the libido that pulls it backward to specific fixation points.

Joseph Sandler: If one wanted to argue the point, one could say that there are certain modes of ego functioning which gave particular forms of *satisfaction* at particular points in development. We could then speak of a functional fixation of the ego, and say that in ego regression the person goes back to, for example, earlier defense mechanisms, or to earlier modes of thinking, that were satisfying or reassuring at the time. This would be different from the way in which you have described ego regression as following a progressive path backward, something I think is more characteristic of organic states.

Anna Freud: I still feel that there is a difference between a mode of functioning that gave pleasure or satisfaction or reassurance on the side of the ego, and the actual libidinal fixation to a libidinal phase. I think that there we have something more direct and basic, but I can quite see the other side.

Joseph Sandler: I have been thinking a lot lately about the way in which the urgent need to deal with anxiety, or with some threat, can be as great as the urgency of an instinctual wish, and may also contribute to regression. The push to function in a particular way characteristic of an earlier period of development, as well as the relief gained by functioning in that way, could be seen to be as great as that we associate with the drives. But of course the pleasure gained may not be as great.

Anna Freud: The pleasure is not the same. What you get is the most effective way of escape from an intolerable situation of strain or anxiety.

Ilse Hellman: When we observed the babies in the Hampstead Nurseries during the war, we thought of ego regression not so much in terms of the pleasure gained as in terms of reducing the stress.

Maria Berger: Can we have libidinal regression without ego regression or vice versa?

Joseph Sandler: If we differentiate ego and id for the purpose of conceptualizing aspects of behavior involving the total apparatus, when there is a conflict of interest between different aspects of the mind, then this must affect our thinking about regression. Miss Freud spoke earlier of the ego collaborating with the id, and I think that in this collaboration there might well be a tendency for the ego to regress when the id does."

Anna Freud: Could we imagine, let's say, an adult remaining on the genital level and still regressing heavily on the ego side?

Joseph Sandler: It seems likely that some people with organic disturbances may show a genital level of functioning but have an ego regression. But apart from that

I am sure that many cases of ego regression allow pregenital impulses, which have been defended against, to
come through. For example, the arteriosclerotic old man
who exhibits himself in the park is letting something
through which may have been very much alive before,
but had been dealt with in some other way.

Anna Freud: Yes, we can say that such impulses are
allowed through to the surface rather than being brought
up by regression.

Joseph Sandler: What seems to have been coming out
in the discussion is a distinction between release and
regression, which might be worth pursuing further.

Anna Freud: And that would give us the answer to the
question of the crime of passion. It is a release, not a
regression.

Joseph Sandler: May we move on now to the question
of repression? We may ask whether or not repression is
an element in all the defenses, one of the basic building
blocks in every defense described. In the first phase of
psychoanalysis, when Freud placed so much emphasis
on childhood traumas, the defense of repression was introduced in relation to the dissociation of affect and the
memories connected with that affect. What would one
say now about the question of repression of feelings? You
have spoken, Miss Freud, of reaction formation in relation to feelings. Would you say that repression, as we
see it now, operates only against ideational content, so
that in consequence associated feelings are not aroused,

or would you say that one can in fact have repressed feelings?

Anna Freud: You know, at the time I wrote this book I was under the influence of the ideas that existed then, and there was much confusion about the whole question of unconscious affect.

Joseph Sandler: The problem must have been made difficult because while we can obviously have preconscious feelings, or feelings in the unconscious part of the ego, as Freud showed in "Inhibitions, Symptoms and Anxiety" in 1926, this does not necessarily mean that we have feelings in the system Unconscious, in the dynamic Unconscious, or in the id.

Anna Freud: This is a difficulty I have always had with Kleinian theory, in that they speak of the deep anxiety in the unconscious, but we only get anxiety if the threatening material reaches the ego.

Joseph Sandler: I think that perhaps Kleinians equate what is descriptively unconscious with what is dynamically unconscious. This leads to a lot of theoretical difficulty.

Anna Freud: Unconscious anxiety is not the same as anxiety in the unconscious. We would have to say that it is only material which reaches the preconscious or the unconscious ego which can be defended against, but this certainly includes feelings, because censorship does not stop at the border between the unconscious and the preconscious. The ego does the defending, including defending against feelings, and this work of defense is done in the unconscious part of the ego.

Joseph Sandler: Isolation has always caused some difficulty. Sometimes we refer simply to isolation, at other times to isolation of affect. When you spoke of isolation, Miss Freud, did you refer to something which is tolerated in consciousness only because the associated feelings have been removed, and which would otherwise be repressed?

Anna Freud: Yes, that was the meaning.

Robert Evans: There is also a conceptualization of isolation as an artificial separation of two contents that belong together.

Anna Freud: I don't think that was the original meaning. The original meaning was the isolation of an affect from the idea that it was originally connected with.

Joseph Sandler: Perhaps what Dr. Evans has referred to is something we put under the heading "splitting," but this is again a term which has several meanings.

Hansi Kennedy: One of the problems with regard to splitting is the question of what happens to the affect. Is a repression of affect involved?

Anna Freud: In isolation the affect is usually displaced, warded off, changed into the opposite, or denied. The important thing is that the result is that the affect isn't connected with the original source, with the original idea.

Joseph Sandler: So we have the possibility of a number of processes resulting in isolation of affect.

Maria Berger: I think that we see isolation when a patient recalls a painful experience and says that he doesn't remember what he felt at the time. However, I remember a particular patient who told me about an unpleasant experience. Although he could not remember any feelings about it, he wiped away a tear. When I asked him about this, he said that it was his hay fever. Although we could say that he used isolation of affect, the affect must have been present in association with the memory or he would not have shed a tear.

Joseph Sandler: One of the problems we have is that when we talk about affect we tend to refer to two different aspects. One is the physiological response, the other is the subjective feeling. Presumably this patient could not defend against the bodily response, but the defense involved was probably directed against the feeling aspect of the affect. This brings us again to the difficult area of repression of feelings. I think that there is a strong argument to say that feelings are mental contents, just as ideational contents are. As one can have memories of feelings, why should one not be able to repress these as well? I imagine that if Mrs. Berger's patient showed tears, his feelings must have been close to the surface.

Sara Rosenfeld: I want to draw attention to the role of the object in such defenses. Some children are told to keep a stiff upper lip, and this may then initiate the particular form of defense we are talking about. We can see how important the role of the object is in fostering certain defenses. This seems to me to be important in the establishment of patterns of defense in children.

Joseph Sandler: I suppose that the influence of the object is different for different defenses. The object may play a bigger role in the development of reaction formations than in, for example, repression.

Ilse Hellman: Denial of affect has probably something to do with socially unacceptable feelings, and is therefore more object related.

Joseph Sandler: Denial of affect has been mentioned several times. It is not in the list of defenses we have been considering, and we might well ask what we mean by it. Is it like the usual denial, in that the affect is there but ignored, or is it what has been called denial in fantasy? Is it the same as isolation of affect? Or do we have in mind that the denial is the outcome of the person's attitude toward the affect?

Hansi Kennedy: What I have in mind is simply that there can be a descriptively unconscious feeling state which one does not allow oneself to experience or to acknowledge in consciousness.

Joseph Sandler: I suppose that one could say that attention has been withdrawn from the feeling, but if it becomes strong enough, presumably the person would have to become conscious of it. I suppose that sometimes there is a counterforce added, and then we would come close to the idea of repression.

Hansi Kennedy: In one's ordinary clinical work it is sometimes possible to put the patient in touch with warded-off feelings quite easily.

Joseph Sandler: It is interesting that you speak of "warded-off " feelings.

Hansi Kennedy: Of course this is very different from what we have been talking about in regard to isolation of affect. When isolation is used it is very difficult to get hold of the affect.

Joseph Sandler: It seems that we have to distinguish between isolation of affect and something like denial of affect or warding off of affect.

Session two

Joseph Sandler: We come now to the mechanism of undoing, which we often refer to as "doing and undoing." The question comes up of whether we should distinguish between simple undoing on the one hand, and doing and undoing as a specifically obsessional mechanism on the other. We sometimes speak of "undoing" when people have to undo something they have done because they subsequently feel guilty, which is certainly not obsessional. We hear occasionally of the person who has a "ruined by success" type of personality, who has to undo his success because he feels guilty. Should we use the term "undoing" for this, or rather keep the term for the doing and undoing of the obsessional?

Anna Freud: Certainly the obsessional who puts a thing in a certain place and removes it again is doing and undoing, but there is something else obsessionals do. An obsessional I treated was very afraid of any sort of aggression leaking out, and he would go over incidents innumerable times in his mind. This was a sort of undoing. He would go through an event up to the moment when the dangerous thing happened, and then he would mentally undo what happened afterward. He would put something else in its place so that the danger was avoided. In this way he was undoing events which had happened.

Joseph Sandler: Does one have to be an obsessional to do that?

Anna Freud: Yes, I think so. Or at least to have an obsessional character. He had to do it compulsively until the dangerous event was removed altogether, until it was really blotted out.

Joseph Sandler: That would be quite different from the sort of symbolic compromise shown in obsessional doing and undoing, where the wish is gratified by an action of some sort, the defense showing itself by the undoing.

Anna Freud: With my patient it was really a belief that an event could be undone psychically after the event.

Joseph Sandler: So you don't mean the obsessional doing and undoing.

Anna Freud: When I spoke of doing and undoing I really meant both.

Joseph Sandler: Would both of these be mechanisms of defense?

Anna Freud: Yes, certainly. In some patients who are not obsessional we find symptoms like compulsive eating followed by vomiting. Is this not a way of undoing what has been taken in?

Joseph Sandler: You mean the psychic significance of the event is undone.

Anna Freud: Yes. You know, children are taught in what is really a very funny way. Let us say that a little child of two or three years of age has hurt another child, then the nursery school teacher or the mother will say, "Now you must go and do this or that, and then it will be all right again." This is really very much like the obsessional symptom, isn't it? A child goes up the staircase and handles the banister roughly. Then he is told he has to go back and stroke the banister to take away the hurt he has caused it. That would be doing and undoing. I remember a little boy at the Hampstead Nurseries, three years old, who used to pull out other children's hair. He took hair and pulled it out, and everyone was horrified. The nurse told him how wrong it was, so he went back to the little girl whose hair he had pulled out in order to put it back on her head again. This was undoing, although of course it wasn't successful.

Ilse Hellman: The question remains of whether there is not a difference between undoing and what one calls reparation, making something "good" again. I think that the two are not quite the same. For instance, if a child strokes a child he has just hurt, there is a feeling of remorse attached to it. It is not the same as just putting the hair back in order to undo the act. There is a feeling that the hurt has to be compensated for in some way. He tries to make the other child feel better again, not just to put the hair back.

Anna Freud: For the child I believe it means to undo the whole event and to give the hair back again. For the adult it means to make good the hurt feeling. What is most interesting is when there is a transition from the physical action into the thought process, with attempts to undo thoughts, as in the obsessional.

Ilse Hellman: There are quite a number of situations where there is undoing in action, but the undoing refers to a thought, not an action. I have a girl patient who has to pick up all banana skins she sees in the street although she hasn't put them there. When she sees a banana skin she immediately gets the idea that someone might be in danger of breaking a leg or getting hurt, and she then has to pick up the skin to avoid that danger. But she searches the street for banana skins. There is clearly a thought that has to be undone.

Joseph Sandler: This is extremely interesting because it makes the link between the reaction formation and the undoing, both of which we associate with the obsessional. I could imagine that what you describe could become a reaction formation of, let us say, overcleanliness.

Anna Freud: And oversolicitousness.

Maria Berger: In past discussions at the Clinic it was said that there is never any undoing without doing. The sort of thing we had in mind was the touching rituals of certain children. To them the wish is so real that from their viewpoint it is an act. The difference between the thought and the act is minimal. I think that we should call the mechanism doing and undoing, and not simply undoing.

Joseph Sandler: But it seems clear that the term undoing includes more than obsessional doing followed by undoing what has been done. If we take up Dr. Hellman's point about reparation as undoing, it is certainly true that we often see how people make attempts to atone, to make amends. This undoing is very different from the undoing we have been talking about. Certainly in the second and third years we do see the beginnings of the child's attempt to placate and appease in an active way.

Ilse Hellman: This links very much with the fear of loss of love and the child's attempt to recreate the situation in which he feels that he is lovable again. It is an attempt to get rid of the feeling of being no longer good enough to be valued and appreciated. It starts, I think, in the preverbal period.

Joseph Sandler: And it may become linked with the feeling of having done wrong, which isn't guilt but is a precursor to guilt, in that it is related to the attitudes of the parents and to the expected sanctions from the parents. Of course, much later in the development of object love this feeling is transformed into concern for the object, but this is relatively late.

Anna Freud: As every mother knows.

Robert L. Tyson: Are there any precursors that we can see in children who subsequently develop the defense of undoing?

Joseph Sandler: To my mind the anal child shows the normal activity of doing and undoing, which is very characteristic of his play. He will constantly put beads in a bottle and take them out and then put them back in again and take them out again. This is part, I think, of his developing a means of testing and controlling his environment. It is a very normal activity, and it seems to me that the defense grows out of this normal activity.

Anna Freud: Yes, he has learned that he can undo. It is very interesting to see the activity shared between two children. I once watched two little ones in the Nursery School, and one of the children was very intent on removing all the dishes from the dining room cupboard. The other child was equally intent on putting them all back. Neither interfered with the other, but the doing and undoing fitted together perfectly.

W. Ernst Freud: I am not quite happy with equating the child's activity of putting things in and taking them out and the defense mechanism of doing and undoing. For that we require some kind of superego and the avoidance of some sort of conflict.

Joseph Sandler: Perhaps one could say that the child's play activity gives him a sort of mastery pleasure, but at the same time it sets the pattern for something which can be used later for conflict-resolving purposes. Children play with doing and undoing, and this is gratifying and reassuring. External play in the anal phase becomes playing with words, and this then turns into playing with thoughts. Would it not meet the point to say that what we see is a mode of functioning which is available to the ego, and if it is used for defensive purposes later on it can then be called a defense mechanism? I could imagine that if this particular sort of activity gave the child a great deal of satisfaction or reassurance, and a feeling of mastery, there might be a later tendency for that function to be seized on for use as a defense.

Anna Freud: One sees certain children who have as much pleasure in tumbling building blocks down as in building them up, and these are perhaps the children who will become obsessional later. It's very difficult to say whether one should call this a pre-stage rather than a precursor of obsessional activity, but certainly defense mechanisms have always to be built on abilities of some sort. Whether or not these are abilities of the ego or something that comes from the primary process is another question.

Joseph Sandler: I am convinced that the defense mechanisms relate to what has been referred to as the perceptual and cognitive style of the individual. A person can have a style of thinking and perceiving which shows the mode of functioning of defenses in latent form. For example, we may see a style of thinking in which there is a great deal of categorizing, and while this is not really obsessional, it may show a predisposition to develop obsessional defenses. There are other people who, in their normal perception and cognition, show a great deal of what could grow into the mechanisms of denial and repression.

Anna Freud: Yes. You remember it was Hartmann who was the first to point out that what we call the obsessional mechanisms are there very early in order to create order in our thoughts.

Vann Spruiell: Wouldn't this also tie in with Hartmann's idea of change of function? What we are talking about may reflect a change of function when it is used in a defensive process.

Anna Freud: You mean a function has been acquired and is then used elsewhere? I would agree with that.

Joseph Sandler: It would be useful to discuss projection now. At present at the Clinic we restrict the use of this term to the attribution of an unwanted impulse to another person, with the impulse then being felt as coming back against the person himself. So if someone is angry with another and uses projection in the way we have defined it, he will feel that the other person is angry with him. We use the term externalization for similar processes lacking this "reflexive" quality. We have, in fact, a very narrow definition, and there would be a good case for arguing that it is far too narrow, for in the general psychoanalytic literature the concept of projection tends to be used to refer to all sorts of externalizations. For example, a person might project an aggressive wish onto a second person, feeling then that the second person has aggressive intentions toward a third. This does not have the "reflexive" quality, and at present we would use the general term "externalization." I am not sure, Miss Freud, that this is the way you saw it when you wrote about projection.

Anna Freud: Historically, the return of the projected impulse back against the self was the first sort of projection that was discussed, and the term externalization was not used. We tended to study only those situations in which the projected aggression or some other impulse was returned to the sender. The idea of externalization or other forms of projection came later.

Joseph Sandler: Historically, then, the concept would apply to paranoid people and to people with phobias, who felt that a situation was too dangerous because they had projected, for example, their own hostile wishes onto it. It would apply to Little Hans.

Anna Freud: Yes. At the time the concept was introduced and first used, it was the pathological and not the normal that was studied. What we now call externalization refers much more to what we discuss in relation to normal development.

Joseph Sandler: Of course, we also see it in the treatment situation, particularly where superego introjects are externalized onto the analyst. We can also see various forms of externalization as aspects of the self-representation being attributed to others, both in pathology and in normal life. A child may write a story and externalize a conflict, inside the session or outside it.

Anna Freud: What you described first as externalization onto the analyst would have, I think, at the time been called transference. It would not have been distinguished sufficiently from the object relationship which develops in the analysis and which we now call transference.

Joseph Sandler: In recent years you have emphasized this distinction, I know.

Anna Freud: But it was not commonly made at that time.

Joseph Sandler: What do you feel, Miss Freud, about restricting the definition of projection to the narrower meaning, in which there is a turning back of the wish or impulses against oneself ?

Anna Freud: My feeling is that the division into projection and externalization really covers all the manifestations, so long as one distinguishes clearly between the two.

Joseph Sandler: Of course, this goes against the general trend in the literature, where the term "projection" is often used where we would use "externalization."

Maria Berger: I have a question about projection or externalization—whatever you want to call it. Often one finds with children a sort of generalization in which the child thinks, "I feel this way, therefore everybody feels this way."

Anna Freud: If that sort of ascribing of what one feels oneself to others did not exist, then individuals would probably never learn to project.

Joseph Sandler: We hear a lot about primitive projection and introjection in the extremely young infant. Is not what is meant something other than what we understand by the defense mechanisms of projection and introjection?

Anna Freud: Yes, the primitive id processes get taken over only later by the developing ego as defense mechanisms.

Joseph Sandler: I want to add to the discussion the idea (of the validity of which I am quite convinced) that a form of very primitive and fleeting primary identification normally persists in adult life. I believe that when we perceive an object we are momentarily confused with it, although the ego then sets boundaries almost immediately. We could speak here of the boundary-setting function of the ego. We see such persisting primary identification in the way we move when we see people riding horses, skating, and so on. If we are not particularly on our guard we move in sympathy with the person we are perceiving. The primary confusion of very early childhood persists in some way. In certain psychotic states, or in toxic states, or when one is not fully aware, we do not set the boundaries so quickly, and can become aware of the confusion.

Anna Freud: There is an interesting parallel to this because we know that with persecuted minorities, against whom atrocities are committed, the atrocities are preceded by a withdrawal of the feeling of sameness. We get the substitute feeling of "we are not the same, you and I." It is a sort of dehumanizing process applied to the victim. Without this preliminary withdrawal or boundary setting what happens afterward could not happen, because of the feeling of sympathy and empathy, of sameness, which has to be done away with.

Joseph Sandler: This would mean that the boundaries become more firmly set, become emphasized so that the benefits of the projection can be all the greater. Then one can focus on differences like color of skin, or Jewishness, and this difference can be exaggerated in order to further reinforce the feeling that there is nothing in common.

Anna Freud: Yes, I think this is a very interesting idea.

Joseph Sandler: May we come back to projection for a little while? I should like to clarify whether it is always the same impulse that is felt to be directed back at one. In some cases it seems to be the same and in other cases it gets modified. Someone might say that the other person is angry with him, but what is being defended against is a death wish which has a different content.

Anna Freud: If you are angry enough it becomes a death wish. I wonder whether it is ever wholly changed. I wouldn't think so. We wouldn't call it projection if it were.

Joseph Sandler: I have never fully understood the projection that Freud spelled out in regard to homosexual wishes in paranoia. The process ends up with a person feeling a sort of penetrating attack, but the change from "I love him" to "he loves me" and then to "he hates me" is a change which has often been referred to as projection, but it seems to be more complicated than simple projection.

Anna Freud: Yes, because if it were simple projection the forbidden love for the other man would come back as a forbidden love from him for the original person. But what happens in between is as you described—the love is changed to hate.

Joseph Sandler: I've never really understood that as part of the projection.

Anna Freud: It's not part of the projection, but a reversal process which gets involved in the projection.

Ilse Hellman: So there is an additional defense in the paranoia that is based on unconscious homosexual wishes. There is not only a projection, but a reversal is included.

Anna Freud: Very little would be accomplished by the mere projection of the homosexual wish. There would still be a homosexual relationship, with the passive and active roles exchanged. In order to make the defense work effectively, the affect has to be changed as well.

Joseph Sandler: One sees the simpler form of projection in those people who believe that others are out to seduce them.

Anna Freud: I think this is more of an externalization. We see it sometimes in prepsychotic states. Someone travels on the bus or on the subway and believes that all the girls are making secret advances to him. These are only his own wished-for secret advances to the girls. We don't call this projection. It is really an externalization of the impulse. The girl does it instead of the man.

Joseph Sandler: But it is his wish to make advances, and he feels instead that they are making advances to him. Why should it not be projection?

Anna Freud: It's getting rid of a criticized drive derivative by ascribing it to someone else. It is something which happens very frequently.

Joseph Sandler: Isn't it the same as projecting the aggressive wish?

Anna Freud: Yes, it is the same, but we don't call it projection.

Maria Berger: Why not?

Anna Freud: I don't know. I'm thinking now of the general usage. It isn't normally called projection. I think that it would be called projection if these other people became persecutors.

Rose Edgcumbe: Do we use projection only in connection with aggression?

Anna Freud: Perhaps only when there has been the addition of aggression.

Ilse Hellman: Isn't the projection also wish-fulfilling?

Anna Freud: Yes.

Joseph Sandler: In paranoid people there is an increase in the narcissistic supplies of the individual because he becomes the center of attention. So a person's idea that all the girls are making eyes at him is one which refuels his narcissism, and perhaps temporarily does away with feelings of inadequacy and helplessness which go along with the recognition of his own unfulfillable sexual wishes. I think that there is also a wish fulfillment through a sort of unconscious basic identification with the persecutor, even though the boundaries between self and other are well established.

Anna Freud: I remember a patient who actually noticed the sexual excitement in these other people, instead of noticing her own. This isn't quite the same as projection, but there seem to be so many marginal phenomena we want to label. I think that one of the problems of constructing a definition is that we feel the need to define the process so that it includes all impulses. Even though the use of the term projection in a wide sense is the common usage, perhaps we ought to stick to externalization for the general class of these processes, and reserve projection for the externalization of a disowned impulse in one's self onto another, an impulse which is felt to be coming back at oneself.

Rose Edgcumbe: Freud gives the example, in his paper "Some Neurotic Tendencies in Jealousy, Paranoia and Homosexuality," of someone who has the temptation to be unfaithful and then believes his wife to be unfaithful. Freud calls this projection, but says that it is not simply putting one's own impulses onto the other person. Also, it involved a libidinal rather than an aggressive drive.

Joseph Sandler: If we follow what was said earlier, we would have to call it externalization.

Anna Freud: There is an element of the impulse returning, because the end of the story is not that the husband is unfaithful to his wife, but rather that she betrays him.

Joseph Sandler: Yes, it would be projection in the strict sense of the definition. But if one were to say that the person is not having conscious thoughts about other women, but believes that the wife is having thoughts about other men, then it would be externalization.

Anna Freud: Yes.

Joseph Sandler: It is a completely arbitrary division, but I suppose it is necessary.

Ilse Hellman: I see projection quite regularly in agoraphobia. I had an agoraphobic woman as a patient, and she told me that every man she passed in the street became sexually excited by her. What she consciously experienced was her fear of being in the street. But it was quite obvious that she projected her wishes and felt them to be coming back at her.

Joseph Sandler: Would we not say that there is always a projection or an externalization in the classical phobic situation? The impulse is put into the external world, and then it can be avoided and controlled, whereas if it were to be recognized as one's own it would not be so readily controlled. But what is projected? Is it the wish or is it the danger situation? And again, isn't it really an externalization rather than a projection?

Anna Freud: I remember a child with a school phobia where it was quite clear from the work in the analysis that the danger for the child was her death wish against her mother. She was unable to move her affection from mother to father, because this meant killing the mother. But this first appeared as a school phobia, as a fear of a boy she felt to be aggressive in the playground. Of course, this means for us that she was an aggressive little girl, but she refused to go out and play for fear he might hurt her. We would say that she was afraid that she would meet her own aggression in him. She then had a fear of a girl at school who had actually told her some aggressive fairy stories, and from then on she refused to go to school. In both instances she feared to meet her own aggressive death wishes in the outside world, but externalized them onto other people so that she could avoid them.

Joseph Sandler: I think people will have to be given license to use projection and externalization interchangeably.

Anna Freud: Until we know better.

Joseph Sandler: One often sees in paranoid people the exploitation of a piece of reality for purposes of projection. Of course there is projection, but often something real is grossly exaggerated. This can lead to difficulties if one has a paranoid patient, because he can always find the evidence that the persecution he is talking about is really there. We also see it in certain character cases, who are not anywhere near being psychotically paranoid, but who have a capacity for selecting particular aspects of what other people do, so that they always produce a bit of reality to justify their own attitudes. They use the reality selectively in order first to externalize, and then to rationalize. Some people do this so skillfully that one can be convinced for a while that what they say is correct. This isn't quite the same as projection, and I've always thought it really needs to be labled a mechanism in its own right.

Anna Freud: Aren't we really talking about a heightened empathy for what goes on in the other person, as something which is part of the necessary background for the mechanism of projection? The reality is detected and used for projection.

Joseph Sandler: I was thinking of a patient of mine who has a partner in his business. For a while everything went well, but now my patient brings excellent reasons why he should dissolve the partnership with the other man, who has not, as far as I can detect, really changed. What he does is that he selects from observed reality for purposes of rationalization. But perhaps with projection there really does need to be a background of empathy to provide the unconscious framework for the projection.

Anna Freud: While the psychotic person may be very empathic and extremely sensitive about what goes on in other persons, he may equally often be completely out of touch with reality. On the other hand the neurotic picks out bits of reality which substantiate his fantasies, and this does not necessarily have anything to do with projection.

Session three

Joseph Sandler: I should like to begin with some comments on introjection. You have mentioned, Miss Freud, that introjection was seen as an instinctual activity at the time you wrote the book. At that time, too, the term was used relatively synonymously with identification. From what I understand, this did not give rise to great difficulty, because it was clear from the context when introjection was used to refer to the setting up of the parents in the form of the superego at the time of the resolution of the oedipus complex. This was quite different from the use of the term for the infant's oral "taking in" of his surroundings. We have these two quite different meanings of the term introjection, but things are made more complicated because there has been a tendency in recent years to distinguish between introjection on the one hand and identification on the other. We are somewhat clearer now about identification, because it can be linked with changes in the self-representation, which is a basis both for perceiving oneself and for action. Things are not quite as clear in regard to introjection, because the double meaning of the term has persisted. In our work on the superego we limited the term introjection to the internalization of parental authority at the time of superego formation. However, Miss Freud, you listed introjection in your book as a defense mechanism, and my guess is that you had in mind the way the person coped with the pain of detaching from the object, with maintaining the tie to the object by internalizing it through identification. Possibly you also thought of it as producing a sort of inner companion which would then form part of the superego. Would that be a correct understanding?

Anna Freud: Not quite. I know very well that at the time I certainly had not thought through the difference between the two terms, or the differences between the processes covered by them. According to my feeling then, the term introjection was rather forced on us, and I know that I didn't feel comfortable with its use, but when writing about identification I felt an obligation to add introjection, because people were using it more and more as a synonym for identification. So I would ask you not to take what I have written very seriously in this connection, because I wasn't very clear about it at the time. Certainly, as you know, the attitude to the term changed later with the introduction of the whole idea of introjects and internal objects, which seems to be a broader idea than identification.

Joseph Sandler: As identification is not mentioned in your list, I suppose we could proceed as if you had put identification there rather than introjection. Wasn't the idea of identification in its defensive sense in current use at that time?

Anna Freud: There is the enrichment of the ego by iden-tification on the one hand, and the defensive use, as in identification with the aggressor, on the other.

Joseph Sandler: Would the ordinary defensive use of identification have been seen at the time as a way of dealing with object loss?

Anna Freud: No, that wasn't the idea at all. That be-longed to the area of enrichment of the personality. One loses the object, but retains something inside, so that one's own person changes and grows as a result of the object loss. The emphasis was not on the defense against the feelings of loss. There was very much the idea, as you know, that one couldn't get rid of objects except by retaining something of them.

Joseph Sandler: What would be a defensive aspect of identification?

Anna Freud: Identification with the aggressor.

Joseph Sandler: I would like to clarify what aspects you had in mind, Miss Freud, when you included introjection as a defense in your book.

Anna Freud: I suppose I meant a defense against feelings of helplessness, of smallness, of impotence in the child, who then appropriated qualities of the adult in order to bolster up the self. I went on to pinpoint this more in the idea of identification with the aggressor. I got the idea from Aichhorn, who was able to show how there could be an identification with a sort of ideal object, a positive object, a powerful object like a hero.

Joseph Sandler: A number of people have asked if we could consider the precise distinction between the internalization (or the introjection) of the parents at the time of superego formation, and the internalization of conflict. You often speak of conflict with the external world being replaced by internalized conflict. Do you link this specifically with superego formation, or is there a separate process in regard to the internalization of conflict? We tend to speak of internalized conflict occurring after about five years of age, more or less at the same time as superego formation.

Anna Freud: I certainly meant that what has been in the outside world before has become internal, so the external part of the conflict, part of the outside world, has in the meantime become part of the internal world. Because of that the conflict with the external object is not an internal conflict with a part of the self.

Joseph Sandler: The idea has been put forward that one can have an internalized conflict before the formation of the superego proper.

Anna Freud: I am sure that this is so. There again it was Aichhorn who brought the idea up first. The internal authority works better in the presence of the external object who is the originator of the prohibition. On his own the child may come to terms quite easily with the conflicting wishes.

Joseph Sandler: This is Aichhorn's story of the child who wanted to steal the fruit . . .

Anna Freud: . . . then he thinks of his father, which means he strengthens his internal superego by the thought of the external figure from whom it's derived.

Robert Evans: If one side of the conflict is in the external world, does this not still mean that the conflict is internalized, because the child has representations of the conflict inside him?

Anna Freud: He can have a representation of the conflict, or of the external figure involved, the one that prohibits, but this does not yet mean that we have an internalized conflict.

Joseph Sandler: Fenichel has pointed out that before the superego exists there is a sort of watchman set up to assess the reaction of the external world. Of course the assessment is distorted by fantasy, by the talion principle, by projection, and so on, so that the child does not have a direct representation of the external world, but for the child the punishing agency is still located outside. This would be different from the externalization of an internal agency, when the child deals with an internal conflict by putting one of the agencies involved in the conflict outside, because it is easier to feel that one has an external conflict than an internal one. So, in a sense, because the child learns to anticipate the reactions of people in the external world (even though these anticipations may be grossly distorted) he has an internal representation, though the conflict is not an internal one.

Anna Freud: I think there are three stages in internalizing conflict. In the first, the prohibiting agent has to be actually present. In the next stage the prohibiting agent can be removed from the scene but is thought of. In the third phase the prohibiting agent is inside.

Ilse Hellman: We had ample opportunity to observe the development of superego internalization in the Nursery, and it seems clear that the awareness of the external prohibition comes much earlier than four or five. We have many observations of eighteen-month-old children finding a way of telling us "the other child has done it" or "the horse has done it." This shows an awareness that something is prohibited.

Anna Freud: I would say the child feels "somebody doesn't like it."

Ilse Hellman: Yes, but it is there at that early age without the prohibiting person being present.

Joseph Sandler: Surely there comes a point where one cannot argue the child out of his guilt feelings anymore. Then one would feel that a firm introjection has taken place. Before that one can usually reassure the child in some way. But I think that we are left with the problem of when the superego introjection occurs, because although we say that the superego gets formed at a particular point, we know that it gets formed over a period of time. In connection with what we were talking about I am reminded of the nightmares of the two-year-old, in which there are certainly reflections of an internalized prohibition against aggression. The aggression is then externalized onto the attacking figure in the dream. For me this has always been one of the patterns for later superego functioning. It seems that even in the child's sleep the prohibitions are effective internally. It is worth exploring to what extent the child can be reassured or argued out of an internal prohibition at, say, the age of two and a half. I think of the child who has always pushed down his aggression, with the constant encouragement of his parents. Perhaps one can explain what goes on in terms of identification (because we know that identification can take place very early), but somehow this does not seem enough to account for this early internalization.

Ilse Hellman: Lots of people can be argued out of their superego convictions via identification, because of some form of attachment to an object.

Joseph Sandler: Isn't there a big distinction between the sort of change one can see in a very young child when one reassures the child, and the sort of arguing out you refer to, in which you usually provide the person with a formula so that he can ignore his superego prohibitions, or gain alternative sources of narcissistic supply?

Ilse Hellman: I thought of it as something similar. The child who enters a delinquent group will sometimes give up certain things which one would have thought were very much part of his superego standards at that point.

Joseph Sandler: We know that drugs do the same. Alcohol does it, and narcissistic supplies from the group will certainly do it.

Anna Freud: Sometimes children do it on their own. I remember a little boy of five who had an enormous wish to have a motorcycle. I explained to him that he wouldn't get it, as his mother wouldn't like it. He said, "All right, then I'll wish for it for my birthday." I said, "No, I don't think they'll give it to you." "All right, I'll wish for it for Christmas; then one gets everything." I said, "No, I don't think you'll get it, it's not something you'll get." He said,

"All right, I'll give it to myself, because I allow myself."
He allows himself, which means that suddenly he was
at one with his superego, and his superego said, "That's
quite all right for you to have."

W. Ernst Freud: It happens all the time when one is
driving. One only observes the speed limit when one
sees a patrolling policeman.

Anna Freud: But all you need do is to put up a dummy
policeman from time to time. People will know it's a
dummy, but it will remind them of the real police, and
that is what happens with these children. They need the
reminder of the prohibiting agent.

Joseph Sandler: One has to distinguish between superego prohibitions and the ego's assessment of reality. It
may not be in one's superego to observe the speed limit,
but the reality may make one do so.

Anna Freud: It *should* be in one's superego. It is really
a question of whether the person is law-abiding. With
the law-abiding person it is in the superego, with others
not.

Joseph Sandler: That still leaves the problem of how
much is ego and how much is superego. I remember
that, many years ago, a friend of mine was given a personality inventory, and one of the questions was whether
he would go into a cinema without a ticket if no one was
watching. He answered that he wouldn't go in. When
he was told that this had given him a point on a "lie"

scale, he was extremely indignant, because he was certainly not lying.

Anna Freud: Then he must be an obsessional.

Joseph Sandler: But, Miss Freud, where do you draw the line?

Anna Freud: Well, I suppose the law-abiding person is law-abiding because he has an obsessional character!

Joseph Sandler: Or he may have a superego which says, "Obey laws, whatever they are."

Anna Freud: Yes.

Maria Berger: I think that all of this has to do with the features of the inner policeman. Is he a kind policeman, or is he a policeman who is always against one, and whom one has to cheat?

Hansi Kennedy: There has to be some flexibility either within the law or within the inner policeman.

Anna Freud: I remember a little schoolboy of six or seven I had in analysis in Vienna. He talked about running on the grass, in the park, something which was one of the most forbidden things. In Austria there were always guards in the parks to see that the children didn't do it. The little boy raised the question in his analysis of why people don't run on the grass, and I said that perhaps they liked the grass to stay nice. He said, "No, that's what they *say*—it's really because the guard is near." This meant for him then that it was only the policeman, the prohibition, which counted, and the other reason was just hypocrisy.

There is another question, one that refers quite specifically to adolescence. I refer to the question of whether the superego in the developing person really becomes wholly independent of the external object, even after the superego has been internalized and the authority of the parent added to it. We have examples from the treatment of children who have gone wrong in their development because, at the age of eight or nine, confidence in the parents has been shattered because the marriage has broken up. This in turn acts on the internalized superego. We have the example in adolescence where, with the loosening of the tie to the parents, the superego gets very shaken. And does that really coincide with our expectations of full internalization? Or does it show us that a link with the original objects and the tie to them always remains?

Joseph Sandler: I think that we ought to try to bring the discussion back a little to the question of the defensive aspects of introjection or identification. We should take into account the point Miss Freud has made about the superego continuing its development, the internalization of aspects of teachers and educators and so on. While I don't think we should go into the specific problems of adolescence here, it is perhaps legitimate to ask whether introjection as a defense might not occur in someone who has a particularly powerful superego and strong internal conflict, and who may then internalize an alternative introject in a superego fashion. This would give an auxiliary superego, a sort of secondary superego to which the person can relate. Perhaps in such a case we could consider later superego-type introjections as a defense.

Ilse Hellman: Do you mean identifications with a new object in adolescence? For example, identification with the leader of a group who is then preferred to the father, identification coupled with the rejection of much or all the father stands for and the adoption of a totally new set of values?

Joseph Sandler: I suppose a lot depends on the use of the term introjection and the meaning one gives it. Certainly we know that identifications can occur throughout life, but I was thinking not so much of the adolescent who identifies with another figure, but rather one who internalizes a figure with whom he can have a sort of internal conversation. As a consequence he can then lessen the influence of the original superego and thereby lessen the pain of his superego conflict. I suppose that the best example of what I am thinking of is the way in which we continue our conversations with our analyst after the analysis. We have, as it were, the ghost of the analyst who says to us, "Well, that is an infantile wish and it is permitted to have it in fantasy as long as you don't act on it." Is such an internalization of the analyst on a par with superego introjection?

Maria Berger: There are certain phenomena which are not adequately covered by the concept of identification.

I think, for instance, of a child who is highly critical toward himself on the basis of having taken in the highly critical attitude of the parent.

Joseph Sandler: I would say that this is identification.

Robert Evans: But suppose he feels that there is something *in him* criticizing him.

Joseph Sandler: That would be introjection.

Anna Freud: A bad internal object.

Joseph Sandler: I suggest that we move on to the next mechanism described, which is "turning against the self." I presume, Miss Freud, you meant turning aggression against the self, because if it were libido you would have spoken of the turning of object libido into secondary narcissism. We have in the past discussed the concept of turning aggression against the self at some length, and found that there were many different varieties. I wonder if you would tell us what you had in mind.

Anna Freud: Well, I really took it from the then current psychoanalytic theory. The impulse, especially, of course, the aggressive impulse, first directed against the outside world, can be deflected from the outside world toward the self.

Joseph Sandler: Do you mean like the child who wants to push the therapist down the stairs but falls down the stairs himself ? This would then be an aggressive impulse of the moment, turned away from the object back against the self.

Anna Freud: Yes. Some people who commit suicide do that to the highest degree. That's the way they try to become good. "I don't murder you, I commit suicide." That's the defense I wrote about.

Joseph Sandler: I assume that you are also using the term here in a relatively broad sense, to include superego aggression turned against the self. But shall we go on to the mechanism of reversal? Nowadays so many different sorts of reversal are described.

Anna Freud: I meant reversal of roles. We had a very good example at the Clinic meeting yesterday of a child of a partially sighted mother who was used by the mother as her eyes to guide her. This, of course, upset the whole mother-child relationship because the child had to mother the mother in certain respects, and in this child it led to a general tendency to reverse roles. For example, in the diagnostic interview she began to question the diagnostician, as she evidently expected to be questioned. She asked, "What's your name?", "Where do you live?", and so on. There can be reversal of roles in other contexts, between victim and attacker, between lover and loved. One always has to imagine a couple in a certain relationship where the individual in question assumes the role of the other and assigns his own role to the partner. That's what I meant by reversal here.

Joseph Sandler: Does one not see it in nurses who have

had deprived childhoods and deal with their wish to be nursed and mothered by becoming nurses, by becoming a good parent to the patient and caring for the patient?

Anna Freud: I was thinking more of the adults who treat their children exactly as they have been treated, only now they are the parents and can take the parents' role toward the child.

Joseph Sandler: We try to distinguish in the Clinic between reversal of roles, identification with the aggressor, and turning passive into active.

Maria Berger: I was taught the meaning of reversal of roles by my very first patient. He was a highly intelligent child with a learning problem, terrified of the school situation, as he was probably also afraid of the treatment situation. He defended against his fear by becoming the teacher or a quizmaster in the sessions, but it wasn't enough for him just to sit opposite me and teach or quiz me. On the table he had to put the ottoman, on the ottoman he put the little chair. He would then sit high up and say he was the teacher and I the pupil.

Anna Freud: This illustrates something else besides. If the defense of reversal isn't sufficient, it has to be repeated, exaggerated and overdone. This shows it up for the defense it is.

Joseph Sandler: What this child does is also to get a tremendous boost to his self-esteem, as well as doing away with his anxiety. I think a very fine distinction will have to be drawn between this and identification with the aggressor, which, although superficially similar, is in fact a different mechanism.

Anna Freud: A more circumscribed one. You know, there is usually more than one defense involved. For example, let us take the child who has been to the dentist and who comes to the analytic hour and now plays dentist. One can say that he identifies with the aggressor because he is now the dentist. But you can also say that it is a reversal of roles. It can also be a turning of passive into active.

Hansi Kennedy: Although we make these distinctions, they're obviously not satisfactory.

Maria Berger: Well, one distinction at least makes sense. In turning passive into active we can say that there is an active repetition of what had been passively experienced.

Hansi Kennedy: This covers the child playing at being the dentist, but only in a specific sense does it cover the reversal of roles, when the child is the dentist and makes the therapist into the patient. But I think all of this is hairsplitting.

Joseph Sandler: I remember a case being treated by a child psychiatrist in a hospital in the United States. The child had been a patient in the pediatric department many times and had received many injections and other physical treatments. He was now being seen for psychotherapy. The child began to play with a toy pistol which shot a dart with a suction pad at its end. He began to shoot closer and closer to the therapist, and it was very clear that the therapist (who was wearing a white coat) was seen as the doctor who might give further "shots" to the child. The child was so terrified of the shots he thought he was going to get that he identified with the aggressor, and shot at the therapist. It seemed to me a very clear example of identification with the aggressor. But I would also say that the child had every right to expect to get shots, because he had got them whenever he had come to the hospital before. This is very different from reversal of roles.

Anna Freud: Yes. Of course, in reversal of roles you can also reverse from active to passive, as in patients who become addicted to masochistic experiences, taking the role of the victim, as a way of dealing with their own aggression. For one reason or another the reversal of roles is for them the most important or the most convenient mechanism.

Session four

Joseph Sandler: We have not proceeded very far into Chapter 4, but we come now to sublimation. You say, Miss Freud, that we have to add a tenth mechanism of defense, one "which pertains rather to the study of the normal than to that of neurosis" (47,44). I would like to begin with the question of whether this was the first time sublimation was regarded as a mechanism of defense, because you say in the text that we now have to add it to the list. We must all be aware that this mechanism is rather like identification, in that it is an aspect of normal ego functioning and important for normal development, but may also be a defense. I suspect that there is still a lot of controversy over whether sublimation is a defense or not. You speak of the displacement of instinctual aims, but there is also the question of the change of aims to a so-called higher level associated with sublimation. This has, of course, led to a lot of difficulty about defining what we mean by higher. Do we see sublimation in terms of what society regards as higher?

Anna Freud: Before responding I want to say one thing about our last discussion. Those present seemed to assume that the formulations about the mechanisms were original contributions made by me, whereas what I did in Chapter 4 was really to sum up the opinions current at the time. You know, I simply took the position as it was then—I needed to prepare the reader for the later chapters—and I summarized the position at this point.

Of course one would say today that it is not only sublimation that belongs to the sphere of the normal, rather than to the neurotic or abnormal. We know very well that regression is normal, that repression is an absolutely essential mechanism in normal development, that reaction formation is normal in character formation. Isolation, undoing, introjection—all also appear in normal development. It is very much a quantitative question whether the outcome is normal or leads to pathology. But perhaps sublimation has a separate and special position in that it is ordinarily always normal, or rather leads to what is normal. If it appears as something pathological, then it has a compulsive quality. If it is used to keep down anxiety, it tends to be overdone, and we would not call it ordinary sublimation. The reason we call it a defense mechanism at all is because if we look at it from the point of view of the drive derivatives it is an interference with a direct gratification which would otherwise arouse anxiety. A sublimation is usually very pleasurable, but can the pleasure derived from sublimation really compete with the pleasure from direct instinctual gratification? I suppose not, and for that reason we need to see it as a defense mechanism.

Joseph Sandler: If I understand you correctly, Miss Freud, as a defense it must have something to do with the resolution of conflict.

Anna Freud: Yes.

Joseph Sandler: And the displacement to so-called higher aims would be a way of resolving the conflict. For example, if someone is guilty about some crude and primitive sexual wish, or an aggressive one, your point would be that in resolving the conflict a certain amount of pleasurable gain is lost. A price is paid for sublimation in terms of giving up some of the direct pleasurable gratification of the instinctual wish. But some of us have a problem in regarding sublimation as a defense because it is so difficult to distinguish the defensive aspects from normal ego development. I imagine that at the time of your writing this chapter the whole notion of adaptation was not in people's minds as much as in the period after the Second World War.

Anna Freud: No, it wasn't. But let us take a very simple example, which was used a great deal at that time. Take the child who smears his feces. If instead of this the child plays with sand and water, or with clay, and begins to build things, then you can compare the pleasures which the little child gets from the two activities. What is lost in sublimation is surely some of the direct sensual pleasure in the primitive activity, the wish to enjoy the dirty object, the feeling on the skin, on the hands, the smell of the feces, and so on. On the other hand, the child then has to cope with the disapproval, the external disapproval followed by internal disapproval. So he does a deal. He gives up some of the pleasure, thereby avoiding some of the disapproval. He has a lesser pleasure, but what he does is much more approved of, so in the end he is better off. But the drive is not better off. The drive has been cheated of some of its gratification. I think it depends very much from what side you look at it.

Joseph Sandler: Would you not say that the instinctual wish gets a symbolic gratification?

Anna Freud: A displaced gratification, yes.

Joseph Sandler: There would also be some sensual gratification if we think of the child modeling clay in place of playing with feces. That would be nearer to the original activity. But if one thinks of the example of, say, stamp collecting, which has been regarded as a sublimation of anal retentiveness, or of hoarding, this is far more removed from physical pleasures.

Ilse Hellman: I wonder whether the idea of a symbolic gratification is really applicable. From the point of view of aggression, we don't approve of people hitting each other violently, but boxing is very violent, and it is allowed and approved of. Now the aggressive gratification is not very different, except that it has to keep to certain rules so that it is socially acceptable. The closeness to the original gratification varies so very much, and an important question is how far removed the activity can be and still be gratifying.

Joseph Sandler: But here comes another question. We can approach sublimation in terms of a transformation of the instinctual energy and a desexualization. But we can also suggest that behind every sublimation there is, at some level, an unconscious fantasy gratification of the instinctual wish. This aspect has not been brought into most writings on the subject, certainly not in the writings of the ego psychologists, where sublimation has been linked so much with the neutralization of instinctual energy. I would guess that the fantasy which might be unconsciously gratified would be much closer to the original activity than the overt sublimation appears to be.

Anna Freud: You are quite right, because Hartmann was very intent on pursuing his idea of secondary autonomy. He believed that the sublimated activity, once removed from the drive, becomes the property of (and part of) the ego, that it gets new roots there and gradually gives up its original roots in the id.

Ilse Hellman: We can study sublimation from the side of what can break through. In the famous chess tournament between Fischer and Spassky, we could see the way Fischer's aggressive behavior broke through in his tantrums. His angry reactions came through and really interfered with the game. One didn't get the feeling that he had a well-settled sublimation, but rather that his chess-playing was very close to the idea of aggressively triumphing over his opponent.

Anna Freud: You know, so much remains in the terminology of games: beating an opponent, capturing pieces, and so on.

Clifford Yorke: I am reminded of Reuben Fine's study of chess players. It is very interesting, because the frequency of breakdown among them is enormous. Ernest Jones once wrote a paper on the problem of Paul Morphy, who came over in 1858 and beat Anderssen, the reigning world champion at the time. Within six months of his return to the U.S.A. as a national hero, Morphy completely gave up chess as an activity, and ended with a paranoid breakdown. Fine has traced the careers of a number of other world champions, and how they performed under stress. Alekhine became an alcoholic and a drug addict, for instance. Chess does seem to be one of those sublimations where the underlying fantasy, which includes murdering the father and a whole lot of other oedipal wishes, does enter symbolically, and apparently can break through relatively easily.

Joseph Sandler: We have to dissect out several things

here. We have learned from Hartmann that an ego activity which may not be derived from a particular set of instinctual impulses may be later sexualized or aggressivized so that it has a completely new meaning and function. This then poses the problem of distinguishing between such a reinstinctualization on the one hand, and on the other the breakdown of a sublimation so that its original instinctual roots and sources show themselves again. In the first instance we have a change of function, and in the second a regressive breaking-down. If we think of Bobby Fischer and his antics during the world championship chess match, we could say that whatever the sources of his chess-playing skills were, whether they were originally aggressive or sexual, narcissistic or based on identification, or had some other origin, we need not assume that these chess-playing abilities had broken down and that the original impulse had broken through. I think the last is very unlikely. In a world champion these skills would have become more or less completely autonomous instruments, which can *then* be used for aggressive purposes. There would have been a change of function.

Ilse Hellman: I know of surgeons and dentists whose sublimations have broken down, and they have not been able to work because the original sadism which had been sublimated could not be sublimated any longer.

Anna Freud: We also have to distinguish here between the breakdown of reaction formations and the breakdown of sublimations. The two are very easily confused.

Joseph Sandler: If we think of a musician, who had developed his musical skills as a sublimation, becoming inhibited in his public playing because of a conflict over exhibitionism or sibling rivalry, the breakdown is not necessarily connected with the original impulses sublimated in his musical skills. To assume automatically that the original impulses broke through or were reinstinctualized would be to risk Hartmann's "genetic fallacy," which is of the utmost clinical importance. What entered developmentally (genetically) into the formation of a sublimation is not necessarily what participates in later conflict involving that sublimation.

Robert Evans: Is the parasitologist who smears feces on his slide to search for parasites always sublimating his anal interest? Is it not what the activity means to him which is important?

Anna Freud: It would also depend on what the motivation was for his choosing that particular profession. It may be that he has simply chosen a profession where he need not be inhibited in certain activities. But there is still the third question, left over from the beginning of our discussion, about the displacement of the aim in the activity of sublimation. You will remember the story my father liked so much of the little girl in a village who walks along followed by a flock of geese. A benevolent traveler comes along and begins to talk to the little girl, and finds out what an intelligent child she is. He feels that it is a terrible pity that her life is wasted in such simple activities, so he pays for her education so that she becomes a teacher. This story was told in a cartoon strip in a newspaper, and the last picture showed the girl, now grown up, walking in exactly the same way as she did when she was a child, followed by a long line of children just as she had been followed by the geese. That is sublimation.

Joseph Sandler: By your definition she would be getting less pleasure from the children than from the geese!

Anna Freud: It's harder work, you know.

Joseph Sandler: Can we touch on the question of what we mean by "higher" aims in sublimation?

Anna Freud: Well, that is very easily answered. One can answer it in two ways. The aims would be more approved of by the superego, or more approved of by the outside world. This is what we mean by higher.

Joseph Sandler: Would you say more removed from direct instinctual gratification?

Anna Freud: But the closeness to the direct instinctual aims would be the reason for the disapproval.

Joseph Sandler: Freud took the term sublimation from chemistry, so we should regard it as meaning a purifying and refining of something cruder. The baser elements, namely the sexual and aggressive elements, are excluded.

Anna Freud: Or are refined. When Aichhorn dealt with

delinquent boys, he maintained that it was extremely important to find a sublimated activity in which to train them that was not too far removed from their instinctual aims. They should not have to take a big step in refining the instinctual aims, but rather a small one which was perhaps possible for them to take. For instance, a very violent boy would be placed in a butcher's shop; a boy who was near the homosexual level might be an excellent tailor and so on. Aichhorn was very successful with this policy. In this we can really see the displacement.

Joseph Sandler: Essentially, then, sublimation means disguising or transforming the activity in such a way that it is socially acceptable or acceptable to the superego, and as a result there is in the activity an absence of direct instinctual gratification. But I imagine that there is always a fantasy gratification at some unconscious level which is much more direct. We also have to distinguish between the development of a skill and the use of that skill for sublimation. Many people have developed skills as part of their ego development, perhaps because of identification, perhaps because they can use a natural talent for adaptive purposes, or for some other reason, but having developed the skill they can readily put it aside. They don't treat it in the same way as the sublimator treats his sublimatory activity and the objects of that activity. I have always held the view that for something to be regarded as sublimation it should be treated as an extension of the self or of the object. For something to be a sublimation people should care for the activity or its products, should be able to pursue and enjoy the activity even when the drives are not aroused. There is some degree of attachment, of affection and concern for the activity, something which parallels the relationship to an object. This seems to me a necessary factor added to the skills involved. From this point of view, certain activities which don't involve great skill might be classed as sublimation.

Anna Freud: What you have in mind is a kind of object constancy toward the activity which then becomes independent of the immediate pleasure gained.

Joseph Sandler: Yes, exactly. In contrast, one could have a sort of need-satisfying relationship to activities. Then the activity becomes something which is undertaken only from time to time, and the person doesn't treat it as if it is something important in his life. This is in contrast to the constant relation to a sublimation, which parallels object constancy as you have described it.

Anna Freud: This is very much along the lines of what Hartmann meant by secondary autonomy, although I was always unhappy when Hartmann took the stand that what we really had to deal with was a change in the energy, from sexual or aggressive energy to neutralized energy. My feeling is that thereby one loses the idea of the compromise character of the sublimation, and the whole question gets pulled over to problems of energy alone, to questions of the quality of the energy. I used to discuss this with Hartmann and Kris.

Joseph Sandler: I would agree very much that the concept of neutralization falls down because it is essentially a descriptive concept which has been given the status of an explanation. This gives the illusion that it is useful. One starts with the description that there is no sexuality or aggression shown in the sublimated activity, and moves to the point that the process of change is one of desexualization and deaggressivization, in other words, of neutralization. This is like saying that someone does not work and therefore is lazy, and going on to say that he does not work *because* he is lazy.

Anna Freud: In particular, the dynamic side gets lost because in reality a sublimation is a bargain. There is the wish to keep as much as possible of the original pleasure and to avoid as much as possible feelings of prohibition, disapproval, or guilt. The sublimation strikes a bargain, but it is a very tricky business. Sometimes something emerges which is near to the original aim, sometimes it is much further removed.

Joseph Sandler: Miss Freud, some people have said that sublimations are essentially the same as reaction formations. Certainly we disagree with this, but there does seem to be an area of overlap. I remember a man who used to advertise in a weekly newspaper that if you wrote to him he would send details of a hundred ways to kill rabbits painlessly. This advertisement appeared week after week. Now I don't think we need to look very far to see the underlying wish and preoccupation of the advertiser. What we see is a reaction formation, and I am sure that this man felt very strongly that rabbits have to be protected from pain. Can we call his activities and his interest in the painless killing of rabbits a sublimation? He was doing something which is socially on a "higher" level, doing "good" one might say, and obviously his work was very highly invested and gratifying to him. Where do we draw the line between the reaction formation and the sublimation?

Anna Freud: You know, sublimation is much more an activity, while a reaction formation is part of the character and personality.

Marjorie Sprince: I was thinking somewhat along the same lines, of the difference in the activity, say, of a Boy Scout and a member of the Nazi Youth. In both you have an adaptation to the social norm, and the attempt to disguise the activity by removing it from its closeness to the original drive. Yet there is a big difference in the activity.

Joseph Sandler: I think that it would be quite wrong to say that the well-intentioned member of the Nazi Youth was not sublimating, if we say that the Boy Scout sublimates. We should not carry our prejudices that far.

Anna Freud: Both are heroes in their own eyes, but they each adapt to a different philosophy of life.

Maria Berger: Can we say that belonging to a group in this way is necessarily a sublimation?

Joseph Sandler: I don't think it is a question of the group, but rather of the activities: perhaps diverting aggression into learning to track animals, into woodsmanship, and whatever other things Boy Scouts do. This, by the way, brings up by association another question, Miss Freud. Why is it that we often see excellent sublimations in people who have a full sexual life, whether normal or perverse? There doesn't seem to be an economic balance between the amount of sexual gratification and the amount of sublimation.

Anna Freud: The answer once given to this point was that we have to distinguish between pregenital and genital activities, and have to restrict the idea of sublimation and reaction formation to the pregenital drive derivatives.

Joseph Sandler: But this is why I mentioned perversions, because they have the pregenital component, and yet at the same time one sees sublimations. One has only to think of highly successful people in the theater and in the arts generally.

Anna Freud: We probably see two quite different efforts to deal with the same drive material.

Joseph Sandler: I think that we talk about sublimation within a framework which derives from a period when the consideration of the regulation of narcissism and self-esteem was not so intensely studied. So many activities, including artistic activities, have as much to do with self-esteem as they have to do with the drives, although developmentally one might be able to argue that they are drive derivatives. In the here and now they may not have all that much to do with the drives. I think that we make a mistake if we think that there has to be a quantitative relationship between the amount of sublimation and the amount of sexuality. We should remember, I think, that the idea of sublimation was put forward, as were so many other concepts, in the attempt to understand relatively gross phenomena, such as the case of someone who is unable to gratify himself or herself sexually, or feels guilty or inhibited about the gratification, and finds an alternative form of expression which is more "refined" from a social point of view. When we begin to look microscopically at the concept, then, as with many other concepts, our theory may break down.

Anna Freud: You know, that applies to all the defense mechanisms. If you look at them microscopically, they all merge into each other. You will find repression anywhere you look. You will find bits of reaction formation or identification. You will find five or six defenses compressed into one attitude. The point is that one should not look at them microscopically, but macroscopically, as big and separate mechanisms, structures, events, whatever you want to call them. Then they will stand out from each other, and the problems of separating them theoretically become negligible. You have to take off your glasses to look at them, not put them on.

Joseph Sandler: Ideally one should have bifocals! Then one could switch from one to the other.

Anna Freud: Yes.

Hansi Kennedy: I think it ought to be said that we should

be very careful about judging what the processes are behind any one activity, because the activity can have different meanings. Certainly it is impossible to say from the activity itself whether it is sublimation or a reaction formation.

Joseph Sandler: It might be worth going back to Miss Freud's point, which was an impressive one, that in speaking of a sublimation we refer to the activity, and when we speak of a reaction formation we refer to an attitude of mind. The two may, it follows, go together, as in someone very involved with the Society for the Prevention of Cruelty to Animals, or who campaigns against cruel ways of killing rabbits. The sadism of the people who rage against fox hunting comes through, of course, in their physical attacks on fox hunters, which are sometimes extremely vicious. If we consider nursing, we can think of reversal of roles, but at the same time the activity might be a sublimation.

Anna Freud: Yes. I think of a patient who is a vegetarian because she cannot stand the idea of killing or eating animals, of being cruel to animals in any way. At one time she even contemplated not eating vegetables because she felt so sorry for the plants. Now that goes, of course, rather far as a reaction formation against cruelty. On the other hand, she is fascinated by the reports of concentration camps and prisons. She has asked herself whether that is a morbid interest, which means to her that she asks whether the cruelty she pushes down in one part of her life shows itself in another part. But then, when she thinks further, she feels so identified with the victims that she is sure that it could not be her own cruelty. When she read the stories about the concentration camps she compared herself constantly with the victims, and felt a certain relief at the thought that they were worse off than she is. The whole thing is quite complicated, and it only seems simple if we look at one side of it at a time.

Irmi Elkan: I should like to ask whether we still accept that sublimation is concerned with pregenital impulses only?

Joseph Sandler: I am sure that Miss Freud has been involved in many arguments about this, because it is a topic which has come up over and over again, and which has not really been settled. Do you want to comment, Miss Freud?

Anna Freud: I would rather let you answer the question!

Joseph Sandler: I don't know the answer either. I do believe that phallic impulses can be sublimated, and that much confusion has arisen because phallic and genital are often confused. By definition something cannot be genital unless it expresses itself in a mature sexual relationship, which involves not only direct instinctual wishes but important object relationship aspects as well. It seems to me that this is often forgotten. Recently we have been trying to draw attention to the existence of a phallic preoedipal phase, a phallic-narcissistic phase distinct from the oedipal phase proper. Phallic impulses have so often been equated with genital sexuality. I am sure that phallic wishes can be sublimated.

Anna Freud: There is another point, an open question. We can ask how early in life sublimations are formed, and whether it is possible to develop sublimations in adult life when genital sexuality exists. Is it at all possible then to make new sublimations? Or do all sublimations date back to a much earlier time in childhood, to pregenital times?

Joseph Sandler: We have to distinguish here very strongly between skills and sublimations. Skills can start very early, but it must be relatively late—four, five or six years of age, I would say—before the child can use the skill for purposes of sublimation. Even then perhaps one has to ask whether or not the gratification is a narcissistic one rather than a more direct instinctual one. You have linked sublimations, Miss Freud, with latency, which is the time that many skills develop. But the pre-latency boy of four or five who plays the piano to admiring relatives and friends may be enjoying enormous pleasure in mastery, in control, in exhibitionism, and so on.

Anna Freud: We used to say to child analysts that they should be careful not to disturb budding sublimations in the child, because if you begin to interpret them, to show up their sexual or aggressive sources, you may nip the whole thing in the bud. We used to think that in the therapeutic process elements the child could not deal with otherwise should be given a push toward sublimation. We felt that we had to be careful of these elements, that something might be going on which did not belong to what one has to analyze. But after a while we saw something else during child analysis, that there are many beginnings of sublimation which come to nothing, or which are transitory. Now we would say that it is far too optimistic to think that a child of, say, five years or so, who develops a special attachment to an activity, will keep that attachment in his later life. On the other hand, I remember analyzing a little boy about forty years ago who was then six years old. He was a clever little boy, with divorced parents, and at times his mother would come to visit him. Whenever she left him again he fell into a sort of depression, and in that state he produced poetry. Well, he dictated the poetry in his analytic sessions. It was very nice poetry, and this boy, after a very stormy career, became a professor of literature. I heard from him recently that he was very interested in seeing his early poems, and as I had treasured them, I had them copied and sent to him. They are quite impressive, and there is no doubt that his present profession and his poetic ability as a child have a very definite link. But at the time we analyzed his poetic tendency, partly in relation to his mother and his feelings of extreme longing and sadness, and partly in relation to his very intense fear of being hurt, which caused him to turn all his attention away from bodily accomplishments to intellectual ones.

Joseph Sandler: This seems to be a very nice example of change of function. The skill develops, and is then used for purposes of sublimation, although it was not necessarily a sublimation at the time it started.

Anna Freud: Well, if he had been a less clever little boy, or less gifted, I suppose he would just have been a little coward because of his fear of physical hurt, and not a poet.

Joseph Sandler: Hampstead Clinic technique has been criticized as being aimed at facilitating the development of sublimation, at encouraging sublimation, encouraging the idea that one does not interfere with sublimation. Now while I think there is a misconception here, it is worth clarifying.

Anna Freud: If nothing worse is ever said about us . . .

Session five

Joseph Sandler: I should like to take up the question of sublimation in regard to a patient who is a woman who had a very Prussian upbringing, and had a very strict Prussian superego. She has a number of stepchildren and suffers from great conflicts about them. She says she would like them to be obedient, but feels that if she were to be strict she would be attacked by the family of her husband's late wife. She has turned particularly against one of the children, a dropout from college, clearly because she cannot bear to see in him the self-indulgence she dislikes so much in herself. Now this lady has a dog that she enters in obedience trials, and the dog wins them all. She has only to lift her little finger, and the dog obeys. She is extremely good at training the dog, and clearly gets relief from some internal conflict by creating a situation in which the dog is perfectly obedient. Would one call this a sublimation or not? Although it could be said that the activity was a drive derivative, we could also say that her strict and punitive superego has attained a certain autonomy, so that the gratification she gets through training her dog and winning the competitions might well be something other than gratification of her aggression. This opens up the question of whether activities which are not indirect instinctual gratifications might be regarded as sublimations. I wonder how you feel about this, Miss Freud.

Anna Freud: It's not sublimation, but rather a displacement and an externalization. What I mean is that her superego demands obedience from her ego, an obedience she demands from the children outside, and this is then displaced onto the dog, where the immediate obedience gives her great pleasure.

Joseph Sandler: That means that we would have to define sublimation rather strictly in terms of finding a new derivative of an instinctual demand, a derivative which is quite removed from the original aims.

Anna Freud: And one more in line with the demands of ego, superego and external reality, one which is more ego syntonic and adaptive to the external world.

Maria Berger: Of course, if the patient was in fact taming her sadistic impulses, then she might really be showing a sublimation.

Joseph Sandler: We need to be very careful here. From

a developmental point of view practically everything can be reduced to instinctual impulses, and we could certainly say that this woman's superego is a sadistic one. However, what entered into its formation need not be operative now. It would not be correct, I believe, to say that every time the superego acted strictly, it was expressing, in indirect form, a sadistic impulse. We have to draw a distinction between what is developmentally true, on the one hand, and what is functionally true in the present, on the other.

Anna Freud: You know, reaction formations get mixed up with what you have described. If we look too closely we may find that several defense mechanisms are contributing to the effect. The source of the behavior might be an underlying sadism, but it also represents other things.

Joseph Sandler: There are many activities, such as teaching and nursing, where one speaks readily of sublimation, but if we look at the activity itself, we may find that it is not a sublimation in the strict sense of the definition.

Anna Freud: With some of these activities, you will find that they don't qualify as sublimations if you take them as a whole, and that only certain aspects can be called sublimation. I was thinking of a remark made to me by a little boy patient, six or seven years old. He was very clever, and in his analytic hour discussed his nursery school teacher. We talked about various methods of nursery school teaching. When we spoke of the Montessori method, in which the children are given a great deal of freedom, he told me that his woman teacher really enjoys commanding the children. He had picked up that what was sublimated in her teaching was the wish to dominate.

Hansi Kennedy: Perhaps he did that because it was not so well sublimated.

Anna Freud: Perhaps, but I think he had a good eye for it. On the other hand, there are many things which the teacher has to do which have nothing to do with controlling or domineering. One could say the same about nursing, of course.

Lore Schacht: Freud wrote that the pleasure the person gets from a sublimation is something much more stable, without the ups and downs, with more continuity in it than the pleasure from instinctual satisfaction. I could imagine that what the little boy picked up as the controlling or domineering aspect of the teacher was the pleasure over and above what one might expect to be appropriate for a sublimation.

Joseph Sandler: It is worth discussing the idea that the so-called aim-inhibited drives are more constant in their pressure than the original instinctual drives. Presumably aim-inhibition (in the sense in which Freud used the term) is an integral part of sublimation. We can well ask, I think, why we can have a more constant pleasure in a sublimation than the sort of pleasure which we associate with the id.

Anna Freud: Yes. We used to discuss this point a lot.

It also arose in regard to masturbation fantasies in which direct sexual discharge was experienced, as compared with derivative fantasies in which the sexual discharge did not end the fantasy. They were much more drawn out and were a more or less constant feature of the person's life, due to the aim-inhibition which existed in the fantasy derivatives.

Joseph Sandler: Surely the striving for certain forms of gratification may get an impetus, a motivation, which does not entirely come from the drives, but might arise as well from the ego's need, for example, to deal with anxiety by chasing after pleasure. And can we not also say that certain activities which yield pleasure, initially by virtue of their relation to the id, go on to acquire a more constant pleasure-giving quality, so that they become enjoyable in themselves? I am thinking of hobbies and other pleasurable interests which people maintain, in which it is almost as if the activities acquire something of the stimulus properties of the drive itself.

Anna Freud: The activity is taken over by the ego. It gets a secondary autonomy. But, you know, it would be good here to go back to the basic question of what happens if a drive is denied its aim, is denied discharge. Two things can then happen, which are quite opposite to each other. One is what we discuss now as sublimation, namely that the ego gets hold of the drive, modifies it, moderates it, makes it different and acceptable, reduces some of the pressure, and finally offers the impulse a moderate, displaced, and reduced satisfaction. That's what we call sublimation. Then it becomes incorporated into the ego, becomes ego syntonic and part of the personality. But, you know, an opposite thing can happen, which has always impressed me very much. An aggressive or sadomasochistic, sexualized aggressive fantasy—a masturbation fantasy in childhood—may be denied its outlet in bodily activity, and then exactly the opposite of a sublimation can happen. The fantasy can stay as it is, can swamp the personality, creating a sort of psychopathic personality.

Joseph Sandler: Is that the so-called impulse-ridden character that Fenichel spoke of ?

Anna Freud: Impulse-ridden, but ridden by one impulse only. An impulse-ridden character is a person who cannot control any of his impulses, whereas these people usually repeat only one and the same impulse and fantasy endlessly. This is, for me, the formula for the psychopath. But I know it is not a generally accepted idea.

Joseph Sandler: Of course there are problems here because of the different uses of the term "psychopathic." Not all impulsive behavior, nor all antisocial behavior, can be regarded as the breakthrough of a drive. Such activity might, for example, represent a need for punishment or a way of dealing with anxiety. We seem to be speaking here only of those people (rather like the cases of traumatic neurosis) who appear helpless in the face of the need to repeat, over and over, a pattern which was a drive-gratifying pattern in childhood. Could that be the point, Miss Freud?

Anna Freud: Yes, it's that. But my feeling is that if one looked very closely at any individual psychopath one would find a pattern of this kind. What strikes me so strongly about cases of this kind is the monotony of the repetition, which is the same monotony we find in masturbation fantasies, which are always the same for any one individual.

Joseph Sandler: Perhaps we should add that the inhibiting of an instinctual wish or fantasy is an active process on the part of the ego. Sometimes the ego may falter in its process of inhibiting or displacing, and the original impulse, or a derivative close to the original impulse, may break through. Alternatively, the impulse may come through in another derivative, in a joke, for example, or in a dream.

W. Ernst Freud: I have always found the concept of "sublimation potential," as we use it at the Clinic, very useful. I think it tells us something about the whole defensive organization.

Anna Freud: It was Kurt Eissler who first suggested that we shouldn't only speak about the child's sublimations, but also of his capacity, his *potential*, for sublimation. This can be picked up rather early, as we have seen from looking at babies, by assessing the willingness of the individual to accept substitutes. A young patient of mine said the other day that she had rather high demands, and if she couldn't have the food she wanted, she would much rather starve herself. If she couldn't have the boyfriend she wanted, she'd rather have no boyfriend at all.

This isn't quite true, of course, but she described something important, namely an unwillingness to accept substitutes. If this happens very early in life, it is an ominous sign in regard to the development of later sublimations. It is interesting to see how some children can gain satisfaction from a substitute offered to them and others can't. They go on screaming until they have their original wish fulfilled. What I think of as sublimation potential is something built up very gradually. It is certainly influenced a great deal by the environment, but I think that there is something basic and fundamental in it as well. Of course, if a baby is too content with the substitute which is offered, or with the person who acts as a replacement, that is also a bad sign.

Joseph Sandler: You describe, Miss Freud, a woman who split her ambivalence, so that her mother was kept as a good object and someone else became the object of her hate or anger (48,45). I wonder whether you meant to include the splitting of ambivalence among the defense mechanisms proper, since you refer to it as a "method of defense" (49,46). Nowadays, of course, we distinguish between defense mechanisms on the one hand, and other defensive methods, measures, or maneuvers on the other. I wonder whether this distinction was beginning to crystallize in your mind at that time, because although you call the splitting of ambivalence a method of defense you don't actually call it a *mechanism* of defense. I don't know if you were conscious of making any such distinction at the time of writing. In the original German you spoke of the *Abwehrtechnik* in this context, so "technique of defense" might be a better translation.

Anna Freud: I didn't count it as a mechanism.

Irmi Elkan: I should like to go back for a moment to Miss Freud's point about the acceptance of substitutes as an indicator of sublimation potential. Ought one not to make a distinction between ego activities and object relations? If you go to an evening institute and the pottery class is full, you might be quite willing to accept a place in the painting class. But this is quite different from accepting someone else if you can't have your boyfriend.

Hansi Kennedy: Perhaps one should not look at the activity alone to get a clue as to whether it is a sublimation or not, but rather at what it really means to the person. One can imagine that some people enter their dogs for obedience trials, or train guide dogs, as a sadistic outlet, or as a reaction formation to sadistic wishes, but others use it as a sublimation.

Joseph Sandler: There are so many questions that arise. For example, does one's need for omnipotent control count as a sublimation if one finds a socially acceptable form for this? By definition it would not, because it is very much an ego activity, even though it might have aggressive sadistic elements in it. And then the question of object relations comes up. If a primitive object relationship is repeated in disguised form in an activity (or in the fantasy accompanying an activity) can it then be a sublimation? It has been said that we talk much less at the Clinic about object relationships than about ego activities.

Anna Freud: Do we? I don't think we do. The object relationships are, after all, almost the most basic subject for us. Really, I don't feel that this is so.

Joseph Sandler: Well, for example, today we have been speaking about the drives and the aim of the drives in regard to sublimation. We know that the object of the drives must come into it, and the relation to the object is very closely connected with the aim of the drive. We speak of sublimation in terms of the vicissitudes of the drive and of the drive aim, but we do not verbalize the fact that there is also a displacement of object and a disguising of the relation to the object in the formation of a sublimation.

Anna Freud: The whole idea of defense is that it is an intrapsychic process, not one connected with the object world. So to the extent that we pursue how the ego defends itself against id derivatives, the object doesn't come into it, except as an instigator—or one of the instigators—of the ego's criticisms of the id.

Joseph Sandler: But what about the intrapsychic object representations, Miss Freud?

Anna Freud: They are in the superego, of course.

Joseph Sandler: Or in the ego.

Anna Freud: Or in the ego, obviously.

Joseph Sandler: In fantasy.

Anna Freud: Only at that point they are not within the scope of the discussion. I do not feel that we have ever neglected object relationships.

Joseph Sandler: I don't think we have, but we neglect talking about them sufficiently. I remember your reminding me once that when one talks about the ego one should always say something about the id, and not assume that the listener or reader is going to take the id for granted. Perhaps the same applies to object relationships.

Sara Rosenfeld: Ernst Kris, in his paper on sublimation, traced back the defenses used by two little girls to their relation to the object. He did this in a very detailed and meaningful way, and I wanted to draw attention to it because of your comment, Miss Freud, that the defenses are not immediately connected with the object.

Anna Freud: Well, they are not immediately tied up with the object, but they are indirectly connected with the object, insofar as we cannot think of ego and superego development without object relationships.

Sara Rosenfeld: Yes, but one can look at the topic more from the point of view of prohibitions, or the wish to please the object, and so on. What Kris does is to examine minutely how the particular defensive structure of the two little girls related to their mothers' own defensive structures, as well as to the interaction between the mothers and their children.

Joseph Sandler: I suppose that one should differentiate here between the motives for defense and the mechanisms of defense as such. When we think of the motives for defense, and the change of aims involved, this must very often involve the object, but the mechanism, the sort of mental machinery involved, might be regarded as independent of the particular object concerned. Of course, the symbolic aspect of sublimatory activities is very often intimately tied to the person's unconscious fantasies in relation to his objects. This has come out in our discussions about sadomasochistic tendencies.

Sara Rosenfeld: Yes, that meets the point exactly.

Joseph Sandler: I should like to mention that our definition of projection, and our understanding of why paranoid projection can satisfy the ego, comes very close to what we say about sublimation. There is a displacement of aim, a transformation, a gratification in an indirect way which is acceptable to the ego. It is true that paranoid projection isn't normally given a high social value, but in some social groups it is. One can imagine that getting worked up about the blacks as a persecuting group in a paranoid way could have a certain social value in a small Southern white community in the United States. This shows how difficult it is for us to make definitions.

Maria Berger: But isn't the amount and type of gratification different in projection and sublimation?

Joseph Sandler: I have always assumed that if one projects an aggressive wish, and then feels attacked, one's own attacking wish unconsciously obtains gratification on a new object, namely the self, even though one may then take further defensive measures against the self-directed aggression. It seems to me that in projection a series of displacements from inside to outside occurs, but the unconscious wish still finds a disguised expression in the paranoid persecutory idea.

Anna Freud: I don't think so. I think that it is only a relief to the ego that the aggression is outside and not inside anymore. Or that the wish that is defended against is outside rather than inside. We discussed such a case the other day in the diagnostic meeting, a boy with persecutory ideas who constantly feels that others derogate him, that they put him in the same category as the street cleaners and make him passive. In reality this means that they make him feminine. But obviously what he defends against strenuously is a feminine wish, the wish to turn into a woman, which at the same time creates an enormous hostility against the mother and against the sisters, whom he attacks. Evidently he thinks that femininity is infectious and he has to ward it off. But he gets no gratification at all.

Joseph Sandler: I would tend to argue that unconsciously he *is* obtaining gratification of his wish to be penetrated, through the idea of being attacked and persecuted. He gets a sexual, feminine, possibly but not necessarily a masochistic gratification.

Anna Freud: Well, this belongs more to what we should really class as the return of the repressed. In the situation he creates he unconsciously experiences all the time exactly what he doesn't want to experience consciously.

Joseph Sandler: At this point I would like to ask you to clarify, Miss Freud, what you understand by successful defense, because this idea comes up very often. I have the impression that people understand different things by the idea.

Anna Freud: I know the question. Others have raised it, with the idea that I meant "successful" in terms of the external world. Of course, I meant nothing of the kind. When I speak of successful defense I look at it from the point of view of the ego. If the ego defends itself successfully, it means that it achieves the aim of not allowing the forbidden impulse to enter into consciousness and that it does away with the anxiety connected with it and escapes unpleasure of any kind. That is a successful defense, although it may also have disastrous consequences for health and for later development. But from the point of view of defending oneself it is successful. You know, if somebody attacks you and you kill that person, the defense has been immensely successful, but it may not be approved of and have very disagreeable consequences. It all depends on your viewpoint. That is what I had in mind.

Joseph Sandler: Perhaps one could add that a successful defense need not have disastrous consequences. Repression can be successful, provided that the impulse defended against is not too strong.

Anna Freud: I would call repression successful if every conscious knowledge of the item concerned has really gone. If the impulse returns from repression, then the defense has not been successful.

Joseph Sandler: But the subsequent defense, which might be projection, for example, might then be successful.

Anna Freud: It might be very successful, although it might also turn the person into a paranoiac.

Marjorie Sprince: Don't we really need some way of differentiating between a defense which doesn't in fact result in pathology, which in a sense would be a successful defense, and a defense which would lead to pathology?

Anna Freud: You know, a wholly successful defense is always something dangerous. Either it restricts the area of consciousness or the competence of the ego too much, or it falsifies reality—we see this best in projection. The defensive mechanisms and measures really undo the excellence of the ego's functions. And I don't think we should introduce values of health or pathology here, but should rather look at the battle between intact ego functions, at the unpleasure or anxiety they generate and at the defenses used against the anxiety. And then we would see who wins, and the consequences for health or illness.

Maria Berger: In what Miss Freud said it seemed important to me that her point of departure was not the person's adaptation to the outside world, but rather to the situation within his inner world.

Joseph Sandler: This brings us to a double meaning of adaptation.

Anna Freud: I can give you an example. Nothing is more dangerous to the later health of the individual than the situation, for example, that we used to meet very often in former times, in which the child defends completely against masturbation in latency, so that it disappears from the scene. This individual may become highly neurotic or even, as I suggested before, psychopathic. We might also get frigidity or impotence, and all sorts of other pathological results. But the breakdown of the defenses every so often during latency, with the breakthrough of normal masturbation, may be a saving feature for mental health.

Joseph Sandler: Is masturbation not almost universal nowadays in latency children?

Anna Freud: It should be universal, but it isn't.

Joseph Sandler: There is the implication in what you have been saying, Miss Freud, that when we come to treat a patient we should bear in mind that his defensive adaptation, from the point of view of his ego, is really a here and now adaptation, which is as successful as he can get it to be at the time, even though it may later result in pathology. If one approaches the patient with this point of view in one's analytic work, it means that one has to bear in mind that one is intervening as the analyst in a system which represents the best adaptation the person can make at the time, given the resources at his disposal.

Anna Freud: That is why patients resent analysis and the interference of the analyst so much, because the analyst is interfering with the patient's best defenses. Only, as far as health is concerned, these defenses have been inadequate attempts and have had disastrous results.

Joseph Sandler: All of this has implications for the way in which we phrase our interpretations.

Anna Freud: Yes.

Session six

Joseph Sandler: Miss Freud, in this chapter you use the phrase "love fixation" (48,45), and I should like to raise the question of the current status of the word "fixation" in regard to an object. We know that Freud spoke of a fixation to an object, as when he referred to a father fixation, in addition to speaking of libidinal fixation during the course of psychosexual development. Of course, when you use the phrase "love fixation" in regard to the child, it is very clear what you mean.

Anna Freud: Yes, it is also clear what the translator meant, but never mind. (*Note by J.S.*: Love fixation is a translation from Anna Freud's German phrase *Liebesbindung an die Mutter*—literally, "love-tie to the mother."

In writing of pregenital fixations elsewhere in the book
[162,148] Anna Freud used the German phrase *prägenitale
Fixierungen.*)

Joseph Sandler: I wonder whether you could say something, Miss Freud, about the use of the word "fixation"
with regard to father fixation, mother fixation, and the
like. We still use the term a great deal, meaning, I think,
that there is a very strong instinctual or emotional investment in the person concerned.

Anna Freud: You know, the term means more, since the
word is used in contrast to the free movement of the
libido. Fixation always means that one is tied to a point
in time, or to an object, when by rights one should have
moved further away. So we wouldn't call a relationship
a father or mother fixation if we are referring to the time
when we expect the child to be attached to these objects.
We call it a fixation when the child should have moved
on. It always means that an undue amount of libido has
been left behind.

Joseph Sandler: The meaning now seems very clear. I've
always been struck by the fact that we tend to use the
term only when the phenomenon to which it applies is
overt. We speak of the grown-up man who still lives with
his mother and doesn't want to leave her to marry, as
being mother-fixated. But the man who does leave, and
who has defenses against his equally strong attachment
to his mother, and who carries this unconscious attachment into his later life and into neurotic conflicts, is not
usually referred to as having a mother fixation.

Anna Freud: Well, I think it is equally applicable to both situations. It always means the libido is tied to the object, whether consciously or unconsciously.

Joseph Sandler: Another point, Miss Freud. In describing the case of the young woman early in Chapter 4, you write, "In order to solve the problem of ambivalence she displaced outward one side of her ambivalent feeling" (48,45). Would it be correct to assume that the word "outward" means "away from the mother," as opposed to the sort of displacement outward which we see in projection?

Anna Freud: Yes. If I were to write this today I would say, "She displaced elsewhere," not "outward." What I describe is really the splitting of the ambivalence.

Joseph Sandler: The term ambivalence is often used to refer to people being in conflict about something. People say that they are ambivalent about doing something, or about going somewhere. You use it here, of course, in a very precise way, Miss Freud, referring to two opposite instinctual attitudes toward an object existing at the same time, and to the conflict over these two separate attitudes.

Anna Freud: I think it always means two opposite feelings existing on the same level, whatever the level may be. But not all ambivalence gives rise to conflict and certainly not all conflict is over ambivalence.

Joseph Sandler: A little later in the chapter you speak

of the little girl's ego resorting to a further mechanism. You say, "It turned inward the hatred, which hitherto had related exclusively to other people. The child tortured herself with self-accusations and feelings of inferiority and, throughout childhood and adolescence . . . did everything she could to put herself at a disadvantage and injure her interests, always surrendering her own wishes to the demands made on her by others. To all outward appearance she had become masochistic since adopting his method of defense" (49,45–46). As you know, Miss Freud, we have recently been discussing the concept of aggression turned against the self, and it would be very useful if you could help us consider some aspects of the topic. The first point is that you speak here of the child's hatred, which represents an object-related feeling, as opposed to the aggressive drive itself.

Anna Freud: I suppose I used the word hatred instead of aggression because she felt so guilty for her feeling, even if it was not accompanied by any action. It was this feeling that she turned against her self. Recently we had a similar case of a child in a situation of being unloved and unhappy, evidently reacting to the situation with anger, hatred, aggression, and death wishes. But what we saw in that child was a very strong reaction against the death wishes shown by her great anxiety when the parents went out. She worried about what would happen to them, and couldn't go to sleep. She had a younger sister, and when she had to cross the street with that sister she was afraid. She didn't want to cross the street because the sister might be run over. She didn't want to be left alone at home with the little sister, apparently afraid of what she would do to her. So she had reaction formations against her death wishes and her hatred. When provoked by other children at school, she would have sudden uncontrollable outbreaks of aggression in which she would hit, pinch, bite, and really hurt the other children. She couldn't control herself. She was afraid of these outbursts, and felt very guilty afterward. But simultaneously this nine-year-old girl would turn the whole feeling against herself and would break into tears, saying, "I'm a total failure, I'm no good, no one loves me, I'm bad." Then she became her own victim, the victim of her own aggression. We felt, although we could not confirm it, that some masochism might have become mixed up with this whole sequence so that she was forced to repeat it over and over again. Whenever somebody approached her lovingly she would bring things to the point where that person would then dislike her. Descriptively we would say this *is* masochistic, but we do not know whether it is *really* masochistic.

Joseph Sandler: You would restrict the term masochistic to situations in which there is a libidinal component in the suffering?

Anna Freud: Yes, so that the suffering becomes an aim in itself.

Joseph Sandler: It is important to clarify this, Miss Freud, because many people use the term masochism for all forms of aggression turned against the self, and if I understand you correctly, the term should be used only where in some way the suffering has been erotized.

People who habitually damage, hurt, or punish themselves may not be masochistic in the strict sense of the term.

Anna Freud: Quite right, because they may just look for relief from guilt, which of course they can get when they turn aggression against the self. That would not yet be masochistic, because they would have to have the secret enjoyment of being the victim. Only then should we call their turning against the self masochistic. Then it is, of course, especially difficult to treat, because one has to interfere not only with the painful situation, but with the pleasure.

Joseph Sandler: I remember that some years ago I suggested that the outlook was less hopeful when there was a masochistic sexualization of guilt or suffering, but you felt then that although the patient might be more difficult to treat the outlook was more hopeful than in cases of turning aggression against the self purely because of guilt. You felt that this was because the superego is so difficult to change, and if there is a sexual reinforcement, at any rate one can get on to that in the analysis.

Anna Freud: Yes, especially because one can interfere with the pleasure by making the whole process conscious. Of course the patient doesn't like to be interfered with because of the pleasure he gains, and he can turn the situation into one in which he becomes the victim and the analyst becomes the attacker, and so on. But if one succeeds in unraveling it, one has a chance.

Joseph Sandler: I have always felt that some of our more active analysts, who interpret a great deal in a very active way, so that they have a sort of to-and-fro conversation with the patient, foster a sadomasochistic relationship, and this may be one of the reasons that their patients stay in analysis for so long.

Anna Freud: I think that is true.

Joseph Sandler: There is another point. The problem we have had about feelings and drives is perhaps not such a big one if we remember that the drives are hypothetical constructs, and that you agreed that what you refer to in your book is essentially the *wish* (Chapter 1). With wishes go all sorts of feelings, as well as representations of the objects or the self toward whom the feelings are directed or with whom they are connected. So when you speak of the vicissitudes of the drive, it seems clear that you refer to the vicissitudes of the wish. If you then postulate that the drive takes a certain path, you simultaneously mean that the wish is modified. So turning aggression against the self automatically involves the displacement of an aggressive *wish* from an object to self. There is clearly an advantage for us to talk of the wish rather than the drive, for then the feeling aspect can be taken as part of the wish. Would you go along with that, Miss Freud?

Anna Freud: Yes.

Joseph Sandler: It may be useful to make some distinctions in regard to the clinical material we have been discussing. In the first place we have the child who specifically does to himself what he wishes to do to the object. So if the child wants to push the object down the stairs, the child, in turning the wish against himself, falls down the stairs. The content of what he does to himself gives us the clue to what he unconsciously wants to do to the object. Then, on the other hand, there are the children who punish themselves because they feel guilty, and what they feel guilty about need have no relation to the punishment they inflict upon themselves. They may feel as guilty about a sexual wish as about an aggressive wish, and punish themselves aggressively for that sexual wish. Here the content of the self-punishment gives us no clue to the unconscious wish which aroused the feelings of guilt and caused the child to punish himself. Then there are also the children who denigrate themselves, who suffer from intense feelings of inferiority or inadequacy. We cannot be sure that this is the result of aggression turned against the self, except perhaps in a descriptive sense, for the child may be identified with a denigrated object, may have problems in regard to regulation of his self-esteem, to the provision of narcissistic supplies. I don't think that we should call this last group aggression turned against the self, because of the big narcissistic component. We may be misled about the pathology.

Anna Freud: I am reminded of a case we had recently of a child who tortured herself, was full of self-reproaches, and who left all the people who interviewed her with a feeling of unease. They felt accused by her in some subtle way, and I am sure that the parents of this child felt accused by the depressive self-torture of the child. So the wish to torture or to punish the object returned in a roundabout way. This is a good diagnostic sign of self-reproaches being deflected from the object. In that child too there was a low self-esteem because the child is unloved, because she is a devalued object in the eyes of the parents. The mother wanted a boy and she is a girl, and so on. Against this background of feeling devalued and having a low self-esteem, which comes from the past, there is then added the aggression which by rights should go outward to the people who denigrate her, who frustrate her and don't love her enough. It is very difficult to say, when we have the finished result, which part of it comes from the feeling of denigration arising from her identification with the parents' image of her, and which is added afterward by aggression turned inward. When you look at the individual case it is, of course, always more complicated than whatever it is we try to extract from it. The position is made even more complicated because the child's attempts to deal with her aggression are so inadequate. In reality she cannot get rid of it, she cannot cope with her aggression, or hate, or whatever you want to call it, against the parents, especially the mother. She tries this and that, she tries to repress, she tries reaction formations, and both of these work to some extent. But then there are breakthroughs and breakdowns; so she becomes desperate. So she tries to turn the aggression against herself, but it is still turned outward to some extent.

Joseph Sandler: Then you would not see the aggressive

aspect of the child's self-reproaches as a secondary gain, as something discovered to be of use by the child.

Anna Freud: No, the aggression that remains toward the parents is part of the whole process.

Hansi Kennedy: I am reminded of the child who talks of killing himself following a wish to attack the parent, and who uses the threat of killing himself as a provocation, or as a way of making the parents anxious or guilty.

Anna Freud: Yes, we find both. There is a little boy we both know who thinks that it is very bad to kill somebody else, and if one is good one kills oneself. But of course, if one kills oneself, the parents are really guilty. So the suicidal thought is an attack, a punishment for the parents.

Joseph Sandler: Perhaps this is important in regard to suicides in children, which seem to be so very different because they so much more often involve the fantasy of punishing the parents.

Anna Freud: Yes, they think how guilty and sorry the parents will be afterward, and how nice it would be to watch that. Mark Twain gave a wonderful example of this in *Tom Sawyer*.

Robert L. Tyson: I was thinking of the forms of self-torture, which we see in adults, which are due to the erotization of anxiety.

Anna Freud: You see this sort of thing in children when it has very much the quality of a flirtation with anxiety. I once described a little boy patient of mine who had terrible anxiety attacks when he was in bed at night because he was sure that a robber was hidden behind the curtains. He was sure that as soon as he moved at all in his bed or, worse still, as soon as he got out of bed to fetch something, or to reach for a glass of water, the robber would pounce on him and destroy him. One felt quite sorry for the child. But I remember I asked him once in the hour, "What do you do if the robber doesn't come out?" And he said: "Then I say: robber, come." Obviously the fantasy was a sexualized one, and playing with the anxiety was a sexual activity.

Maria Berger: Probably it's quite normal at certain periods of development for anxiety to be mixed with excitement—the child who loves to be tossed in the air, for instance.

Joseph Sandler: I remember a patient who had eczema as a child. His mother would come and put a soothing lotion on him at night. His later life consisted in large part of having to have little irritations and to scratch away. He couldn't bear the thought of not having something in his life go wrong. I think that the pain from the eczema was erotized very early on in his life, and this must be true for many children with skin complaints, where there has been painful scratching, or something similar.

Anna Freud: Of course, the pain may be erotized, but also the ministrations to the pain.

Mahmoud Sanai: One often comes across erotization of depression. Many poets have spoken of "sweet sorrow." If one looks at the lives of poets one can see that there is a certain enjoyment in being depressed in some of them.

Anna Freud: In the Hampstead Nurseries we saw that many young children stopped reacting to pain the moment the pain stopped, but in others the reaction was dragged on for a long time, long after the pain had stopped, as if the child could not disengage himself from the pain. I think this is a step along the path toward erotization of the painful situation.

Joseph Sandler: I should like to note the role of the maintenance of feelings of safety in people repeating what looks like purely masochistic behavior. The behavior may create an unconscious feeling of the presence of the love object, even though in order to do this the person has to do something unpleasant to himself. Somehow what is conjured up in fantasy is the feeling of the existence of the object close by, and this can produce a feeling of safety in addition to other gratifications.

Miss Freud, in describing the patient who turned her hatred inward (49,45), you speak of the girl's ego finding relief from the sense of guilt by using a defense mechanism. I want to ask you to what extent we should think of defense mechanisms in connection with the doing away of guilt feelings. And do we oppose the defensive measures or defensive maneuvers used when guilt is involved to other defense mechanisms? You speak of projection giving the child relief from the sense of guilt, and yet I have a feeling that sometimes we hesitate to speak of defense mechanisms when guilt is being dealt with.

Anna Freud: You know, it depends on how you look at it. We can look at it from different ends. Let us say the child has a sexual or aggressive impulse, and that this is followed by guilt. Now the child would like to remove the guilt, but the best way to remove the guilt is for the child to institute a defense against the impulse. So if we start at the end of the impulse, we can speak of a defense proper. The impulse may be defended against by projection, and the child who feels guilty for a certain impulse then has no need to feel guilty about it if someone else has it. It would be incorrect here to say that the defense is against the guilt. The defense is against the drive derivative.

Joseph Sandler: I suppose I really want to get you to extend the formulation in Freud's "Inhibitions, Symptoms and Anxiety" about the anxiety signal initiating defense to any painful signal as the instigator of defense. This would include guilt, fear of the outside world, and so on.

Anna Freud: I think I say that in another chapter.

Joseph Sandler: So that a stab of guilt could equally bring into play defense mechanisms against the impulse which gives rise to it?

Anna Freud: Yes. You know, people can do different things in relation to guilt. Some people cannot turn against the impulse that makes them feel guilty, but indulge in the guilty action, and then deny or repress the guilt. What they really ought to do is to attack the reason for the guilt feeling, and not deal with the outcome, the conflict.

Joseph Sandler: I am rather puzzled, Miss Freud, when you speak of what people should *really* do.

Anna Freud: When I say things like "what they should really do" I always speak from the point of view, not of the outside observer, but of the internal conflict. What certainly works best is to remove the reason for the guilt. But to remove the reason for the guilt means a great loss of pleasure, satisfaction, or relief of tension. So some people are quite reluctant to do that, and want to have their pleasure, but their pleasure makes them feel guilty. Sometimes patients come for analysis, and say—especially homosexual patients—"All I want to do is to continue with the things that give me pleasure and not to feel guilty about them." They have tried using measures that didn't work. And what did they do? They went on with the activities that make them feel guilty, and then denied the guilt, or used a rationalization—only these methods didn't work.

Joseph Sandler: Are there cases in which they can work?

Anna Freud: I think rationalizations work very well. But there are other methods too. For instance, such people may provoke their environment to actions which then justify them in reacting with the impulse they would otherwise feel guilty about. I suppose there are thousands of ways of defending like this, and I suppose the individual tries them out until he finds one that suits him. It doesn't really suit him, of course, because he wouldn't want to be in analysis if it worked.

Joseph Sandler: Yes, I suppose that is the point. There are many people who do in fact manage, by some trick or defensive method, to deal with their guilt feelings, and don't end up in analysis, don't develop symptoms, and feel that they are coping quite well. Also, I suppose that if the guilt arises from some wish that is not necessarily put into action, and the person then deals with the guilt in one of the ways we have been discussing, the way of dealing with the guilt might be called a successful defensive activity, and be regarded as quite normal. For example, the guilt might be dealt with by the use of projection within the person's fantasy life. If this works, then the person is in luck, and we don't see him in our consulting rooms.

Anna Freud: One could add that the patients who come for help, but who try to keep their pleasure and have the guilt removed, usually get greatly disappointed in analysis at the start, because the more one analyzes them, the more guilty they feel. They lose the methods they have used so far against the guilt, and feel the full weight of the guilt. So in the end it all comes back to dealing with the impulse, and to seeing whether it is appropriate or inappropriate to the present situation.

Joseph Sandler: If we take into account the distinction between what is descriptively unconscious and what is dynamically unconscious, we can, of course, speak of feelings which are descriptively unconscious. So anxiety or guilt can be kept away from consciousness, and people with a lot of unconscious guilt may go through life either punishing themselves or dealing with the guilt feeling in some other way. They are not aware of feeling the guilt, but in fact it is there. Such people may appear on the surface to be anxiety-free or guilt-free characters, and analysis may transform them into people who experience guilt and anxiety quite acutely. Would you say that if they have these feelings after analysis, this is better for them although somewhat less comfortable?

Anna Freud: Yes.

Joseph Sandler: Miss Freud, in this chapter you compare hysteria and obsessional neurosis, and say that "we will assume that the problem is the same in each case: how to master that hatred of the mother which springs from penis envy. Hysteria solves it by means of repression" (50,47). Could you amplify the point about the hatred of the mother springing from penis envy?

Anna Freud: For simplicity's sake I chose two types of child, one with an obsessional makeup, and another with a hysterical makeup, and I chose the same situation which was intolerable to them. Each of them blamed the mother for their not having been made into a boy. That is the usual hatred of the mother on the basis of penis envy. The two different sorts of little girl are now confronted with the need to deal with that feeling. What I left out was that this is not the main problem in an obsessional child, as I only wanted to show how differently the two types of child deal with the same situation.

Joseph Sandler: So the hatred of the mother springing from penis envy is the resentment toward the mother for not having provided a penis.

Anna Freud: Yes.

Joseph Sandler: You say, Miss Freud, that "the aggressive impulses associated with hatred and the sexual impulses associated with penis envy may be transformed into bodily symptoms, if the patient possesses the capacity for conversion and somatic conditions are favorable" (50–51,47). I was struck when reading this how much the formulations of the earliest phase of psychoanalysis about dammed-up affect finding its expression in conversion symptoms remain in our theory when we think of drive impulses being transformed and discharged into hysterical symptoms. Presumably the defense involved is repression. But what I particularly want to ask you about, Miss Freud, are the so-called phobic defenses. We know that many defenses enter into phobias, yet we seem to treat "phobic defense" as if it were a unit in itself worth giving a title to. We hear colleagues speak of the patient using phobic defenses against their aggression, or against their exhibitionism.

Anna Freud: We could also call it an avoidance. It is an avoidance of the situation in which the conflict or feeling arises, and the consequences of that avoidance, or the way in which it is carried out, we call the phobic mechanism. It involves a withdrawal from the situation.

Joseph Sandler: So one should speak of phobic avoidance.

Anna Freud: One should speak of phobic avoidance, yes.

Maria Berger: Does this not give us a problem, in that such avoidance has the features of a symptom?

Anna Freud: It has and it hasn't. If you look at it from the normal side, we don't know how many of our moves in life are really avoidance of situations which we dread. If we look at this closely we would have to call it phobic avoidance, only the required intensity for it to be a symptom isn't quite reached.

Maria Berger: What does such avoidance defend against?

Anna Freud: Earlier I referred to the example of a little boy patient who developed much castration anxiety on the football field, and in every sport. He was so afraid of bodily hurt, especially hurt to his penis, that he became quite unable to do any sports. But this never became a phobia in the usual sense, because he simply avoided the area of sport altogether, and developed great intellectual and poetic abilities instead. So he wouldn't have noticed that he was phobic. I knew in his analysis that if he weren't so afraid of the situation of being hurt,

he would probably be less of a poet and a better sports-
man.

Joseph Sandler: When does a food fad, for example, become a symptom? Wasn't it Wilhelm Reich who said that
behind every character trait lies a phobia?

Anna Freud: There is an avoidance of something, so you
develop something else instead. It is a very interesting
line to follow.

Joseph Sandler: Especially in regard to the question of
what is normal and what pathological. Here we have a
mechanism which is in a sense quite irrational but is so
frequent that it can be considered normal. It certainly
has a function for the ego.

Anna Freud: What people call, rather optimistically, all-
round development, really means that no aspect of development is interfered with by such little phobias. But
who can achieve that? If one looks at people closely we
find that there are always things they avoid and things
they favor. What we are talking about also lies at the
basis of what I have called ego restriction. As the ego
develops it tries to avoid the worst areas and to go into
the most comfortable ones. This is very interesting for
normal psychology.

Hansi Kennedy: Is it not a question of how widespread
such restrictions are within the individual? I think, for
instance, of such things as failure in sports. If the child

particularly wants to be a good footballer, then he may have real difficulties.

Anna Freud: He doesn't entirely want to be a good footballer, because at the same time he restricts the wish. But let us look at it in another way. If, for instance, what he is afraid of in sports is the competition with others, because to lose means to him a complete destruction of his whole personality, he might then withdraw from the sports field and turn to the intellectual field. But then there is every chance that the fear of competition will follow him there, not any more in the physical sense, but in the mental sense, and he will feel just as destroyed if someone writes a better essay, or accomplishes a better poem. So he has to leave this particular area, and again look for another one, and in the end he will not find safety from competition anywhere. There are all shades of normality and pathology in these things.

Joseph Sandler: Freud, of course, distinguished between an inhibition and a neurotic symptom, but it is so often difficult to make the distinction. It is clear that a central aspect of the inhibition is stopping the activity which represents the gratification of an instinctual wish. By not entering into a particular area, the conflict is not aroused, and I understand how this is opposed to the idea of the symptom as a compromise formation. But often what is, descriptively speaking, an inhibition, as we see it in our clinical work, has the qualities of a symptom in the sense of being a compromise formation. We speak loosely, of course, of all sorts of things as symptoms. But it gets very difficult, for example, when we see a withdrawal from a situation because of a phobic anxiety. From one point of view we see an inhibition, but from another viewpoint the phobia is a symptom.

Anna Freud: I think an inhibition is really meant to be an unfinished symptom because there is the move forward of the wish, and then there is the counterforce against it. That is the inhibition. I think the characteristic of the inhibition is that the wish is kept alive, and very often remains conscious. People are very unhappy about their inhibitions, because they want to perform well. With a phobic withdrawal the person is not unhappy anymore. He has given up the wish, at least in consciousness. The symptom is only formed if a compromise is found between the wish and the guilt, so it is a step further removed. For instance, the boy who is so afraid of the football field might become an umpire. He can stand in a safe position and judge what the others do, he can send them off the field, and so on. Or he may become one of those boys who are crazy about watching football on television, and be quite safe in that—which means he fulfills some of his interests and at the same time guards against injury. That's a compromise. I suppose one might even call it a sublimation.

Joseph Sandler: It might be a sublimation if he is an umpire. If he throws bottles at the players at football matches, we wouldn't call it sublimation. But I still have a problem, Miss Freud, if I think, for example, of a man who is impotent. We say he has a sexual inhibition, but we know it isn't always an inhibition. The person who can't approach girls, who is afraid, may turn out in analysis to be phobic, with the women representing a vagina dentata, or a castrating mother, or something like that. He has put an enormous amount of unconscious fantasy distortion into the situation of being with the girl. What we may see is a phobia which shows itself like an inhibition, and I have the feeling that when we get down to analyzing the patients who are sent to us with inhibitions, it very often turns out that they have phobic avoidances.

Anna Freud: Yes, you know that in the case of the young man you describe we would choose a term for his disturbance according to how near he can get to the girl. If, like some of our patients, he can never go anywhere girls might be found—I remember a boy in treatment who couldn't stand in line next to a girl in school because he might catch femininity from her—then we would call this a phobia, a phobic retreat. If he can come closer, and can even dance with them, only can't have intercourse, or if he is ready for intercourse but can't have an erection, we would probably call it an inhibition. The terminology is quite elastic—you can stretch it.

Joseph Sandler: Before ending today's discussion I should like to put forward a question about the way anxieties that are essentially phobic can be of either defensive or adaptive value. I think of someone with a street phobia in which he is repeatedly exposed to the phobic situation, but always retreats from it. We can see the way in which he has to deal over and over again with the conflict aroused by the wish represented by being in the street. But if, by contrast, we think of someone who has a fear of heights, which we also call a phobia, the fear may not be experienced at all unless the person goes to the top of a tall building. He might do this once a year or once in five years. There seem to be some anxieties which look phobic in structure, but don't appear to have an ongoing function in dealing with some persistent or frequently recurring unconscious wish. This seems to be rather different from the person who always thinks about his need to go out into the street and then feels frightened and doesn't go out, so he constantly avoids the activity which represents something forbidden.

Anna Freud: I would put the question the other way round. Why are these people able to choose situations which they meet so seldom? Why is such a person afraid of an insect which does not exist in Europe at all, and not of the common fly or a bee or a wasp which he might meet all the time? I have the feeling that the centering of the fear on something that is easily avoided is really a clever move of the ego. Think of the fear of heights as an example. We find it very often in our patients. I have a feeling that if they choose height to be afraid of, then it is something which they do not actually have to experience. It is far away and can easily be avoided. It therefore lends itself to symbolization. I remember one highly obsessional patient who had obsessive avoidance symptoms which were very cleverly placed. They never interfered too much with his life. He would say to himself, for example, "If it were to involve my books, then how could I study?" So he chose something that lay a little outside an important area—a chair, for example, because he could then sit on another chair. He was highly plagued by his symptoms all his life, but his professional and daily life were not really actively interfered with, because he placed his symptoms that way.

Joseph Sandler: But he would have to be in contact with these situations regularly. I wonder whether an approach to such things as fear of heights might be to say that finding oneself on top of a tall building might concretize something that was previously well contained in fantasy. Then one finds oneself suddenly in a situation in which the threat is much greater and cannot be contained by the fantasy, so there is an anxiety attack. Then of course it might not really be a phobia.

Anna Freud: I remember my obsessional patient saying (he had fears of pollution by different objects), "Of course my key doesn't bother me. If it did I wouldn't be able to get into my apartment." So the key was free from pollution, and something a little less necessary to his life was polluted instead. But one could say that he was a highly developed obsessional who knew how to manage his obsessions! What he did with his obsessions some people do with their phobias.

Session seven

Joseph Sandler: Could you elaborate, Miss Freud, on the question of concern about the other person's safety as a reaction formation (51,47–48)?

Anna Freud: Worrying about safety is a form of concern for the object, and the most frequent examples are to be found in those children who can't go to sleep when the parents are out in the evening. They worry that something might happen to the parents. If they are in the theater, a fire might break out. If they are in a car, they might have an accident. If the parents are on a trip and flying somewhere, the plane might drop out of the sky. This means the child is afraid of his own death wishes coming true, and so develops an overconcern for the safety of the object. On the other hand, we know that mothers who are overly concerned with the child's safety also have a reaction formation against their own hostile wishes.

Joseph Sandler: You have said, Miss Freud, that one should use the term reaction formation to refer only to an aspect of character.

Anna Freud: The fears of the child become ego syntonic. What the child feels is, "I love my mother or my parents so much that I couldn't stand it if anything happened to them. I have to be continually concerned with their safety." This is completely ego syntonic, and it is on the border between a character trait and a symptom.

Maria Berger: I think that we should distinguish between a reaction formation of excessive tenderness, and the constant worrying and overconcern for the parents that we have just been talking about.

Anna Freud: I suppose now we make more subtle definitions and would have to say that something is a reaction formation when it extends from the original objects for whose sake it was erected to a general attitude to other people. Then it becomes part of the person's character or personality, so that the person is tender toward everybody, overconcerned for everyone's safety, and so on. It's an important feature of the reaction formation that its aim is to keep an opposite part unconscious or repressed, and of course overconcern does exactly that. Instead of having the bad wishes toward the object in consciousness, the child has good wishes in their place, and in that sense it is a reaction. It acts as a counterforce against the repressed.

Joseph Sandler: What I find so interesting is that, just as with aggression turned against the self, reaction formations, particularly against aggressive wishes, can nevertheless result in the child or the adult being aggressive although they have the reaction formation as well. I remember a lady who was very obsessional, who had had many abortions but never had any children. She unconsciously hated children and babies as she had hated her younger siblings, but was passionately devoted to her dog. When she was in her menopause she decided that the dog—a bitch—was sexually frustrated and had to be mated. The dog gave birth to puppies, and she was very concerned that these puppies should survive. In order to ensure this she regularly cleaned the nipples of the mother with a strong disinfectant to make sure that they were free of germs, and all the puppies died. It seems that even though there was a strong reaction formation against cruelty, the unconscious wishes broke through.

Anna Freud: Yes, one often sees that.

Joseph Sandler: Could you comment, Miss Freud, on the relation of reaction formation to superego formation? You speak in your book of the moral code of exaggerated strictness as being a reaction formation. Presumably this is because of the exaggeration, but I think that we all feel that there is a strong link between superego functioning and ordinary reaction formations. When we speak of superego development, we refer so often to cleanliness and bowel training. We also know that reaction formations begin in the anal phase, before the formation of the superego proper, but it is not clear what the continuity is between the reaction formation which a child establishes relatively early in development and the later superego. There is an interesting area here, because so many of our ideals and moral prohibitions are in the nature of reaction formations. We feel an inner injunction to be kind, to be concerned. I think we would have to call these things reaction formations, even if they are not excessive. Would you comment on the connection between reaction formation as a defense mechanism and an aspect of normal character development, and superego formation?

Anna Freud: It was Ferenczi, I think, who talked about sphincter morality, which we would call the child's response to a presuperego demand, to a command which has been taken over from the parents, especially the command to be clean. The predecessor of the superego is there to be seen. But the mechanism by which the demand is fulfilled is the reaction formation. The demand alone wouldn't bring about the cleanliness.

Joseph Sandler: I've always understood something different by sphincter morality. I have always assumed that the child on the pot, experiencing what has been called the "battle of the bowel," will obey during the anal phase on a purely pragmatic basis. In other words, it is not that the child does this or that because he knows it to be right, but he does it because he knows he will get disapproval if he doesn't do what the parents think is right, and it is entirely tied to the approval or disapproval coming from the real parents. In more than one sense it is morality on a business basis.

Anna Freud: Sphincter morality is, so to say, a lower form of morality.

Joseph Sandler: It seems to be almost an "as if " morality before the child becomes fully identified with the parents' morality.

Anna Freud: It isn't meant that way. As far as I remember, it meant that the earliest form of morality is to be clean, to control the bladder and the bowels. And what is built up at that time is repeated on a higher level in regard to functions which are no longer bodily functions. I think that is how it was meant. Also, in regression, the higher commands are thrown off first, and in psychosis even the sphincter morality is lost.

Joseph Sandler: So the reinforcement of a repression by

its opposite, as in a reaction formation, would in your view be seen as beginning in regard to the control of messing in the anal phase, with the same mechanisms being later applied to other impulses. And then that aspect of the superego which relates to the ego's own attitudes to the self and to the child's own impulses, attitudes based on reaction formations, would be something that has grown out of this. Would that be a correct statement?

Anna Freud: Yes. Ferenczi added something very interesting which always impressed me. He said that all morality begins as hypocrisy, which is certainly true. He illustrated it in the anal sphere with the child's first liking the smell of its own excrement, and being quite uninterested in the smell of a flower. But then the child learns to imitate and later to identify with the adults who show him a rose and say "how nice," and who say that the smell of excrement is "nasty." And the child imitates hypocritically, but gradually acquires that attitude. Schilder once said to me that the worst thing about giving official psychiatric lectures at the medical school is that when you have done it a few times you believe it all.

Donald Campbell: Would sphincter morality, then, inhibit a biting impulse, which is oral rather than anal, and which would have developed earlier in the child?

Anna Freud: The inhibition of the biting impulse of the child goes very differently. The child likes to bite, and the child bites the mother. There are some simple and primitive mothers, even in our society, who have the

idea that the child will never stop biting unless the
mother bites it back. In the Nurseries during the war
we had to dissuade many mothers from using that
method, which was based on the idea that the child
would be taught that biting hurts. Well, without necessarily doing that, mothers do give signs of displeasure
when they are bitten by the child, and the child will
then respond to the displeasure of the mother. "I mustn't
do it or mother will get angry." But I think that's all that
happens there. The child will then, in spite of that inhibition, use biting as a weapon with other children until,
I suppose, the second or third year of life. We get worried
if this behavior lasts longer, but the biting impulse as
such is not disapproved of by the child after its first
experience with the mother. We would never speak of
a reaction formation to the biting impulse when it is only
inhibited in certain situations.

Joseph Sandler: It's hard to imagine a reaction formation
to biting. What could it be?

Anna Freud: Certain eating disturbances, where the
child won't chew, I suppose. But that is more an inhibition than a reaction formation.

Joseph Sandler: I think that what complicates things is
that struggles over feeding are at their height in the anal
phase. You have often pointed out, Miss Freud, that the
battle over food is very much an anal struggle, although
in analytic reconstruction some analysts see these conflicts as occurring much earlier. So perhaps reaction formations might be set up during the anal phase against

all forms of aggressive behavior, including biting. I suppose one might get a reaction formation against hostility which is so widespread that the child becomes a passive child who appears to have given up his aggressiveness altogether. What I find particularly interesting is the thought that one could get reaction formations against *derivatives* of early oral impulses. For instance, a later derivative of biting might be sarcasm, and I could imagine a reaction formation then developing in which there is excessive concern about the effect of one's words on other people, as a defense against the aggressive wish, which could be in turn a derivative of the original urge to bite.

Anna Freud: Yes, and there one could ask whether the person sees such remarks as biting or cutting, because with biting we would say it is an oral impulse, but with cutting we would have to say that it is phallic. But in any case, it is certainly aggressive.

Joseph Sandler: Yes. And again, there is the danger of the genetic trap in reconstruction. Something may start off being oral, but become very much anal or phallic while still retaining the oral mode. I think, as you have put it, Miss Freud, there is a change of tool involved. And, conversely, the same tool can be used for different purposes.

Maria Berger: One of the reasons why there is no need for excessive reaction formations against biting impulses is that people do have a real-life outlet for such impulses. People bite when they eat, they may like crunchy foods;

the basic drive impulse can find expression that way. And of course this is not frowned upon socially, as is the direct expression of anal impulses.

Anna Freud: Yes. I once tried to show how wrong it was to look at both anal training and the handling of feeding difficulties in the same way, because the wish for food is something that always remains, whereas pleasure in anal matters has to be removed altogether in the course of development. There is an enormous difference between the two.

Joseph Sandler: It is worth commenting at this point that our use of the term ego dystonic is not always consistent. Perhaps we should use "consciousness dystonic," because the term usually refers more to consciousness than to the ego as a whole, as a structure. Certainly Freud used the terms "ego syntonic" and "ego dystonic" long before he put forward the structural theory. If we look at it from the side of the gratification, we might find that there is an unconscious gratification in an impulse, but it is at the same time ego dystonic, in the sense that the person does not want to accept the impulse consciously as part of himself. From this point of view the ego may play a very big part in the development of a symptom, which may finally represent a solution which is quite acceptable to the unconscious part of the ego, but because it is not in accordance with the person's conscious standards and ideals, it is felt to be alien, ego dystonic.

Robert L. Tyson: I've often wondered about the developmental position of repression in regard to the other defenses. Is it early, or does it appear relatively late in development?

Anna Freud: That is a question that's been asked very often and is very difficult to answer. We know it's not terribly early. It seems likely that all the major repressions in a particular individual are probably set up within a certain period—perhaps the oedipal period. Because later on you can't repress, except in highly abnormal states.

Joseph Sandler: I should have thought that a certain amount of repression was normal in ordinary functioning throughout life.

Anna Freud: It goes on from the past, but repressions are not newly established. You can re-repress what returns from the repressed, and in treatment, when people suddenly forget what has happened in the treatment hour, what has occurred is that you have opened up something with the patient, but some patients have the ability to close it off again immediately. This is certainly a repetition of repression, and not a new thing.

Joseph Sandler: I think there may be a confusion about the way the term is used. The question would be, it seems to me, whether the defense mechanism of repression can be employed later on in life. I think the answer must surely be yes. If we speak of the content of what is repressed, which might otherwise be unconscious or preconscious, one could say that it gets repressed because it becomes attached to the impulse which is in itself the subject of repression, and so the defense mechanism of repression acts against the newer content as well. Surely we need to be constantly repressing derivatives of the past which threaten us?

Anna Freud: The question is whether we make new repressions of areas which have not been repressed before, or of instinctual matter that has not been repressed before.

Irmi Elkan: What about ordinary forgetting? For instance, when one doesn't want to pay a bill, one might forget to write out the check or post the letter. Isn't this an indication of repression?

Anna Freud: It's between what is conscious and preconscious, and is not a repression.

Joseph Sandler: But in 1900 and later in 1915, Miss Freud, Freud pointed out that repression, or the censorship, can exist between the conscious and preconscious.

Anna Freud: Yes, the censor is working all the time, and in every dream, in every slip, in every lapse of memory, you can see that it is certainly there. But what I had in mind is that the big repressions come early.

Joseph Sandler: I think that we have often asked ourselves the question—certainly people outside analysis often ask it—whether or not the essential conflicts in later life are revivals of earlier conflicts over oedipal and preoedipal wishes which have returned from repression. Is what comes later simply a derivative of what occurred earlier? It has been said that in adolescence fresh wishes which may be conflictual may emerge. It has been questioned whether all adult conflicts are simply childhood conflicts being reenacted on a different stage, so to speak. I personally think it is a caricature of psychoanalysis to say that we see everything the patient brings in the present as being a replication of something from his early childhood. As we do have very real new conflicts in later life, we can legitimately ask whether the mechanism of repression is available to the ego in order to deal with such conflicts.

Anna Freud: Let me give you an example. We know what happens to infantile death wishes against the love object, especially the parents: such wishes can be repressed, reaction formations can be built up, they can be displaced, they can be turned against the self, they can be answered phobically, or all sorts of other things can happen. But one of the things that can occur is that they are merely repressed, so that the individual knows nothing about these wishes. Now take a man of, let us say, thirty or forty, a fairly peaceful man all his life, who has good reason for developing hate and death wishes toward a rival, perhaps someone who has a superior position to him. He battles with those death wishes because he does not want to become a murderer. But can he repress them? I think he can do this only if the wish or impulse emerges with the old death wishes against the parents, and then he can treat those in the same way.

If it is only a new impulse, and it might easily be a new impulse, I don't think he can repress that anymore.

Joseph Sandler: What happens if he doesn't want to be a murderer in regard to the new impulse?

Anna Freud: He has many ways to deal with it. He can avoid his enemy, he can leave the country, he can try never to see him again, he can hide his hostility, he can become superficially friendly, he can avail himself of the other defense mechanisms at his disposal. But I don't think he can repress the impulse.

Joseph Sandler: It seems that if such a wish arises toward a competitor, it will appear to be very much more dangerous if childhood death wishes are revived. In that case the person has to deal with a much more intense wish, one which has a much more primitive form for him. He has then the very urgent task of defending against the wish, and his first attempt may be to throw both the new and the revived wishes out, to keep them under, to put them under lock and key, just like the old ones. So he would use repression, but if that is unsuccessful, he may resort to other mechanisms. He may become persecuted, for example. A lot must have to do with the intensity of the impulse he faces because of childhood wishes having been revived and added to the new death wish. But this is not quite the same as saying that all adult impulses are new editions of the old ones. We are talking about the old wishes becoming mixed in with the new ones, which is something quite different.

Sara Rosenfeld: I wonder what the effect is of the social setting in which the child lives. I think of the situation in which the home environment is not particularly well disposed toward the establishment of firm superego structures, and does not encourage the use of repression. You told us, Miss Freud, that if repression has not been established early on it cannot be established later; the mechanism is not available. You have made a similar point about parental introjects in superego formation. Can we get differences in the way the environment facilitates the development of repression?

Anna Freud: I know the sort of case you have in mind. We both know of a child in whom the parents have failed to instill any sort of sphincter morality, which means that what should not be consciously expressed anymore, let us say through soiling, has remained available to him, even though he is already of school age. I would see this lack on the part of the parents as causing a developmental interference in the child. If, at the age when he should be helped to establish certain internal structures, he is not helped to do so, then we get such an interference. We see quite a number of children like that nowadays.

Joseph Sandler: I think that perhaps we should not link together inextricably the use of repression and the formation of the superego, because one could imagine a child in whom repression doesn't work well, but who has a very critical superego. It seems that superego formation will occur in most children in one way or another at a particular age, by about the age of five or six, whether or not the oedipus complex has been resolved, whether or not the child has experienced the normal massive repression at about the age of five. Somehow, the superego seems to some extent to have a life history of its own. Possibly the strong link between superego formation and repression was made because, together with the so-called resolution of the oedipus complex, they were seen to occur at the same time, and consequently it seemed that they were all parts of the same process, with no aspect occurring on its own. Perhaps nowadays we would say that they are separate processes which are very much interconnected, but which normally occur at the same time.

Anna Freud: We have to think of the different borders between the psychic structures, because what is out of order in these children is not the border between ego and superego, but the border between id and ego. The repression—or rather the censor, if we can still call it that—lives on that border.

Joseph Sandler: And there are also children who have very strong guilt feelings, but have to react massively in what looks like an impulse-ridden way in order to deal with their guilt feelings, because they can't deal with their guilt in any other way.

Hansi Kennedy: Very often these are the children from so-called progressive homes, in fact. But there are at least two types. There are those who have excessive guilt and are tormented by conflict, and there are those who act out in order to deal with the guilt.

Joseph Sandler: You once told us, Miss Freud, of the experiences you have had with the children of analysts. You said that at one time it seemed to analysts that it was the best thing for their children to let them do everything they wanted in order not to encourage any inhibitions.

Anna Freud: Yes, that was bad, because the child's ego was then afraid of being destroyed by the id impulses. This is different from the fear of the ego that has not obeyed the commands of its superego.

Sara Rosenfeld: I want to draw attention to the fact that in borderline children we often find that repression is one of the mechanisms that are not available, or not available in the normal sense. This gives us a useful diagnostic clue in regard to borderline cases.

Anna Freud: Yes. There is a mistake here in the book in this connection—I don't know whether it is mine or the translator's, but I may have been wrong—where I call repression the least normal or the most pathogenic of the defense mechanisms (54,50). I shouldn't have said that, because all normality is based on the availability of repression at early ages. It can, of course, then easily lead to neurotic conflicts, but I agree that what is so abnormal in the borderline children is that they do not have repression at their disposal in the usual way.

Session eight

Joseph Sandler: Miss Freud, in this chapter you say that repression should be placed side by side with the other specific methods of defense, but it nevertheless occupies a unique position. You point out how strong a defense it is, that it is "capable of mastering powerful instinctual impulses, in face of which the other defensive measures are quite ineffective" (53,49). You then describe how repression acts through the application of an anticathexis, and represents a "permanent institution demanding a constant expenditure of energy" (53,49–50). The other defense mechanisms, unlike repression, are brought into operation "whenever there is an accession of instinctual energy" (54,50). There's a problem, isn't there, about the nature of the permanent barrier, the permanent anticathexis, because in the energic theory, if it is permanent it would have to be considered to be "bound" cathexis, but this contradicts the idea that the instinctual impulses behind the repression barrier are free-floating, subject to primary process, and pushing forward for discharge. Would we not have to say that repression represents a barrier which can, at any time, be applied and reapplied? But then one has to wonder how this differs from the other mechanisms, which can also be applied and reapplied. Should one conceive of repression as a sort of heightened stimulus barrier? A further question arises in regard to your reference to the possibility that certain mechanisms have to be used when the repression fails. How does one reconcile this idea with the notion of repression being the most powerful form of defense? Do you think of "powerful" in the sense of the strength of the energies involved, or in the sense of effectiveness? Projection can be seen, I suppose, to be more effective in certain circumstances than repression, and certainly it involves less of an expenditure of energy. It is true that it involves doing more violence to reality, because one distorts the external world so much, and it might be more effective then, although in a sense less powerful. There is something which has to be clarified here.

Anna Freud: Well, I think the meaning is pretty clear. Repression is a one-time happening. It isn't done whenever the instinctual demand comes up. On the other hand, what secures the repression demands a constant expenditure of energy. I think I can't say it in different words than those I used in the book, but there is to my mind quite a difference between the process of repression, which happens once, with a constant countercathexis, which is an ongoing process or an ongoing structure, and the other methods of defense. If we are dealing with a reaction formation, it is certainly a structure which has to be maintained, but it doesn't work in the same constant way as repression has to work to keep the instincts down. As regards the question of effectiveness, my idea was that repression can deal with more powerful quantities. But, of course, even a powerful process doesn't always work, and every so often the machinery is defective, and we know then that we get a return of the repressed. It may reach consciousness, but invite re-repression, as it does very frequently in analysis, or it may call for the action of some other defense mechanisms. We find an initial attempt at repression as the basis of most other defense mechanisms.

Joseph Sandler: Is it that repression, after a certain level of development has been reached, is the first mechanism that is tried, perhaps with the exception of denial, which is a simple withdrawal of attention?

Anna Freud: Developmentally, of course, repression is not the first. Other mechanisms like projection are used long before repression.

Joseph Sandler: Presumably because repression needs a considerable amount of strength on the part of the ego in order to work.

Anna Freud: Well, it needs structuralization of the personality, which isn't there in the beginning. If you haven't yet built the house, you can't throw somebody out of it.

Joseph Sandler: Nor keep him locked in the basement.

Anna Freud: Neither. You have to have the structure first.

Joseph Sandler: There are one or two questions relating to this which have bothered me for some time, and I have referred to them before. We know that Freud found it necessary from time to time to postulate a censorship between the system Unconscious and the system Preconscious, and a further censorship between the Preconscious and the Conscious. So a wish which found its way past the first censorship was still liable to modification in the Preconscious before it reached the second censorship, at which point the decision would be made about whether it should be admitted into consciousness or not. Now, if we transfer this idea to the structural theory, which is your essential frame of reference in the book, we would have to say that there is a repression barrier on the periphery of the ego, on the border with the id. The properties of secondary process thinking and other means of transformation previously ascribed to the Preconscious would now be allocated to the unconscious ego. The ego would be aware that a wish or its derivatives might constitute a threat to consciousness, because of the arousal of the anxiety signal. Then further defenses, including repression, might be instituted. This then provides a possibility for the repressed being constantly added to by derivatives which have been formed in the unconscious ego but which have not been allowed to reach consciousness or motility. They may have had quite an elaborate development before being re-repressed and added to the original infantile wishes, which had earlier succumbed to the major repression we associate in time with resolution of the oedipus complex and superego formation. The question that then comes to mind is how the ego knows what to repress. Does it not first sample the instinctual wish by allowing it some entry, and then because of the anxiety signal say no? Doesn't this process have to occur over and over again, because the repressed wish has to be recognized in order to be defended against? After all, not all instinctual wishes are repressed, so some sort of selection must occur. And I think we have to ascribe such a process of recognition and selection to the ego.

Anna Freud: I don't see any difficulty here, although evidently you do. But I'd like to correct one thing. You say I use the structural model in my book, but you know, I never know whether I use the structural or the topographical theory because I take from each what is useful. Does the conflict look so different when you look at it from the points of view of these two theories? But whatever way we use the theory, it has always contained the idea that there is constant movement in two directions in us. There is an upward movement toward consciousness, which implies the striving for satisfaction, whether in the id or in the unconscious—it does not matter which way you want to put it. On the other hand, there is a reaction from the unconscious ego to push down impulses or memories, or whatever, which are trying to rise up. We have to take both movements into account, and certainly my idea would be that there is a great sensitivity at the border. We don't take it for granted within the analytic process that the patient becomes anxious before material that we are trying to make conscious has really risen into consciousness. He feels it coming, and the resistance against it arises with it, and we take this as a sign that something is going to happen of which he is afraid. Of course, the anxiety really begins before full consciousness is reached, and this is, I think, what you have in mind.

Joseph Sandler: I suppose my thoughts about this are affected by an increasing realization of how important the system Preconscious or the unconscious ego is in mental functioning. The more we know about how the mind works, the more we see the extent to which there is unconscious functioning which uses secondary process. This unconscious activity is involved in the formation of derivatives of infantile wishes of all sorts, it forms and elaborates highly organized fantasies, and so on. I think we are much more aware nowadays of the role of the Preconscious or of the unconscious ego, both from a theoretical and a technical point of view. Earlier on, because the term "ego" referred so much to consciousness, or to the conscious self, the ego tended to be confused with consciousness. One even sees it in something you have said in this chapter, Miss Freud, namely, "Repression consists in the withholding or expulsion of an idea or affect from the conscious ego. It is meaningless to speak of repression where the ego is still merged with the id" (55,51). Isn't there a contradiction here, if you maintain that repression must occur ultimately at the border between ego and id? Would you agree that repression can also represent a holding back of a threatening impulse or wish at any point in its path through the ego or through the system Preconscious, a holding back that is directed against the wish, or whatever is associated with it, reaching consciousness?

Anna Freud: Yes. You introduce here the question of quantity. Something may come toward the border of consciousness, but because it is of low instinctual quantity it is not considered to be a danger until it is near consciousness. Whereas if it is highly cathected at that time, then it is a great danger, and is reacted to more quickly. We cannot think of these movements without taking into account the quantities involved.

Joseph Sandler: Is it not more than a quantitative question, Miss Freud? Isn't it as if the ego might say, "I will tolerate this as a preconscious thought, but I will not allow it into consciousness"? What I have in mind are such thoughts as those which patients have between sessions, thoughts that are repressed, presumably repressed in the same way as infantile material is. Can you say something about this?

Anna Freud: You know, children say it quite openly. They don't mind some things as long as they are not put into words, which really means put in secondary process terms. And they warn you, or they get furious, if you put it into words for them in the session. They get furious because the words arouse anxiety. But if the anxiety is only there on a vague level, they can tolerate it.

Joseph Sandler: What about repression in the forgetting of a name, for instance. Is it the same mechanism?

Anna Freud: It is a loss from consciousness, but into the Preconscious.

Joseph Sandler: Therefore, in the structural model, into the unconscious ego.

Anna Freud: Yes.

Joseph Sandler: I think that we should consider repression to be a defense mechanism that the ego uses outside consciousness like all the defense mechanisms, one which is applied in proportion to the threat the wish represents. If the threat is recognized very early on, as a dangerous oedipal wish, for example, then it might be repressed more or less as soon as it is recognized. Or it might be tolerated as part of unconscious thinking, or of unconscious fantasy life in the ego, but if it comes too near to consciousness, a pushing back occurs. The content may reemerge, and then there might be a re-repression and this could happen over and over again.

Anna Freud: There are some patients who are threatened all the time by a low but worrying amount of anxiety. I think they feel threatened because what should be quietly in the id, in the system Unconscious, rises all the time to be very near to consciousness. It isn't quite there, and we don't know why they feel so threatened. Of course, they are quite right to feel that at any moment something may break through. It is already at the door, and I suppose you would say it has become preconscious and near enough to consciousness to arouse anxiety but not near enough to be perceived.

Joseph Sandler: This would be an active holding back, but fairly late in the passage of the wish through the unconscious ego.

Anna Freud: Yes, but if in the person we are talking about there is a reaction formation, as in the obsessional, what he would do, quite instinctively and automatically, is to reinforce the reaction formation. He'd become more orderly or more clean or more slowed up, because he feels that the dam isn't quite strong enough. He says, "I must add another stone to it, perhaps it will then keep the flood back." Now this is certainly at a fairly high level of mental activity. We lose too much if we leave out the topographical view altogether.

Joseph Sandler: It seems that a great deal was gained with the structural theory, but the dynamic of the back and forth movement in the system Preconscious seemed somehow to be lost with the introduction of the concept of the ego as a structure.

Anna Freud: But it is lost only for the people who confine themselves to the structural theory. There's no need to.

Joseph Sandler: I don't think we need to say who they are.

Anna Freud: I'm reminded of the teacher at school who used to say, "I'll mention no names, I'm not pointing at anybody and it isn't even the person I'm looking at."

Joseph Sandler: Can we take up again, Miss Freud, the question of the massive repression that occurs before latency, and that results in the infantile amnesia? It seems clear that repression can be used again as a separate defense mechanism, although perhaps it doesn't have the same force later as it did early on. But there may be an exception in regard to traumatic experiences. One gets the same sort of massive repression if a trauma has occurred, the defense being against the revival of the traumatic experience. Perhaps the same massive repression also leads to hysterical fugue states or to other states which are equally gross.

Anna Freud: What you mention in regard to traumas or fugue states is really the operation of something different from repression. It is a failure of the ego to perceive, which is not quite the same as withdrawing attention from something.

Ilse Hellman: Not long ago I interviewed someone whose infantile amnesia extended to the age of eight. He said he really had no memories at all up to that age, and it became clear that if he had perceived what was happening around him this would have overthrown everything he wanted to hold on to. So he didn't perceive what was happening. The man he grew up with wasn't his father, as his own father had been killed before his birth. He was never told this as a child, but later realized that there were a number of signs that he must have perceived and understood. But he had no indication that he had noticed or observed the facts about his father, until someone told him purely by chance. That is the non-perception, I think.

Anna Freud: I once described a case that I analyzed many years ago where a whole year—it might have been two years—between the ages of about seven and eight, was absolutely blotted out from the memory of the patient, who otherwise had the normal childhood memories. The period was completely missing, as if it were a full childhood amnesia. What came out in her analysis afterward was that she had lost her father very early, and had built up a theory of her mother being forever faithful to the father. During those one or two years of her childhood the mother had a relationship with a man who lived with the family, and was a very good father to my patient. But this man represented someone who could destroy the idea of the mother's faithfulness to the father. It was a very fascinating case. It was quite clear why, in order to keep an ideal she had built up, she had to remove a whole section of her life, all the evidence, positive and negative. I suppose that if something like this happened later in life, it would be similar to a fugue state, wouldn't it? There would be the removal of conscious awareness of a whole part of one's life for a certain period.

Joseph Sandler: When we consider the mechanism of repression and also its relation to denial we run into a number of problems. Classically we regard the mechanism of denial as being simply the withdrawal of attention from something significant that for one reason or another is unwelcome. But you have pointed out, Miss Freud, that denial is really the failure of the ego to perceive, and that this is different. It looks as if from a clinical point of view we have to consider a whole range of "denials" in which any withdrawal of attention is reinforced by a counterforce, by a countercathexis, if you will. What I mean is that if denial were simply the withdrawal of attention, then it would be relatively easy to point out to the person concerned what he is denying and to get him to see it. But we know that there are people who strenuously avoid looking at something painful or threatening, and even though it may be pointed out, maintain the denial. This is usually in regard to something in the external world, and seems parallel to the process of repression, which we normally conceptualize as involving both the withdrawal of attention and the application of a counterforce. But, of course, we don't usually speak of repression in regard to the perception of something in the external world. Then we also have the so-called scotomization, in which something which would normally be seen is blotted out by a sort of blind spot. Some things are simply not seen. The person looks but he does not see, and this is somewhat different in quality from other forms of denial. And there is repression proper, which is usually conceived of as a sort of "horizontal" repression, in the sense that attention is withdrawn from some mental content, a counterforce applied, and the offending content kept down. But there is also what we might call a sort of "vertical" repression—some people would call it a split—in which one part of the person's life is kept completely separated from another. I do not think this is at all uncommon. I remember a patient who kept out of her analysis a full-fledged obsessional neurosis which was restricted to the bedroom. When finally I quite accidentally got a hint of this, and managed to pull it into the analysis against severe resistance, she reacted with rage, maintaining that this part of her life did not really belong to the analytic work. Her defense had the force of a repression, except that she was conscious of the warded-off part. In a sense she had separated her consciousness, her life, into two areas. In energic terms, we could say that there seem to be a number of ways in which countercathexis is applied, repression being the most important of these. I don't know whether you have any comment on this, Miss Freud.

Anna Freud: I remember a very lively discussion many, many years ago when the term "scotomization" was first introduced, because scotomization meant not seeing something that was there. If it was not seen it did not have to be repressed. Current theory was that certain things were repressed because they had been perceived. It is a way of keeping things out of consciousness, but in order to keep something out it has to be there first. If it isn't there at all, then we don't need to repress it! We'd call it denial now, I think.

Joseph Sandler: The problem has become more complicated nowadays because of the emphasis, in recent years, on unconscious awareness. This has perhaps been influenced by all the work on subliminal perception, and the knowledge that perceptual input is examined first in some unconscious way before being structured into a conscious percept. I think we would now tend to say that both scotomization and other forms of denial involve a recognition, but an unconscious recognition. And with denial we have the problem of whether we should regard it simply as a process whereby the unconscious ego pretends to consciousness that something isn't there, or as a much more active rejection of the perception. The whole area needs to be clarified.

Anna Freud: Because the original German term *Verleugnung* really means disavowal, it implies that you've seen it and then you say you haven't. You say it isn't there when you first had the impression it *is* there. Disavowal is a much better term than denial.

Joseph Sandler: A word about the chronology of defenses (54,50). It is clear that no one feels completely satisfied with the state of our knowledge about this. We could ask whether we should apply the notion of lines of development to defenses, rather than to maintain a view of them as separate units which come into being at particular times. I don't know why we have such difficulty with chronology. Is it that the little child cannot speak?

Anna Freud: I think we know a little more about it now than we knew at the time of the book. I remember I warned myself not to say more about it than I knew, which was very little. I suppose at that time it was not sufficiently brought into connection with structuralization. Nowadays we could probably say in much greater detail at what time every one of the defense mechanisms would have a chance to be used, because preparations for it have been made. You remember we said before that to speak of repression makes no sense before there is a division between conscious and unconscious ego, between ego and id, and so on. To speak of projection or externalization makes no sense before a differentiation between the inner and the outer world has been established, because if there is no outer world for the child, you can't assign anything to it. On the other hand the very fact that you can assign certain sensations or happenings to another place *creates* the distinction between inner and outer. I think we should ask what the preconditions are for the working of the various different mechanisms. Identification really makes no sense before the merging period is over, because then you and the object are one anyway, so why trouble to identify? You are already there!

Joseph Sandler: None of the mechanisms makes sense without the idea of displacement, which must be one of the very earliest mechanisms. For example, identification implies a displacement of a mental representation.

Anna Freud: Yes. I think that would be the way to go about it. But that is far further into the study of childhood reactions than we were then.

Joseph Sandler: As far as the chronology of defenses is concerned, I am not sure we are much further now.

Anna Freud: Only because we haven't used the knowledge that we have for this specific purpose.

Maria Berger: We are on uncertain ground when it comes to precursors of defense. There are so many things one is tempted to call precursors of defense, and the whole thing can become very complicated.

Joseph Sandler: One of the things we do need to straighten out is the whole concept of the precursor, because it may be that we are using the wrong concept. Perhaps we ought to be looking for "necessary conditions" instead, because there is a tendency for the precursor of a defense mechanism to become equated with the mechanism itself. But there is a question I would like to ask in regard to the development of repression. How is it that hysterical symptoms can occur in two-year-olds, as you have pointed out, Miss Freud? I have seen an hysterical paralysis of the arm in a child of two based on an identification with the mother who had a sprained wrist and had her arm in a sling.

Anna Freud: Yes, there is no doubt that hysterical symptoms can occur in children of two, especially leg and arm symptoms. But I think that what the symptoms make use of very much is the easy interchange between mind and body in the first year of life, in the psychosomatic world of early childhood. I think this serves as the earliest basis for hysterical symptoms where the symptom has meaning. But we have never collected knowledge in regard to this in any systematic way.

Joseph Sandler: Perhaps because we tend not to get such young children in the Clinic. I should now like to ask about the link which is so often made in the literature between the defense mechanisms and the vicissitudes of the drives. For example, parallels have been drawn between the expulsive and the retentive aspects of the anal drives, and the defense mechanisms that show some of these qualities. As a result, developmental links have been postulated between drive vicissitudes and defense mechanisms—projection linked with expulsion, and so on. I wonder if you would care to make any comment on this?

Anna Freud: Of course there are some defense mechanisms which grow out of primary process functioning. Displacement is a good example, and the turning of passive into active is another, where the opposites are really the same. There you can see the influence of the primary process. There are certain underlying models, shall we say, out of which the defense mechanisms can emerge. But I think that to equate projection with expulsion, as you describe, goes much too far. It destroys again the difference between id activity and ego activity, and by undoing the differences we don't get any further in clarification.

Joseph Sandler: I have a note here of some further questions. One refers to the degree to which defense mechanisms can be taken over through identification. If they can be taken over in this way, then which mechanisms are more easily taken over? In a family of deniers, for instance, how much of the use of denial would be based on identification?

Anna Freud: We can ask the same question about a family of obsessionals. On the one hand there are underlying similarities of personality between parents and children, and on the other certain basic characteristics can be taken over by imitation and identification, and out of that can grow similar defense mechanisms. But where defense mechanisms are really only taken over, first by imitation and then by identification, they are easily given up in analysis, because they are not the person's own.

Joseph Sandler: They must be very different qualitatively. But I suppose that there is a whole range of mechanisms that can be reinforced in a selective or differential way by other members of the family. These would then be mechanisms which actually belong in the first instance to the person concerned, but whose use would be greatly increased because of family support and reinforcement.

This sort of differential reinforcement wouldn't be identification.

Anna Freud: No.

Joseph Sandler: Do you still hold the view you expressed here, Miss Freud, that it is possible that "repression is preeminently of value in combating sexual wishes, while other methods can more readily be employed against instinctual forces of a different kind, in particular, against aggressive impulses"? (54–55,50–51).

Anna Freud: It was a speculation, because I wasn't too sure then whether repression could equally be used against aggressive impulses. We knew so much less about the ego's dealing with aggression than with libido. Certainly repression can equally be used against aggression.

Joseph Sandler: The point you make in this chapter is that possibly each defense mechanism is first evolved in order to master some specific instinctual urge. Do you think one could say that it is evolved during a particular phase when a specific drive dominates the picture? It might otherwise sound as if you postulate a special link between the mechanism and the partial instinctual drive, and I don't think you meant that.

Anna Freud: I think I meant it as an open question. There are periods of life when particular instincts are dominant, and therefore also special dangers and special tasks of mastery for the ego. This certainly makes a link between the two. I think I also thought at that time that the obsessional defenses were particularly directed against anal sadism, either against the anality or the special sadistic qualities of that period. Don't we say this now too?

Alex Holder: The question of the extent to which the use of a defense is dependent on ego development is still an open one. Is it just a coincidence that certain defense mechanisms are used against anal drives and others against oral drives, simply because the ego is in a particular phase of development?

Anna Freud: Hartmann has always made this point. He pointed out that obsessional defenses are very often in use at a time of life before the battle against anality has begun at all, because in ego development they are present in order to master certain thought processes. So what you say is certainly there as well.

Vann Spruiell: I should like to ask whether there is any pleasure gained from defense mechanisms. Can some defenses be traced back to pleasurable activities?

Anna Freud: Is there ever pleasure in the defense mechanisms? Only in the result, I think.

Joseph Sandler: Perhaps there may be a so-called function pleasure and a feeling of relief, which is a most powerful reinforcing agent. But this is of course not the same as a sensual pleasure. Possibly the pleasure in mastery might come into it, but again this is of a different quality. What we can be certain of is that we can take pleasure in celebrating the end of our long discussion of this chapter.

CHAPTER **5**

Orientation of the
Processes of Defense
According to the Source of
Anxiety and Danger

Anna Freud introduces the fifth chapter with the sentence: "The instinctual dangers against which the ego defends itself are always the same, but its reasons for feeling a particular irruption of instinct to be dangerous may vary" (58,54). The first of the motives for defense against the drives is *superego anxiety*. This forms the basis of neurosis in adults. An instinctual wish seeks to come into consciousness and be gratified. The ego would assist it, but the superego protests. Because of this the ego turns against the instinctual impulse, its motive being fear of the superego.

The defense against instinct seen in adult neurotics

shows how the superego prevents the ego's coming to terms with the drives and how it is the main cause of neurosis. It builds up an ideal in which sexuality and aggression are condemned. The sexual and aggressive restrictions imposed deprive the ego of its independence and capacity for enjoyment. As a result, analysis of the superego, with the aim of reducing its harshness, plays an important part in the therapy of neurosis.

There are some who hope that by appropriate education of the child a gentler superego may be formed and neurosis prevented. This view holds that the parents should set an example of tolerance toward the drives and give up their overstrict moral code. The child's aggressiveness should find an expression externally, so that it does not have to be turned inward through a cruel superego. But, from a practical and theoretical point of view, the hope that neurosis might be prevented in this way is false.

Anna Freud draws attention to *objective anxiety* as an important factor in the infantile neurosis. While adult neurotics have superego anxiety as a motive for defense, small children defend against their drive impulses in order to obey their parents. The fear of castration yields the same result as superego anxiety. But the outside world is the source of the child's fear.

This fear causes the development of the same symptoms as can be seen in adults as a result of superego anxiety. Knowing this leads us to an understanding that in neurosis it is the anxiety which starts the defensive process, irrespective of the origin of that anxiety. The symptoms which develop do not indicate the sort of anxiety that caused them. From the point of view of objective anxiety as a motive for defense, there might be some hope that neurosis can be prevented by reducing the sources of objective anxiety, by not threatening punishments or anything reminiscent of castration, and by allowing the child's instincts to be gratified. But such an educational hope of eradicating infantile neurosis is also doomed to failure, because of the existence of the third motive for defense against the drives, namely, *instinctual anxiety*. As the ego develops, its original friendliness to the drives diminishes, and it becomes "alien territory to the instincts" (63,59). If instinctual demands become excessive, or if the ego feels itself abandoned by the superego or the outside world, its hostility to the drives as a source of anxiety is increased. The ego fears that it may be overwhelmed, defense mechanisms are brought into play, and neurosis results.

Anna Freud then adds the ego's need for synthesis to the three motives for defense against instinct. The ego's harmony is destroyed by conflict between opposite tendencies such as homosexuality and heterosexuality. She then goes on to speak about the motives for defense against *affects*. In the same way as the ego is prompted to defend against the drives, it also defends against the affects associated with the drives. It is enough that an affect be connected with a prohibited instinctual wish for the ego to defend itself against experiencing it. But there is a further relation between affects and the ego, one determined by the pleasure principle. The ego welcomes pleasure and will be more ready to defend against unpleasant affects such as pain, longing, and mourning than against pleasurable ones.

In analytic practice the reversal of a defensive process

allows the factors that contribute to it to be seen, including the instinctual impulse and the motive which stimulated the defense. As a result of analysis the id derivative, previously defended against, enters the ego, accompanied by the affect which prompted the defense.

The therapeutic implications of these ideas are now clear. By the analyst reversing the defense the instinctual impulse or affect is allowed into consciousness, and the ego and superego can reach a better solution. The outlook is best when the motive for defense has been superego anxiety, especially if the identifications behind the superego have become accessible to analysis. When the defense is motivated by objective anxiety in the child, analytic therapy also has good prospects. Having reversed the defenses in the child's mind, the therapist can then try to influence reality so that the objective anxiety is diminished. Alternatively, the objective anxiety may be shown to be based on the memories of past experiences or on fantasy distortions, and can be "unmasked" by analysis (69,64).

If the motive for defense is to avoid pain or unpleasure, the child has also to learn to tolerate increased amounts of unpleasure without invoking his defense mechanisms, but this is more the work of education than of analysis.

Where the defense is a reaction to the patient's fear of the strength of his drives, there is a danger that the defensive measures may be done away with without our being able to help the patient's ego. In that case, there may not be a favorable reaction to analysis. Normally we reassure the patient that his drive impulses are more controllable when conscious, but this may be an illusion in those cases where the main motive for defense is the fear of the strength of instincts. An analysis can strengthen the ego by making unconscious drives conscious, but it may weaken it by immobilizing the defensive processes by disclosing them, and this may then "advance the pathological process" (70,65).

The Discussion

Session one

Joseph Sandler: It is clear, Miss Freud, that when you speak of superego anxiety you refer to anxiety caused by superego introjects, rather than an anxiety that is somehow within the superego itself. It is an anxiety the ego experiences in relation to its superego. I mention this only because some people are not clear on this point.

Anna Freud: Yes, you are right.

Joseph Sandler: We tend to talk of the instinctual wish obtaining gratification through reaching consciousness, and there is a relative neglect of motility, of the behavioral aspect. Ought we not say that an instinctual wish, in pressing forward for gratification, moves not only toward consciousness, but simultaneously forward to motility and action? Or is there an implication that one has the thought first and then secondarily acts on it?

Anna Freud: No. The idea here is that motility is under the control of the ego, and perhaps I should have distinguished between the instinctual wish which presses upward and overruns the ego, going straight into action, motility and fulfillment, and, shall we say, the tamer wish which knows that the safe way to obtain gratification is to enlist the cooperation of the ego. The ego then controls motility, puts it at the service of the wish, and in this way achieves gratification.

Joseph Sandler: Perhaps at the time you wrote the book, the distinction between the ego and consciousness was not made as rigorously as today, and the role of the unconscious ego was not given as much importance.

You speak in this chapter, Miss Freud, of the superego protesting, and I should like to ask whether you think that it is the superego which actually protests, or is it rather that the "protest" is a way of referring to the ego's anticipation that it is going to be punished from some internal or internalized source? Perhaps referring to the superego protesting is simply a useful way of speaking.

Anna Freud: It's a way of speaking, because the idea is that if the notion of protest were not included in the superego, the protest wouldn't happen. So saying that the superego protests is a shorthand way of saying that the ego feels that this disapproval would come from the superego.

Joseph Sandler: This brings up the whole question of whether the superego itself should be regarded as an active agency, or rather as a set of beliefs and images and memories organized in a particular way so that it functions as a frame of reference for the ego, one which leads the ego to think, in certain circumstances, "If I do this

I will be punished, or lose love, or some other sanction will be applied."

Anna Freud: It's good that you remark on this because it shows how history has to be taken into account. At the time of the book much more activity was ascribed to the superego than now. We have shifted the active moves to the ego, and see the superego much more as a set of notions, as you have said just now. You know, that was also the time in analysis when certain people advocated smashing the superego. They had the idea that one had to remove the superego of the patient, and only then would he feel comfortable. I never shared that idea.

Joseph Sandler: I should like to take up the point you make about the ideal standard set up by the superego (59,55). On the whole you have followed Freud in emphasizing the aggressive aspects of the superego, and the compliance it demands. I wonder if you would care to comment on the feeling of security provided by the superego, which is more in the picture nowadays. What I mean is that the superego can also be seen as being like a parent standing behind the child who encourages him, saying, "What you are doing is right, I approve of it." The emphasis in the chapter tends to be on the superego as critical conscience, but I think it can also be an internal encouraging parental substitute.

Anna Freud: But that wouldn't have fitted into this chapter, because I was concerned with showing the superego as providing a motive for defense in that it arouses anxiety. But you are quite right to comment on the missing aspect because each little section of the chapter refers only to one particular idea. You know, there were also people at that time who regarded all anxiety as anxiety caused by conflict with the superego, and in the first part of this chapter I follow that idea and try to show that the superego is by no means the only source of anxiety. I want to say, "Let us look at other possibilities."

Joseph Sandler: I don't think you anticipated at the time how closely the text might be examined!

Anna Freud: No, I really meant it to be a discussion. I remember that the idea of objective anxiety wasn't at all well regarded at the time. The idea that fear of the external world could, at any time of life, cause similar results as the fear of internal agencies, was a more or less heretical revolutionary idea.

Joseph Sandler: May I ask you about superego severity? How do you see the modification of the strict superego through analysis? I imagine that you don't agree with people like James Strachey, for example, who suggested that all therapeutic success depends entirely on superego modification. Nevertheless, we all believe that it is to some degree through a modification of the severity of the superego that the neurotic conflict comes to be diminished. How do you see this coming about? Is it a modification of the superego introjects, or is it a modification of the ego's anxiety about the dangers which the superego represents? To put it another way: is the voice of conscience lessened, or is it that the ego doesn't pay so much attention to the voice of conscience? After all, in our therapeutic work we direct ourselves toward the ego, and my own impression is that gradually one begins not to hear the irrational prohibitions against infantile wishes so loudly, so to speak, because one gets them into perspective. The change occurs in the ego rather than in the superego introjects. But we still call this a lessening of superego severity, and I wonder if you have any thoughts about this.

Anna Freud: I think that in large part the so-called superego change comes about because of the analysis of aggression. After all, we ascribe the severity of the superego to a turning of aggression away from the external world, and attaching it to the inner world, so that the aggression is then used by the superego against the ego. If, in the analysis, the course of the aggression is changed again, and what belongs to the outer world is directed there again and freed, I think that in itself lessens the severity of the superego very much. And, of course, there is the differentiation that one establishes in analysis between the past and the present. What is considered a sin in infancy is insignificant in adult life, and so on. Also, with advancing age, the wishes in themselves become less dangerous. You know the story of the rider and the horse—well, Grete Bibring once said that it's not only the rider who gets older, but also the horse.

Joseph Sandler: Yes, but one wonders why the superego doesn't get less severe with age—at least, I haven't noticed it yet.

Anna Freud: You have to wait.

Joseph Sandler: You think there's some hope? I'm very happy to hear that.

There is a question about the relation of aggression turned against the self and the superego. We are all familiar with Freud's view that the superego extends deeply into the id, and that the instinctual aggression gets deflected back against the ego via the superego. What I wonder about is how we integrate this with the observation that the introjects do not actually duplicate the real parents, but contain projections which have occurred before the process of superego introjection has taken place. I mean here projections of the child's own aggressive wishes, so that there are attacking or persecuting figures in fantasy, figures which are now vehicles of the child's aggression, and which clearly later enter into his superego. As a consequence, very kind parents may bring about a severe superego because the child pushes his aggression down in order to protect his relationship to his kind and loving parents. What puzzles me is that although this makes sense from a developmental point of view, can we be sure that the person's *current* aggressive wishes are directed back through the superego against the self ? Does the superego become more strict at points in time when the person's unconscious aggressive impulses are greater? I mean that if the superego is built upon aggression turned inward, is it more severe in later life whenever more aggression is aroused? Is it not the case that if a person has developed a hostile, critical, and punitive superego, it will remain consistently severe, creating a high degree of superego anxiety, even if the person is not threatened at the time by an aggressive wish? What happens when the threat arises from a libidinal wish? How does one resolve this problem?

Anna Freud: I would think that by analyzing the history of the superego, by calling it back into consciousness, one shakes its foundations. As you know, the kindness of the parents who appear as monsters in the child's fantasy, and who become the child's strict superego, makes it so difficult for the child to feel aggressive toward them. Partly this is because of the conflict of ambivalence, partly because it seems to the child to be irrational. But, whatever the cause, the parents block the outlet for the child's aggression toward them. Now, if in the unfolding of the infantile history it can be shown how much aggression really went toward these nice parents, and how the child not only loved them, but hated them and wished them dead, and revolted against them, and fought against them, then this shakes the whole superstructure.

Joseph Sandler: I suppose that there is no real problem if we say that through insight the patient becomes aware that the unconscious inner voices (if one can use such a term), which sound so critical, represent externalized aspects of the patient's own aggressive self. And this comes into the analysis as it is revived through regression and appears in the transference, so it can be analyzed in the present even though it belongs to the past.

Anna Freud: Yes, but I think that we could even illustrate what happens with an example that doesn't return to childhood at all. We know that even outside analysis, let us say in a normal unanalyzed person's life, a very strong guilt feeling may disappear when the person realizes that he is really very angry. Through this release of anger against somebody, the guilt decreases. In answer to your question about the relation of aggression to the superego after childhood, I believe that even later in life this communication between guilt, which is fear of the superego, and anger, or restriction of freedom of aggression, remains. And, on the other hand, people often use an attack on someone else to relieve themselves of intolerable feelings of guilt. This is certainly a very widespread method. One often says to patients, "I don't think you are as angry as all that. You feel bad about something you have done yourself." This means that attacking an outside person communicates in some way with the attack of the superego on the ego.

Joseph Sandler: As you say, Miss Freud, one sees this mechanism very often, but I wonder if one could not describe it in a different way. Someone feels guilty, and then externalizes the "bad" aspect of himself onto another person. Through this he identifies with his own superego introject, not only gaining a good feeling through having got rid of the crime he feels guilty about, but also getting an enormous feeling of virtue through the identification with his superego. There is a double gain. Sometimes we see this in extreme form in the aggressive behavior of extremely guilty children, or in children who feel intense or even what I call "catastrophic" shame. The guilty or shameful aspect of the self is displaced onto someone else, and then there is something like identification with the aggressor, that is with the aggressive superego, resulting in a great deal of reassurance and satisfaction. I think we know nowadays that not all impulsive behavior (as in the so-called impulse-ridden character) derives from weak control of the drives by the ego.

Anna Freud: Well, take a very simple example. You've given a very bad lecture. The audience wasn't attentive, they've coughed, they've sneezed and whispered to each other, and you have the terrible feeling that you haven't come up to your own expectations, that you've said stupid things. You've stumbled over words and you feel terribly guilty; you haven't prepared yourself well. What an enormous relief to have the realization that the people there were just stupid. Suddenly you are whitewashed, and the whole guilt is spent through the attack on the other people. I think this is the child's usual way of defending himself, but it is also a way we adults have.

Joseph Sandler: It doesn't work as well in adult life as in childhood.

Anna Freud: It works quite well. It is, of course, what we call self-righteousness, which so often hides guilt feelings. All of this is part of the everyday behavior of people.

Joseph Sandler: Do you want to comment now on the use of the term "objective anxiety," Miss Freud?

Anna Freud: It is *Realangst* in German, which means fear of the external world. It means justified fear. Probably that is why it has been translated as objective anxiety. It means that there really is some danger existing in the external world.

Joseph Sandler: Here again, as with superego anxiety, you are talking of the source of the anxiety, and if I understand you correctly you do not mean that the anxiety has any sort of special quality. The increasing emphasis on the experiential world of the child, as opposed to the real world which exists outside his experience, and our better knowledge about how perception is distorted by memory and fantasy, puts us on shaky ground nowadays when we talk about real anxiety, so we have to be careful. Obviously you mean something very different here, Miss Freud, from an anxiety which has its source in neurotic conflict or in something that is linked with a fantasied danger from the past. But what about the case of the child who has an anxiety because he's been traumatized, let us say, or frightened by something he didn't understand? Then for him the real world *is* frightening, although from our adult, reasonable point of view it isn't. Is his anxiety objective? Do you mean by objective anxiety that the source of the anxiety is understood by the child as being the external world? If so, we might get into trouble when we consider phobic anxieties, or other anxieties imputed by the child to the external world, which then seem to him to be objective.

Anna Freud: At the time my idea was much simpler than that. I was really thinking of the fear of loss of love or of the fear of loss of the object, or of castration fear, before these have become internalized. It's really turning the wheel back from the internalized dangers to their sources.

Joseph Sandler: Let us consider castration anxiety for a moment. In this chapter you suggest that some echoes of more primitive anxiety are aroused by what actually happens in the real world—if we think of books like *Struwelpeter* there is plenty of evidence that there is enough in the external world to arouse castration anxiety in the child. Yet we also know that castration anxiety is so often stimulated by the child's own sadistic wishes, and his own wishes to castrate the father, which he projects and experiences as a threat according to the talion principle. The more he would like to castrate his father the more afraid he is that he will be castrated. Perhaps you would restrict objective anxiety, the reality anxiety, to things the child would reasonably, within his own mind, taking the state of his ego and of his knowledge into account, consider as belonging to the external world.

Anna Freud: Attribute to the external world, yes.

Joseph Sandler: Well, "attributing" might include projecting, and I was trying to get out of that problem, because projection starts much earlier than superego internalization.

Hansi Kennedy: Would objective anxiety be the anxiety aroused when the little boy sees a little girl without a penis, for example?

Anna Freud: Yes, that would be an example, because

there is the realization that the genitals can actually look like that, which means to the little boy that castration can actually happen. You wouldn't call that objective (I never used the word objective myself, but I was translated this way), but for the child the perception is a fact of the external world.

Joseph Sandler: That puts it very clearly.

Ilse Hellman: The way I usually think of it is that the perception of reality confirms the child's fantasies and fears, which are based on projection. It seems to me that objective anxiety refers to the anxiety aroused by confirmatory real things, such as the little girl without a penis, or a really threatening mother. But are these things the real originators of the anxiety? We wouldn't think in those terms today.

Joseph Sandler: I'm not sure that Miss Freud would agree with you here.

Anna Freud: You know, the fear of loss of love is certainly for the child real anxiety. He realizes that "this can really happen."

Ilse Hellman: You mean, when mother shows anger toward him?

Anna Freud: Exactly. It's no more than that. You mustn't forget that by the time we analyze the person all this has been overlaid. We don't really meet *Realangst* anymore in adults. It is a preparatory phase for anxiety about something internalized. And, anyway, castration anxiety isn't the best example, because castration anxiety is at its worst when structuralization has already taken place. Here I speak of earlier phases.

Hansi Kennedy: I always understood castration anxiety as being related to the sort of chance observation of the different genitals of a child of the opposite sex. Such an observation lays the foundation for the type of anxiety experienced later in phallic conflicts. This means that the element of the anxiety that would enter into the development of the "real" anxiety or the objective anxiety could enter at quite a different time.

Joseph Sandler: Aren't we talking of a number of different things? A trauma is something we know can be aroused by the intensity of external circumstances leading to the person being overwhelmed. But we also know that children seek out their traumas, as Abraham pointed out many years ago, when he wrote about the experiencing of sexual seductions as a form of sexual activity. So the particular preoccupations of the child will determine the significance of the child's observation of reality, or of his understanding of the memory of that observation. Also the child regards as facts things seen but interpreted in his own particular idiosyncratic way. There might be a problem with Dr. Hellman's formulation, in that one could push it to the notion of fantasies being first and reality second, which is not at all what I understood Miss Freud to mean. There is a risk that one might get into the position that everything starts with fantasies, and that reality experience is secondary. On the other hand, we may have a chicken and egg problem here, because of the interaction between fantasy and reality. But I think that none of us has any doubt that real experiences can have a very profound effect. I have a patient who, at the age of five, was present at his new brother's circumcision. Whatever his fantasies of castration were, they really paled beside the actual experience of seeing what was for him the penis being cut off, with all the blood, and so on. After that his castration fantasies played a much more significant role in his life. But it is, of course, very likely that what he saw would have had no significance for him if he had not been in a phase in which his penis was so very important to him.

In this chapter, Miss Freud, when speaking of the role of anxiety in the development of neurotic symptoms, you suggest that "in the formation of neurosis it seems to be a matter of indifference to what that anxiety relates" (61,57). Do you mean that the form of the neurosis is the same whatever the source of anxiety, or that in the development of a neurosis the ego really isn't concerned with the source of anxiety? These seem to be two different things.

Anna Freud: What I meant was that the formation of a neurosis starts with the anxiety, from whatever source it arises, because the defense is directed against that anxiety. But you know there is a much more important question behind this little section of the chapter, a question I tried to pursue again very many years later. I mean that the first clashes in the child's life are between the instinctual wishes and impulses on the one hand, and the frustrating agencies and powers in the external world, on the other. And only later does this become an internalized process and an internalized conflict. This idea is really foreshadowed here.

Joseph Sandler: Are you using the idea of neurosis here in the sense of the neurotic formations which occur after, say, five years of age, or do you include earlier infantile childhood disturbances as well, disturbances which do not have the classic neurotic structure?

Anna Freud: Of course we didn't know very much about those disturbances at that time. What was meant here is that the structural development of the individual neurosis begins with the arousal of the danger and the anxiety, and as a consequence, the wish to get rid of the anxiety. This then arouses the defense and the regression that occurs to avoid the new conflict on the new level; and in turn there is the compromise formation which leads to symptoms. This is what I understood by the development of the neurosis, the *Neurosenbildung*. For that process the existence of the anxiety is the main starting point, not where it comes from.

Joseph Sandler: Even though the particular anxiety and its source will affect the content of the neurosis, and the particular defenses used?

Anna Freud: Yes, of course.

Joseph Sandler: I wonder whether you would care to comment, Miss Freud, on how it is that the little girl who has never seen a penis, whose parents have never shown themselves to her naked, who has no brother, who didn't go to the modern sort of nursery school where it is possible to peep into the lavatory, and so on, will still, in the phallic phase, run around with a broomstick between her legs and do the "phallic" things which we take to show penis envy. Freud thought of inborn or inherited fantasies or memories, but I think one still has to ask where this knowledge comes from.

Anna Freud: We used to wonder in the Hampstead Nurseries why children who have never witnessed adult intercourse, where there was no primal scene because there were no parents, still made intercourse movements. You would find the little boy lying on a little girl, acting out a primal scene. Where did he learn it? Possibly from animals.

Maria Berger: But was it then a primal scene for him?

Anna Freud: No, for us. For him it was a wish for sexually exciting release.

Ilse Hellman: I suppose that if little boys get sexually aroused and have erections, irrespective of whether they have parents or not, they experience a sensation which in turn leads to an urge to *penetrate*.

Joseph Sandler: It looks as if there is a biologically based urge which takes over, and which the child may rationalize into something else if it needs to.

Anna Freud: I remember that it was quite surprisingly impressive in the Nurseries.

Joseph Sandler: Perhaps it's a little different when we turn to castration anxiety, because that is such a specific fear. One has to ask why it is so ubiquitous.

Anna Freud: Yes.

Joseph Sandler: If we move now to instinctual anxiety—the dread of the strength of the instincts (63,58)—a problem comes up of whether we should distinguish between the fear of being traumatically overwhelmed and the fear of giving in to impulses without being able to control them. Perhaps the two are the same.

Anna Freud: You know, the idea I put forward wasn't popular at all at the time—I mean the idea of the ego's concern for its own intactness. And what wasn't popular either was the idea that the ego as such is hostile territory to the impulses and drives. But that was very much my idea there.

Joseph Sandler: Although we have discussed this before, in Chapter 1, it would be interesting to pursue the question again of whether this is an innate hostility of the ego or whether it is something secondary to the need of the ego to protect its own integrity and its feeling of being in control. This last would cause the ego to regard anything unexpected or so powerful as to be potentially overwhelming, whether from drive sources or not, as a threat. I think that you are very often misunderstood in this connection, Miss Freud, and perhaps you would like to clarify whether or not you take the view that there is a basically hostile attitude of the ego, hostile on principle, so to speak, toward the drives. It is different if we say that the ego feels that the drive represents a specific threat which would overwhelm the ego if it were to submit to it.

Anna Freud: You know, secondary process functioning in a sense threatens the unhindered road to gratification. What happens in the secondary process is that thought is put between impulse and action. Well, from the point of view of the impulse that is an impediment. It is so much easier for the instinct to reach its aim when there's no thought. The thought can only delay it, and if the ego looks at the consequences and weighs up whether the result would be good or bad, from the point of view of the external world and the superego, then we get a slowing up, an arresting of the impulse. But what the impulse wants is to break through and fulfill itself.

Hansi Kennedy: Doesn't the impulse need many aspects of the ego to collaborate with it in order to achieve this?

Anna Freud: That is a different aspect. To be safe and to avoid dangerous consequences the impulse would need the collaboration of the ego, but the impulse itself doesn't really care. What it needs is motility and gratification. It needs to get hold of motility, but not of all the secondary process thinking which later goes with the ego control of motility. You know, the crime of passion, as it is called, is an action committed without benefit of ego activity. The term means that the passion, the impulse, is of such magnitude that every other consideration apart from its immediate fulfillment is disregarded.

That is what I meant, but people never understood that. They thought that my reference to the ego's innate hostility to the drives has some moral aspect, but there is no moral aspect in this at all. There is a very simple example that one constantly meets in analysis, when one sees, for instance, how thinking hinders orgasm in intercourse. That is not the moment to think, it is not the place to think, and so far as the impulse is concerned thinking is quite superfluous.

Joseph Sandler: Then the functioning of the one system and the functioning of the other do not have the same aims or the same interests.

Anna Freud: This is one of the difficulties, namely that the various areas of the personality pursue quite different aims. Naturally, for harmonious functioning we like them to get together and to find the best way for peaceful coexistence. Sometimes they do, but very often they don't.

Joseph Sandler: Would you say whether it is a correct understanding that the ego doesn't mind instinctual wishes as long as they behave themselves and don't cause trouble? What has been read into the idea of the hostility of the ego is that *in general* the ego is not sympathetic toward the fulfillment of instinctual aims. But I think you have made it very clear that the ego will go along with these aims so long as they do not constitute a threat.

Anna Freud: Yes. And you can also put it the other way round. The impulse doesn't mind the ego, is not hostile to the ego, so long as the ego contents itself with helping the impulse. But the moment the ego becomes an obstacle and a hindrance there is hostility between the two.

Session two

Joseph Sandler: Last time we discussed the question of the ego's fear of the instincts, and whether this reflected an innate hostility to the drives. Certainly we can see a sort of cautious attitude on the part of the ego toward anything that has a thrusting or peremptory quality from the side of the drives, because of the ego's fear that it might be overthrown before it has time to examine whether the impulse is overwhelming or not. There is a sort of guardedness against assault, so to speak. The ego wants to see what is going on before cooperating with demands made on it. Do you want to add to that, Miss Freud?

Anna Freud: Well, I suppose what one could add is that what is felt is not always dread on the part of the ego. There is sometimes a feeling of relaxation, of comfort, when the ego can let go and let the id take over, as for example at the beginning of sleep. I remember that at the time there was a novel in German that attracted quite a lot of attention. It was called *Holidays from the Ego*. It had nothing to do with psychoanalysis, but described a kind of sanatorium where people went to have a holiday from the ego. It was a very comforting place, because the discarding of the secondary process, and whatever comes into the ego from the side of the superego, as well as all the other demands for delay, were, well, on holiday. So one can look at it from two sides.

Joseph Sandler: You raise an important point here, Miss Freud, that the ego structures and functions can be put aside temporarily without damage, provided that certain reassurances are given from outside.

Anna Freud: Reassurances that one can put them back in place again.

Joseph Sandler: So under certain circumstances there is a license to regress, from the side of the ego.

Anna Freud: Of course, daydream fantasy provides special conditions for the ego, because although it keeps to the secondary process, in so many ways it approaches the primary process and permits the instinctual demands.

Joseph Sandler: But there's still a censorship.

Anna Freud: There is still a censorship.

Ilse Hellman: The difference is that the ego has an awareness of its control over the ending of the daydream. So the fear of loss of control is lessened.

Joseph Sandler: The daydream fantasy also has the stamp of unreality. It is known to be imagination, so it can be differentiated from reality.

Anna Freud: We have heard a lot about orgies lately. The orgy is, after all, a voluntary throwing off of the ego's controls which is not accompanied by anxiety. We know that some experiences with drugs may be similar.

Joseph Sandler: You mean because they put the ego's controls out of action?

Anna Freud: And it is done with a great feeling of relief and no anxiety, unless the whole thing goes so far that anxiety has to be aroused. Perhaps we can put together alcoholism, drug-taking, and the orgy as examples to show that what is aroused by the ego's relaxation of controls can be a pleasurable feeling and not anxiety.

Ilse Hellman: One shouldn't generalize about this. I think that what happens is that there is a conscious decision to enter into things, but what happens does often in fact lead to anxiety and panic. We see this sometimes with people who take LSD. The experience of being out of control can become very frightening at a certain point.

Joseph Sandler: This whole area has been opened up around the question of the ego's hostility to the id. Clearly there seem to be states in which any such hostility disappears. Perhaps it is only the need to adhere to the reality principle that forces one to keep oneself in control, to retain the feeling that one is functioning at a higher level. Perhaps such a need to preserve the ego's functioning creates what looks like an innate reserve or apprehension on the part of the ego about instinctual demands. Would that fit the case? It does seem that if we knock out certain of the ego institutions, under special conditions, the ego can quite happily go along with the id, as in early infancy.

Anna Freud: But it then loses most of its characteristics, and that is quite a price to pay.

Joseph Sandler: Perhaps one could say that ego and id function then as a joint apparatus, a combined system.

Anna Freud: With the id in control, not the ego. Then the whole question arises of whether the id has control of motility or of the thought processes. It is a very interesting area to study, and it is not considered at all in the book.

Joseph Sandler: A friend of mine had an interesting experience which might be relevant. He used some mushrooms from his garden to prepare a meal, but the mushrooms weren't ordinary mushrooms and contained some hallucinogenic substance. The whole family started to hallucinate. My friend had the most acute anxiety attack, brought on particularly by the wish he had to fling his arms round the neck of the physician who was attending him in the hospital, to give him a big kiss. This aroused acute homosexual anxiety, and he was in quite a panic. This is quite different from the person who knows he has taken LSD, has someone with him to guide him, who is voluntarily suspending control and feels in a safe situation. It again points in the direction of the ego being willing, but only under certain conditions, to give the id control, as you would say, without there being any evidence of hostility to the drives.

Anna Freud: Yes. You know, perhaps "innate hostility" is not the best description, because it puts everything onto the ego. If we were to say that the ego is alien territory for the id, this would be much better. The id then feels uncomfortable in ego territory, because the conditions are not what it really wants.

Joseph Sandler: I have to wonder how the id can feel uncomfortable if the ego is doing the feeling!

Anna Freud: Well, if you imagine some wish entering the ego from the id, with the one purpose of finding satisfaction, because that is in its nature, and if you personify things a bit to make them simple, it is the ego that says, "Wait a little, let us think first what the outcome will be. Perhaps it isn't really very wise to get that fulfillment." Well, if we still personify, the wish would feel, "What has that to do with me? I know what I want." The id wish would feel very uncomfortable in the ego because it is in alien territory. If we give the id a voice, it would say that all it wants is discharge. And then it's held up, it's admonished and told to do what is not in its nature to do, namely to consider the consequences.

Joseph Sandler: Perhaps you mean, Miss Freud, that it *ought* to feel uncomfortable!

Anna Freud: Well, if it *could* feel, it would feel uncomfortable. If you personify both, you would talk of their relation to each other.

Joseph Sandler: Of course, while it is useful to personify ego, id, and superego, this does create a number of problems. For example, there is the question touched on before of whether it is the id or the ego which feels the pleasure if the ego assists the id to gain gratification. We might spend hours arguing about that, getting nowhere if we forget that id and ego are only theoretical concepts referring to different aspects of the functioning of the whole mental apparatus. But if we remember that we *are* referring to concepts, then it is very useful to personify. So we can then speak, for example, of the hostility of the ego to the id being balanced by the idea of the ego's innate friendliness to the id, prompting it to find appropriate and satisfying vehicles for discharge of instinctual wishes. We could then say that the id can give the ego a lot of pleasure! On top of this there are, of course, all the nonsensual pleasures which the ego derives from its effective functioning.

Anna Freud: Yes. Of course, when ego and id work in harmony it is difficult to say what part of the pleasure belongs to the ego and what part to the id, because they all blend together.

Robert L. Tyson: I have a question about the developmental aspect of instinctual anxiety. It seems to be an anxiety that can arise only after some development of ego structure, and I wonder whether it can be experi-

enced as anxiety very early in life by the infant, as the
first structures of the ego are being built up.

Anna Freud: I think the situation is different before and
after what we can call a character has been formed. Character is a more or less permanent balance between, let
us say, id and ego, with a balance between the quantities
involved, and with a more or less permanent mode of
relating to each other. Then anything that upsets this
balance—a weakening of the one or a strengthening of
the other, for instance—would arouse anxiety and discomfort. On the other hand, before the establishment
of this character there is probably a greater tendency for
what goes on to be altered. If you look at the very small
child, at one moment the id wishes may be in ascen-
dancy, and the ego has very little to say. On another day
the ego may be rather strict in controlling the instinctual
impulses. The situation shifts until a permanent and habitual way of finding a balance between the various agencies has developed.

Maria Berger: Can one not say that there is in the ego
a need to regulate not only the instinctual strivings but
also the affects? One sees children so often who have
strong defenses against sad feelings, and when these are
analyzed one sees the fear of crying, a fear of dissolving
into tears.

Anna Freud: There can be defenses which prevent affects
reaching a particular level of experience. But here again
we have the same contradiction we discussed before. For
most individuals there is also a pleasure in delivering

themselves to an overwhelming emotion, whether the emotion is pleasurable or not. So you have both aspects. Too much may be frightening, but there is also a relief in letting go of control. We often say that it is a relief if a person can begin to cry when he is really sad. It can also be a relief to laugh. The affect takes over.

Maria Berger: Thinking back to your remarks about the orgy, Miss Freud, isn't there a point at which some people would become afraid of madness?

Anna Freud: This would depend on the individual. What has always interested me very much is that in some ways the person worst off at an orgy is the onlooker, who doesn't share the orgy. While the people involved get drunk, or are under the influence of a drug, the onlooker is not. So from the point of view of his intact functioning ego he looks at the loss of ego control in others, and that can be very frightening and very uncomfortable. For the people involved in the orgy, certainly a private fear of madness might be aroused if it is there. But such people would in any case probably be very reluctant to enter into orgiastic pleasures.

Joseph Sandler: I think we may be talking about different sorts of orgy. Nowadays people usually think of sexual orgies, and there the madness may not be so much the threat as the temptation to perversion. The onlooker may also enjoy the situation, from a voyeuristic point of view, more than he might as a participant. It seems to me that different sorts of danger are involved, and that different people have different fears about letting go.

Ilse Hellman: We have not talked about the orgasm, and the difficulties patients have in experiencing it. We can learn a great deal from them. We all know the woman patient who has to count a pattern on the ceiling in order not to be carried away by sexual excitement.

Sara Rosenfeld: When we talk about adults who fear being overwhelmed or going mad because they cannot control the level of their drives or feelings, is that not what the small child experiences when he is unable to cope because of the relative weakness of his ego? Surely the adult who is afraid of being overwhelmed is afraid of the revival of the childhood experience of being overwhelmed.

Anna Freud: But what is revived is something that was not frightening in the same way in childhood.

Sara Rosenfeld: I was thinking about the child in a situation where a limiting, protecting, and containing object was not present, and the child in consequence experienced tremendous anxiety about being overwhelmed.

Anna Freud: We have other examples from children in the Clinic. I mean the children who have a poor ego development and very uncertain impulse control. What little they have is very precious to them. They are quite unable to enter with pleasure into any games, like fantasy games, which involve losing ego functioning. So they cannot allow a change of name in the course of the game, because they feel that by doing that they lose their personality, which means they hold on to their precarious ego functioning. Any situation that lessens the efficiency of their egos can be nothing but frightening to them.

Sara Rosenfeld: Does this not have to do with the uncertainty of their self-object boundaries? If the boundaries are weak and are threatened, such children cannot allow themselves to pretend in games nor can they let the adult join in, because for them this comes close to confirming what is normally only pretended.

Joseph Sandler: I think we might have to draw a distinction between two sorts of threat. There are those threats which have a specific content, which involve a danger situation which can be visualized by the child, and which are analyzable in terms of the memories and fantasies of the child. But there are also the threats which I think you are alluding to in this chapter, Miss Freud, which are simply threats of being overwhelmed, threats which are nonspecific, which may be devastating for the infant in that they are connected with a terrifying loss of control. The moment a fantasied danger situation comes into the picture, we may be dealing with something completely different. So when we are confronted with the threat of loss of boundaries we would have to ask whether we are dealing with a relatively basic fear of disintegration or a fantasy of something which represents a specific threat to that particular child, either because of his picture of reality or because of his fantasies.

Anna Freud: It's a more primitive fear that I had in mind, a primary fear of disintegration.

Joseph Sandler: Would this fear be similar to the primary traumatic situation of being completely passively overwhelmed, the experience of so-called automatic anxiety?

Anna Freud: Yes.

Mahmoud Sanai: When young people join a radical group and reject society, they may adopt a new father figure and their superego then functions differently. But in doing this they create a new external world for themselves, and actually perceive the external world quite differently. Then they may feel safe in doing what the group wants them to do, without fear of being out of control in regard to the very same impulses or activities that before were experienced as threatening.

Anna Freud: Yes, what we see is then a complete reversal of attitudes in regard to sexual activities, to the idea of dirt, of violence, and so on. But this is a change in the ideal, and therefore a change in the conflict which prompts the defense.

Joseph Sandler: Miss Freud, you speak of both the ego's need for synthesis and the ego's requirement for some sort of harmony between its impulses (64,60). I should like to ask whether you see the need for synthesis as something intrinsic to the ego, or as something the ego has the capacity for—in other words, as something the ego can employ as necessary. There has been a tendency to speak of the synthetic function of the ego as something rather like an urge to synthesize, or a need to synthesize, whereas my feeling is that it is more a capacity for synthesis which the ego uses in order to be able to function smoothly. If the ego doesn't have to, I do not think it synthesizes. There are so many contradictory beliefs and attitudes which we do not bring together because we don't have to. It is only when we are faced with a contradiction which causes discomfort that we make use of our capacity for synthesis. In view of the fact that you used the rather ambiguous phrase "the ego's need for synthesis," perhaps you would care to comment.

Anna Freud: At an International Congress not so very long ago, Charles Brenner made a very good contribution about our overestimation of the synthetic function. He pointed out that the function was there, but people did not make all that abundant use of it, and could really tolerate many contradictions. I was very impressed with that, because it is perfectly true that we greatly esteem the tendency to synthesize. Our expectation of the well-functioning harmonious adult is that he makes full use of his synthetic function, and it is very interesting to be alerted to the fact that people can get by without doing this. I suppose that what I said at this point in the chapter was really too optimistic. I assumed that people do what they should do.

Joseph Sandler: Perhaps if you had said "necessity for synthesis" instead of need, it might have been better.

Anna Freud: What I wrote in German was *Bedurfnis*,

and "need" may be a misleading translation. But there was behind this the idea that a properly behaving ego should synthesize. But in fact the ego can very well survive without it.

Joseph Sandler: How can it, Miss Freud?

Anna Freud: It's just a less good ego. Take as an example the idea that a thoroughgoing scientist should also be an atheist. There are plenty of scientists who are not.

Joseph Sandler: I suppose we are thinking at different levels. If one is thinking at the level of the microscopic psychological functioning involved in such activities as perception, no ego would develop unless the child made use of the capacity for synthesis.

Anna Freud: Of course, what you say is quite clear. The child would be a schizophrenic, which means split into a great many bits that don't fit together. But what you are speaking of is the basic integration. On a higher level, many contradictions can remain.

Joseph Sandler: But only to the extent that the person can function adequately without resolving such contradictions.

Anna Freud: But the person can't function properly without the basic integration because no feeling of identity and of self would emerge without it.

Maria Berger: Perhaps the ego's capacity for synthesis

is one of the tools it uses in order to achieve the harmony you speak about, Miss Freud.

Joseph Sandler: That would lead to the idea that the function of synthesizing, or the activity of synthesizing, might yield some sort of good or pleasurable feeling. This is, of course, different from saying that there is a drive or need to synthesize, but fortunately it is not incumbent on us to prove or disprove the notion of such a drive or need.

Anna Freud: Well, just one remark. I find it most dangerous to call a capacity a drive, because it confuses the issue.

Joseph Sandler: Turning now to the question of harmony, I should like to ask whether you see it, Miss Freud, in terms of the smooth functioning of the apparatus, or whether you refer here to a *feeling* of harmony. I ask this because, to my mind, such a feeling is extremely important. Threats to such a feeling can provide an important motive in ego functioning, leading to the development of all sorts of methods aimed at protecting the good feeling that I think goes with harmonious ego functioning. The feeling of harmony is certainly something other than a sensual pleasure, something more than the absence of anxiety, and also more than Karl Bühler's *Funktionslust*, isn't it?

Anna Freud: It comes the nearest, I would say, to the feeling of safety you have written about, the feeling that things are in order.

Joseph Sandler: Perhaps something a little more than safety, but a type of pleasurable well-being?

Anna Freud: Exactly. It is well-being. It's the feeling that all is going well.

Joseph Sandler: I think this has many implications, because we can then say that the ego defends in order to preserve the feeling of harmony and well-being, and that the ego would synthesize or not, depending on how the lack of synthesis affects the feeling of harmony. Harmony is not, of course, the same as synthesis.

Anna Freud: Just a comment about the translation. The English version says that the adult ego *requires* some sort of harmony, but the German original says the ego *demands* it. There's no perfect translation that gives the nuances of the thought behind the words. We always used to say that the most satisfactory translations are the Japanese, as we can't check them.

Session three

Tom Lopez: I wonder whether the idea of a drive to synthesize was dismissed too lightly last time. Nunberg pointed out that a manifestation of the synthetic function of the ego is the need to attribute causality, and that this need, though not an instinct, has the same compelling force. He goes on to say that we can assume that the need for causality is a sublimated derivative in the ego of Eros. Further, he says that the tendency to unite two beings that we see in the id shows itself in the ego as a tendency to unite ideas, thoughts, and memories. There are a number of studies which point to tendencies within the individual, for instance curiosity, which have a drive-like quality. Cannot this be marshaled as evidence for something like a drive to synthesize?

Joseph Sandler: I don't think that the existence of motivations for behavior such as curiosity is evidence for a drive to synthesize, although no one would dispute that there are other motivational forces in the individual apart from the instinctual drives. And, speaking personally, I do not find Freud's speculations about Eros, as a general tendency to unite things, very convincing. I suspect that Nunberg's idea of a binding, uniting tendency in the ego, as a sublimation of Eros, is a hangover from the days when practically all behavior was seen and understood as drive-derived. Rather, I think that when one is confronted with contradictory states which lessen the ego's feeling of harmony, and when as a result the ego has to resolve the contradictions or ambiguity, the urge to apply the capacity to synthesize might be very strong and might have a peremptory quality. But if the contradictions don't disturb the person's well-being, he won't feel the urge or need to synthesize. On the other hand it is certainly true that the infant does seem to have, alongside curiosity, an urge to explore that involves pulling things apart and putting them together, and we know that this plays an important part in building up his world. In the small child it certainly does look as if this has the quality of an urge of some sort, but for the rest of it I think that the synthesizing is something forced on the child in order to adapt to reality. But I do not know how important all of this is.

Anna Freud: I would express it in another way, not in the drive way at all. When we speak of the need to synthesize, I think of it more in the sense in which Edward Bibring spoke of the different tendencies in the human being, one of them being a tendency to complete his development, a tendency to reach the next stage. If there is a tendency to, let us say, complete ego development to the best possible functioning level, given what is inherent in the individual, the synthetic function would certainly be extremely necessary. You don't get a proper ego without the use of the synthetic function, and you get a split or schizophrenic or inefficient ego if the synthetic function is in any way damaged. So I would see the need more in the sense of the ego saying, so to speak, "I need to exercise this particular capacity to reach my particular aim."

Joseph Sandler: This raises issues about the need for functions and capacities to be exercised, once they exist either in developed or embryonic form. As you have pointed out, Miss Freud, while there is a sort of tendency, it seems, for functions to develop in particular ways, such a tendency isn't in fact a drive as you understand it. But what you have said about the exercising of the synthetic function would presumably apply to other ego capacities as well, and we haven't looked at those all that closely.

Maria Berger: There must be many tendencies which

we can call ego needs, that have quite a peremptory quality, starting, for example, from the intolerance of ambiguity, the intolerance of something the ego can't fit together. One can see this working in children very easily, when the child asks questions to close the gaps in his understanding and perception.

Anna Freud: What you describe is the synthetic function in action, because before there is the capacity for integration and synthesis the child is quite content to have things disparate and in contrast to each other.

Maria Berger: Precisely. The disruption of the ego's harmony creates the need, and this then mobilizes the synthetic function.

Joseph Sandler: I think it is important that functions and capacities that can be mobilized in a peremptory way—in order to preserve comfort and safety, for example—should not be confused with the drives. Such functions can look as if they are driven, but are actually relatively automatic ways of dealing with anxiety or unpleasure. One of the major threats to the feeling of harmony that we experience continually is the pull toward regression, the pull to operate at a simpler level. We would all do this very readily, except that it is normally too threatening. To regress would lead to much lesser integration and synthesis, and normally we then become anxious and counter the regressive move by making use of such things as the synthetic capacity as well as many other functions.

Ilse Hellman: I think the use of such capacities as the

synthetic function is very much related to the need to defend against anxiety about not understanding, against the danger of being overwhelmed by chaotic and unintegrated experiences.

Joseph Sandler: This is very important, because we aren't all drooling schizophrenics at the moment, precisely because it would be so traumatic for us to allow this. So we keep ourselves functioning at a higher level. Not to synthesize and not to integrate is enormously threatening.

Anna Freud: What you have been saying refers to all the functions. After all, there is a reason why the ego develops out of the id, or why the id-ego separates into two different parts, and there is a reason for the ego to want to maintain its integrity. If there is a tendency in us to maintain secondary process functioning in the ego, all the necessary ego functions have to be kept more or less intact. The best way to look at it is to compare the ego with the id and with primary process functioning, or with dreams or certain psychotic states, and then to get an idea of what would happen if the secondary process level were not maintained.

Joseph Sandler: As Dr. Hellman pointed out, we would be chaotically overwhelmed, and terrified, because it is extremely threatening to give up one's contact with reality.

Anna Freud: It would be interesting to apply the same sort of argument to the function of memory. You know how lost we would feel if suddenly this function were to be interfered with, and we had to meet the outside world or the inner world without any memory of what had gone before. I have always found interesting those stories that depict people with a loss of memory, and which describe their absolute anxiety and disorientation, and their inability to cope with the world around them. We could try working this out for every ego function, and we would then see how useful it is to have a functioning ego!

Joseph Sandler: Perhaps it's also rather a burden sometimes.

Anna Freud: Still, I think it's an advantage in the long run.

Joseph Sandler: I suppose the discussion has centered on the synthetic function because in some way it has been given a special place. It has always been singled out as a special function of the ego.

Anna Freud: I was reminded of something about memory. We have heard the recommendation made in our psychoanalytic society by Dr. Bion that one should meet every patient's analytic hour without having in one's memory anything that has gone before, in order to ensure freshness of mind and objectivity in receiving the material. How absolutely disoriented one would feel if one could do this, as if one had lost one's own contact with oneself !

Joseph Sandler: The suggestion involves the idea that

one can do away not only with conscious memories, but with many functions of the unconscious ego, functions which work automatically to structure our perceptions.

We come now to the question of conflict between opposite tendencies such as homosexuality and hetero-sexuality, passivity and activity (65,60). I am not sure whether you refer specifically here to true internal conflict within the id, Miss Freud. Where I have some difficulty is that were it not for the ego and all the ego functions we have been talking about, the id could readily reconcile the opposite tendencies you mention. I think that there is no real conflict from the point of view of the id.

Anna Freud: Of course, because there is no synthetic functioning in the id. There is no need to harmonize opposing instincts, and the whole conflict begins only when development has reached the point where these things clash with each other in the ego.

Joseph Sandler: I am very glad to hear you clarify the point that internal conflict between two opposing id tendencies is really a conflict within the ego. One could say that it is a conflict for the ego about which of the two tendencies to collaborate with.

Anna Freud: I never thought that could possibly be misunderstood, because the coexistence of opposing tendencies in the id is one of the prerequisites for the understanding of the id, I always thought. We know this from dreams and from child development, before ego development has reached a certain level. The clash can only be on the level of the ego, within the ego.

Joseph Sandler: Perhaps one should comment that the ego has the capacity to reconcile opposing tendencies of the sort we have been talking about quite readily were it not for such things as guilt. It could find, for instance, a compromise solution between homosexuality and heterosexuality, passivity and activity, and so on. In normal sexual intercourse, for example, identification with the partner usually gratifies the unconscious homosexual aspects of the person's bisexuality. This is quite normal, and is a way in which the ego can (and often does) find a reconciliation and gratification of two opposing tendencies.

Anna Freud: But of course the whole of psychoanalytic therapy is based on the fact that the reconciliation between opposing tendencies can happen only when they are lifted into consciousness. Why should we try so hard to make them conscious if they could be brought into harmony while they are unconscious? One of our basic presuppositions in analytic therapy is that conflict exists only in the conscious ego.

Joseph Sandler: Not in the unconscious ego?

Anna Freud: Yes, you are right. The better way would be to say that in primary process functioning there is no conflict, but with secondary process functioning there is. Then it becomes a secondary question, of whether the conflict is in full consciousness, or is preconscious, or whatever.

Joseph Sandler: Presumably the conflict may or may not reach consciousness, depending on whether it's been resolved one way or the other before it reaches the surface. If the conflict has been dealt with preconsciously, only the solution may reach consciousness, but surely there can be both conscious and unconscious conflict? One may not know at all that one has been in conflict, because the solution has been found unconsciously —perhaps a solution through using one or other of the mechanisms of defense.

Anna Freud: You know, it is easiest to show what happens with love and hate during the course of child development. You know how both tendencies can coexist in the beginning, before the synthetic function of the ego is there. Then you get a next stage when love and hate are still there, side by side, but the hate is objected to by the ego because to kill the loved object means that the loved object isn't there when you want it again. This is a low level of conflict, but it comes to a higher level where the ego says that to hate any loved person is forbidden, that the love and hate are absolutely incompatible, not because of their outcome but because of their opposing nature.

Joseph Sandler: Miss Freud, you go on in this section to say that if the instinct "could achieve gratification in spite of opposition by the superego or the outside world, the result would . . . be primarily pleasure but secondarily unpleasure, either as a consequence of the sense of guilt . . . or of the punishments inflicted by the outside world." You add that "when instinctual gratification is warded off from one or the other of these two motives, the defense is undertaken in accordance with the reality principle. Its main purpose is to avoid the secondary pain" (65,60–61). So essentially the reality principle has to do with the preservation of the ego from pain, and presumably the maintenance of a feeling of harmony within it. In order to preserve the ego from loss of well-being, reality has been taken into account.

Anna Freud: What I am implying here is the definition of the reality principle as we took it over then. Quite simply, the reality principle is a modified pleasure principle, a way of guarding against unpleasure by taking reality into account.

Joseph Sandler: I have the impression that there is a slightly different emphasis here. The emphasis seems less on the reality consequences if the pleasure principle is followed, and more on the feeling states—pain or unpleasure—that would arise if reality were not taken into account.

Anna Freud: It's really terribly simple. On the one hand there is the pleasure principle, which means that the individual thinks, "I feel good if I do that," and on the other there is the reality principle, which is, "but I will feel bad afterward for one reason or another." The reason we speak of the reality principle is because reality is taken into account.

Joseph Sandler: Is the reality principle not then based on the need both to avoid pain and to preserve a good feeling in the ego, with the taking of reality into account being secondary to the regulation of the feeling state of the ego? I should like to reinforce the link with the feeling of well-being.

Anna Freud: Isn't it really the same? It is as if the ego says, "I feel good unless I feel bad, and I avoid feeling bad so that I can continue to feel good."

Joseph Sandler: We come now to the defense against affect. There is perhaps a problem here because the affect is seen both as a drive derivative and as a motive for defense. Isn't the motive always related to the affect that accompanies the drive? Isn't it, in fact, an affect which is ultimately defended against, a painful feeling state? If the wish did not create a painful affect in some way there would be no motivation for defense, it seems to me.

Anna Freud: Yes, I think that's exactly what I mean. If you look at the text, you will see that it says that there are two motives for defending ourselves against affect. One is the close association of the affect to the drive to which it belongs, so that if we are suspicious of the drive, and ward it off, we ward off the affect at the same time. The other reason brings us to pleasure or unpleasure again. Because in so far as affects are unpleasurable or painful, we defend against them.

Joseph Sandler: Were you at this time including anxiety among the affects?

Anna Freud: Of course. As you can see, it says in the text, "If the ego has nothing to object to in a particular instinctual process and so does not ward off an affect on that ground, its attitude toward it will be determined entirely by the pleasure principle: it will welcome pleasurable affects and defend itself against painful ones" (66,61–62). And anxiety is an unpleasant affect which provides a motive for defense, according to the pleasure-unpleasure principle.

Joseph Sandler: I think I understand. On the one hand, there are such affects as sexual or aggressive excitement, which are linked with the impulse, and the defense against experiencing the excitement will be determined by the content of the wish and the fantasies bound up with the excitement. On the other hand, there is the affective criterion of pain or unpleasure which prompts the ego to initiate defense against the particular impulse that gives rise to the unpleasant or uncomfortable feeling.

Anna Freud: Yes. The whole thing seemed much simpler to me when I wrote it. My meaning was that the drive could be forbidden even though it could lead to pleasure, but it is never allowed to get as far as that. The drive is defended against, and so the pleasure is also forbidden. On the other hand, we could be dealing with a perfectly respectable impulse, against which there is no objection from anywhere, but it leads to pain or unpleasure, and because of that it will have to be warded off as well. This may be an oversimplification, and I think we would express it differently today, probably more precisely. At that time we thought in terms of drive, anxiety, some other affects, the pleasure principle, and the reality principle. I am not even sure if we really thought in terms of signal anxiety at the time—I suppose not, but now we are aware of signal anxiety, of signal feelings of other sorts, and we have more of an affect theory than we had then. That may be the difference.

Joseph Sandler: Would you say, Miss Freud, that really we don't so much defend against the affects themselves, but rather against impulses in order to avoid the development of unpleasant affect, to stop such affect reaching consciousness.

Anna Freud: Yes, we defend against unpleasure, and this includes anxiety.

Joseph Sandler: One small point. Referring to the affects which are warded off, you say, "for the ego is never allowed to experience them exactly as they are" (66,61). Do you use ego in the sense of consciousness here?

Anna Freud: Yes.

Joseph Sandler: Later in this chapter you begin the discussion of considerations bearing upon psychoanalytic therapy by saying that "this survey of the defensive processes gives us a very clear idea of the possible points of attack for analytic therapy" (68,63). You then speak of the reversal of the defensive processes, a forcing of a passage back into consciousness for the impulses or affects which have been warded off, and you go on to say that "it is then left to the ego and the superego to come to terms with them on a better basis" (68,63). Presumably this would be facilitated by the more reasonable perspective which the ego will have about the reemergence of the infantile past, and this would then be followed by a process of working through.

Anna Freud: Of course in children the maturation of the ego has also taken place in the meantime. This is true of adults, too, since the more mature adult ego is in a very different position for coping with impulses than the child's ego was.

Joseph Sandler: You use the phrase "the conflict is genuinely endopsychic" (68,63), and I wonder whether you could clarify this.

Anna Freud: I meant that the influence of the outside world is excluded here, and it is something going on within the personality. In contrast to adult neurosis, in the infantile neurosis there is still a quantity of objective anxiety, so it is not wholly endopsychic. I wanted to contrast the two.

Joseph Sandler: Could you say something a little more, Miss Freud, about the tolerance of pain? The development of this tolerance would presumably be part of normal development.

Anna Freud: Certainly in normal development we expect a child from year to year to tolerate pain to a greater extent without immediate panic reactions, or immediately having to bring defense mechanisms into operation.

We do not expect the very young child to have any tolerance of pain in that respect.

Joseph Sandler: You say that it is the role of education to teach the child to tolerate pain better, but I think that there are some analysts who feel that this is a wrong approach.

Anna Freud: You mean who don't teach their children that pain or unpleasure has to be tolerated. The expectations of the environment play a big part here. We all know the overanxious parent who wants to remove every source of unpleasure immediately in order not to let the child experience it. But this doesn't allow the child to develop methods of coping with it, and one may then get an eight-year-old reacting to any unpleasure as if he were still one year old. We see a lot of this. Perhaps I should have said "upbringing" rather than "education." The role of the external world is very important.

Joseph Sandler: I think we should encourage analysts not to feel guilty about telling their children, "Well, you'll just have to put up with it."

Anna Freud: You know, there are analysts who never succeed in getting their children to go to the dentist. They have never created in their child the understanding that unpleasure has to be tolerated, that one has to cope with it.

Joseph Sandler: Thank you very much, Miss Freud.

Part II

Examples of the Avoidance of Objective
Unpleasure and Objective Danger:
Preliminary Stages of Defense

CHAPTER 6

Denial in Fantasy

This chapter begins with Anna Freud pointing out that
the methods of defense so far discovered all function to
help the ego in its struggle with the instincts, and are
motivated by instinctual anxiety, objective anxiety, and
superego anxiety. In addition, "the mere struggle of conflicting impulses suffices to set the defense mechanisms
in motion" (73,69). In all conflicts (whether with id, superego, or external world) the ego attempts to repudiate
a part of its own id, but what varies in this situation are
the *motives* for the ego's defensive activities. All such
defensive measures are ultimately directed toward making the ego safe and toward protecting it from experiencing unpleasure. This unpleasure arises not only from
threatening drive stimuli, but also from sources in the
external world. The more the external world is a source
of pleasure and interest, the more possibility there is of
unpleasure arising from it. Because of the ego's imma-

311

turity and dependence on the external world, it tries in many ways to protect itself against the unpleasure and dangers that arise from it.

From the point of view of the psychoanalysis of the neuroses, attention has in the past been directed predominantly to the inner struggle between the drives and the ego. The infantile ego's defenses against "objective" unpleasure by "directly resisting external impressions" (75,71) are normal, not pathogenic, and are not the main focus of attention of clinical observation.

Anna Freud cites Freud's case of Little Hans to illustrate defense simultaneously directed both inward and outward. Little Hans's oedipal conflicts and castration fears caused him to employ displacement, reversal, and regression as mechanisms of defense. Consequently his incestuous love for his mother and his hostility toward his father disappeared from consciousness. The symptom allowed him to deal with his castration anxiety. In the analysis the defense mechanisms were reversed, leading to a cure of his neurosis. But afterward little Hans's mental processes were still disturbed. He had to deal with the reality that his body (and especially his penis) was smaller than that of his father, who remained a rival. Further, he envied the pleasure shared between his mother and her baby. To accept the unpleasure arising from these real causes was too much to expect from a five-year-old. Nevertheless, two of Hans's daydreams revealed that he had found fantasy fulfillment of the wish both to have a genital like his father's and to have children from whom he could gain pleasure as his mother did. Hans's fantasies helped him adapt to reality, just as the neurosis had allowed him to deal with his id. He transformed reality by denying it by means of fantasy. Only then could he accept it.

Little Hans's displacement of his aggressiveness and anxiety from his father to horses is a normal process, and need not be pathogenic. Anna Freud cites the case of a seven-year-old boy who developed a series of fantasies about owning a tame lion. He could use these fantasies to deny painful reality in a way that did not lead to neurosis. A ten-year-old boy had intense and extensive daydreams of taming savage wild animals, and it could be shown that he used his fantasies to defend against disagreeable reality, a number of defense mechanisms being employed in this process. The same mechanisms can be seen in stories told by children, as well as in fairy tales, folklore, and books written for children. In all of these a pleasurable quality is gained through total reversal of the real situation. As Anna Freud puts it, "The child's ego refuses to become aware of some disagreeable reality. First of all it turns its back on it, denies it, and in imagination reverses the unwelcome facts. Thus the 'evil' father becomes in fantasy the protective animal, while the helpless child becomes the master of powerful father substitutes" (85,79–80). This is a normal mechanism of childhood, but if it occurs as a delusion in later life it indicates serious mental illness. What happens in psychotic delusions shows us why denial of objective sources of anxiety and unpleasure is not used more extensively. Such denial is inconsistent with the important and valued function of reality recognition and reality testing, but such an inconsistency is not disturbing in early childhood.

In adults the daydream has the quality of a game and

the original function of defense against objective anxiety is diminished. There is a greater degree of reality testing and intolerance of opposites. Fantasy is not so highly prized, but if there is considerable investment in fantasy, it can become incompatible with reality. So, for the adult, if an instinct irrupts into the ego and finds gratification through hallucination, this spells psychosis. Denial in fantasy as an attempt to avoid neurosis puts an abnormal strain on the individual, especially on the ego's relation to reality.

The Discussion

Joseph Sandler: In the very first paragraph of this chapter, after you have pointed out, Miss Freud, that the defensive methods are motivated by three principal types of anxiety, you add, "In addition, the mere struggle of conflicting impulses suffices to set the defense mechanisms in motion" (73,69). I wonder if you could clarify this.

Anna Freud: We should add "as soon as they reach the ego."

Joseph Sandler: Presumably, then, such conflict could be related to any of the three major sources of anxiety, as well as to the need for the ego to protect its own integrity.

Anna Freud: Yes, the conflict is always within the ego.

Joseph Sandler: In the second paragraph, which deals

with the way in which the investigation of defenses has developed, you say, "In all these situations of conflict the person's ego is seeking to repudiate a part of his own id. Thus the institution which sets up the defense and the invading force which is warded off are always the same; the variable factors are the motives which impel the ego to resort to defensive measures" (73,69–70). Could you amplify this point?

Anna Freud: I suppose what I wanted to stress here was the specific point that what the individual repudiates and would like to exclude from his own consciousness is part of his own self, and that's why the words "of his own id" are there. It really means of the id, which is a part of himself. That's all I meant.

Joseph Sandler: Were you using "ego" in the sense of the individual, the person himself ?

Anna Freud: No. I used it in the sense we use it now, as the agency in the mind which sets up the defense. The whole process is so difficult for the ego because what it wants to exclude is not a foreign body to the ego as agency. The word "institution" in the second sentence of the quotation is a bad translation. I meant the *agency* in the mind, what we call in German *Instanz*.

Joseph Sandler: Is it always the struggle between the ego and id that is involved in the defense? Would it be right to say that in this chapter you have extended the view that the defense is always against the instinctual impulses?

Anna Freud: Yes. Later I say that the aim is always to secure the ego, to save it from experiencing unpleasure, and by that I include all the painful affects.

Joseph Sandler: Perhaps you could comment on the phrase "borrows its love objects" in the sentence "The ego is in close contact with that [outside] world, from which it borrows its love objects and derives those impressions which its perception registers and its intelligence assimilates" (74,70).

Anna Freud: What I really mean is that the ego *takes* its love objects from the outer world.

Joseph Sandler: When you go on to discuss Little Hans, Miss Freud, you speak of his love for his mother and of his consequent jealousy and aggressive attitude toward his father, which in turn conflicted with his affection for him. This gives us a good opportunity to return to the question of ambivalence, because not all mixed feelings are ambivalence. We know that it is only after a certain point in development, after the child begins to relate to the so-called whole object and knows that it's the same person toward whom he feels love and hate, that we speak of ambivalence. Of course, what you describe here is a *conflict* of ambivalence, and one can ask why it is that the child can't find a solution to this as readily as he can to other conflicts. You say, Miss Freud, that it's because of the intensity of the feelings at the time, so that the child feels really torn in his ambivalent attitudes to his father.

Anna Freud: It's also because the negative side of the child's feelings toward his father goes so very directly to his death wishes. Then it becomes a matter of killing the person whom at the same time he really loves. Such a conflict is, of course, not open to a solution anymore.

Joseph Sandler: Not an easy one, anyway.

Anna Freud: Not an easy one, no. So one of the two sides has to be repressed.

Joseph Sandler: When you speak, Miss Freud, of the child's castration anxiety being aroused, perhaps it would be better to say rearoused. I mention this only because of the work which has been done at the Clinic in recent years showing that castration anxiety occurs in the phallic-narcissistic phase, which occurs before the triangular oedipal situation has arrived.

Anna Freud: Yes.

Joseph Sandler: The next point is a question about the fact that you use the term objective anxiety here in terms of the conscious experience of the child, whereas before you had been using it predominantly in terms of the *real* external source of anxiety. What you say here is that objective anxiety is anxiety that the child now feels or believes was aroused by something in the external world. The child externalizes his castration anxiety and while this may have been objective anxiety previously, surely afterward it was not.

Anna Freud: He thought it was real, so for him it was real anxiety, namely objective anxiety, whether it was so in fact or not.

Maria Berger: We still have a problem, because although you refer to castration fears as objective anxiety, such fears may have to do with the projection of the little boy's own unconscious wishes. This is very different from the other instances of objective anxiety you cite, where there is something in reality of which the child has, so to say, a right to be afraid.

Anna Freud: I wouldn't think so. If you think of the way the child feels it to be, it is for him a danger which threatens from the environment. He believes that somebody will come and do something to him. Whereas if it is a conflict, let us say, over his own femininity that threatens his masculinity, then his femininity is not a source of objective anxiety.

Maria Berger: So you broaden the idea of objective anxiety to include not only what is objective to the onlooker, but what seems like an objective source of anxiety to the child.

Anna Freud: Yes, it's fear seen as coming from outside.

Joseph Sandler: I think we have to be careful here, Miss Freud, because normally we wouldn't call objective anxiety something felt to be coming from the outside in consequence of the projection or externalization of some inner anxiety. We would add the qualification that it is *experienced* as coming from outside, which is what you have just done. You have made the point very convincingly that there are sources of anxiety for the child, which had previously tended to be neglected by analysts, and which are based on actual threats. Perhaps there was a vicious parent, perhaps threats actually made to the child in regard to castration, for instance by a nursemaid. Or the child may have been reading *Struwelpeter* at a time when he was particularly vulnerable.

Anna Freud: If you stretch a point you could say the child is afraid of the father. The father is there in reality. So far as the oedipus complex is concerned, the father is in real possession of the mother, which means that he is the real rival. So that what the child experiences as a threat coming from the father to his masculinity is something real, even if the father has not said, "I'll cut off your penis if you do this or that." In that sense it's real for the child, so it is objective anxiety.

Joseph Sandler: What happens if the child is projecting his own wish to castrate the father?

Anna Freud: That's a different matter. And that's not taken into account here. Of course we know that the father may be out of the way, or that he is the mildest person in the world, and the child will need some figure to project his own aggression and castrating wishes on, so he sees the father as a castrator.

Joseph Sandler: But he still experiences it as objective anxiety.

Anna Freud: He will still experience it as coming from outside, yes.

Maria Berger: I think this is broadening the notion of objective anxiety, because we now look at it from the child's point of view.

Joseph Sandler: We may be running a risk here if we broaden the concept too much, Miss Freud, because you made a very fine distinction earlier in the book between the different sources of anxiety, and if we now include in the notion of objective anxiety the end results of a defense such as projection we may be in danger of undoing the earlier clarification. Of course, one could certainly say that the anxieties of the child are very often a mixture of his fantasies and externalizations on the one hand, and the reality on the other, and that they all combine in creating for him a particular source of anxiety. But what I think you had in mind, Miss Freud, was that the primary threats from the drives, from the superego and from the outside world, have to be differentiated, without taking into account the subsequent changes which occur as a result of defense. It is certainly clear that we do have to be careful when we speak of the child's castration anxiety in the oedipal phase, because that is now anxiety which was originally objective, and has then had added to it externalizations in consequence of the child's defenses against his own aggressive wishes. In some way we should differentiate between anxiety *attributed* to the outside world and anxiety which has its actual *source* in the external world.

Ann Hurry: When Freud first wrote about this, he didn't really see the anxiety as being the result of a defense, but rather as a result of the child's reasoning at the time.

Joseph Sandler: From the point of view of the child's primitive thinking the talion principle would certainly make castration fears objective anxiety. But from the point of view of the child's own projected sadistic aggressive wishes, it would not be objective anxiety. I think we would give less weight nowadays to the child's idea that there must be a retaliation as the dominant or only feature in castration anxiety. I don't know what you think about it, Miss Freud.

Anna Freud: I like that formulation. *We* know the father wouldn't have done it, but the child didn't know. The child took it as a reality, and that element in the castration anxiety was objective anxiety.

Joseph Sandler: This is, of course, what worries us, that such fears, as well as phobic anxieties, which are posited by the individual as external to himself, would come under the heading objective anxiety.

Anna Freud: Certainly not.

Joseph Sandler: We have a basis for a distinction if we differentiate between elements of objective anxiety proper, and sources of anxiety defensively attributed to the outside.

Maria Berger: What do you mean, Miss Freud, when

you refer to the "methods employed by his neurosis," mentioning displacement and then the "*reversal* of his own threat to his father, that is to say, its transformation into anxiety . . ." (75,71)? Did you mean here the process of reversal implied in projection, or did you mean some other form of reversal as a defense?

Anna Freud: It's a turning against the self. Instead of threatening the father he feels threatened by the father, so he has turned it against the self.

Rose Edgcumbe: And reversed the roles.

Anna Freud: Reversal is only another word used for it.

Joseph Sandler: Would projection be more appropriate?

Anna Freud: Well, you could also use that.

Joseph Sandler: Because that is the sense in which we tend to use projection now, with reversal being restricted to reversal of affect or reversal of roles. Where a hostile impulse is involved, and is dealt with by being externalized so that it is felt to be coming back at the subject himself, we tend to say projection although, as we have seen, the term is used in many different ways.

Anna Freud: Yes, you could say projection, but the important thing is that the process should be understood.

Joseph Sandler: When you describe Little Hans, Miss Freud, you show very clearly how he maintained the phobic anxiety as a symptom. He then experienced the anxiety as arising from outside, but could take steps to avoid the external situation. This allowed him to control a much greater threat, the threat of being overwhelmed, for example, or of castration. I want to draw attention to the phobic anxiety as an anxiety which has been constructed so that the individual can protect himself by avoidance. This is, as we know, at a completely different level from signal anxiety, the internal unconscious indicator of a threat of some sort.

Maria Berger: So you would say that the anxiety experienced as a signal then instigated the construction of a phobic reaction in order to avoid the full experiencing of a threat from inside?

Joseph Sandler: Yes. Our experience at the Clinic is that there are some children who have ego defects of one sort or another, who cannot restrain their signal anxiety to the level of a signal, and then experience anxiety attacks. They are flooded by anxiety and the panicky feeling that they cannot hold themselves together. There seems to be a whole continuum from signal anxiety to the automatic flooding anxiety, but all of this is completely different from the anxiety of a phobic child who creates an anxiety situation precisely in order to enable him to avoid an external situation which represents the internal danger that has been put outside for defensive purposes. He needs the phobic anxiety in order to protect himself by avoiding it.

Anna Freud: But does he in fact create it? Doesn't he

merely displace it? Little Hans wanted to save his re-lationship with his father, and succeeded in saving it. But he acquired another enemy to battle with instead, namely the horse. Then the anxiety followed the dis-placement from the father to the horse, so that now he has his father, but he can't have a horse. To avoid the horse he has to stay at home, but it would be much worse if it weren't the horse and if, for instance, he were unable to be in the same room as his father, because he would then have outbreaks of anxiety or panic.

Joseph Sandler: You raise an interesting point, Miss Freud, when you suggest that it could be the same anx-iety. I have a hesitation about seeing it as a displacement, because it seems to me that the unconscious ego actively constructs a symptom here. It may be that the ego *uses* the displacement, actively transferring the anxiety for its own purposes. Then what the child does is to set up an anxiety situation rather than experiencing panic when-ever the threatening wishes or the threatening punish-ment comes into his mind. I see the construction of the phobic situation as an active process on the part of the unconscious ego.

Anna Freud: I think that what you describe fits the school phobia very much better, because we know that the fear is located in the home and in the family, and the school phobia is a way of dealing with the child's own threat-ening attack on the mother. What it represents is really the fear of the mother's death, of the wish to kill the mother. Then the child cannot leave the mother alone because he is afraid that this might come true, and therefore he cannot go to school. But what is set up next is the dangerous situation in school, which is not a displacement of the anxiety the child felt at home. Usually what appears on the scene is either a threatening teacher, but more often it is another child who is threatening. To avoid this threat the child now has to stay at home to protect the mother, which is the earlier wish. But my feeling is that this isn't quite the same as what happens in the animal phobia, where the animal is much more the direct successor to the parent with whom the struggle is really going on. You see that in the next paragraph, where I talk about the analysis of Little Hans's phobia, I refer to it being "discussed, allayed, and shown to be without objective foundation" (76,72). That means that the reality has been taken out of the objective fear, so the child doesn't feel anymore that the father is a threat.

Joseph Sandler: Presumably to show that the fear is without objective foundation would not be sufficient to deal with it. The child would have to be able to tolerate the fact that he has angry feelings toward his father as well.

Hansi Kennedy: He would also have to accept that his father is bigger and stronger. Isn't that an aspect that you always stress, Miss Freud?

Anna Freud: Yes.

Hansi Kennedy: Well, how can this be allayed so easily? I mean, the father remains bigger and stronger.

Anna Freud: I suppose that what would be shown is that

the child's mind has exaggerated the fear enormously. There is a danger, and that makes it objective anxiety, but it is not as dangerous as all that.

Joseph Sandler: You mean that Little Hans would have to realize that the father had no bad intentions. I rather think that Little Hans had to find that his *own* bad intentions were not going to be so powerful after all.

Anna Freud: The real attempt of this part of the chapter was to show, on the one hand, how many defense mechanisms are used in a particular phobic disturbance, and to go through them as one would have to do in analysis. But in this particular chapter I wanted to show what was left at the end. What was left was something much more normal, childlike, effective but still defensive, namely the two fantasies that helped Little Hans bear an unpleasant reality (77,73).

Joseph Sandler: And the preceding part of the chapter is in a sense a preamble.

Anna Freud: It is a preamble to show, not that Little Hans becomes so sensible in the end, and says, "Well, I'm small and he's big, and perhaps some day I'll grow up and I'll also be big, that's just how children are." Not at all. It is to show that he now has two nice fantasies which console him, which comfort him. "I am a mother" and "I am a father," and we are content to leave it at that because, after all, that's how children feel. We saw an interesting case recently where a little boy, at the age of eight, comforted himself with fantasies in order to deal with the real situation of having a very unhappy home life, with a psychotic father whom he loved. The illness of the father is denied, and the father is described as getting better all the time, and is wonderful, and can do many things. The fantasies comfort the boy, but of course one can ask what the expectations are for a child like this for whom life is built on denial in fantasy at that age.

Joseph Sandler: The question arises of whether the child is only using denial in fantasy, or is developing other methods of comforting or defending as well. After all, we all lead a very active fantasy life which helps us to turn away from unpleasant reality. On the whole these fantasies are preconscious, perhaps occasionally conscious, but they don't dominate our lives as they do in the child who withdraws into fantasy. That leads us to a major question about the name you have given to the mechanism. Is the mechanism one of a particular type of denial or disavowal, or is it that denial is the consequence of the retreat into fantasy? From a descriptive point of view, of course, the child succeeds in not thinking about something which is painful, in comforting himself with something else, so he effects a denial through fantasy, but the denial isn't done in the fantasy.

Anna Freud: No, it's denying by means of fantasy. You know, when I talk about the boy with the tame lion (78,74), I say that he used to amuse himself with the fantasy, by which I did not mean that he lived his life through it, but it just made his life more pleasant.

Joseph Sandler: So we should add, shouldn't we, Miss

Freud, that fantasies can give pleasure that counterbalance pain. So even if the child cannot quite pretend that the unpleasant reality isn't there he can to some extent do away with the pain of that awareness by indulging in a pleasurable fantasy.

Anna Freud: I must say I was fascinated at the time by animal fantasies, and I always regretted that we didn't make more of a collection of them, because they are really marvelous. I particularly like the fantasy of the boy who has the tame lion. It's obviously a lion, but then he dresses the lion up as a person. This means the dangerous person reappears in the lion, only it's now the other people who would be so terrified if they knew that this person was really a lion.

Hansi Kennedy: It is interesting that this particular defense is very different from the sustained denial which we see so often. Perhaps we should call the way in which daydreaming can be used in order to take flight from painful reality something other than denial. The child may realize what is going on, but he comforts himself, he makes himself feel good, he amuses himself in a way. It is very much a latency activity.

Anna Freud: These were latency children I described. The child with the lion was seven, and he was a very amusing boy. I suppose in a sense he knew what he was doing, that he was playing with the fantasy. When I was seeing him, at a time when he was very engaged with his lion story, my father walked through the waiting room which he and I shared, and the little boy nodded to me and then said, in reference to my father, "also a sort of lion." So there he knew and he didn't know, but he used the fantasy to make his life more pleasant.

Joseph Sandler: I think that the prevalence of animal fantasies has perhaps changed. I suspect that nowadays footballers and supermen and other television heroes have taken the place of animals in children's fantasies.

Anna Freud: Now it's television monsters, space creatures, whereas at that time it was what the children saw in the circus and heard about in their fairy stories. They had different sources.

Joseph Sandler: Of course it is crooks and detectives, cowboys and Indians nowadays as well. It is an interesting topic.

Anna Freud: For me it was fascinating. Think of the child who couldn't go to bed without the dog to protect him, but then couldn't go to sleep because the dog might bite him. The change from protector to attacker was a very easy one. All of this connects with the child's enormous interest in the very big animals. It's well known among teachers of young children that you can get the child's interest, when you are teaching natural history, if you start talking about the big and dangerous animals. The whole class will be with you, but if you talk of cats and dogs or insects, it's very difficult. We haven't studied the child's involvement with the big and dangerous animals enough yet.

Joseph Sandler: At the end of the chapter you comment, Miss Freud, on the difference between the child's fantasy and the adult's delusion (87–88,81–82). Could you comment further on the distinction?

Anna Freud: I would say that what happens is that with development there is a change in the aim of the daydream, or in the function of the daydream, which is reduced more and more to a pleasant, harmless accompaniment of one's daily life. This happens as the ego matures and reality testing becomes more important. Before that the fantasy can play a much more important part as a precursor of defense. The question for me is where the dividing line is between the two. Are we right to be very concerned if, let us say, an eight-year-old relies too much on his fantasy life? Or do we say that it is still all right to have fantasies to that extent until the end of the latency period? We know that it's quite in order up to the age of five, and we know that children can distinguish between fantasy and reality even at that age, but they aren't too concerned about the distinction. They know the fantasy isn't real, but it's still very important to them. There is this marvelous example in the Winnie the Pooh books, where Winnie sits at the table and imagines himself in all sorts of roles. He is a sailor and he's a soldier, he flies in the air and has all sorts of megalomanic fantasies. But at the end comes the very sad phrase "and then I pretend I'm only me." This is a big drop back to reality. I have known children up to adolescence who have maintained daydreams in a so-called continued story, a subject I was very interested in at one time. In a case I'm thinking of as many as twenty-two people were engaged in the service of the daydream, each with his own characteristics, each having his own fate and interaction with the others. The reality life of that child wasn't affected at all, but she would change from her reality back into the continued story daydream, without losing any part of it at all.

Joseph Sandler: But surely the question of pathology lies in the other things that the child does or doesn't do? In itself fantasy is not pathological, but it seems to me that it's only if other things don't develop, or pathological structures do, that we have to worry. Of course, if the child spends all his time daydreaming then one is concerned, but I imagine that what normally happens is that the daydreams become preconscious and find further derivatives in sublimatory activities and other forms of interest and activity.

Anna Freud: In reality it should be a question of quantity. If too much is invested in daydreams, we would expect the investment to be missing somewhere else. This has been discussed at length when we considered the imaginary companion. Of course we haven't sufficiently studied people who have elaborate daydreams, because usually when we get them in analysis their lives have been damaged because their attention has been directed all the time to their fantasies.

Joseph Sandler: The crucial thing seems to be the degree to which the child consciously withdraws from the outside world in the process of getting lost in conscious fantasy. This is quite different from the situation in which the child has a great many preconscious fantasies, or when he retains the capacity to switch off the fantasy to attend to reality. It seems to me the critical and possibly pathological aspect is the giving up of reality.

Anna Freud: Yes, we often get children at the Clinic with the complaint that the child sits at school, daydreams, and cannot learn. But what about those children who can daydream in a very vivid way, and in whom everything else is left intact? I've never found out how they do it.

Hansi Kennedy: I think very few children actually tell us about those daydreams which are absolutely ego syntonic. The daydreams aren't disturbing, and the child feels that it's his private life and his own private concern.

CHAPTER 7

Denial in Word and Act

In this chapter Anna Freud continues her discussion of denial. She points out that even though the ability to test reality is not impaired in the young child, it can "get rid of unwelcome facts by denying them" (89,83), using this capacity not only in its thought and fantasy, but also in action. The child's ego uses "all manner of external objects in dramatizing its reversal of real situations" (89,83). Denying reality is a strong motive in children's play and in games involving playacting. It is easier to construct a pleasant world of fantasy, she says, than to take in the facts of reality.

Adults commonly reverse the real facts when dealing with children, for example telling a small child that he is a big boy. They use such reversals of reality to comfort the child. Similarly, many presents given to children involve the same reversal, and help the child pretend to be grown up. Educators have the problem of how much they must encourage the child to assimilate reality and how far they can allow the child to turn from reality to the world of fantasy.

Adults expect that the child can turn quite readily from the denial of reality in play to appropriate reality-directed activity. They expect him to be able to put aside his fantasy play very quickly in order to do what they expect of him. The fantasy play has to remain a game and not become an obsession, a tendency which could be seen in a little girl who was acutely unhappy about her lack of a penis, and who denied this by lifting her skirts and exhibiting herself. In this way she called on others to admire something which she did not have. Another child might have displaced the concern further through an interest in beautiful clothes or in gymnastics.

The little boy lion tamer of the previous chapter turned more and more to denial in fantasy as an attempt to master his growing castration anxiety, and had increasingly to belittle everything around him. He became constantly facetious, and this activity developed an obsessional quality so that he could not be free from anxiety unless he was joking. Similarly, a little boy put on his father's hat and clung to it, resisting taking it off indoors. Such activity is different from that of the child who simply plays at being a big man. The child who carried the hat everywhere finally thrust it into the front of his trousers in order to leave his hands free. He returned it, says Anna Freud, to where it originally belonged.

The sort of behavior described is not obsessional in the strict sense. What we see is a defensive measure directed against the frustrating external world and not against the instinctual wish. Denial allows the ego not to become aware of something painful from without. Such denial of reality can then be reinforced in fantasy or behavior by a reversal of the real facts, and this is different from the way in which reaction formations are maintained in true obsessions. In what Anna Freud describes here the child consistently provides proof of the opposite of reality, and if the persistent proving is impeded, the ego experiences anxiety and unpleasure.

As the ego matures it is not easy for denial to exist side by side with reality testing. Maturation imposes a further restriction on denial in word and act. Whereas in fantasies a child can be supreme, if he wants to dramatize his fantasies he will need a stage in the real world on which to do it, so he is limited by the degree to which those around him will go along with his dramatization. The judgment by others of the abnormality of an activity is related to the degree of its conspicuousness. The child who went about everywhere with the hat was conspicuously odd, but when later he carried a pencil in his pocket, he was regarded as normal. What he did with the pencil was now as reassuring as his previous activity, but had become socially acceptable. If the external world does not tolerate the particular protective measures developed by the child, an internal conflict may arise that may eventually lead to neurotic manifestations. Anna Freud warns us, however, that it is "dangerous to try to guard against infantile neuroses by falling in with the child's denial of reality" (99,92).

The Discussion

Joseph Sandler: This is a very clear chapter, but there are a number of points we might discuss. You start the very first sentence, Miss Freud, by saying that "for some years the infantile ego is free to get rid of unwelcome facts by denying them, while retaining its faculty of reality testing unimpaired" (89,83). Presumably it is only after a certain point in development that the need for reality testing comes into conflict with the use of denial. It seems that for a certain time it is possible for the two to coexist. Is this what you meant, Miss Freud?

Anna Freud: Yes, the child denies by pretending, which is, after all, not the same as believing.

Joseph Sandler: Later in the chapter you say that "the infantile ego resorts to denial in order not to become aware of some painful impression from without" (96,89). Do you take the view that denial always refers to perception of the external world, whereas repression and many other defenses apply to the revival of wishes, memories, and associated affects that derive from the past and arise from inside?

Anna Freud: At the time I found it a useful distinction to make, because if we talk of denial of internal stimuli, where do we draw the line in regard to repression?

Joseph Sandler: Repression is regarded as involving the use of a counterforce or, in energic terms, a counter-cathexis. Does denial involve a counterforce in the same way?

Anna Freud: No, but we could say that the pretense that

is set up acts in the same way toward the denied fact as the countercathexis does toward the repressed content.

Joseph Sandler: Throughout this chapter, Miss Freud, you have used denial not simply in the sense of ignoring painful reality, but as involving a reversal of the facts. One reality is substituted for another. We have tended in the past to see denial as unconsciously pretending to oneself that something isn't there, rather than that the *opposite* is there, which involves more than a simple withdrawal of attention. Perhaps we should distinguish denial from scotomization, the creating of a blind spot with the result that a piece of reality is simply not seen.

Anna Freud: We should look at the meaning of the word denial. If you deny something that someone else says, you not only do away with what he says, you say by implication that the opposite is true. You say that what he says is wrong, and that the opposite is right. Unlike Laforgue's idea of scotomization—I remember the arguments very well—in denial something is first perceived and is then done away with.

Joseph Sandler: According to the way you see it, the denial is accomplished by the substitution of something else, a fantasy or an action, or something of that sort.

Anna Freud: Yes.

Joseph Sandler: I have always had a feeling of unease about regarding denial simply as a withdrawal of attention. We know that when we draw the attention of a child to something he doesn't want to see, he very often doesn't simply ignore it, but does something else to reinforce the idea that the unpleasant thing does not exist. It has been suggested that if we draw attention to what is denied the child will then perceive it fairly easily, but we know that this doesn't happen in reality. Denial, certainly from a clinical point of view, involves some sort of resistance on the part of the child or adult to seeing something he doesn't want to see.

Anna Freud: We can see this in the way the adult world colludes with the child's wish to deny. We don't say to the child, "You are not a little boy." We say, "What a big boy you are," which means we put the bigness immediately in the place of the smallness which he resents. We don't say, "This won't taste bad," but we say, "It's quite good, try it." This is the way we fall in with the way the child denies unpleasant facts.

Marjorie Sprince: When we say that denial only applies to external reality, does this mean that the child who says, for example, "I'm not unhappy," when he *is* unhappy, is not using denial? Surely there is a denial of his affective state. Are we saying that denial doesn't apply to affects because it applies only to the external world?

Joseph Sandler: I imagine that if the affect is a reality for the child, and he substitutes something else, he is showing the sort of reversal Miss Freud described here as denial, and the term would then be appropriate. But your question does raise the point of where to draw the line in relation to external reality. If we say that feelings are part of reality, then it follows that we can think of denial as applying to subjective experiences such as the feeling of anxiety. There are some rather difficult problems about reality involved here.

Maria Berger: We often see, in quite little children, a magical doing away with reality. One also sees this in psychotic children. On a dark day such a child may be frightened of the dark outside and, seeing lights on in the house, might insist, "It's morning time, it's morning time." This is not only a denial of the darkness, it's a bit of magic, a conjuring away of what seems to him to be evening time. This would fit with what you have said, Miss Freud, about substituting something in denial, because the unpleasant darkness becomes the morning time, for instance.

Joseph Sandler: It is probably time that someone had another look at the whole group of the "reversal" defenses, because many of the distinctions we make are very arbitrary. When we think of the definition of denial we have been using, then the idea of reversal of affect would also fit the situation in which someone who feels anxious replaces the anxiety with excitement or elation. The so-called reversal of affect is, in this context, the same as denial of affect. But then we have the person who does something that denies an external source of anxiety, and this is not the same as reversal of affect. Probably we have to look at the context in which we use a particular term. I think Miss Freud has been speaking in the context of the external world, of the reality outside the person himself.

Anna Freud: Yes, when the child uses magical thinking, it has at its base a denial of real facts. The magical thinking is then added. So we could either say that it is part of the denial or that it reinforces the denial.

Joseph Sandler: I was intrigued that you have said that denial is a precursor of defense, Miss Freud, and that makes a great deal of sense if we think of denial simply as a withdrawal of attention from something unpleasant or threatening. However, would the mechanism not be entitled to full status as a defense if we use it in the way you have used it here?

Anna Freud: When I called denial a precursor of defense, my idea was that the child learns how to defend against stimuli that come from the internal world on the basis of his dealings with the external world. Once he has had the experience of denying external stimuli, repression of what comes from the internal world is greatly facilitated. That was my idea.

Joseph Sandler: If we see defenses in a broad context—and it was you, Miss Freud, who first generalized the notion of defense to include defenses against the external world—we would have a very good basis for calling denial a defense in the full sense of the term, as a mechanism of defense against the external world.

Anna Freud: Yes. If we include defenses against external reality, then we have to consider denial to be a mechanism of defense. It is very interesting to see how denial goes on to connect with magical thinking, and we can then ask when denial becomes lying.

Joseph Sandler: And also rationalization. Perhaps we ought to think in terms of a developmental line here.

Anna Freud: Yes, it would be interesting.

Joseph Sandler: It is interesting too that the type of defensive activity you describe in this chapter is different from what we normally understand by acting out. This is not the sort of activity in which an unconscious wish, coming from the inside, finds its expression in action rather than in consciousness. What you describe is more the defensive use of action in order to do away with something painful and unpleasant. It is not the enactment of an unconscious wish.

Anna Freud: In German it would be *handeln* and not *agieren*.

Joseph Sandler: In many of the examples you have given, Miss Freud, you have illustrated ways in which the child can get the illusion of being strong or being grown up. The reality brings about a narcissistic wound, a feeling of inadequacy, and the fantasies and reactions of the child, the denials you describe, represent ways of restoring the child's narcissistic supplies, restoring his well-being, giving him a pleasurable feeling through identification with the grown-ups.

Anna Freud: But, of course, it is also the fear the parents or adults have of hurting the child's narcissism that leads them to do a great deal of this kind of pretending through reversal during the child's upbringing. In order not to hurt the child one falls in with the child's methods, which in the long run is not helpful to the child.

Joseph Sandler: But up to a certain point it must be very useful for the child.

Anna Freud: It's pleasant for the child. The question is whether it helps the child's adaptation to reality, something which, after all, he has to undertake at some time.

Joseph Sandler: But do we not give the child a feeling of security by using such methods of pretending and reversal from time to time?

Anna Freud: We do, but it is a false security. The very young child needs it, but the question is for how long. Sometimes reality is brought in too late, after the child has become accustomed to comforting himself with pretense.

Molly Mason: In a good nursery school one watches for the overuse of this sort of pretense. I am reminded here of those children who always choose to be the baby rather than being more grown up. One worries about them.

Rose Edgcumbe: If we think of a situation in which there is an unpleasant external fact which brings about lowered self-esteem or anxiety, then are the denial of reality and the denial of affect not alternative ways of dealing with such a situation? On the one hand there is the alternative of denying the reality and substituting something more pleasant which gives rise to nicer feelings. But there is also the other alternative, which is to accept the reality and to deny the feelings about it. I wonder if the denial of affect could be seen as a later development, used when it is no longer possible to deny reality because this would strain one's sense of reality too much. Could we think here of a developmental sequence, in which there is a move from the denial of the external reality to the acceptance of external reality, but with denial of the affect which has been aroused?

Anna Freud: I would think so, because so long as the denial of reality works, the affect doesn't appear. If it doesn't work, the affect arises, and then it has to be denied. I am reminded of something my father said, which you probably know, when he spoke of how we bring up our children. He said we supply them with a map of the Italian lakes and send them to the North Pole.

Maria Berger: There is another side to what one does when one tries to use the technique of denial with the child. The child may see the hypocrisy of what we are doing, and may, at that moment, not want to be big or clever. He might want to be a baby, for example.

Anna Freud: This comes up very much whenever the child is ill, whenever he has to get an injection or take medicine. Children resent it enormously if the mother camouflages the bad medicine with something sweet and will distrust the mother afterward. They will distrust the sweet and good because who knows what is hidden underneath it. The opposite method, and I believe the right one, would be to say, "This will taste very bad, but. . . ." I think then the child will respect the adult more and will feel safer.

Joseph Sandler: I am sure that we all agree that the tricks played by the parent which the child must inevitably discover, like saying that something isn't going to hurt when it will hurt, can only be harmful to the child's development. However, the sorts of denial in action which you have described in this chapter, in which the parents participate by giving the child grown-up presents, help his narcissism enormously. He can get a feeling of magical identification in later life in badges and uniforms which bolster narcissism, as well as in the symbolic identifications with admired figures. I imagine that in part this is directly traceable to the earlier techniques of denial through the grown-up play initiated by adults. The child who doesn't get this sort of thing probably also suffers in his development.

Anna Freud: Yes, such a child is pushed too early into reality. It's very difficult to know what is the right time for the children who grow up with the idea that all adults are nice, are good uncles and aunts, to realize that they aren't. At some time the child has to take notice of this. There are thousands of ways in which the child's denial of his smallness and of his limitations is colluded with, is helped along.

Hansi Kennedy: I should like to come back to Rose

Edgcumbe's point. If there is a developmental step from denial in reality to denial of affect, could we not say that denial in fantasy represents a further step? The fantasy is put in place of action, so some unpleasant reality is replaced by a pleasant fantasy. We have a sequence there as well.

Joseph Sandler: If we are to speak of a developmental line here, we should keep in mind something that is general to developmental lines, that is that the earlier steps do not disappear—rather, the later levels get added to the earlier ones. What we call a developmental line is really a sort of developmental branching. So we might see denial of external reality as something that starts early, and after a certain point denial of affect, which is more difficult and complicated for the child, might become possible, and the child might then use either method as necessary. With the development of thought and fantasy, he might then also use denial in fantasy, which is more sophisticated than denial in action. Incidentally, in this particular context, I am not at all sure that denial in fantasy comes after denial of affect. I don't think that we can postulate a developmental line from denial in action to denial of affect to denial in fantasy.

Anna Freud: The ability to pretend without action comes later developmentally than pretense through action, which needs a tool for the action, usually a toy. Later on this tool can be disregarded and the denial can take place in fantasy. The three-year-old in the nursery school, who plays at being a policeman, needs a helmet for that activity. The eight-year-old, who has a fantasy of being a policeman, needs no helmet.

Joseph Sandler: He can be a plainclothes policeman!

Rose Edgcumbe: He also doesn't have to chase other children; he can just sit still and think.

Joseph Sandler: There is something which one sometimes sees in very young children, and I wonder whether you would include it under the heading of denial. I remember a ten-month-old child crawling on the floor, knocking its head, crying for a moment, and then deliberately knocking its head against the table leg again. Of course one thinks immediately in terms of active mastery of a passively endured painful experience, but in a sense this is also like a denial, a reversal, as if the child says, "I am not the one who is at the mercy of the environment."

Dorothy Burlingham: I think it is his interest in what happens that makes him do it again.

Anna Freud: And also the wish for mastery. It is both together.

Dorothy Burlingham: But I don't think it's a denial.

Maria Berger: I am rather bothered by the thought that we may be losing sight of the fact that we are talking about a defense. In all fantasies there is a denial, and when we talk about denial in fantasy, I think we have to try to distinguish this from the denial that exists in the ordinary pleasurable fantasying of any child. Otherwise we would have to regard all fantasies as defenses.

Joseph Sandler: We have a real difficulty here, because fantasies certainly help us to turn away from unpleasant reality, and in children's fantasies the role of narcissistic gratification is perhaps the biggest factor, in addition to the satisfaction of instinctual wishes. I think that you have introduced here, Miss Freud, the notion of defense against narcissistic hurt, without saying so explicitly. We know how important this is in our clinical work, and how important it is not to think that every defense is a defense against an instinctual wish. But this does leave us with the problem of drawing the line between denial in fantasy as a defense mechanism on the one hand, and the ordinary comforting and gratifying role of fantasy on the other. Probably there is no clear-cut line to be drawn.

Anna Freud: I suppose we tend to call it defensive when the child prefers to turn to such denial in fantasy or in action to an unusual degree, at the expense of coping with the real world.

Joseph Sandler: In this chapter you use the phrase "work it over" (92,86), Miss Freud, when you speak of the little girl who has to deal with the painful comparison between herself and her brothers. I wondered what you meant there.

Anna Freud: Probably having to find some solution, to cope with it. The German is *Verarbeitung*, and what I really meant was that the child has to cope with the problem in a constructive way. "To assimilate it" would convey the right sense.

Joseph Sandler: The whole question of the use of denial in relation to penis envy is intriguing because of its universality, even in little girls who haven't actually seen boys or animals. You refer in a footnote to Rado's idea of the "wish-penis," an hallucinatory reproduction of the penis by the little girl. It makes one wonder whether there is not a penis built into the innate neurological plan for the body schema in both boys and girls.

Anna Freud: It is an interesting idea.

Joseph Sandler: In this chapter you give examples of exhibitionism being used defensively, and the question of defensive exhibitionism versus instinctual exhibitionism is one which is of particular psychoanalytic interest. You describe the little girl's need for reassurance and the defensive demand "Look under my skirt" or "Look at me" in order to deny the feeling of being castrated. I don't think we have ever differentiated clearly enough the instinctual drive aspect from the defensive aspect in such activity. We know how often children become exhibitionistic when they lose the parent's attention (when a sibling arrives, for example) and how wrong we can be if we see this as only instinctual. How do we bring this together?

Anna Freud: You know, it has been discussed a lot in regard to masturbation. Masturbation can be seen as the satisfaction of an instinct, but it is also a means of reassurance to the boy that he is intact, that the penis works. One is an instinctual use, the other is a defensive use, and the same is true for exhibitionism.

Joseph Sandler: Perhaps we can say that the child harnesses his natural exhibitionistic impulses in the service of the defense. From a technical point of view, however, the distinction is very important, because it affects what we interpret. A lot of what has been taken as instinctual exhibitionism seems to me to be essentially defensive.

Anna Freud: But not in the phallic phase.

Hansi Kennedy: There was a child at the Hampstead Nurseries, who has also been discussed by you, Miss Freud. She was very exhibitionistic, and used to lie on the floor at night before going to bed, with her legs spread open, inviting the boys to look at her or to play with her. Then she developed very acute penis envy, and didn't want to expose her genitals. She was still very exhibitionistic, but stopped exposing her genitals directly.

Anna Freud: But I remember that whenever I came to the Nursery she would come up to me and say, "Come and see my Sunday dress." Or she would display something on her finger of which she was proud.

Joseph Sandler: Certainly, as you say, Miss Freud, in the phallic phase the two seem to go hand in hand.

Anna Freud: But above all there is the reassurance that there is no defect.

Joseph Sandler: You say in this chapter, Miss Freud, that denial "can be employed only so long as it can exist side by side with the capacity for reality testing without disturbing it" (97,90). I wonder to what degree denial is discarded in normal life. I have been impressed more and more by the way in which as analysts we do not easily become aware of successful denial in our patients, unless we get some independent report coming from the outside. Then one realizes how much the patient omits in the analysis. Obviously the capacity for denial remains, and it must be a useful adaptive mechanism, even in the adult. I wonder to what extent the use of denial gets limited in adult life. The capacity to deny certainly seems to remain.

Anna Freud: The capacity remains. You know, in our everyday dealings with other human beings, we find their denial of reality extremely disturbing. We find that it's terribly difficult to convince somebody of something which they have denied, or to get them to alter their behavior if they are using denial. We complain greatly and say, "It is impossible to deal with that person, he has no sense of reality." This means that what he does is nonadaptive, or rather it is felt by others to be non-adaptive.

Joseph Sandler: But intrapsychically it is, of course, a very successful adaptation at times.

Anna Freud: Very, but only if that person is the only person in his world.

Joseph Sandler: Obviously a good adaptation for one person isn't a good adaptation for another.

Maria Berger: Of course denial is a good adaptation to a limited extent only. So when one is ill, and denies the seriousness of one's illness, then this isn't an economic defense.

Joseph Sandler: But it is a good adaptation in the here and now, just at the moment, without taking a long-term view. What is a good adaptation at the moment may not be a good adaptation in the long term.

Anna Freud: Which explains, of course, why it is so easy for children to use denial, because they never take the long-term view. For the purposes of the here and now, denial is a most useful mechanism.

Molly Mason: I am intrigued by the way denial in action can be built into the personality. I remember a little girl who was in treatment with me and who had very strong penis envy when she was three. She used to pull her clothes up the whole time, saying, "I have got one." After treatment she did well, was successful at work, and eventually became a model. I felt that this was based on the same sort of denial.

Anna Freud: On the other hand, people who use denial a great deal in adult life are very threatened by reality, if they are confronted by the reality directly. The reality does not fall in with their method of coping, and they suffer very badly.

Joseph Sandler: Although you distinguished compulsive denying activity from truly obsessional behavior, Miss Freud, I wonder whether you would say that the urge to deny, of the sort you described in this chapter, has a peremptory quality.

Anna Freud: Yes, that's what I meant really. It's not an urge, but it has the quality of urgency, of peremptoriness.

Joseph Sandler: Could you elaborate on the very last sentence of the chapter, where you say of denial, "When employed to excess, it is a mechanism which produces in the ego excrescences, eccentricities, and idiosyncrasies, of which, once the period of primitive denial is finally past, it is hard to get rid" (99,92). "Excrescences" doesn't really sound like one of the words you use, Miss Freud.

Anna Freud: The German word is *Auswuchse*, which means outgrowths, really. *Sonderbarkeiten* is eccentricities, but *Eigenheiten* is personal qualities, perhaps peculiarities rather than idiosyncrasies. What I meant is that one can accommodate this particular mechanism in the structure of the adult personality if we don't mind distorting that personality to quite a considerable extent.

Joseph Sandler: Yes, perhaps in the politician or in the

bigot, or in someone in whom we would say there is a distorted ego, one can see the use of denial. I mean the sort of polemical, mob-rousing politician. The denial goes over into lying and falsification.

Hansi Kennedy: They may not believe what they say themselves.

Joseph Sandler: Beyond a certain point perhaps they do.

Anna Freud: Oh yes, they do. I don't know how this fits in with the idea of the impostor, but I suppose it has something to do with it. He presents himself as big, but he feels that he is small. Then the question is whether he believes what he says or not. I suppose many impostors really believe themselves after a while.

Hansi Kennedy: Isn't that rather the same sort of thing we associate with denial in the child? The child looks at something and says it isn't there, and we can say that at one moment he half believes it, but at the next moment he can be brought back to reality.

Anna Freud: In the adult it would be much more fixed. In the child there is a swing between fantasy and reality, between denial and realization, and it is much more fluid. Whereas if the adult builds a great part of his life on denial, he has to do it very firmly. By the way, it is what many children, especially adolescents, complain of in their parents. They say that they can't make their parents see reality, that they deny the whole time, that they see things in too rosy a light, and so on.

Joseph Sandler: Sometimes the parents complain about the child as well! But in regard to the question of whether impostors and demagogues believe in what they say or not, it is perhaps relevant that the ego, during the course of development, does not learn to put a label on reality, but rather to impose the label of "unreality" on certain experiences. So if the ego is not specially attentive, or if it is in some way seduced, the label of unreality is temporarily not applied, and everything is treated as reality, just as it was for the child at the very beginning. We have to do work and be on the alert to label things as unreal.

Robert L. Tyson: I would like to ask about people one sees who are persistently optimistic and hopeful, where one wonders how they keep it up. Would that be seen as a defense?

Anna Freud: Yes, just as the comedian who is really a depressive lives on the defense of reversal of affect.

CHAPTER 8

Restriction of the Ego

Anna Freud showed previously that denial is used in situations in which the child cannot otherwise escape some unpleasant external impression. When the child is older he finds ways of avoiding such impressions, and there is then no need for denial. The ego can "refuse to encounter the dangerous external situation at all" (100,93). This is the "restriction of the ego" discussed below.

Now Anna Freud describes a child patient who dealt with situations in which he saw himself as competing with the analyst by abandoning the activity concerned. He could not tolerate comparing his performance with another's, and avoided this by giving up the activity, losing pleasure and interest in what he was doing. But at the same time he would become preoccupied with activities in which he felt himself to be superior, and spent much time on them. "He restricted the functioning of his ego and drew back, greatly to the detriment of his development, from any external situation which might possibly give rise to the type of unpleasure which he feared most" (102,95). There seem to be many intelligent children who do not have the usual inhibitions in relation to learning, but who avoid entering into activities in regard to which their achievements can be compared with those of other children. Such a comparison devalues their work in their own eyes, and they become disinclined to repeat the attempt. As a result "they remain inactive and reluctant to bind themselves to any place or occupation, contenting themselves with looking on at the work of the others" (103,96).

Anna Freud contrasts this sort of withdrawal with neurotic inhibitions, in which certain harmless ego activities have become connected with past sexual impulses that have been warded off. Because the ego activities have become sexualized they are defended against. Ego restriction differs from such inhibitions, however, because the children who give up their capacity for work as a consequence of ego restriction regain it if external conditions are changed. This is not true for neurotic inhibitions. One can see a complete "turning about" of an ego restriction in those cases where children cannot learn at school, but do extremely well with private coaching, where there is no comparison of their work with that of other children.

Restrictions of the sort described are not only imposed by the ego on itself for the purpose of avoiding an unpleasant realization of inferiority. There can be other reasons, such as the fear of the aggression which might arise from the envy of competitors. Anna Freud cites the case of a young boy who played football very well but became afraid of the bigger boys in case they might be jealous and aggressive. His passion for games was lost, and by becoming no good at games he avoided the situation which aroused castration anxiety in him. Simultaneously he developed his literary skills. She refers further to a girl of ten who went to her first dance, full of excitement, and fell in love with the handsomest boy there. She fantasied that there was a secret bond between them, but was then teased by the boy when they were dancing together. This was a humiliating disappointment, causing her to avoid parties and lose her interest in dress and dancing. But she then turned to intellectual activities and won the respect of boys in that way. Although it later emerged that the disappointment at the dance repeated an earlier traumatic experience, what she took flight from was the real situation that caused the intense unpleasure.

Anna Freud points out that in neurotic inhibition the defense is against the translation of some internally forbidden instinctual impulse into action. Although the inhibition seems to be related to the external world, it is the inner processes that the person is afraid of, as can also be seen in the phobias. On the contrary, in ego restriction it is disagreeable impressions from the outside, arising in the present, which are avoided, because they might revive similar impressions from the past. While in inhibition the ego defends against its own inner processes, in ego restriction the defense is against external stimuli.

In the inhibition there is a constant struggle against an instinctual wish, with the expenditure of much energy, and the bond between the unconscious wish and the inhibited activity persists. There is no such bond in restriction of the ego. What is important is not what the activity represents or symbolizes, but whether it produces pleasure or unpleasure. If the activities produce unpleasure or anxiety, the ego does not want to engage in them further. Whole areas can be given up, and the ego might then "throw all its energies into some pursuit of an entirely opposite character" (111,102).

Ego restriction is not a form of neurosis, but is a normal developmental phenomenon. It is only when it has become too marked that it results in disturbance of development. Anna Freud suggests that modern methods that give the child a great deal of freedom of action in choosing his own activities and interests may be misguided because they underestimate the determination of the child to avoid unpleasure. In many cases children would, if not given guidance, choose activities only on the basis of the aim of avoiding unpleasant feelings. The result of freedom of choice may be "not the blossoming of personality but the impoverishment of the ego" (112,103).

The child's ego may defend itself against the formation of a neurosis by checking the development of anxiety through an ego restriction and consequently deforming itself. But the person who uses restriction of the ego may find himself confronted with anxiety situations if, for some external reason, he has to change his way of life. Then the loss of a protection against anxiety through restriction of the ego may be a precipitant of a neurosis.

Anna Freud goes on to point out how the external world can affect the development or otherwise of inhibitions or symptoms in the child by diminishing or facilitating opportunities for ego restriction. Finally, she describes how parents may protect their children from anxiety by restricting their activities, and this may lead to an absence of symptoms. Often "it is impossible to form an objective judgment of the extent of a child's symptoms until he has been deprived of his protection" (113,105).

The Discussion

Joseph Sandler: The differentiation between neurotic inhibition and ego restriction that we discussed in Chapter 4 has been made very clearly in this chapter. At the start you say, Miss Freud, in reference to denial, that on it is based "the fantasy of the reversal of the real facts into their opposite," and that it "is employed in situations in which it is impossible to escape some painful external impression" (100,93). So for denial, as for the other mechanisms discussed so far, we have to assume that there has been an unconscious perception of something painful or threatening, a sort of pre-perception, a subliminal or unconscious perception. At some level the person has to become aware of what he is defending against. Does the same thing happen when we have ego restrictions? I ask because the person clearly makes a decision at some level to avoid situations which, for one reason or another, he does not like.

Anna Freud: Restriction of the ego deals with unpleasurable affect that is aroused by an external experience. The idea is that after the child has once had the experience that such an affect can be aroused, the easiest thing for him is not to enter into the same situation again.

That is what I had in mind when I said that this is by no means a neurotic mechanism, but really one of the mechanisms which help us to build up our different personalities. From the earliest time there is a more or less automatic avoidance of the disagreeable, and after all why *should* we have disagreeable experiences? The ego feels that there are other things that one can do instead.

Joseph Sandler: This seems to be specially relevant to the crucial distinction between phobic avoidance and ego restriction.

Anna Freud: You know, I had great trouble at the time making people understand the difference. They didn't want to understand it. They thought I was destroying something that was a very good psychoanalytic concept, namely the idea of phobic avoidance. Actually, in the beginning an ego restriction looks very much like phobic avoidance, but the crucial question relates to what is avoided in the phobia. We know that what is avoided is an inner situation, an inner urge, which is projected outward, displaced outward, and then avoided in the external world.

Joseph Sandler: And as a result the phobia has to stay alive, in order to fulfill its function. The person needs to be preoccupied with it, but this isn't the case in restriction of the ego as you have described it.

Anna Freud: Yes, the wish has to stay alive in order for the phobic avoidance to be there. But in restriction of the ego, it's an external situation that arouses the unpleasant affect. The situation can be avoided and the activity given up, and the situation is then not specially cathected, as in the case of the phobia. In the course of time, the wish for that particular activity is dropped altogether and the cathexis is turned elsewhere. This is quite different from the phobic process, where the investment remains firmly attached to the avoided activity or situation, and an anticathexis has to remain in place just as firmly.

Joseph Sandler: This is important technically, Miss Freud, especially if we take a developmental point of view in our psychoanalytic work. I have a patient at the moment who has had a thyroid deficiency since birth. He was taken to see many doctors and has never really worked at anything. He has had lots of therapy, but it seems quite clear that his lack of incentive to work is not a neurotic disturbance. He simply never developed an interest in working and any analysis in terms of phobic avoidance, of fear of success, or something similar, is quite inappropriate. His lack of enthusiasm for work is, it seems to me, not at all neurotic.

Anna Freud: His main attention was probably on his body.

Joseph Sandler: Yes, I am sure that was so, and also on his relationship with his mother. Although he is a very disturbed man, his problems are rather the end product of a restriction of the ego fostered by his physical illness and his mother's overindulgence.

Anna Freud: But, you know, it's terribly difficult to make this difference clear to people.

Joseph Sandler: It is possibly worth mentioning that the phobic avoidance we have been talking about refers to a particular group of irrational fears which involve externalization of a constantly recurring inner wish and a subsequent continual avoidance of the feared situation. Unfortunately there is also the practice of labeling every irrational fear a phobia, and this has led to much confusion. There are some fears which are called phobias in which the person experiences anxiety when he finds himself in certain situations but, different from the situation in the phobia proper, he is not tied to these situations. Such fears look like phobias but they do not have the function of representing an unconscious wish in externalized form, so the person does not need to be preoccupied with the danger all the time. But could not the phobic avoidance of particular situations of this sort eventually cause an ego restriction?

Anna Freud: Yes, but with the ego restriction there is no fear left, so it is not phobic avoidance. The ego retreats from the frightening situation, and the child then feels indifferent to it. This is shown in the example I gave of the little boy and the football game. He first experienced fear on the football field, but then he dropped his interest in football and turned to a completely different side of life. There was no fear of football left, but he would wonder why other people wanted to play football. He saw it as something boring.

Marjorie Sprince: What would happen if a child like that were then forced to play football?

Anna Freud: He would play very badly.

Marjorie Sprince: Presumably he would not be frightened, because the aggression was no longer attached to it in the same way.

Joseph Sandler: I think we would have to say that there would be at least a little signal of anxiety!

Anna Freud: Well, he would probably again be frightened of being hurt.

Maria Berger: When you say that the outcome of ego restriction is not neurotic, I understand what you mean. For example, the little boy who didn't want to compete with you in drawing opted out, and I think then the opting out can become a pattern so that it can create a personality which is based on avoidance, on restriction. Even though it is not necessarily neurotic, we would see a disturbed personality.

Anna Freud: The boy who opted out of playing football I have mentioned before. He is now a professor of literature and very successful in his work.

Maria Berger: Then you were describing isolated phenomena rather than patterns of personality development in the examples you gave?

Anna Freud: Well, no. What I described was the way in which this particular mechanism can be responsible for different directions of ego development.

Hansi Kennedy: For example, whether the boy becomes a footballer or a professor of literature?

Anna Freud: Yes. After all, such a decision has to be made at some time in life and this particular experience may be decisive. It wasn't that he was a weak boy. I suppose that if he had had no castration fear he would not have shied back from, let us say, football playing. But he had the usual castration fear, and this became decisive for him in regard to the direction in which his interest was turned. He was a strong little boy, and could have been a good footballer, but he was also gifted intellectually. In one area he met anxiety, so his ego said, "Why expose myself to that? There are other things I can do."

Joseph Sandler: I suppose one can distinguish between the effect of ego restrictions which cause an individual to develop in one direction rather than another, like the boy we have been talking about, and those which limit the activities of the individual so much that we get a disturbance of personality development, an ego distortion, constriction, or impoverishment. In the first case we wouldn't say that there was anything wrong with the person, from a psychopathological point of view, but in the second case we might feel that there is a severe disturbance.

Anna Freud: Yes. If such a person meets fear again in another area, and retreats from that as well, no choice may be left to him. My idea was that early in the life of the more or less normal child there are really many choices for him as to how he will distribute his libido. The choices are determined by events of the kind I described earlier.

Joseph Sandler: Then I suppose we have to add, Miss Freud, that society regards some activities as compulsory or essential, and if these become restricted, rather than nonessential activities, the child may develop a neurotic disturbance and be referred for help. But essentially the processes involved are the same.

Anna Freud: Yes.

Ilse Hellman: I think we have to make it clear when we advise people about their children who give up activities that the ego restriction is not in itself pathological.

Anna Freud: Where it is potentially pathological we don't get any sign of the child excelling in another field; there is no transfer of libidinal interest from one field to another.

Joseph Sandler: Our criteria for pathology in children are so socially linked, and embedded so much in the disturbances caused in the parents, that we tend only to get children referred when the child has an actual problem which brings him up against his environment, when he fails examinations, and so on. Of course, if the parents are analysts then we may get the opposite!

Anna Freud: We shouldn't forget that the sort of children you are referring to may be neurotically inhibited, not necessarily restricted in their ego. We should distinguish between the two.

Marjorie Sprince: I wonder what the precursors to ego restriction are. What causes some children to restrict themselves, and others to attempt to master the threatening situation?

Anna Freud: Probably they have a different attitude toward anxiety, tending to withdraw from it rather than trying to master it.

Joseph Sandler: You also touch on this, Miss Freud, when you refer to the children who are allowed to withdraw from activities at school. The attitudes of people around the child play a very big part in determining whether the withdrawal is permitted, whether coaching is given, or whether a change of teacher or school is advised. From what you have said it seems that this can have a profound effect on the child when we are not dealing with a neurotic inhibition but rather a withdrawal from something that arouses anxiety or unpleasure.

Arthur Couch: I wonder if we shouldn't differentiate between restriction of the ego and restriction of ego activities. Merely restricting activities such as playing football, for instance, does not mean that the ego is restricted in its thinking about the area. There may be a withdrawal of overt activity rather than a blotting out of all interest in that aspect of things.

Anna Freud: You are quite right, but we also have to remember that at the time the term ego was used very much as a synonym for the self, and what I really have in mind here is that the shifts between the ego activities create different kinds of personalities, different kinds of selves. But you are right in that I meant the restriction of the activities, not of ego functioning as a whole.

Joseph Sandler: One could add, though, that if the child withdraws from a certain activity—let us say mathematics—then by giving it up, his mathematical skills will not develop further. And, of course, in the light of what you have said, Miss Freud, this is not an inhibition but a lack which is a consequence of a restriction. The point seems to me to be important from a practical, technical point of view in both child and adult work.

Anna Freud: To me it seemed then that the most important distinction was that in the case of inhibition the wish survives, even if it cannot be put into action and cannot be fulfilled. Whereas in what I called the ego restriction the wish is, for all practical purposes, abandoned.

Joseph Sandler: I suppose one can also see this sort of restriction in things like food fads later on. If the child isn't presented with tapioca pudding, or whatever he dislikes, then he has no problem. He doesn't feel anxiety in the absence of the pudding.

Anna Freud: Unless there is an underlying wish for the tapioca pudding!

Joseph Sandler: When I referred to the technical importance of your ideas about ego restriction a little earlier, what I had in mind was the ease with which we can fall into the trap of the genetic fallacy, making the assumption that something like a food fad always represents an underlying wish or phobia which still exists actively in the present. Sometimes this leads us to a very wrong interpretation when we are dealing with a structural alteration, an atrophying of interest or a character trait of some sort. What we see is that it is only when the person is put into the anxiety-creating situation that he shows the anxiety and the withdrawal, even though the developmental roots of the anxiety or avoidance may have involved other wishes and conflicts. I suppose what I am leading up to is the idea that we can also get ego restrictions which have started off as inhibitions or phobias, and have then become autonomous, so to speak.

Anna Freud: Certainly what you say is quite right, but I think we gain a lot when we look for the dividing lines. The distinction seemed to be an important one for me, namely that in the one instance the wish is there, with a constant countercathexis kept up, while in the other instance the personality has developed away from the unpleasant activity.

Joseph Sandler: You set up the distinction you wanted to make very well in this chapter. It was refreshing to read it.

Anna Freud: For me, too.

Joseph Sandler: At the beginning of the chapter you say, Miss Freud, that "instead of perceiving the painful impression and subsequently canceling it by withdrawing its cathexis, it is open to the ego to refuse to encounter the dangerous external situation at all" (100,93). By "cathexis" do you mean attention cathexis or a libidinal cathexis?

Anna Freud: I mean the libidinal cathexis. In the German it is *Besetzung*, which refers to the charge of energy. What I really mean relates to the affect, to the emotional cathexis, the emotional investment.

Joseph Sandler: Sometimes we say that we don't cathect something and we mean a mixture of withdrawing attention and interest from the side of the ego, as well as withdrawing instinctual cathexis. When we speak of emotional investment we certainly mean something more than the investment with instinctual energy.

Anna Freud: Yes.

Joseph Sandler: A little later in the chapter you refer to a child patient who lost pleasure in what he was doing and gave up the activity. In contrast, he would get very taken with activities in which he could feel himself to be your superior (102, 94–95). Is this not also denial in action as you described it in the previous chapter, Miss Freud?

Anna Freud: No, it's not the same, because here we see an avoidance mechanism which is very much to the detriment of the child's development. This means that he withdraws from one situation after the other, due to his inability to face competition, and is left with very little in the end.

Joseph Sandler: So here he is not undertaking something in order to push something else away. You are not putting emphasis on the substitution of a second activity for the first.

Anna Freud: No. Turning to the other activities he could enjoy is not defensive. He simply undertakes them because he is not threatened in doing them. What this child does away with are those activities where he was not sure whether or not he would come out on top.

Ilse Hellman: What is interesting is that this child gets no pleasure from the activity as such, it seems, but is really only interested in the experience of winning.

Joseph Sandler: I think we should mention that the withdrawal shown in the restriction of the ego isn't the same as the "giving up," the abandoning of activities, shown by a depressed person. In ego restriction the child turns away from one activity, but he might well devote a great deal of energy to something which does give him satisfaction.

Anna Freud: Yes, but this isn't so for every child. This is why I divided the process here into two parts. First there is the mechanism of withdrawal from the thing which arouses unpleasant feelings, and then there may be the compensations. Those who only take the first step are damaged, not in a neurotic sense but in a developmental one. They have somehow cut off many possibilities for normal development. But then, of course, there are those who achieve the second step. The libido they have withdrawn from one activity is displaced onto something else. It is a sort of compensation, we might say. So these children are not damaged, but become good in another area. Still, they have cut out a part of life. After all, it would be nice to play football at weekends and be a professor of literatue during the week. It would be nice to have the all-round development, and the question really is—why not? Why should we not develop on the two sides, in physical ways and intellectual ways? We have had the example of the ten-year-old girl who withdrew after the shock she experienced at her first dance, but who became a very good and clever scholar afterward. Wouldn't it have been nice if she could also have gone dancing? That's why I called this an ego restriction.

Marjorie Sprince: I think there must also be limitations to what one can do that are based on reality. You can't spend your time doing everything, so you choose the thing that you are good at. Does this mean an ego restriction?

Ilse Hellman: Don't we think of ego restriction when a whole area is left out?

Hansi Kennedy: We have to consider the effects of the particular culture on the total personality, and the part played in this by the ego restriction. I remember when we discussed the choice of a phobia not so long ago, and it was mentioned that if someone living in England has anxieties about climbing mountains, he can very easily avoid the feared situation. But if he has an agoraphobia or a fear of traveling on underground trains in London, this may substantially interfere with his life. I think there is also something like that in regard to ego restriction. It is as important to understand the way the restriction impinges on the total functioning of the person as to understand the structure of the restriction itself.

Joseph Sandler: Yes, it's like the tapioca pudding. There are some cultures where you don't get served it, and an ego restriction in regard to eating it doesn't cause any problems.

Hansi Kennedy: You can easily avoid tapioca pudding, but if you are unable to eat fifty different sorts of things it's not so easy. It's no longer ego restriction, but a symptom.

Joseph Sandler: The question of what we call a symptom is another problem, and a big one at that.

Sara Rosenfeld: I think we shouldn't forget the influence of the parents' choice of lifestyle and the child's identification with the parents' particular ambitions and interests. This also contributes to the preferences of the child for certain activities rather than others.

Anna Freud: This book is about the relations between ego and id on the one hand, and the defense mechanisms on the other. The defenses are described as possibilities the child has for dealing with something that has already been influenced by imitation, internalization, conflict or agreement with the parents, admiration of them, and so on.

Maria Berger: In clinical practice, of course, we don't get the sort of child that you discussed in the chapter. What one finds more often is the child with further problems arising from the ego restriction.

Anna Freud: Yes. The boy I was talking about didn't come into analysis because he couldn't play football, he came for very different reasons. But during his analysis it became very clear to me why there was a withdrawal from the physical area and an enormous involvement with the intellectual field. This discovery was a by-product of the analysis.

Joseph Sandler: You refer in this chapter, Miss Freud, to children who withdraw from activities and "behave as if they were intimidated." You say, "The mere comparison of their achievements with those of the other children robs their work of all its value in their eyes. If they fail in a task or a constructive game, they conceive a permanent disinclination to repeat the attempt. So they remain inactive and reluctant to bind themselves to any place or occupation, contenting themselves with looking on at the work of the others" (103,96).

I find it interesting to see how you anticipated something which we now see more grossly, namely those disruptive children who react in a very aggressive and disturbing way at school when they are humiliated, when their self-esteem is lowered through failing at something or being criticized or shamed. These children don't get bored but become disruptive, yet are very much like the children you describe. They reject the activity in a violent way, as if to say, "I don't care at all for your silly nonsense."

Anna Freud: That produces more restriction of the ego than neurotic inhibition.

Joseph Sandler: I should like to make a comment in regard to the sexualization of an activity which then makes the activity the target of the ego's defenses, with the consequent development of an inhibition. It is worth noting, I think, that such a sexualization need not involve the same sexual impulses or wishes which entered into fostering the development of the particular activity or skill which has now been affected. The sexual or aggressive wishful fantasies which prompted the development need not be the ones which later seize hold of the activity, leading to an inhibition. So we don't necessarily see a recapitulation in the development of an inhibition, or a regression along the lines of development, but rather, as Hartmann has pointed out, a new sexualization or aggressivization once the activity has achieved relative autonomy. A good example, and one which has been cited very often, is the way masturbatory wishes can be deflected into the playing of a musical instrument. Later the musical skill might become inhibited because it becomes a way of, say, aggressively killing a rival, or of fulfilling some aspect of an oedipal wish. If we assume that it is the original wishful fantasy that is involved in the sexualization later on, we again fall into the genetic fallacy.

I have a question which relates to your statement that "children in the latency period may attach more importance to the avoidance of anxiety and unpleasure than to direct or indirect gratification of instinct" (111–112,103). Could you elaborate on that remark please, Miss Freud?

Anna Freud: The idea is that prelatency children, the under-fives, would always give precedence to the gratification of instinct. But, later on, when their instincts are already under control, they may be guided in their behavior by the need to avoid anxiety and pain, and this can be much more important than gratification. I was trying to emphasize, when I wrote what I did, that after a certain age the freedom of choice the educationalist may offer the child may lead to an ego impoverishment. The child prefers to avoid unpleasure, and withdraws from activities. You know, I was really referring to school-age children. We see a change again in puberty. The point I really wanted to make had to do with the idea that children in progressive schools who are given the opportunity of developing in an all-round way will often surprise us. They might want to do only one thing, and the one thing was often not what they liked best, but what would be safest to do. Here is Dr. Sandler's "safety principle." They would be safe from anxiety and unpleasure, from competition and jealousy, and so on. This is one big argument against the idea of the "free" school.

Free schools can be quite all right, but they can also have a most restrictive influence on the kind of children I have been talking about.

Joseph Sandler: The last point you make in this chapter (113,104–105), in relation to the role of the environment in producing symptoms of disturbance, is very important because it shows us that the symptom can remain quite latent until something brings it into the open, or rather lets the child's individual idiosyncrasy turn into a symptom.

Anna Freud: You see it with food fads. The mother may give in fully to the child's food restrictions, food fears, or whatever you want to call them. Then they don't appear as disturbances because the situation is under control for the child. There is no problem unless the child is presented with the foods he has been avoiding, and then one realizes how severely restricted or inhibited he is.

Hansi Kennedy: That is a secondary sort of conflict and may be very different from what was originally avoided through the ego restriction.

Anna Freud: The conflict now gets forced on the child, when in the first instance the child was spared the conflict by the restriction, with the collusion of the environment.

Part III

Examples of Two Types of Defense

CHAPTER 9

Identification with the Aggressor

In introducing the topic of identification with the aggressor, Anna Freud remarks that the ego's habitual defense mechanisms may be seen relatively easily when they are employed separately and in relation to some specific threat. It is not so easy when defenses are combined, or when the defense is used alternately against internal and external forces. Both these problems are illustrated in the process of identification which, as a factor in superego formation, helps toward mastery of the drives. But identification is also "one of the ego's most potent weapons in its dealings with external objects which arouse its anxiety" (117,110). Anna Freud recalls that Aichhorn once described a boy who had a habit of making faces that would cause the whole of his class to laugh. Aichhorn discovered that it was not that the boy was making fun of the schoolmaster, but rather that "the

379

boy's grimaces were simply a caricature of the angry expression of the teacher"; when the boy faced a reprimand from the teacher, "he tried to master his anxiety by involuntarily imitating him." This imitation of the teacher was unconscious, but by means of the faces he pulled "he was assimilating himself to or identifying himself with the dreaded external object" (118,110).

Anna Freud goes on to recall the little girl mentioned in Chapter 7, who dealt with a fear of crossing the hall in the dark by running across it, making peculiar magical gestures. She mastered her anxiety by making the movements she thought a ghost would make and pretended to be the ghost she might meet. This sort of behavior also occurs in primitive religious ceremonies. It can be seen as well in children's games in which there is identification with a frightening object. But the imitation of such an object is only one aspect of a more complicated process.

A six-year-old boy came to his analysis after having been to the dentist, who had hurt him. He attacked various objects in the room, cut a piece of string into pieces, and went on to sharpen and resharpen pencils. He broke off the points and sharpened them again. He was identifying "not with the person of the aggressor but with his aggression" (120,112). The same boy once arrived just after he had hurt himself by running against the fist of the games master while playing. The next day he came dressed in military style with a sword and pistol. He was not imitating the teacher he had run into, nor was he copying his aggression. Rather, the masculine military weapons were symbols of the master's strength and could help the child identify with the manly adult.

In this way he could "defend himself against narcissistic mortification or actual mishaps" (121,113).

These examples illustrate the way the child introjects an attribute of an anxiety-producing object, and in this way "assimilates" an experience of anxiety he has just had. Identification or introjection combines with the impersonation of the aggressor, and the child "transforms himself from the person threatened into the person who makes the threat" (121,113). This is linked by Anna Freud with Freud's description, in *Beyond the Pleasure Principle*, of the way a child can change a passive experience into an active one as a means of mastering anxiety. Freud refers specifically to the way in which a doctor's frightening examination can later be reversed in a child's game by way of mastering the unpleasant experience.

Anna Freud points out that the transformation described can relate to a frightening anticipated event. A little boy always angrily rang the bell of the children's home where he lived. He would then criticize the maid loudly for being slow. What happened was that, after pulling the bell, he was frightened in case he would be reproached for ringing loudly; so he criticized the maid before she could complain about him. His aggressiveness was here a measure of his anxiety, and he turned his aggression against the person from whom he expected attack. Anna Freud cites a further case, of a five-year-old boy who became very anxious when masturbation fantasies were touched on in his analysis. He became very aggressive, laid about him with a rod, and brandished kitchen knives, threatening his mother and grandmother. This was not the release of his masculinity; he "was simply suffering from anxiety" (123–124,115).

Identification with the aggressor is a common stage in normal superego development. By identifying with the parental threat of punishment, the child takes an important step in superego formation through internalizing the criticisms of others. Repeating the internalization of the qualities of the adults about him provides the child with superego-forming material. But this "internalized criticism is not yet immediately transformed into self-criticism" (125,116). A new development occurs. Identification with the aggressor is followed by what Anna Freud describes as "an active assault on the outside world" (125,116). This is exemplified by a boy who, through identification with the aggressor, criticized his mother passionately, complaining in particular of her curiosity. It emerged that the curiosity was his own rather than his mother's, and he had particular difficulties in mastering it. What he had done was to reverse the roles completely, taking over his mother's feared indignation and then going on to ascribe his own curiosity to her.

Another patient complained that her analyst was secretive. But this patient had consciously been secretive, had suppressed something very personal, and expected a rebuke. Her defense was to accuse the analyst of secretiveness.

What can be seen in these examples is a phase in superego development in which external criticism had been internalized but the offense is externalized. Identification with the aggressor "is supplemented by another defensive measure, namely, the projection of guilt";

Anna Freud refers to this as "a kind of preliminary phase of morality" (128,119). After that the superego turns its severity inward, and the person normally becomes less intolerant of others. However, with this development the ego has to endure the unpleasure of self-criticism and guilt. There are those who never move on to the further stage, and although aware of their guilt "continue to be peculiarly aggressive in their attitude to other people" (129,119). Anna Freud suggests that failure to move from criticism of others to self-criticism may reflect "an abortive beginning of the development of melancholic states" (129,120). She comments that in such cases "the behavior of the superego toward others is as ruthless as that of the superego toward the patient's own ego in melancholia" (129,119). Identification with the aggressor may also represent a step in the development of paranoia, resembling it in regard to the mechanism of projection.

Both identification and projection are normal ego activities, and the outcome of their use will vary according to the material upon which they are used. The special combination of the two involved in identification with the aggressor is normal only while the ego uses it to deal with the anxiety aroused by external authority. The defensive activity becomes pathological when it enters into love relationships. So the husband who projects his unfaithful wishes onto his wife and then reproaches her has introjected her reproaches and projected part of his own id. He defends himself not only against her aggression but also against the breaking of his love attachment to her as a result of his own unfaithful wishes. The outcome is "projected jealousy" (130,120).

Projection can be combined with other mechanisms

when it is used as a defense against homosexual impulses. The reversal of love into hate can result in the development of paranoid delusions. In the defense against both heterosexual and homosexual love impulses the choice of a target for the projection is determined, as Freud put it, by "the perceptual material which betrays unconscious impulses of the same kind in the partner."

The analysis of identification with the aggressor "enables us to distinguish in the transference anxiety attacks from outbursts of aggression" (131,121). The analysis of the aggression based on the identification with what is supposed to be the analyst's criticism can reduce the aggression only when the fear of punishment and of the superego has been reduced. Abreaction of the aggression will have no effect on it.

The Discussion

Session one

Joseph Sandler: We have come to a famous chapter, which has been very influential. It would be useful for us to look at it in terms of the time when it was written. We will also need to consider in our discussion the problem of the relation of identification with the aggressor to projection and to other forms of reversal. But first there are one or two points which need some clarification before we get fully into the discussion. At the beginning of the chapter you make the point that some defense mechanisms are "employed separately and only in conflict with some specific danger" (117,109). It would be correct, wouldn't it, to assume that you don't mean specific in terms of the *content* of the danger, but rather the specific *source* of the danger?

Anna Freud: Yes.

Joseph Sandler: The next point is that you make use here of the idea of external and internal conflict, and it is clear that by internal you mean, in general terms, conflict between different parts of the mental apparatus, and I suppose that we would now say that what we call internalized conflict is included.

Anna Freud: Yes, of course.

Joseph Sandler: External conflict is then linked with the idea of objective anxiety, the fear of what might actually happen from the direction of the real world.

Anna Freud: Yes.

Joseph Sandler: A little later, when speaking of the boy who mimicked the teacher's anger and copied his expression as he spoke, you say that the boy identified himself with the teacher's anger, although the copying was not recognized by him. You then say that "through his grimaces he was assimilating himself to or identifying himself with the dreaded external object" (118,110). I wonder if you would care to say something about what you meant by the phrase "he was assimilating himself to."

Anna Freud: The German word is *Angleichung*. The child becomes like the teacher. "Assimilating himself " is a rather clumsy translation. But, you know, the best example I now have of this process is one which I didn't possess at the time. It came later, at the Hampstead Nurseries, from the little girl who had a small brother who was so afraid of dogs that she said to him, "*You* be doggy and no dog will bite you." That is a perfect expression of the whole thing.

Joseph Sandler: You come near to it with the example you give of the girl who tells her little brother that there is no need to be afraid in the hall. He just has to pretend he is the ghost he might meet. But is the child turning things around, reversing the roles, or is he in a sense only assimilating himself to the ghost? In other words, is he saying, "If I am also of the class of ghosts I won't be attacked"?

Anna Freud: You know, there is the example in Kipling's *Jungle Book* where there is the protective—one could say defensive—cry Mowgli is taught when he goes through the jungle. Whenever he meets a dangerous animal he has to call out, "We be of one blood, ye and I," and then nothing will happen. That is the assimilation to, or the approximation to becoming the aggressor, or becoming like the aggressor.

Joseph Sandler: It sounds exactly like what you have described as identification with the aggressor. But it does seem to be very different in quality from the child who is frightened of the dentist and then plays dentist with his little brother.

Anna Freud: That is turning passive into active. What I describe is more of an identification. But the two are very near to each other. You know, at the dentist it would not help you at all to pretend that you are the dentist. Whereas with the dog and the wild animals it evidently helps on the spot.

Joseph Sandler: In all of this we have to distinguish between the reversal of the aggression in identification with the aggressor, and that form of identification, which is an important part of normal child development, in which he progressively identifies with the strong—one could say aggressive—aspects of the parents. There it isn't a way of dealing with fear by turning someone else into the helpless one.

Anna Freud: Yes. But in identification with the aggressor it isn't a reversal. If the boy is frightened of the dog, identifying with the dog doesn't mean he will bite the dog. It means he also is a dog, so no dog will bite him.

Ilse Hellman: I remember a child who always barked when a dog passed in the street. That had the same meaning.

Anna Freud: It's the same mechanism.

Joseph Sandler: He masters the anxiety certainly, and we can be sure of that because we can see how the identification is used as a defense. But I suppose the child might get a certain narcissistic gratification, or a gratification of the feeling of mastery as well. I'm not sure that this will be something which always happens, but I can imagine that some children get a supplementary benefit, so to speak, from identification with the aggressor. I think again of the child who "shot" the therapist because he was afraid of getting "shots"—injections which he had previously received at the same hospital. This seems to me to be very different from what you describe, Miss Freud.

Anna Freud: Yes, because what you are talking about is turning passive into active.

Joseph Sandler: But surely when you say it is turning passive into active you mean that it is a form of identification with the aggressor which includes the component of passive into active. It is certainly not simply the mechanism of turning passive into active on its own, is it?

Anna Freud: Well, that mechanism is very near to this one, but the identification with the aggressor does not need to go as far as changing passive into active. The child changes into the aggressor in order to protect himself, but doesn't necessarily now direct his aggression toward the former aggressor. That is why identification with the aggressor remains different.

Hansi Kennedy: I recall a child in the War Nurseries who was afraid of dogs when we went for walks. Once after returning from a walk she played at being a dog and explained, "I'll be doggy so doggy don't bite me." This example suggests that this mechanism only works to protect the child against anxiety, but not against anything which approaches an attack. A dentist is a person who attacks, and that is different.

Joseph Sandler: Wouldn't it help the child who is due to go to the dentist the next day, and is afraid of that, to deal with his current anxiety about going to the dentist if he plays a dentist game with his little brother? Isn't he there dealing with an anxiety, even though it wouldn't be effective at the time that he has to visit the dentist?

Anna Freud: There's no doubt that identification with the aggressor and turning passive into active are very near to each other, and still they don't completely coincide.

Marjorie Sprince: I wonder if you could say something, Miss Freud, about the differences between the child who has to imitate the frightening teacher, and the child who consciously pretends to be a ghost. Would you put these under the same heading?

Anna Freud: We would put them under the same heading. The difference is in the degree of intensity of the anxiety, of the automatic response, of the extent to which the child acquires the response as an habitual one, and so on. The little girl, who was only four or five years old at the time, and who advised her little brother to "be doggy and no dog will bite you," was taking it from her mother, I believe. Her mother certainly barked at her and the little girl herself became a very sharply talking child.

Joseph Sandler: I think we should add, Miss Freud, that we can legitimately speak of identification with the aggressor when it occurs in fantasy. I suppose that that is probably its largest domain, isn't it? The child, in an anxious situation, very often has fantasies which involve the sort of mechanisms we have been discussing, and this is quite different from the denial in fantasy.

Anna Freud: It's interesting to compare it with other mechanisms, or with the devices children use to overcome fear. I remember a little boy in analysis, who was about five or six, who was very frightened of my Alsatian dog. But he didn't become a dog, or bark at him. He once said to me that he now knew that if, from the door onward, he smiled at the dog, the dog wouldn't bark at him. This means appeasement, which is very different from identification with the aggressor.

Marjorie Sprince: It is interesting to consider how the two mechanisms make for different sorts of pathology later on. The placatory child has a very different development from the child who identifies with the aggressor.

Joseph Sandler: Identification with the aggressor can also show itself in the form of identification with the superego introject. One may well deal with it, and with one's fear of it, by turning on someone else and attacking them. This is not quite the same as identification with the frightening object, but it is the same as the child who identifies, for example, with a critical parent and criticizes his little brother for the very thing he feels bad about. Would that then be identification with the aggressor?

This is what you have called the projection of guilt, I think, Miss Freud. We have seen it so very often in the Nursery. A child who feels criticized for doing something naughty may turn around and criticize another child.

Anna Freud: It's more an externalization. The bad part is externalized and the good part is now free to criticize the bad part which has been put out onto someone else.

Joseph Sandler: But it is on the basis of identification with an authority figure.

Anna Freud: Well, this identification is part of the superego, after all.

Ilse Hellman: I think what we see in the many examples of this is an intermediate stage toward the superego working really internally.

Joseph Sandler: I have a certain hesitation about allocating identification with the aggressor or similar mechanisms to particular stages. You see the mechanism even when the superego is highly developed. Some people who have very strong guilt feelings identify with their superego introjects and attack others for the very things they feel guilty about themselves.

Anna Freud: What I question here is only the use of identification in this context. What I mean is that it is a general experience that to criticize others is so much more comfortable than self-criticism is. With some people it remains that way throughout their lives, but others learn to bear self-criticism. We probably should think in terms of a stage in development, because little children are not self-critical.

Ilse Hellman: What I was thinking of was the stage when children try to be good, but are not able to be, so they take sweets which belong to other children, knowing quite well that it is wrong, but doing it nevertheless. The fault is then always put outside until they reach a particular point in development when the attempt to control is successful, although for a while it occasionally doesn't work.

Anna Freud: We used to ask ourselves in child analysis about the time children begin to have enough confidence in their analyst to confess what they do wrong. You know how this begins. It is when the child says that the child sitting next to him in school has done something very wrong, and this is only one step before confessing what they have done wrong themselves. So the move is gradually from others being in the wrong to admitting that they are in the wrong themselves.

Joseph Sandler: All this is tied up with the question of the degree to which the conscience is felt by the person to be part of his own self, or as a voice inside him which is in some way apart from him, alien to him. If he feels criticized by such a voice he might then deal with it through something like identification with the aggressor. Probably the way in which one functions in relation to one's superego introjects varies from time to time, and perhaps also from individual to individual.

Anna Freud: And there may be, as Ilse Hellman has said, an in-between stage when the voice begins to be one's own, but is not yet listened to with any degree of attention.

Joseph Sandler: There is the issue of whose voice the voice of conscience is. Is it the child's own voice or the voice of introjected authority? We can say that the voice starts as one's own, as with the child who slaps his hand and says to himself "naughty." But then we may ask whether that gets dissociated and becomes experienced as part of the introject. Or is it the memory of the parents' voice which is heard again?

Arthur Couch: I have a question about the similarity in what the child identifies with to the actual nature of the frightening person or object. If, in facing the little dog, the child becomes superman, are we not seeing an identification with the frightening power of the object rather than an imitation of the nature of the object itself?

Joseph Sandler: I think Miss Freud possibly covers this when she suggests that there are both sorts of identification with the aggressor. Perhaps we ought to think in terms of having subclasses of this mechanism, because it might well be that children who don't give away the content of their fear in what they do are very different from those who identify much more closely with what they are afraid might happen to them.

Anna Freud: There are surely all kinds of gradation.

Joseph Sandler: What is becoming clear is that we are dealing here with a whole class of phenomena which come under the heading of identification with the aggressor. Could we turn to a point which comes up fairly early in the chapter? You refer to the "primitive ego" (119,111), and it seems that you raise here the problem of whether we can equate the primitive society with the primitive child. The way you use the term "primitive ego" is ambiguous.

Anna Freud: How is it in German?

Ilse Hellman: Das primitive Ich.

Joseph Sandler: Perhaps at that time analysts went along with the view that there was a line of development in regard to different societies just as there is in the individual. This isn't a view that is generally held now. Although we find magical practices in many primitive societies we can equally find them in our own society. But to return to Mr. Couch's point. You actually say, Miss Freud, about the child who played at "dentist," "There was no actual impersonation of the dentist. The child was identifying himself not with the person of the aggressor but with his aggression" (120,112).

Donald Campbell: I think the child also identifies with the distance in the relationship. The father or the dentist is so much bigger and more powerful, so the child establishes a distance equally as great by becoming the superman or something like that.

Joseph Sandler: One could say that the boy who cuts off bits of string, who breaks the pencil points, who sharpens them and breaks them off again, is not playing at dentist, nor is he impersonating the dentist. But if one looks at the unconscious fantasy of what the dentist would do to him, we are not very far from an identification with the castrating aggressor.

Anna Freud: Yes, only he doesn't do it to the dentist. That's what I wanted to emphasize.

Joseph Sandler: I think one might get a clue in an analysis to what the child was worried about from the things he was doing. So in the dentist example the child is doing a little more than simply identifying with the power of the dentist. There is a content symbolically involved as well.

Anna Freud: You know, we differentiate between the child who identifies with the aggression of the aggressor and not with the aggressor, and the child who actually identifies with the aggressor. If the child is identifying with the aggression of the aggressor he may feel that he can go one better, so to say. It doesn't cost him anything.

Joseph Sandler: I suppose that in the case of children who identify with frightening dogs or lions in order to deal with their fear, there may be a history which determines the choice. Perhaps visits to the zoo.

Anna Freud: I remember from the Hampstead Nurseries how the mothers would come and fetch the two-year-old children for outings on Sundays, taking them either to Madame Tussaud's or to the zoo. Once when such a little one came back and we asked her how she enjoyed the animals at the zoo the mother said, "She tried to frighten the lions." This meant that in front of the lions' cage she became a lion. What she did was to turn things around completely. Instead of being frightened she had the idea that the lions were frightened.

Joseph Sandler: As you have given us this example, Miss Freud, we should perhaps note the difference between what you have described and those counterphobic mechanisms in which someone constantly exposes himself to a danger situation in order to master the anxiety. That is quite different from the child who responds to a danger situation with identification with the aggressor.

Anna Freud: If it becomes habitual one would probably identify it as counterphobic.

Joseph Sandler: What has always struck me about counterphobic behavior is that the person seeks out the anxiety situation.

Anna Freud: Because he has constantly to prove to himself that he is not afraid, which is of course not true of these children.

Joseph Sandler: And in the children who show identification with the aggressor there's more of an internal source of anxiety than in the counterphobic person.

Anna Freud: Yes.

Joseph Sandler: A little later in the chapter, you say, Miss Freud, "A child introjects some characteristic of an anxiety object and so assimilates an anxiety experience which he has just undergone" (121,113). Can you clarify again what you mean by assimilate in this context?

Anna Freud: I meant that he copes with or masters the anxiety. The German is *verarbeitet*.

Joseph Sandler: Somewhat later you say "the child transforms himself from the person threatened into the person who makes the threat" (121,113). I want to raise a small point for the record here. Of course, the child does not become the person who makes the threat; he becomes *like* the person who makes the threat. The boundary between himself and the other person is not lost. Of course, in ordinary speech, one often says that one becomes the other person when one means "becomes like the other person."

Anna Freud: Or that one appropriates the quality of the object, or an aspect of the object.

Joseph Sandler: If there is an ego defect, and boundaries are not easily maintained, then one does see, particularly in psychotic and borderline children, confusion between oneself and the other person. This must be very different from identification with the aggressor, which is a much more organized defense. There must always be an interval, however short, in which the anxiety signal occurs.

You spelled it out, Miss Freud, in regard to the child who became afraid after he had rung the bell vigorously.

Anna Freud: Also, in this example, we see a whole process carried to its logical conclusion, which is that the attacker becomes the attacked and the attacked person becomes the attacker. It ends with a change of roles and, of course, we can't really say whether this is then passive into active, or identification with the aggressor. You can take your choice.

Joseph Sandler: It seems to me that there always has to be in some way a reversal of roles with the attacker as a necessary condition for identification with the aggressor. We still have to ask the question of where the aggression comes from when a child's aggressive behavior is defensive. Whose aggression is it when we see identification with the aggressor? Are we talking of a reserve of aggression at the disposal of the ego? Do we see a mobilization of an aggressive drive? I ask this because you make the point that "the child's aggressiveness could not be construed as indicating that some inhibition on his instinctual impulses had been lifted" (123,115).

Anna Freud: No, it isn't drive aggression. I don't think I went into the question of where it comes from at all. The child is not an aggressive child really, but an anxious child who can mobilize aggression when he is anxious, and it serves him well in mastering his anxiety. But where he mobilizes it from was left open at the time.

Joseph Sandler: A little further on you say of the child,

"He had introjected the aggression of the adults in whose eyes he felt guilty . . ." (124,115). Presumably you mean that he had copied the adult, using the term introjection in a descriptive rather than in a more strictly technical sense.

Anna Freud: Of course we used the terms identification and introjection absolutely synonymously. What I say in the text is that he exchanged the passive for the active part. This means that he copied the aggression in going over into the active to substitute for the passive.

Joseph Sandler: What I would like to have clear is that it isn't the parental aggression as such which has been introjected. Perhaps identified might be closer to what was meant, especially now that we distinguish more between the two.

Anna Freud: He appropriates it, I would say. He uses it but it isn't really his own.

Joseph Sandler: You mean he appropriates the idea, but he must be using his own aggression.

Anna Freud: Well, if he had no aggression at his disposal he couldn't use it. But we have the example at the Clinic of a boy who commits the most terribly aggressive acts, which we think is a reaction to or an identification with the father's aggression. The father is not only aggressive to him, but also to the mother, particularly when he is drunk. Now what is it? Is it the father's behavior which arouses the child's own aggression, so that he then commits these violent acts? Or does the father arouse his anxiety to an extent that can only be mastered by mobilizing his own aggression? These are very tricky questions, and perhaps we would say the therapeutic outlook is better if it's an imitation of the father's aggression than if it's his own enormously aggressive nature. But I would say these are unsolved questions.

Marjorie Sprince: I suppose one can look at it in the same way as one looks at the sexual excitation of a seduced child. If a great deal of aggression is experienced by the child before he is able to bear it, perhaps it can mobilize his aggressive drives before they would develop in the ordinary way.

Joseph Sandler: I think we have to take into account the fact that although ultimately it might be the child's own aggression that makes him so frightened, his aggression having been projected onto the attacker, this does not give us cause to assume that the aggression he uses as part of the defense of identification with the aggressor is the same aggression he projected earlier. Here we have to take the issue of the developmental layering of the child's mental organization into account.

Anna Freud: You know, in wartime, when we discussed the Hampstead Nursery children, we had the question very often in mind of how we could teach them to control their aggression when they saw everyone around them being aggressive. The soldiers and the pilots were aggressive.

Ilse Hellman: And got medals for it.

Anna Freud: Yes, aggression was, so to say, the order of the day, and children don't really differentiate between the big aggression in the outside world and the small aggression in themselves. I remember one of our children passing a house in one of the streets that had been completely bombed. He looked at the bombed house and said "naughty, naughty." There was no difference for him between what he broke to pieces and what they broke.

Ilse Hellman: I remember one of the little boys saying about the Marie Curie Hospital, which was bombed, "Me not done it."

Anna Freud: Probably in all these cases there is really insufficient distinction between the child's own aggression and the aggression in the outside world.

Joseph Sandler: Nor, perhaps, enough development of the superego to enable the child to allocate guilt sufficiently to the enemies in the war.

Anna Freud: Another example was in the house we were evacuated to in the country. One of the children wrote to his American foster parents about the latest bomb attack in Essex, and the child dictated, "but it was a kind German, he didn't drop the bomb on our house." This definition of kindness is rather egocentric, perhaps, but I hope you'll put it all in a paper on aggression!

Joseph Sandler: We'll do our best. As you get toward the end of the chapter, Miss Freud, you make the point which is often discussed, that identification with the aggressor is a precursor of the superego, a stage in its development (124,116). When one reads this it's extremely clear, but five minutes later one is puzzled again. It feels, when one thinks about it, as if some point is missing which ought to be there. Of course one understands that criticizing oneself, or criticizing somebody else and then criticizing oneself can be a pre-stage of feeling criticized by one's superego. But there are so many intervening questions. Is it that the view that you held of superego formation at the time you wrote this was essentially that it was based on identification, and that the superego was an aspect of the self that became differentiated? The problems lie, I think, in regard to the way in which the feeling of being criticized is transformed into self-criticism.

Anna Freud: Well, you know, you must not take it too literally. Of course what I say is that identification with the aggressor is an aspect of superego formation, but we know very well that this is not the whole story, because what is turned back from being directed to the outside world is then added to the outside world. But I don't deal with that question here. What I say is that the process of dealing with the aggression or criticism from the outside may—and you see, I don't put it too definitely here—collect, so to say, the material which the superego then uses in its building operations. It's like the birds who collect little bits of straw for their nests. It's not more than that. But when this goes on for a long time, quite a lot collects within the child, and then the next step is that while it's there already, it's not yet effective, because it does not yet really criticize what the child does himself. This is another step that is a very gradual one, and it is a rather painful task to turn the inner institution or agency, which is being built up, truly against the inner processes rather than toward the outside world.

Joseph Sandler: Did you then take a specific element among many processes, that is, identification with the aggressor, or identifying with anticipated criticism, and narrow down your focus to its particular role?

Anna Freud: Yes.

Joseph Sandler: Then what you do is to limit the process to what you have just said, that in a way there are bits and pieces of mechanism and content that become the raw material for the criticisms of the conscience later on, among other things.

Anna Freud: Yes.

Ilse Hellman: At the time there was a considerable emphasis on the role of the object relationship because of the central part played by fear of the loss of love. I think we have to see the whole development of the superego in terms of the development of object relationships and the subsequent internalization of the mother and the establishment of the internal relationship as something which does not depend on being good or bad. In other words, superego development depends on the fear of losing the mother's love if one doesn't do exactly what she says. I think that gradually all the criticisms, plus the good aspects of the mother, become internalized.

Joseph Sandler: I think that at the time Miss Freud was writing, the supporting, loving aspects of the superego were not stressed. Freud had introduced the superego concept after World War I, and the aggressive side was very much in his mind.

Anna Freud: They were, as far as the defensive operations were concerned, of course. They were motivated by fear of what the superego might do. But where the child does not criticize himself, and is not concerned about losing love, then the whole process of building up an inner criticism may be delayed.

Joseph Sandler: Then dealing with external criticism by identifying with the critical parent becomes part of ego development, eventually crystallizing in some way in the superego, although other factors come in as well.

Anna Freud: Yes. If you want to make a very sweeping statement, you could say, "What else is the superego than identification with the aggressor?"

Maria Berger: It also contains identification with the benefactor.

Anna Freud: That's a different aspect of the superego.

Session two

Joseph Sandler: We are still on identification with the aggressor. The first point I have to raise is in relation to the example of the little boy who ascribed his own curiosity to his mother (125–126,116–117). We would all agree that he projected his curiosity onto his mother, but in this case you speak, Miss Freud, of reversal of roles. You say, "The reversal of roles was complete. He assumed his mother's indignation and, in exchange, ascribed to her his own curiosity" (126,117). You are clearly referring to something more than projection, because you add his assumption of his mother's indignation, which is presumably why you describe this in the chapter on identification with the aggressor. If he simply put his own curiosity out onto her, presumably that would be only projection.

Anna Freud: He gives her the sin and assumes the critical role.

Joseph Sandler: So it is both a straightforward projection and at the same time an identification with the mother.

Anna Freud: What it means is that the boy appropriates the indignation. He takes it over.

Joseph Sandler: This is particularly interesting because it seems to be a much closer linking of reversal of roles with the mechanism of projection than we had tended to make in the past. What we see here is a combined identification and projection, and I think it is worth commenting on. We tend to use the notion of reversal of roles rather more broadly—where we see, for example, someone who wants to be mothered taking a mothering role. What I mean is that although he will project his need onto someone else, and identify with the wished-for mothering person, he won't necessarily do this with the mother. He might do it to someone else.

Hansi Kennedy: We sometimes see this where the therapist is treated as the patient and the child assumes the role of the analyst.

Anna Freud: But real reversal of roles means changing places. This is what children do when they play horse and rider—"now *you* be the horse and *I'll* be the rider."

Joseph Sandler: Well, no, Miss Freud, because that means that the horse will be the rider.

Anna Freud: Well, that's how it is when two children change places. They reverse the roles. It's usually not horse and rider, it's usually a coachman—the driver and the horse, and then the roles get reversed in play. The one who was the horse becomes the driver. You don't do it with a real horse but children do it. I have always made the point that so long as the children do it it's very healthy play. But if one of them gets fixed in his role, and always has to be the horse who is driven and whipped and has to serve the driver, that's a bad sign. He has to take a holiday from that by reversing roles.

Joseph Sandler: Perhaps we see its parallel in the sex

play of children when they say, "Now you'll be mummy and I'll be daddy."

Anna Freud: Yes, also mummy and baby.

Maria Berger: You have put this, Miss Freud, into a chapter on identification with the aggressor, but the mechanism is different.

Anna Freud: As you see, in this chapter I try to deal with some of the complications. There are variations in the processes. They are not all the same.

Joseph Sandler: I think this example does belong here, not because of the projection of the curiosity but, as you have emphasized, because of the taking over of the mother's indignation. So the particular reversal of roles could be said to fit into the general class of identifications with the aggressor. Turning to another point, a little further on, you say, Miss Freud, "She introjected the fantasied rebuke and, adopting the active role, applied the accusation to the analyst" (126,117). Just in order to be tidy, let us note again that this isn't what we tend to call introjection nowadays, but rather is an identification with the fantasied rebuke.

Anna Freud: What I meant was what I said before. She takes over the rebuking.

Joseph Sandler: Later you say, in relation to a pre-stage of superego development, that "the moment the criticism is internalized, the offense is externalized" (128,118).

This would mean that the mechanism of identification with the aggressor can be supplemented by another defensive measure, namely the projection or externalization of guilt. Could you elaborate a little on what you called the projection of guilt? We use the term, I think, to refer to a way of getting rid of guilt feelings in oneself by accusing another person, or making the other person into the guilty one. Of course, you touch on it again at the beginning of the next chapter.

Anna Freud: What I am really talking about here is a developmental phenomenon. When the child begins to internalize the criticism of the parents we get the feeling "all right, now he will act appropriately," but there is an extreme reluctance in the growing child to recognize internal conflict and to suffer its consequences. We now get the criticisms inside, and the child asks himself what he can do to prolong the happy state of not feeling guilty. So he puts the guilty action outside, and he is almost as well off as before. Then he has no internal conflict, and the recognition that conflict is inside is a very gradual and very slow process. I think it is much slower than we usually believe, and we can see how the child defends against it with whatever means he has at his disposal. One of these is to say to himself, "All right, I recognize this shouldn't be done, but I am not doing it, somebody else is."

Joseph Sandler: There are some people who cannot bear to maintain an internal conflict of any sort, and throughout their lives will externalize conflict.

Anna Freud: What this means is that the gradual acceptance of internal conflict should be one of the developmental lines that I have set up. What we are talking about is an intermediate stage in which the child already knows what's wrong, but undoes it because he doesn't want to know that he is doing something wrong.

Marjorie Sprince: You wouldn't use the word "projection" today, would you?

Joseph Sandler: Defining projection as attributing something unwanted in oneself to someone else and then feeling that it is directed back at you is a very narrow definition, and this is perhaps something of an idiosyncratic usage particular to the Clinic. We use it in this narrow sense and use the term externalization for all other forms of "putting outside." But in fact, there is a general usage of projection . . .

Anna Freud: Yes. Projecting into the outside world.

Joseph Sandler: Which is quite legitimate, of course, although a bit confusing. It doesn't have to involve the unwanted impulse, say, being directed back at oneself, but it might refer to other people doing something we disown in ourselves. But projecting or externalizing guilt is rather different from other forms of projection. When we speak of projection it is very clear when we think of it in regard to an ideational representation, but the projection of guilt is not the projection of a feeling that the person is experiencing, but rather an externalization of a responsibility. What happens is that we don't project the bad feelings of guilt, but do away with them by externalizing the responsibility.

Anna Freud: Or the actual committing of the forbidden action.

Joseph Sandler: Yes, my point is that it is not an affect which is projected.

Anna Freud: No, not at all.

Joseph Sandler: We certainly have a big problem with definitions in this area. For example, we have tried to separate off a very narrow concept of projection, one in which there is a "reflexive" element. But that leaves us with the term "externalization" as a very broad one indeed. One can externalize guilt, in the way we have just discussed it—really the externalization of responsibility. One can externalize an aspect of oneself onto another person without it qualifying for projection in the narrow sense, because it isn't turned back against oneself. One can externalize an introject, so that someone outside is felt to be the critical authority. Indeed, we could say that one can externalize any one of the major psychic institutions, as Miss Freud has pointed out. So we have the problem that the narrower we make the definition of projection, the bigger the ragbag of externalizations we have. We have made some attempts to deal with this at the Clinic, but none has been very successful.

Anna Freud: There is just a point about projection of affect. Frequently we do project an affect onto another person. Anger is very often attributed to another, and we have those cases where we believe that the other person is feeling guilty toward us, which is quite different from what we usually mean by the projection of guilt. An actual feeling is attributed to the other person, which is quite different from the misdeed being attributed to the other person.

Joseph Sandler: So perhaps projection of guilt has to be a little more precisely defined.

Anna Freud: Anyway, here it's not the guilt that is projected but guilt that is avoided.

Joseph Sandler: You say in this chapter, Miss Freud, that "vehement indignation at someone else's wrongdoing is the precursor of and substitute for guilty feelings on its own account" (128,119). This indignation gets worse when the person is about to perceive his own guilt, and you say that this stage is a sort of preliminary phase in the development of morality. You go on to say: "True morality begins when the internalized criticism, now embodied in the standard exacted by the superego, coincides with the ego's perception of its own fault. From that moment, the severity of the superego is turned inward instead of outward and the subject becomes less intolerant of other people" (128,119). I know we've discussed this before, but I'm still not quite clear about the meaning of your statement that true morality begins when the criticism internalized in the superego coincides with the ego's awareness of its own faults.

Anna Freud: Yes, there are very moral people—I refer here to hypocritical morality—who are indignant about what other people do and ignore the fact that they do it themselves. But many moral people, of course, stop there. It is the next step that creates the true morality, namely the perceiving that it's I myself who does it, and it's I myself who criticizes it. I thought this passage was rather clever!

Joseph Sandler: But I think the rest of us have some difficulties. It does seem to me that there is an enormous jump between the stage that you describe in which the person projects (or rather externalizes) his own indignation in order to deal with the feeling of having done wrong, on the one hand, and the internalized morality on the other. There must be other stages as well, and the relation of one to the other is not at all clear, at least to me. For example, the feeling of having done wrong which exists in the presence of the parents, would also have to be a pre-stage in superego formation. So the affect of guilt is not the critical element in superego development. It seems rather that the internalization of the authority is.

Anna Freud: We don't call it guilt but fear, or perhaps shame, or fear of loss of love, before it becomes guilt. We use the term guilt only when we consider the superego. But the feeling gradually becomes internalized even when it is still connected with the external object, and it remains after it has been externalized. When we look at it developmentally, there are very many moral young children. I would even say moral toddlers, but their indignation is always about what somebody else does. There are no guilty toddlers, I think. Not in the true sense of the term.

Joseph Sandler: So your point is that the term guilt should be linked with internal conflict, with the superego.

Anna Freud: I think that's the usual meaning.

Joseph Sandler: My question would then be whether the identical feeling might be there before there has been a true superego introjection, but when the parents are still the authority figures. From a developmental point of view I wonder if the identical feeling cannot be there earlier than true superego formation. I can recall when I was a first-year student at the Institute, when we still had Institute seminars with you in your house, and I asked you about a dog I had who liked to get onto the bed, but when he heard someone coming he would get off the bed and have his tail between his legs. I asked you then whether the dog did not feel guilty. And you said that he didn't feel guilty, but he felt a consciousness of having done wrong.

Anna Freud: The crux of the matter would be—how would the dog feel if no one came in? I think he would feel very comfortable. Which means if there is not the fear of discovery, if there is the certainty that no one has seen what you have done wrong, before there has been full internalization, the child doesn't feel guilty. The child may feel ashamed, but he will feel guilty only according to the degree of internalization.

Joseph Sandler: If I may persist a bit, I think my point is that the transformation of the fear of punishment or of the fear of loss of love into a feeling of having done wrong may occur before we put the label "guilt" on this feeling, but the affect may be the same. It is a particular sort of unpleasant anxiety, I think, that we feel when we have done something wrong, but also before superego formation, when punishing authority approaches.

Maria Berger: I agree with you because there does seem to be a stage when the child feels uneasy, but will still do the thing he knows he mustn't. This is particularly important because that is where some psychotic children get stuck. I remember a girl of about eight who would pick up dirt from the floor, say "You mustn't eat dirt," and put it into her mouth. I suppose the next step is the knowledge that you mustn't and you don't, but that didn't occur with this girl. That's why I think there is a stage before the full internalization of parental authority.

Joseph Sandler: I wasn't thinking as much of this as a separate stage, but rather as something very simple. The three-year-old who has a guilty look when caught, quite different from having a frightened look, does, it seems to me, experience the same affect as the one we later call guilt.

Anna Freud: But don't we call it a guilty look because an adult in the same situation would feel guilty?

Ilse Hellman: We have recently discussed an adolescent who is aware of his homosexual wishes, and who has made a sort of plea to the analyst to make sure he will help him control them. He feels that what he wants to do is wrong, but is also aware that he can't rely on his control. He needs an external person to make sure it won't happen. The next step will be, we hope, that not wanting it, the awareness that he can stop it, and the external person not being needed anymore will come together. I am reminded so much of the little children who said to me that it was my fault that they had eaten all the sweets, because I went out of the room for a few minutes. If I had been there, they wouldn't have. The child is aware that he cannot yet control himself.

Anna Freud: I remember a little girl who blamed her mother, in an outburst of anger, when she cut herself with scissors during play. She said to her mother that she should have known that one doesn't let little children play with such sharp scissors.

Joseph Sandler: Yes, that might be anger, but it might also be a reproach—the externalization or projection of guilt that we were talking about.

Anna Freud: But what the child said was that the mother should have prevented her from doing what she shouldn't do.

Hansi Kennedy: I was also reminded of young children who often have an awareness of having done something wrong but then defend against that in different ways.

For instance, there is the child who has taken something he oughtn't to have taken, and then comes and simply says that he hasn't taken it. He covers up in some way, but that does indicate that there is an awareness of having done wrong. I don't know what we call that.

Joseph Sandler: It's so difficult to define a feeling state, of course. The words one uses are never exactly right, and we are guessing about the child's feelings. We guess that there is a consciousness of having done wrong which may or may not be like a guilt feeling, before there is a superego, when the authority is still vested in the parents. I think the child must have much the same feeling as he does later when he feels guilty.

Anna Freud: You could look at it another way. Before the existence of an efficient superego, the child tries by all means to escape the criticism of the parents. He does things in their absence, he hides what he does from them, or lies, and may even try to placate them with confessing another act. He may try to amuse them, and so on. All these maneuvers are repeated with the superego.

Marjorie Sprince: I wonder whether the child doesn't experience, before there is guilt, shameful situations that are not associated with guilt. Perhaps shame in the sense of feeling unable to deal with impulses.

Anna Freud: Yes, there is an area where this can be studied very positively. That is the relation of children to their own excrement. We know the great difficulty we have in leading the child from considering his body products to be something very nice and valuable, toward making him disgusted by them or indifferent toward them. But whatever result you achieve with the child, you achieve it only when the child is in the presence of other people. The child (and perhaps even the adult when all alone) has a completely different attitude to his body products. This is an interesting aspect of the problems about guilt feelings we have just been discussing.

Joseph Sandler: And we can add to this that even after superego formation we may still have the sort of shame, a bad feeling, that is dependent on the presence of the other person, and on other people knowing what one has done or thought. I think that there is a sort of guilt that is related to the presence of other people, even with the full establishment of the superego. Of course, we can also have a shaming superego, which complicates things. I had a patient yesterday who confessed to wanting to do something wrong which was very trivial. He said that what had held him back was a feeling of shame. As the work in the session progressed it became clear that it wasn't simply a dependence on the presence of other people, on fear of what the others would think of him, but that he has a particular sort of conscience which seems to say, "It's all right as long as other people don't know about it." Which is quite different from feeling ashamed in front of others.

Anna Freud: Yes, there is a wide variety in types of conscience.

Joseph Sandler: For example, some people feel that something is all right at home, but the neighbors mustn't see it. This can be internalized as part of the superego.

Renate Putzel: Isn't there an enormous development of the superego in adolescence that involves part of the rebellion of the adolescent against adult standards? They are very concerned about what is really right and wrong, and what they can accept and cannot accept. I think the autonomy of the superego depends to some extent on the outcome of the period of adolescent struggle. It seems to me we can't speak of its formation being completed in early childhood.

Anna Freud: Yes, this is very controversial, because what one finds in adolescence is a sort of group conscience, so that something can be quite all right within the adolescent group that is not all right when confronted with opinions from outside the group. It's a very complex problem.

Joseph Sandler: Complex also because one sees the remains of the infantile superego in adolescents and adults. Yet at the same time throughout life we get ideals being formed which can give the person narcissistic supplies that might otherwise have to come from the superego. They can come from the group, and one can get supplementary external superegos, so to speak, which lessen the severity of the earlier superego. But my feeling is that the essential childhood structure remains, and whatever else exists is added to it, but we cannot really undo what is created early on. But do we assume that, from a fundamental point of view, changes can occur? I think you made the point, Miss Freud, in your 1927 book on the technique of child analysis, that the superego can be modified by teachers and by other educators. I don't think you've ever withdrawn that statement, have you, Miss Freud?

Anna Freud: No.

Joseph Sandler: The next point for discussion relates to the statement that "it is possible that a number of people remain arrested at the intermediate stage in the development of the superego and never quite complete the internalization of the critical process. Although perceiving their own guilt, they continue to be peculiarly aggressive in their attitude to other people. In such cases the behavior of the superego toward others is as ruthless as that of the superego toward the patient's own ego in melancholia. Perhaps when the evolution of the superego is thus inhibited, it indicates an abortive beginning of the development of melancholic states" (129,119–120).

Would you see things in quite that way now, Miss Freud? I wonder if you would not say that in the cases of the people who are so aggressive toward others there can be a full internalization, but the amount of guilt they experience is far too severe for them to stand, so we get the further step of externalization. This would be very different from an arrest at a pre-stage of superego formation. It seems to me possible that what we see is a later mechanism, added on when the guilt is really intolerable. Then, in the next paragraph (129,120) you point out that although identification with the aggressor

represents a preliminary phase of superego development, it can also be seen as an intermediate stage in the
development of paranoia. Presumably that would be
linked with projection, and the feeling of being persecuted. Do you still see identification with the aggressor
as an intermediate stage in the development of paranoia?
Or do you mean that if we were to put these things in
order of complexity, so to speak, this puts identification
with the aggressor in the middle somewhere, without
it necessarily meaning that it is going to be a stage in
the development of paranoia?

Anna Freud: No, I don't mean that. What I meant was
only that since the mechanism of projection is employed
rather freely at this time, if you intensify the use of it,
you may end up with a paranoid state because you project
many things which are then felt to be coming back at
you from the outside world.

Joseph Sandler: I think it worth noting that you did not
mean that an early stage in the development of a paranoid
illness is identification with the aggressor, because if that
were so we would have a lot more paranoid people about.
And, of course, you do point out in the next sentence
that identification and projection are normal activities.

Anna Freud: Yes.

Joseph Sandler: Toward the end of the chapter you speak,
Miss Freud, of the mechanism of reversal, specifying
that you mean specifically the reversal of love into hate
(130,121). You have spoken before of reversal of roles,

and of reversibility in terms of the drives. Love and hate are, of course, more complicated than sexual or aggressive wishes, and I wondered whether you wanted to differentiate between sexuality and aggression on the one hand, and loving and hating, which involve more of an object relationship, on the other. Was it simply that you wanted to use different words because you had spoken of sexuality and aggression before? Were you pointing to something specific here?

Anna Freud: What I meant was the change from hate to love, and not the change from libido to aggression.

Maria Berger: A so-called reversal of affect.

Anna Freud: Yes.

Joseph Sandler: It's very different from the other sorts of reversal. It is more a substitution of one affect for another.

Anna Freud: In German I wrote *die Verkehrung ins Gegenteil*, which is a turning round into the opposite.

Joseph Sandler: There is something which has always puzzled me about the steps in the development of paranoia. I mean the steps from "I love him" to "I don't love him" and then "I hate him," or "He doesn't love me, he hates me." I feel there is something unexplained there, and I've never been able to pinpoint quite what it is that is missing in the process of getting this complete substitution by the opposite.

Anna Freud: You get very many examples of it in normal life, quite especially with adolescents or preadolescents. I remember a young adolescent patient who would come into the room and say that she had met, in the waiting room or on the stairs, or in the street, an absolutely hateful man. She could hardly bring herself to think of him. He immediately aroused her violent hate, but what it meant was that she was sexually aroused by him. She liked him, but she had to ward off the loving feeling, leaving the hate. And with children you can find that quite often. The unwelcome love manifests itself as hate.

Joseph Sandler: I think I can be a bit more precise now. Doesn't the girl in the example you have given hate her own feelings and then turn this hate for herself into hate for the object?

Anna Freud: Well, you can use the word hate, but you can also say she disapproves of her own feelings, or she feels guilty about her feelings. She wards them off. You could put it this way. She acknowledges the importance of this object, but since she is unable to acknowledge the positive feelings, she puts it in the opposite terms.

Joseph Sandler: And then, descriptively speaking, it's a reversal of love into hate. It is, of course, so typical of adolescents, for example, for a girl to say, "I hate him, I hate him," and we all know very well that she's interested in the boy.

Anna Freud: Yes, and it's quite safe to emphasize the hate, because until the girl is quite sure the boy is interested, she has to save herself from the narcissistic humiliation.

Joseph Sandler: Would you care to elaborate, Miss Freud, on the last sentence in that paragraph, when you say that the target the ego chooses for its unconscious impulses is determined by—and here you quote your father—"the perceptual material which betrays unconscious impulses of the same kind in the partner" (130,121). Could you expand on what you meant in that context?

Anna Freud: Yes. I meant that the more normal the person is in whom this happens, the more he will pick out people or moments in the outside world where there is some rational foundation for an externalization, and he will use these, but will not externalize onto somebody where it absolutely does not fit. But the slightest sign that the other person would be a good person to attribute that feeling to will cause him to use the mechanism extensively.

Joseph Sandler: Yes, and of course this is one great difficulty we have with paranoid people, that there's always some truth in what they say.

Anna Freud: And this is why what paranoid people say is so hurtful, because they have usually caught something true.

CHAPTER 10

A Form of Altruism

Anna Freud starts this chapter by commenting that projection breaks the link between the ideas that represent dangerous drive impulses and the ego. In this it is like repression, in that both act to prevent the instinctual process being perceived; other defensive processes affect the instinctual process itself. Projection is also like repression, in that it can be motivated by any source of anxiety.

Little children use projection to disown their own acts and wishes when these threaten, by allocating responsibility to others who may be put forward as "whipping boys," or accused of wrongdoing. Anna Freud remarks that "in either case it [the ego] dissociates itself from its proxies and is excessively intolerant of its judgment of them" (133,123).

While projection disturbs our relationships with others, it may also consolidate them. It does so through a "normal and less conspicuous form of projection," a form of "altruistic surrender" of one's own drive impulses in favor of others (133,123). An example of this is the case of a governess who since childhood had wanted, and fantasied having, beautiful clothing and a number of children. She also wanted to do everything better than her older playmates, and to gain admiration for this. As an adult she was unassuming and modest. She came to analysis unmarried, childless, and dressed rather shabbily. She showed little envy or ambition, and it would have been natural to assume that her wishes had been replaced by reaction formations extending to all her instinctual life. In analysis, however, it became clear that she satisfied her own sexual wishes by "an affectionate interest in the love life of her women friends and colleagues" (135,125). She was very interested in her friends' clothes and devoted to their children. Also, "she was ambitious for the men whom she loved and followed their careers with the utmost interest"; as Anna Freud puts it, "She lived in the lives of other people, instead of having any experience of her own" (135,125).

Analysis showed that she had developed a severe superego so that her own wishes could not be gratified. Her ambitious masculine fantasies and her feminine wishes were prohibited, but rather than being repressed, the impulses found "some proxy in the outside world to serve as a repository for each of them" (136,125). She projected her forbidden instinctual impulses onto suitable other people, but did not dissociate herself from them; rather she identified with them. While what she did was egoistic, "her efforts to gratify the impulses of others . . . could only be called altruistic" (137,126). The development of these attitudes could be traced to incidents in her childhood in which she had dealt with the frustration of her own wishes by ensuring that some other child was satisfied instead.

Another young woman, who was particularly fond of her father-in-law, reacted to the death of his wife by offering to dispose of her clothes. She took no garments for her own use, but put aside one coat as a present for a poorer cousin. When the mother-in-law's sister wanted to remove the fur collar for herself, the patient flew into a blind rage. In analysis it was seen that it was guilt that prevented the patient from taking anything that had belonged to her mother-in-law, as this would have gratified the wish to replace her. After renouncing the wish, she felt disappointed, but could gain its fulfillment through the poor cousin. Her superego accepted this wish as long as it was not the patient's own.

There are many instances of projection and identification combining in this way for purposes of defense. There are two purposes served by this defensive process. The subject can "take a friendly interest" in the gratification of other people's drives, and thus indirectly gratify his own. It also frees the activity and aggression associated with the fulfillment of instinctual wishes, so that these can be used on behalf of others. "The most familiar representative of this type of person is the public benefactor, who with the utmost aggressiveness and energy demands money from one set of people in order to give it to another" (141,130). A similar process occurs in the assassin "who, in the name of the oppressed, murders the oppressor" (141,130). The object of the aggression is always a representative of childhood authority which imposed renunciation of the drive.

There are special features which favor the selection of particular objects for such projection. One of these is the perception of the forbidden impulse in the other person. Usually the object has once been envied, and by displacing wishes onto objects who can better fulfill them, altruistic surrender can be "a method of overcoming . . . narcissistic mortification" (142,131). This latter point is often a factor in the girl's choice of a man, for whom she may be very ambitious, but with whom she does not have a true object relationship. Parents are often both egoistic and altruistic in the same way in regard to their wishes for their children's achievements.

After citing Rostand's *Cyrano de Bergerac* as an excellent study of altruistic surrender, Anna Freud goes on to consider altruistic surrender in connection with the fear of death. Such a fear can be dealt with by excessive concern for the safety of the love objects, upon whom the subject has displaced his instinctual wishes. It is a mistake to suppose that this is an outcome of the warding off of death wishes consequent on suppressed rivalry. It is due rather "to the subject's feeling that his own life is worth living and preserving only insofar as there is opportunity in it for the gratification of his instincts" (145,133). When the drives are transferred to others, their lives become more precious than the person's own.

In a long footnote Anna Freud draws attention to the similarity between altruistic surrender and the conditions determining male homosexuality. The homosexual "makes over his claim on his mother's love to a younger brother whom he has previously envied" (146,134). What can be added is that the pleasure in giving and helping in altruistic surrender is itself a gratification of instinct. Passivity is turned into activity and narcissistic mortification is overcome by a sense of power; the "passive experience of frustration finds compensation in the active conferring of happiness on others" (146,134). Finally, Anna Freud wonders whether a genuine altruistic relation can exist, and asserts that projection and identification are certainly not the only ways to acquire attitudes that appear altruistic. Another route is that of masochism.

The Discussion

Session one

Joseph Sandler: We can start by assuming that there are a number of different forms of altruism, taking it in its descriptive sense, and that we need not consider it to be some innate tendency within the individual. In other words, what you describe here, Miss Freud, is a particular form of activity which is the result, the outcome of a set of transformations. Would that be correct?

Anna Freud: Yes, you mean you don't think anyone is born altruistic.

Joseph Sandler: Or even *becomes* altruistic, out of the goodness of his heart.

Anna Freud: No, it's out of the badness of his heart.

Joseph Sandler: I often wonder about people who dedicate themselves in their work for others—the excellent secretary we are always looking for. Some of the qualities involve so much dedication that one wonders what the difference is between that sort of application to one's work and masochism.

Anna Freud: I think that in the end there is a very close link to masochism.

Joseph Sandler: Right at the beginning of the chapter you say, Miss Freud, that projection breaks "the connection between the ideational representatives of dangerous instinctual impulses and the ego" (132,122). You then say that, of all the defensive processes, this most closely resembles repression. I suppose one can assume that by "ego" here you are referring to consciousness, but I wonder whether there are not many other mechanisms that also break the connection between the idea and the wish behind it. I can see the point you make in regard to something like the displacement of an aggressive wish, where the wish remains as one's own but the object is changed. The wish is accepted, although the object is displaced. But, in the light of our previous discussions, wouldn't a mechanism such as reversal involve the sort of break you mention?

Anna Freud: It is fairly simple. What we do either in repression or in projection is not to change the instinctual process, which in reality remains the same. What we change is the perception or the feeling that it belongs to the self. But in the defensive processes such as reversal or turning against the self, turning something into its opposite—for example, passive to active, love to hate—the instinctual process itself is altered.

Joseph Sandler: And a mechanism such as isolation of affect—would you see a break there as well?

Anna Freud: Well, there we get the division between ideation and emotion.

Joseph Sandler: My difficulty came from the fact that you are using ego in the sense of self-representation, and referring to identification of oneself with the impulse.

Anna Freud: Yes. What I really had in mind was projection. The person says, "I don't mind aggression as long as it is not I who am aggressive. Somebody else can be aggressive." The impulse doesn't change.

Joseph Sandler: It's a dissociation of oneself from the wish.

Anna Freud: Yes.

Joseph Sandler: If we think of dissociation of something from one's self-representation, we have to think of the confusion that exists about the concept of inner world as opposed to outer world, because the child builds up a knowledge of the outside in his mind to form part of his representational world. The boundaries between inside and outside are then gradually built up in the world of the child. So when you say that in repression "the objectionable idea is thrust back into the id, while in projection it is displaced into the outside world" (132,122), presumably what this means in projection is that the unwanted content is displaced from one's representation of oneself to the representation of the outside, of a person outside. In that sense, projection is a form of displacement.

Anna Freud: Doesn't that make it more complicated than it needs to be? The feeling of the individual is, "This is no longer I, it is the person who is out there in the outside world." The feeling is not "It's a representation of that person," but "It's that person."

Joseph Sandler: Yes, that is of course the person's belief. I am sorry for my pedantic tendencies . . .

Anna Freud: And my simplifying tendencies . . .

Joseph Sandler: It might be better to say simply that in projection the content is felt as belonging to the outside world rather than to oneself.

Anna Freud: I know what you mean. You know what I mean. It's only a different way of expressing it. And I think the way I express it actually corresponds to the feeling of the person in whom the process is going on, who doesn't feel that he has ascribed something to an object representation in himself. The feeling is, "It's you, and not me."

Joseph Sandler: Just as the feeling is that something that one perceives outside oneself does belong to the outside world.

Anna Freud: Yes, and it does, doesn't it?

Joseph Sandler: It's a very good hypothesis that it does! But it *is* relevant that all we know consists of representations, and on the basis of our experience we have built up a division between inside and outside, which serves us very well because it corresponds with our hypothetical external reality. But I don't think we should have an argument about this, Miss Freud.

Maria Berger: Perhaps we should, because it's an essential problem.

Anna Freud: To me it sounds like what the German philosopher said: "How lucky it is that in cats the slit in the fur is just in the place where the eyes are."

Joseph Sandler: I get your point, Miss Freud.

Anna Freud: Luckily the inner representation coincides with the object in the outer world, if our reality testing is in order. If the reality testing is affected, it's not so.

Joseph Sandler: That touches on a point I want to make. If we think in representational terms, it allows us to bring into this framework the understanding of the products of the breakdown of psychotic patients, or the problems of psychotic children when their boundaries get confused. It also forces us to look at things a little more developmentally, so that we can take into account what you yourself have pointed out, that there can't be projection until there is a boundary between self and notself. This boundary is, of course, in the mind of the child. In regard to repression, as you have put it, repression thrusts the impulse right out of the realm of conscious experience, and we can say that projection thrusts the wish into what is the external world for the person. It does seem to me to be possible to say a great deal about defenses in terms of what the defenses do to mental representations.

Anna Freud: I suppose so.

Joseph Sandler: You mention in this chapter the view of the English school that projection can come about early. We know that the English school started in a very un-English way with Melanie Klein.

Anna Freud: Yes, absolutely. At the time it began it wasn't called the Kleinian group. There was the British Society, the English Society. I tried to keep this book nonpolemical, and there are only very few points where I touch on the controversies. I do so in this chapter because according to what we believe, as you said just now, projection does not come into being until the division between outer and inner world is established. Whereas with the Kleinians, it is thought to be one of the earliest mechanisms, and when I have tried to make a chronology, I put it rather late.

Joseph Sandler: You say, Miss Freud, "At all events the

use of the mechanism of projection is quite natural to the ego of little children throughout the earliest period of development" (132–133,123). In the earlier edition you had put "infancy" instead of "development" and in the original German *Infantilperiode.*

Anna Freud: I don't mean the first year of life there. I meant childhood. The first year of life didn't play such a great part then.

Joseph Sandler: Whereas now, if we say the earliest period of infancy, we mean the first few weeks.

Anna Freud: Yes, that has changed a great deal.

Joseph Sandler: I wonder if you could say something about the chronological development of projection, Miss Freud. Would it coincide with the development of boundaries, possibly being something which grows out of the fluctuating confusion that the child feels, so that perhaps projection and its correction becomes part of boundary formation? This would allow us to say that the two go hand in hand as development progresses.

Anna Freud: Of course, I go very much by the child's speech, because what one says about the child before speech is so much without proof. According to the development of verbalization—well, the earliest I would put it is eighteen months. I mean what we now call the toddler age, eighteen months to two and a half years. The constant need of the child to put the blame on others is very early, but we don't really know about it before the child can speak.

Joseph Sandler: I suspect that some people would put it earlier than that, and I wonder what you think of the hypothesis that one can't have secondary identification—I don't mean primary identification or fusion or anything like that—without projection, because really they are opposite sides of the same coin. Where secondary identification can exist, it must also be possible to project, because in identification an attribute of the object is taken over into one's own self-representation, and in projection the reverse occurs. So if we put the two things together, possibly the observation that such identifications have occurred can provide evidence that projection can also occur, because they are so close in form, except the direction is different. If all this is so, one would expect to see this sort of thing toward the end of the first year, I think.

Anna Freud: Only we have no proof of it before the child speaks. It may be, or it may not be.

Joseph Sandler: I was thinking of the child of nine months who feeds his mother—I know this is not an easy example—but certainly one sees deliberate copying of the object quite early. My thought was that perhaps from that time one could imagine attributing to the object things one doesn't like in oneself.

Anna Freud: If you want to take it from a theoretical point of view, and without any proof from the child, you could say that throwing out or disowning what is unpleasant, for whatever reason, is a very early tendency. Something is thrown out, which means away from the self, but it is only after boundaries between self and object are established that the object is seen as a convenient place to put what's thrown out. But there has to be a logical connection between an action and its consequences, between an action and the unpleasant feelings aroused by the action. It's that which makes the child want to get rid of his wishes, as well as the idea that the wish is forbidden. I wouldn't put it too early. But, of course, in our imagination we can place it anywhere in development. The question is whether we can get proof. And, anyway, whatever we call projection in the book, we would probably call externalization now. Only the term didn't exist at the time.

Joseph Sandler: That brings us directly to the next point, Miss Freud. You say that projection "disturbs our human relations when we project our own jealousy and attribute to other people our own aggressive acts" (133,123). Could you explain that a bit more? Do you mean that we then begin to act in an irrational way toward these other people, and as a result that disturbs our relationships, or do you mean something more than that?

Anna Freud: I mean something much simpler. We don't like the other people any better after they've become the carriers of what we don't like in ourselves. It makes them unpleasant, open to criticism, and we don't like them at all.

Joseph Sandler: So it is because of what we project onto others that our good relationship with them gets disturbed.

Anna Freud: Yes, that's what I mean.

Joseph Sandler: When you go on to say that it may work in another way, enabling us to form "valuable positive attachments" (133,123), you refer specifically to the mechanisms of altruistic surrender, I think.

Anna Freud: Yes.

Joseph Sandler: There has been a lot of talk recently about projective identification and empathy, and I wonder whether we could say that the normal process of projection—as opposed to its defensive use—in association with identification might contribute something positive to development in regard to our empathic understanding of other people. Usually we think of projection as a way of getting rid of things we feel are bad in ourselves, but could not projection apply also to things other than aggressive wishes, and thus help us to understand how other people function on the basis of a realization of how we function?

Anna Freud: Yes, but if it's projection of unwanted impulses such as aggressive ones, or forbidden sexual ones, what we externalize along with them is our criticism of these impulses.

Joseph Sandler: So you are speaking here specifically of

the defense mechanism of projection, not of the general process. Freud distinguished, I think, between projection as a defense and as a general psychological tendency.

Anna Freud: Yes, I do here too, because it certainly helps to build up relationships. But what appears first is the criticism of others as we discussed it in relation to the last chapter. Self-criticism is put out onto others. So we do not get empathy. It can be empathy only if we externalize onto others what we like in ourselves. That is the difference between the projection of what we dislike in ourselves and the form of altruism I discuss here.

Maria Berger: Does one in fact externalize what one likes in oneself ? Doesn't the form of altruism you speak about relate not to what people like about themselves, but what they wish for? If one talks about externalization as a defense, what would be the purpose of externalizing?

Anna Freud: I think I can answer that. One likes the wish, but one doesn't dare fulfill it in oneself. That is the reason one externalizes it. Because what one externalizes with it is an enormous urge to get the wish fulfilled, only it is through somebody else now.

Joseph Sandler: There are, of course, many ramifications of the idea of projection. Apart from it being a defense, at an age when he is very egocentric a child will understand other people's behavior in terms of what he understands about his own. In a sense we could call this a form of externalization, although it's very different from what we usually understand by externalization.

Anna Freud: I remember a little boy who just couldn't understand that the grown-up people who had money and could spend it as they liked would not spend it all on sweets, which at that moment was the thing he wanted most.

Marjorie Sprince: I remember someone once saying to a child patient, "When you are able to like yourself, you will be able to like me." Isn't this externalizing good aspects of the self ?

Joseph Sandler: When one uses the phrase "good aspects of the self," I suppose it means the parts that one can accept, the wished-for parts and other attributes that one likes, or sees as good. But, of course, there are still aspects of the self which feel good, but which also give rise to anxiety, so that they then feel bad. This is quite a problem.

Hansi Kennedy: There would be a conflict.

Maria Berger: The question is whether or not some aspect of the self is acceptable to one. If it is acceptable, would one then want to externalize it?

Joseph Sandler: I wonder about the situations where people seem to have a compulsion to force their opinions on others. I suppose that would reflect an anxiety about the validity of their own opinions, so that they need external confirmation, or a need to control everyone else for some reason, or something like that. There are people

who get really upset if they can't talk people around to
their own way of thinking.

Anna Freud: That's something quite different.

Joseph Sandler: Perhaps because it would be a way of
trying to get corroboration rather than being a projection.
There is something I should like you to comment on,
Miss Freud. In the first case you describe in this chapter,
of the woman who surrendered everything for the family
where she was a governess, you say that analysis of her
relations to her parents showed that her early giving up
of instinct "resulted in the formation of an exceptionally
severe superego, which made it impossible for her to
gratify her own wishes" (135–136,125). Here we can assume that the pushing down by her of her aggressive
wishes contributed to the formation of a harsh superego.
You then go on to describe how her sexual and ambitious
wishes found proxies in the outside world. There seem
to be different forms of altruistic surrender, and you have
described one of them extremely clearly here, but I
wonder if you would comment on the relation of what
you have described to reversal of roles, and on the part
played by identification—you refer in this chapter to Paul
Federn's idea of "sympathetic identification." Clearly
what is going on is more than just projection.

Anna Freud: It would be much better if we dropped the
term projection and talked only of externalization. What
I really saw was the contrast between those people who
deal with the prohibition of their own wishes by a strict
superego in this particular way, and others who use the

opposite way of condemning all the people in the outside world who have similar wishes, because they can't stand seeing the forbidden wish being fulfilled. In that case the superego criticism that is felt inside now goes out to all the persons outside whom they, so to say, seek out to blame. But in the type of altruism I described the person seeks out the wishes in the outside world to represent his own wishes, and instead of blaming, fulfills it there. This is to me the important thing—the individual is not critical of the fulfillment so long as it is not his own person involved, and the superego (which is so critical of, let us say, exhibitionism) says, "Well, for the other person it's quite all right, it's nice." From that comes the vicarious pleasure.

Joseph Sandler: This vicarious pleasure is presumably gained through observation.

Anna Freud: Yes, and identification.

Joseph Sandler: So identification with the proxy avoids the superego's strictures, because it's not oneself fulfilling the wish. But we would have to say that it occurs at some unconscious level so it is not consciously felt as being in the self through an identification.

Anna Freud: Yes. As in all these defensive maneuvers, a whole row of defense mechanisms is needed to bring about the result. What I find so interesting is that at every step in the process the whole thing can turn into the opposite, namely into the negative direction. The person outside who is now the carrier of, let's say, the exhibitionistic wish, could be envied enormously, and envy and jealousy could consume the person whose wish it originally was. He may say, "If I can't have any beautiful clothes, no one should have them." Whereas the altruist in my chapter feels that everybody, or especially some particular person (or probably more than one person), should be dressed beautifully, and enjoys it. The same applied to my patient's wish for children, and the same to her wish for professional success. So you could say it's an escape from envy. But I don't think, at least not from what I've seen in analysis, that it begins with envy and is a warding off of envy. I think it's another way of solving the situation in which somebody has what one hasn't got oneself.

Joseph Sandler: Does not the same mechanism which you have described in this form of altruistic surrender in fact apply to a much broader group of attitudes, of which altruism is only one example? I was thinking, for instance, of a person I know who goes on a diet to lose weight from time to time, and is then strongly compelled to feed other people more. In some ways she gets gratification from this, but I don't think it could be called altruism.

Anna Freud: It's a vicarious pleasure.

Joseph Sandler: Well, how does that differ from altruism by proxy?

Anna Freud: Altruism is always by proxy. It's not usually directed toward one person only, because it becomes a character trait, which means that it is then distributed toward a larger number of people. Do you remember the little girl we discussed the other day who, when there is a program on the television she likes, insists that her sisters watch it? I thought that was really an example of altruism in the child. But somebody said, "Oh no, she's just bossy." Now the altruists are bossy, because the urge that is usually behind the fulfillment of one's own wishes is now placed behind the fulfillment of the wishes of the other person. And the wishes have to be fulfilled in a certain way, namely in the way the altruist would like to fulfill them for himself or herself. And, after all, the bossiness of so-called do-gooders is proverbial, and we get all the gradations there right up to those insupportable people who dictate to others just what they should do to be happy. So bossiness is, I think, a hallmark of altruism, but it can be kept at a low level or it can go very high. The altruist can be a very pleasant person, or with the increase in the need to control, can become a most unpleasant person.

Maria Berger: The type of person you describe is one we knew very well on the Continent before the war. They were usually older women who attached themselves to wealthier families, and lived by proxy through the lives of the children, trying to control whom they dated, the way they dressed, whom they went out with, and so on. Some of them were seamstresses, some governesses, but whatever they were they found a niche for themselves in the family.

Anna Freud: You know, all these things have other aspects attached to them—the vicarious pleasure, the masochistic surrender of one's wishes to others, and particularly the feeling "I'm not good enough, I don't deserve it, others do deserve it." We can follow this back to two solutions to the penis envy of girls. One is that of the girl who becomes someone who can't stand not having the masculinity she is striving for, really hates men for it, and verbally castrates and destroys the man. But another is that type of woman who fulfills her own ambitions via the masculinity of the man, which is very different. You can see this very clearly in the different types of women in public life.

Hansi Kennedy: The role of envy must be crucial in this.

Anna Freud: It's very crucial, and the question should be: does the altruism circumvent envy altogether, or is it perhaps a warding off of envy? I remember that one of the cases I described in this chapter was a very possessive, jealous little girl, who then took the turn toward altruism. With others the envy may be either not conscious, or not noticeable.

Joseph Sandler: Yes, or avoided through control.

Anna Freud: Yes.

Joseph Sandler: It's probably always there in the background.

Hansi Kennedy: One sees it in very young children in a very special situation—I mean those children who are quite happy to participate in something by watching, and those who have to be actively involved. It's something we can see very early, even in the second year of life. There are children who like watching, and there are others who get bored by just having to watch an older child or parents do something, and really want to do it themselves.

Anna Freud: A third alternative would be to become the sort of person who helps others fulfill what they have set out to do. That would then be an altruistic stage. I must say I was fascinated at the time I wrote this by all these distinctions.

Joseph Sandler: Reading the chapter has revived this fascination for all of us, because I think we tended to simply take the view that there isn't such a thing as real altruism, that it is a reaction formation, and had forgotten the details of what you have written. The mechanisms involved are extremely important. I am thinking of the use of a proxy, of what we called years ago the "Sabbath goy" mechanism.

Anna Freud: But he had to do the forbidden tasks, and he is a lower figure, and these people are not. We have talked of the women who have different ways of solving penis envy, but you can see it with men. Men who teach, for example, can have different sorts of relationships with younger colleagues or students. There are those who feel enormously threatened by the young and then defend themselves against the threat with anger or some other reaction. But there are also those who find great pleasure in helping young students fulfill their aims. I remember that Ernst Kris, for example, had enormous vicarious pleasure in seeing one of his young men attain something. That was altruistic pleasure. But the next question is how many of these things are defensive processes to ward off resentment, anger, fear, or envy.

Maria Berger: There is another type of altruism, which is a sham altruism built on reaction formation.

Anna Freud: It's quite different from that.

Joseph Sandler: The distinction between the form of altruism you have described, Miss Freud, and reaction formation is an important point. There is also the difference between the reaction formation which is built into the character, and an attitude adopted more or less as a conscious or contrived posture. These are what I call the sugar and the saccharin reaction formations.

Anna Freud: I am talking of the sugar reaction formation. What I mean is that it's built into the character. A very pleasing example of this is in the Schumann song *Frauenliebe und -leben*. The bride calls on the younger sisters in a friendly way to help her dress up for her great day. This really means they should not envy her, should not think that they would like to be in her place, but should put all their wishes also to be brides aside, in order to help her.

Joseph Sandler: In the last sentence of the footnote right at the end of the chapter, you refer to "another and easy route to the same goal . . . by way of the various forms of masochism" (146,134). Could you elaborate on the point about masochism?

Anna Freud: What I meant about masochism is that you find people who masochistically have a very low opinion of themselves, so that what they feel is that they are not good enough to get what they want; a better person deserves it. This looks exactly like the altruistic reaction, but is based on a masochistic view of the self.

Joseph Sandler: And I suppose it shouldn't be called altruistic except perhaps in a broad descriptive sense, because it's usually accompanied by enormous resentment of the other person, although that can be unconscious.

Marjorie Sprince: I want to take up the point mentioned earlier about dieting. I have been very puzzled by two anorectic patients who have a need to feed everyone else in an excessive way. They say that they're not good enough to have the food themselves, the other person should have it; but they convey a sense of having to suffer at the same time. There seems to be a masochistic element in the pleasure of watching other people eat, but not allowing themselves to do it themselves.

Joseph Sandler: With anorectics one has to take into account the fact that they usually have a latent bulimic tendency, and that the urge to eat may then have to be externalized onto another person.

Anna Freud: I remember in that respect that Max Eitingon, many years ago, told of a case of a very severe alcoholic he was treating by analysis. At one point it looked very much as if the patient had got hold of the urge, and the drinking had stopped. But then the patient would get up in the night and put out water for the cat. So the thirst was there, but it was displaced onto the cat, and he had to satisfy it.

Joseph Sandler: I am reminded of that wonderful cartoon of the weary father trudging back to bed in the middle of the night, saying to his wife, "Her doll was thirsty."

Session two

Joseph Sandler: Looking back at the chapter on altruism it seems that there are still a number of things we haven't fully gone into. First, in relation to the altruist's aggressiveness, you say, Miss Freud, "This defensive process serves two purposes. On the one hand it enables the subject to take a friendly interest in the gratification of other people's instincts and so, indirectly and in spite of the superego's prohibition, to gratify his own, while, on the other, it liberates the inhibited activity and aggression primarily designed to secure the fulfillment of the instinctual wishes in their original relation to himself " (140,129). I don't understand what you meant there.

Anna Freud: It's so easy. If you can't get what you want yourself and enjoy it yourself because it's prohibited by internal conflict, well at least somebody else can get it, and you can enjoy it there through what you call vicarious enjoyment—which is certainly worthwhile. But that isn't all. At the same time the process liberates, or creates an outlet for, the aggression. What I meant was that originally the individual wants to pursue his or her instinctual aims aggressively. "I want it, I'll have it, I'll fight anybody who won't give it to me." This aggression becomes impossible and forbidden when fulfillment of the wish becomes impossible and forbidden, but now, with the altruism, you can fight for somebody else's fulfillment of the wish with the same aggression, with the same energy. So you have both your libidinal vicarious pleasure, and you have the outlet for your aggression. It's surprising that not more people are altruists!

Joseph Sandler: Are you then saying that one of the purposes of aggression is to secure the fulfillment of non-aggressive instinctual wishes? This is very interesting.

Anna Freud: It is a use for aggression.

Joseph Sandler: Just to clarify things—the aggression you are referring to here is aggression at the disposal of the individual that he would normally use, if he were not having to defend against it, in order to gratify all sorts of wishes. This throws some light on the problem of aggression, I think.

Anna Freud: It's so obvious. I can give you a good clinical example I had just yesterday. By the way, this is always suspicious. You know, Stekel was known in the Vienna Society for always having had a patient just that morning who brought the very thing someone else was describing.

We used to call that the Wednesday patient of Stekel. But anyway, yesterday I had a clinical example of a young patient who has great guilt feelings when she fights with her parents for the fulfillment of her life's wishes. She has plenty of opportunity to fight her parents, but she always has many guilt feelings about it. But suddenly she came out with the following sentence in the analysis with a great deal of feeling: "I wish I were a Negro, or an American Red Indian, and then I could really fight for the liberation of these people." This meant to fight without any guilt feelings, and in a way which was quite ego syntonic and superego syntonic, she could release the whole aggression against the authorities which she now has to keep in check. If she had the disposition, she would, I suppose, be an altruist. Now she is an egoist. But, to return to your question, I think it has always been obvious that aggression can be in the service of libidinal fulfillment.

Joseph Sandler: It has been very useful for us that you put it this way, because we have tended to say libidinal and aggressive wishes, and to treat them as if they were simply parallel, which hasn't made the struggle we have had with the whole concept of aggression any easier. To say that one of its functions is to obtain, in a forceful way, the gratification of other wishes of all sorts is very clarifying.

Anna Freud: You know, I think you would find it in the old literature, which describes the inner processes of "do-gooders." I mean people who are extremely active in good works, but at the same time extremely aggressive in pursuing their aims. I think it has always been assumed in psychoanalysis that they satisfy, or rather employ aggression on behalf of others which originally they would have employed for their own benefit.

Joseph Sandler: Of course we see this in the antivivisection and anti-foxhunting groups, in the Society for the Prevention of Cruelty to Animals, and so on. Their members sometimes use the most aggressive means to pursue their ends.

Anna Freud: Yes. There's a famous example of a teachers' convention where the subject was corporal punishment. The argument was so heated that they came to blows about it.

Joseph Sandler: It struck me on reading this chapter that you used the phrase "narcissistic mortification" (142,131), which was certainly used a lot later on, but I wonder whether you introduced it here. Was this a term coined by you? Of course, the idea of the narcissistic wound is there in Freud and Abraham.

Anna Freud: In German it is *narzisstische Krankung*, which I suppose I would have called in English a narcissistic hurt. It is the same.

Joseph Sandler: It is interesting how words can get into the literature through translation, because mortification means something a little different from hurt.

Anna Freud: It means a hurt that is humiliating at the

same time. Something that hurts your pride is a mortification.

Joseph Sandler: When you discuss altruistic surrender
from the side of the fear of death you point out that the
altruist is not really concerned for his own life in the
moment of danger. You say, "He experiences instead
excessive concern and anxiety for the lives of his love
objects" (145,133). Now we can see the development of
your thoughts in terms of the use of the proxy, as well
as of the concern for the object. On the other hand, we
have very often brought this type of concern and anxiety
about others under the heading of reaction formation.
Would you care to say something further about that?

Anna Freud: Well, this is quite different, of course. The
reaction formation is a defense against hostile wishes
toward the other person. But what I have been describing is a sort of identification with the other person on
the basis of shared instinctual wishes. Identification is
not even the right word, but the moment you give your
main wishes to another person, you and the other person
are in some way one. And then of course you have to
keep the other person alive to keep yourself alive. Or
rather, your concern for your own life changes to concern
for the other person's. And there is no hostility included
in that. By the way, I wonder if everyone here is familiar
with *Cyrano de Bergerac*, because, as you can gather
from this chapter, I was highly struck by the marvelous
picture of the altruistic surrender to the rival on the basis
of the rival's better physical endowment. It was one of
my favorite plays for a while. You know, Christian, Cy-

rano's rival for the love of a woman, is handsome, whereas Cyrano is ugly. He helps the handsome man who represents him get to the woman he loves. And then, of course, there's the tragic end with Christian dying, being killed in battle. It's a beautiful picture of what is meant by altruistic surrender and the reason for it. I used to know *Cyrano de Bergerac* by heart at one time—I can still recite it, because it's beautiful language, and it's a beautiful play.

Maria Berger: We have clarified the distinction between altruism and reaction formation. Shouldn't one also see the place of masochism in all this? I have a feeling that the altruists you talk about are not necessarily masochistic altruists because they get a lot of vicarious gratification, as you have shown us, whereas the masochists don't. There is the altruistic do-gooder, the reaction formation do-gooder, and, I suppose, a masochistic do-gooder who doesn't get vicarious gratification but gets a feeling of mortification instead.

Anna Freud: I would say the altruistic person escapes the masochistic position, because he cannot fulfill his own wishes because of internal conflict. But this does not lead to the enjoyment of his suffering or deprivation. He looks for a substitute and finds the substitute in helping others fulfill their wishes. So it's a turning away from the masochism.

Joseph Sandler: This brings us back to what is for me one of the most important questions in all of this. That is, the question of how an instinctual wish, for example, gets its gratification via a proxy. There must be an unconscious fantasy in which the object is equated with the self, and this must happen in a way in which there can actually be adequate gratification. This must mean that the perception of something happening gives the gratification. This is very different from the basic model of instinctual gratification tied to zonal stimulation and discharge, and it raises fascinating questions.

Anna Freud: It is, of course, not like hysterical identification, and it needs quite a level of ego and superego development to take that particular course. But I agree it's a very important item to study.

Joseph Sandler: It does face us with the problem of how the drives get gratified if we use a frame of reference in which we say that the instinctual wish is powered by instinctual tension mounting, and then through activity of some sort there is a reduction in the tension. Here we see a reduction in instinctual pressure through a substitute representation, and the implications for our theory of drive gratification are tremendous.

Anna Freud: What we see in altruistic surrender is a very refined form of drive gratification. I mean refined in the sense that ego and superego have a great deal to do with it. On the other hand, if you look at the aggressive side there isn't much refinement, because the aggression is the same, and it can be rather crude aggression, only in the service of someone else.

Joseph Sandler: Of course, there are cases where people

use others as props for their own aggression, as tools, and there we would have a different situation.

Anna Freud: They are not altruists. We have just seen a case at the Clinic where a very shy and apparently unaggressive boy uses a brother for the expression of his aggression and antisocial tendencies. That's quite a different matter.

Joseph Sandler: The idea of substitute or symbolic gratification ties in with sublimation, and perhaps understanding how that occurs would give us further insight into the way in which a sublimated activity, just like a gratifying activity undertaken by another person, could also yield instinctual gratification.

Anna Freud: But in altruistic surrender the original wish really remains the same. It's not deflected, it's not torn down. It's exactly the same as you see, for instance, in the Cyrano de Bergerac example. The wish is to be loved by that woman. And that remains the same for him and his proxy.

Joseph Sandler: I think that there are two schools of thought about sublimation. In one the idea is that the wish has changed, that the energies involved have been transformed, while in the other there is the assumption that the wish is still alive, but unconscious, and that it is gratified in a disguised form, perhaps in a much more refined form. In the second case one would see a greater similarity with the vicarious gratification in the form of altruism you describe, or in symbolic gratification.

Anna Freud: In altruism we are not dealing with anything symbolic. It is only that someone else has the nonsymbolic pleasure.

Joseph Sandler: I am still bothered by the problem of how one gets a reduction of tension in oneself through the proxy.

Anna Freud: And there is the question of why one should be so good if one gets nothing out of it. I mean, there has to be a reward for this enormous renunciation!

Joseph Sandler: I suppose we have to say that a lot of things are gratified. I am thinking of mastery and control, in particular. There is also the hostility which one sees sometimes in people who are altruistic, sometimes toward their protégés, sometimes toward the people who are seen as obstructing their protégés. There is, of course, another route the process can take. The thing can go slightly wrong, and the aggression doesn't come out against the frustrator, the aggressor, but against the proxy, forcing that person to certain actions. That's where the altruism has gone wrong.

Maria Berger: But don't you think that there must be an enormous amount of gratification in fantasy, and the identification with the object is probably spun into a fantasy? If we think of the governess, the fantasies could be of two kinds. In one she gets so much pleasure through the other person vicariously, but she might also have fantasies in which maternal feelings are gratified.

Anna Freud: Which leaves the question of why she can be maternal toward the child who represents herself, because the maternal instinct should go toward children in general. There are so many shades in all these things.

Joseph Sandler: One day we shall have to get to grips with what the Kleinians are trying to encompass under the concept of projective identification. And, I think, we should take careful note of the fact that you said in 1936, in relation to the case of the governess, "She gratified her instincts by sharing in the gratification of others, employing for this purpose the mechanisms of projection and identification" (136,126). And in the footnote to that remark you refer to Paul Federn's idea of sympathetic identification. Could you tell us a little of your thoughts on that subject?

Anna Freud: What I will tell you is why I put the footnote in, because such footnotes were made by Ernst Kris at the time. He would say, "Don't forget, you should quote Federn here." Then I said, "Well, what should I quote?" Then he gave me the quotation. So I don't remember.

Part IV

Defense Motivated by Fear of the
Strength of the Instincts
Illustrated by the Phenomena of Puberty

CHAPTER 11

The Ego and the Id at Puberty

In this chapter Anna Freud points to the interest in the psychological changes in puberty and to the contradictions apparent in the mental life of adolescents. They are "excessively egoistic, regarding themselves as the center of the universe . . . and yet at no time in later life are they capable of so much self-sacrifice and devotion"; they make "the most passionate love relations, only to break them off as abruptly as they began them" (149,137). They enter "enthusiastically into the life of the community" but long for solitude (149,137–138). They can submit blindly to some leader, but defy authority. They are "selfish and materially minded and at the same time full of lofty idealism" (150,138). They are ascetic but can be instinctually self-indulgent. They may be inconsiderate, but at the same time can be touchy. They can be light-heartedly optimistic, but very pessimistic. They "work

461

with indefatigable enthusiasm and at other times they are sluggish and apathetic" (150,138).

These phenomena can be seen as the result of physical changes or as being due to purely psychological factors, independent of physical processes. All agree, however, on the importance of puberty in development.

Anna Freud points out that the psychological problems of puberty were relatively neglected by analytic writers. This is because psychoanalysis does not agree with "official" psychology that sexual life begins at puberty. We see it as beginning in the first year, and regard puberty as one of the phases of sexual development, in which there is a "recapitulation of the infantile sexual period" (152,139). Although infantile sexual life is repeated in later phases, each phase adds something, and in puberty genitality predominates over pregenital component drives. Thus adult sexual life has two beginnings: one in the first year, the other at puberty. In the climacteric there is a further recapitulation, but genital impulses "flare up for the last time and pregenital impulses come into their own again" (152,140).

All three of the periods mentioned are similar in that "a relatively strong id confronts a relatively weak ego" (152,140). While there is a relative lack of change in the id, the differences between the periods arise from changes in the ego. In infancy and puberty the ego uses different defense mechanisms, so the comparison between the two periods will throw light on ego development. In the small child instinctual demands and the associated affects and fantasies are intense, but his relatively weak ego has a powerful ally in the external world. He is strongly motivated "by the hope of love and the expectation of punishment" (154,142). Children learn, over the first years, to control their instinctual life to a considerable degree. The field of study of the way the ego is caught between the id and the outside world is that of education, which looks for ways to join the external forces and the ego together in their struggle against the drives. The young child develops internal conflict involving "objective anxiety," the anticipation of punishment from the outside. This anxiety is strengthened by the turning of instinctual forces against the self and by anxieties originating in fantasy. This means that "objective anxiety" may have a relatively loose tie with reality.

The attempts to solve the conflicts that then arise in the mind of the young child may give rise to the symptoms of an infantile neurosis. Moreover, in small children "the ego is the product of the conflict itself " (156,143). In later life the ego is more rigid, and the first childhood period can be regarded as being over when "the ego has taken up the position it intends to occupy in its battle with the id" (157,144).

During latency it is as if a truce has been called between the drives and the ego. The ego has time to develop and strengthen itself. The superego has been created and the main conflicts come to involve superego anxiety—the anxiety of conscience together with a sense of guilt. The ego has an ally in the struggle against the drives in the superego. But with puberty there is a drastic change in the balance of forces because the drives are stimulated and inner conflicts flare up. There is an increase in libido and aggression, and submerged instinctual interests reappear. Reaction formations acquired during latency threaten to break down. Oedipal wishes are revived, as well as castration ideas and penis envy. What is then revealed is "the familiar content of the early infantile sexuality of little children" (159,146). But by puberty the ego is much more consolidated, and if it allies itself with the id, it comes into conflict with the superego. Its one wish is to "preserve the character developed during the latency period, to re-establish the former relation between its own forces and those of the id" (160,147). It uses all its mechanisms of defense, and in the immediate prepubertal period we can see the different phases in the conflict with the drives revived.

With puberty proper the genital impulses predominate and there is an apparent improvement. The previous turmoil seems to have disappeared. But this does not mean that the previous conflicts have been solved; rather they are overlaid. They may well reappear and produce problems again. When phallic wishes have predominated in childhood, however, the increase in genitality at puberty can lead to an abnormally exaggerated genital masculinity.

What is at issue in the struggle of the adolescent is the nature and fate "of the psychic structure in childhood and latency" (163,149). There are two opposing extremes of outcome of the adolescent conflict. The id may overthrow the ego, leaving no trace of the previously developed character. At the other extreme the ego may be the victor, and the character formed during latency "will declare itself for good and all" (163,149). In the latter case there will be a restriction of the id impulses, with much energy expended to hold the libido in check. This is "permanently injurious": "Ego institutions which have resisted the onslaught of puberty without yielding generally remain throughout life inflexible, unassailable, and insusceptible of the rectification which a changing reality demands" (164,150).

Finally, it cannot be said that the strength of the drives during puberty gives an indication of the final outcome. What has to be taken into account in addition are the strength of the instinctual impulses, the ego's tolerance of the drives (which depends on its development during latency), and "the nature and efficacy of the defense mechanisms at the ego's command" (165,151).

The Discussion

Joseph Sandler: I think that nowadays we speak more of adolescence than of puberty, and there is a legitimate distinction between the two. In the immediate prepuberty phase we do get adolescent characteristics, but as we tend to speak of preadolescence as well, the distinction is not as clear as it might be. The eleven- or twelve-year-old child is very different from the latency child, but possibly the physical changes will not yet have occurred to the same degree as a little later. Certainly there are psychological changes before the child actually reaches puberty. But of course puberty *will* occur no matter what the level of psychosexual development, and in that sense there is a clear distinction between adolescence and puberty. And nowadays we tend to speak of adolescence as going on into the early twenties, don't we?

Anna Freud: There's an interesting point here. The term "extended adolescence" was first used by Siegfried Bernfeld, but he was referring to the difficulty that some people had of entering into sexual life proper, to those people who postpone sexual gratification in adolescence and thereby prolong adolescence. But we know how early sexual life begins in adolescence nowadays, and yet we see a prolongation of adolescent behavior and of the whole adolescent upheaval in spite of this. So evidently the connection between the beginning of sexual gratification and the ending of adolescence is not as valid as we once thought.

Joseph Sandler: You speak in this chapter, Miss Freud, of puberty being the first recapitulation of the infantile sexual period (152, 139), and you say that a second recapitulation takes place later in life, at the climacteric . . .

Anna Freud: I think it was Ernest Jones who wrote about that first.

Joseph Sandler: You say that the genital impulses flare up for the last time, which is certainly a menopausal tendency in some women, but not in all, and then you say that the pregenital impulses come into their own again. Do you still take this view, Miss Freud?

Anna Freud: Again, I think I took up something here that played quite a part in the psychoanalytic literature at the time. I mean that, for example, women who had come to the end of their proper genital sex life might show anal-sadistic tendencies, which come into the foreground again. There used to be much talk about this sort of thing, but I haven't seen it in the literature recently.

Ilse Hellman: It comes up when we talk about the treatment of older people.

Joseph Sandler: You say later, Miss Freud, that "a man's id remains much the same throughout life" (152,140). Did you mean man as opposed to woman, or did you include women as well?

Anna Freud: I'm sure I meant a person, a human being. You know, when this book is reprinted again I want to go through the translation. What would Women's Liberation say today, if *Mensch* were automatically translated by "man"?

Joseph Sandler: Would you still say, Miss Freud, that the id remains much the same, because on the face of it one would expect it to die down with age. What you say might be a comforting thought, but if it is a fact, then is it equally true for sexuality and aggression?

Anna Freud: There are certainly changes in intensity, both for libido and aggression.

Joseph Sandler: Would you say that the wishes remain essentially the same?

Anna Freud: Yes, that's what I really had in mind. The big changes don't happen in the id. The whole chapter is about the balance between id and ego.

Joseph Sandler: Yes, you compare the immutability of the id with the mutability of the ego. You point out also that in the ego's "conflicts with the instincts it makes use of different defense mechanisms in the different periods" (153,141). We all know this for early development, and we also know that there are some defenses that are characteristic of adolescence—for example, intellectualization. You also say later that the defenses of adolescence are earlier defenses exaggerated, but is there anything particularly special in regard to defense mechanisms during adolescence that we would connect with, for example, the adolescent revolt, and the need to reject the parents?

Anna Freud: Yes, but those would be defenses against the external world, or rather defensive behavior toward the external world, not defense mechanisms directed against the id. If we think of the changed defenses against the id, what is characteristic for adolescence are such mechanisms as intellectualization.

Joseph Sandler: Can we really say that it is the defense against the external world, Miss Freud, if we think of the way the adolescent defends against closeness with his parents?

Anna Freud: It's a defense against a tie to the parents.

Joseph Sandler: And at the same time against his wish to regress and to be a child. This puts the conflict between the wish to be an adult and the wish to be a child at the center of the adolescent's internal concerns.

Anna Freud: But I don't think he uses the usual defenses

such as turning into the opposite, changing passive into active, or denial. I don't think there is a new range of defenses either. The tendency to intellectualize, however, is an important defense and a dangerous one.

Joseph Sandler: But also a normal one to some degree.

Anna Freud: Normal for adolescence.

Maria Berger: Wouldn't you say that there is an upsurge of externalization, Miss Freud? The conflicts felt inside always seem to get attributed to the outside in adolescence.

Anna Freud: Yes. On the other hand, externalization is used to a large extent early in life. It's not a new defense mechanism.

Joseph Sandler: You refer to the main fear of the ego as being that of loss of love or of punishment, and you follow Freud in this. I wonder if you could comment on the role of the fear of helplessness and of being unable to cope at various ages. It seems that such a fear could well be put on a par with the fear of loss of love and of punishment or castration. I mean the fear of simply being helpless, as something existing in its own right.

Anna Freud: Both the fears I mentioned are based on helplessness—not only the fear of helplessness, but on the actual helplessness of the child. The child is in the power of the parents, and it is this feeling of being in the parents' power that predisposes the child to the fear of object loss and the fear of loss of love, with all the consequences which follow.

Joseph Sandler: I was thinking of something a little more than that, more like the fear of being helpless in the face of being overwhelmed by something uncontrollable, the fear of the traumatic experience, which can then get connected with a danger situation of some sort. I wondered whether there can be a fear of helplessness as such, as a potent threat at different ages. The danger would be essentially the danger of the devastating experience of loss of control.

Anna Freud: What you refer to is the child's inner realization of his need for the object. This, of course, leads to the fear of object loss, which then creates the situation of being helpless vis-à-vis the external world, and also being helpless vis-à-vis the internal world. This is because the role of the object in the child's life is to protect him against both external and internal dangers.

Ilse Hellman: I think that the actual experience of helplessness we are talking about gets very closely linked to the danger of object loss, to the parents' part in giving the ego the support that is needed to avoid helplessness. The helplessness itself is frightening but is soon experienced as being the outcome of object loss.

Anna Freud: You know, we see it clinically very much in the case of children with only one parent, where the other parent is either dead or has gone away for some reason. What you see very clearly in the child is the fear that the second parent could go too, and what would happen then?

Joseph Sandler: I was very taken with your use of the word "forepain" (155,143). It presumably stands in contrast to forepleasure in the context of precursors of superego development. You link it with objective anxiety here, and with the actual behavior of the parents, Miss Freud. Couldn't one also link it with what comes from inside as well?

Anna Freud: It's really signal anxiety.

Joseph Sandler: In the German original it is *Vor-Unlust*, and what it suggests to me is that you were thinking of something more than just an anxiety signal. Possibly there is a content attached to it which contains a threat connected to the parents as authority figures.

Anna Freud: Yes.

Joseph Sandler: You take the view in this chapter, Miss Freud, that the drives decline during latency. This tends to be questioned nowadays. There are those who think that the latency child has a very active sexual life, but disguises it and deflects it into sublimated activities and the like. It is often said that if one gives projective tests to latency children, what they produce is full of oedipal conflicts and sexual preoccupations, fears of castration and so on. This seems paradoxical, and I remember that some colleagues who tested children used to conclude regularly that children who brought material like this weren't in latency, although they were by every other indication latency children. The question of what happens to the drives during latency comes up for discussion again. I don't think we would question that there is an upsurge of drives in puberty, but the idea of their decline during latency has perhaps to be modified.

Anna Freud: I think that, clinically speaking, I would take the same view as before, that there is a decline in instinctual pressure and an upsurge in the ego's free deployment of its energies. I don't think that the decrease in the instinctual pressure is due to the ego's activity. I really think it is the other way around. For example, there is definitely a decrease of masturbation in normal latency.

Joseph Sandler: Some people might disagree with you about that, Miss Freud, and would say that it becomes more hidden, that the real change is that there are more kinds of activities which allow for instinctual gratification.

Anna Freud: I wouldn't say that our experience with latency children confirms that. When you have a child in analysis at age four and five, you can see the changes very clearly when the child goes over into latency.

Joseph Sandler: I don't think there is any doubt that there are marked changes on going into the latency period.

Anna Freud: The question is what is the cause and what the effect.

Maria Berger: One change which lets us recognize the arrival of latency is that children remove themselves from home. They go to their friends and play in the street. This is very noticeable.

Joseph Sandler: In this chapter you do refer, Miss Freud, to the changes brought about by the internalization of the principles held up to the child by his parents and teachers. You say, "In his inner life the outside world no longer makes itself felt solely in the form of objective anxiety" (157,144), and you speak of the setting up of the superego. It seems to me that, despite the changes we can observe from the outside, we can still ask whether the pressures involved in the unconscious fantasy life of the child diminish. Could one not say that, relative to what happens later on, and relative to the directness with which the oedipal child shows his sexual and aggressive wishes, the latency child conceals them much more? Heinz Hartmann would have said they were neutralized more, I suppose. I don't know whether there is a diminution in instinctual pressure or not, but I do know that there are different opinions about it.

Ilse Hellman: I think it's extremely difficult for us to judge this. What blurs the picture nowadays is that there has been such a change in adult attitudes that what is internalized in the form of rules and regulations means something different. We don't see what we used to see as latency, because certain attitudes are not offered or expected nowadays. What is expected from the child by the adult world is so very different, and I think this may very well be the reason why we do not see latency as such a well-defined stage as we used to. The change when a child went into latency used to be quite dramatic. On the other hand, we know that there is certainly a change in the child's preoccupations, and an increased interest in matters removed from immediate sexual or aggressive concerns.

Anna Freud: This is due to the nonsuppression of infantile sexuality.

Joseph Sandler: The question about latency seems to be how much the change is in the id and how much in the ego. Perhaps there is a tendency more recently to put emphasis on the ego factors in the changes.

Dorothy Burlingham: Isn't there nowadays a tremendous rush from one period to the other, without the child staying for any length of time in latency?

Anna Freud: Yes, a child hardly enters latency before he's already in adolescence. So if you don't look at the right time you may miss it!

Maria Berger: I have been struck by the way latency-age children play games in a rather stereotyped way. I am thinking of schoolgirls playing repetitively with their jump ropes, going on and on. There is a certain stereotype of behavior and defenses belonging to that period.

Joseph Sandler: Are you referring to defenses, or to the fact that the children get a disguised form of instinctual gratification in skipping and skipping?

Maria Berger: Do you think they get instinctual gratification from walking in a certain way to avoid the cracks in the pavement?

Joseph Sandler: I wouldn't be surprised.

Ilse Hellman: It has obsessional defensive content.

Maria Berger: This is what I mean.

Dorothy Burlingham: I was wondering, although it is not quite on this point, whether we couldn't compare the results we get from projective tests now with those we got in the past. Possibly we would see quite a lot of difference between thirty years ago and now.

Anna Freud: It is a different world altogether now. The question for us is what creates the difference and where it starts. With the id, or with the ego?

Joseph Sandler: We can certainly say that at some point a desexualization of some sort occurs. The question seems to be at which point, and whether this is through the lowering of instinctual pressure or not.

Anna Freud: Well, you know, the whole thing has changed so enormously and the difference is in the masturbation conflict. Because that was the big thing that changed when the child entered latency in the past.

CHAPTER **12**

Instinctual Anxiety During Puberty

Anna Freud now deals with the topics of asceticism, intellectualization, object-love, and identification in puberty. She begins the chapter by commenting that there are phases during which increased libidinal cathexis occurs which are of interest in the study of the ego because then its mechanisms stand out more clearly. Two of these ego attitudes deserve special attention because they are increased at puberty—asceticism and intellectuality.

In adolescence there is at times "an antagonism toward the instincts which far surpasses in intensity anything in the way of repression which we are accustomed to see" (167,153). It is an asceticism comparable to that of religious fanatics. Unlike many neurotic conditions, in which only one aspect of instinctual life is defended against, a different picture is met when instinct as a whole is repudiated. The starting point of this process is the turning

477

against the incestuous fantasies of prepuberty and the masturbation associated with them. It then extends to instincts in general, and it seems that the quantity of instinct rather than its quality is feared. "They mistrust enjoyment in general and so their safest policy appears to be simply to counter more urgent desires with more stringent prohibitions" (168,154). It can extend from the drives to ordinary physical needs. The renunciation extends "to things which are harmless and necessary" (169,155). We see young people depriving themselves of ordinary protection against the climate, mortifying the flesh, reducing food intake, depriving themselves of sleep, and deferring anything which represents giving in to physical needs.

Whereas in neurosis we see substitute expressions of the particular instinctual wish that has been defended against, in the repudiation of instinct found in adolescent asceticism "no loophole is left for such substitutive gratification" (170,156). But there is a later "swing-over from asceticism to instinctual excess" (170,156), which can be taken as a transitory sign of spontaneous recovery. Where the drives continue to be repudiated we get a sort of "paralysis of the subject's vital activities" of a psychotic sort (170,156).

A distinction can be made between the sort of asceticism described and repression. In the former the fear is of the amount of instinctual drive rather than the content of any particular impulse. A relatively more primitive process seems to be at work than in repression. The "asceticism of puberty must be interpreted not as a series of repressive activities . . . but simply as a manifestation of the innate hostility between the ego and the instincts, which is indiscriminate, primary, and primitive" (172,157–158).

In puberty we see a development of intellectual interests, particularly in abstract ideas. Sometimes this is intense, and may be the basis for adolescent friendships. "They will argue the case for free love or marriage and family life, a free-lance existence or the adoption of a profession, roving or settling down, or discuss philosophical problems such as religion or free thought, or different political theories, such as revolution versus submission to authority, or friendship itself in all its forms" (174,159–160). It is surprising to find how removed these discussions are from the actual life of the adolescent, and it becomes clear that his concerns are not attempts to solve his real problems. But the very subjects in which the adolescent is so passionately interested are the same concerns "as have given rise to the conflicts between the different psychic institutions" (176,161). Intellectualization can then be seen to be a means for "thinking over" the instinctual conflict and solving it in that way. Anna Freud says, "Their mental activity is rather an indication of a tense alertness for the instinctual processes and the translation into abstract thought of that which they perceive" (177,162). It is possible that the intellectualization of puberty is simply an exaggeration of a more general ego attitude, and this phenomenon in adolescence, as in psychotic illness, may be an intensification of a normal way of mastering the instincts by thought. Anna Freud suggests that this might explain why instinctual danger appears to make people more intelligent. During quiet periods the person can allow himself some stupidity, and in this regard instinctual anxiety acts like objective danger.

Anna Freud adds that the decline in intelligence of children when they enter latency may be due to the prohibition of their interest in sex, resulting in an inhibition which becomes more general. Therefore it is not surprising that with the reawakening of sexual drives in prepuberty, intellectual abilities are stimulated. On the other hand, as intelligence has the function of helping one master instinctual danger, in latency and adult life the person can relax his efforts "to intellectualize the instinctual processes" (180,164). But the adolescent's mental performances, however remarkable, are on the whole unfruitful.

In both asceticism and intellectualization the ego is afraid of the quantity of instinct. Such anxiety belongs to very early ego development, when the ego is being differentiated from the id. The fear of the strength of the drives helps maintain the separateness between ego and id, and both mechanisms have the aim of controlling instinctual processes at a time when there is an upsurge of libido. The primitive dread of the strength of the drives is revived, and other drive and ego processes are affected.

We can see a conflict between two opposing tendencies in adolescents in connection with their object relations. The general hostility to instinct is usually first directed against incestuous fantasies, and as a result the ego turns against the members of his family as though they were strangers. Similarly, the superego, being still invested with libido coming from the earlier parental relationship, is treated as "a suspicious incestuous object and falls a victim to the consequences of asceticism" (182,166). So there is also an estrangement from an aspect of the superego, and this may lead the adolescent to become asocial, although early in puberty there may be an overinvestment of superego contents, and this is the probable cause of the idealism of adolescence. But, as Anna Freud puts it, "We now have the following situation: asceticism, itself due to an increase in instinctual danger, actually leads to the rupture of the relation with the superego and so renders inoperative the defensive measures prompted by superego anxiety, with the result that the ego is still more violently thrown back to the level of pure instinctual anxiety and the primitive protective mechanisms characteristic of that level" (183,167).

At the same time we get many new attachments taking the place of the old. While one person can readily be substituted for another in this, the form of the relationship gets reproduced over and over again. The adolescent aims less at possessing the object than at "assimilating himself as much as possible to the person who at the moment occupies the central place in his affection" (184,168)

Adolescents will change in many aspects, depending on whom they admire at the time. They change their views, while still holding them firmly. Anna Freud links the adolescent here with the "as if" personality described by Helene Deutsch. She recalls a young girl who had many successive friendships, but became indifferent to each abandoned love object and conceived a violent dislike for that person. It was discovered in analysis "that these feelings toward her former friends were not her own at all" (185,169). Whenever she changed her object she copied the views of the new friend and no longer experienced her own emotions. The resulting love relationships are not object relations at all but primitive identifications. So the fickleness of adolescence is a step back on the basis of an early type of identification.

Anna Freud then relates the case of a fifteen-year-old girl who was very concerned with being loved, and who fell violently in love only to show very quickly how shallow this love was. What one sees in adolescence is a sort of "delibidinizing" of the external world, and the adolescent may show a regression from object love to narcissism. The efforts to recontact the external objects are "convulsive," and may only be by way of the narcissistic route, through identifications. In this way there is a further resemblance to psychotic patients in the adolescent's attempts at recovery. In both adolescence and psychosis there is a quantitative change in cathexis, and in both the increased investment from the id adds to the danger. This causes the ego to make greater efforts to protect itself. And in puberty and psychotic illness there is "the emergence of primitive defensive attitudes which we associate with the ego's dread of the strength of the instincts—an anxiety which goes further back than any objective anxiety or anxiety of conscience" (189,172). Finally, the normality or abnormality of the processes in any adolescent can be judged on the basis of whether one or another of the characteristics previously mentioned is dominant. So the ascetic is normal if his intellect functions freely and he has healthy object relations. Something similar is true for adolescents who intellectualize and are idealistic, and for those who move from one object to another. But if any one attitude overshadows the others, the problem is posed of how much is a normal transition and how much pathological.

The Discussion

Session one

Joseph Sandler: At the beginning of the chapter, Miss Freud, you say, "Owing to the heightened cathexis, wishes, fantasies, and instinctual processes which at other periods occur unnoticed or are confined to the unconscious emerge into consciousness, surmounting, when necessary, the obstacles placed in their way by repression and becoming accessible to observation as they force their way into the open" (166,152). When you say "confined to the unconscious" I suppose you really mean the unconscious part of the mind rather than the system Unconscious of the topographical model. Your use of the phrase "the unconscious" would presumably include the possibility of preconscious contents.

Anna Freud: Yes, I merely meant that they were not conscious, and nothing more.

Joseph Sandler: In fact, in the German original you said *unbemerkt oder unbewusst*, which means unnoticed or unconscious in a descriptive sense. Here one can really see the hazards of translation! When you say that the contents emerge more directly and become accessible to observation, presumably this is after some modification. Or do you feel that they come through directly, without change?

Anna Freud: In adolescence it is pretty direct.

Joseph Sandler: Could you give an example?

Anna Freud: Yes. You know, with adolescents you get direct fantasies of, for example, intercourse with the mother. There are thoughts of direct sexual assault on the mother and her body, without any modification.

Joseph Sandler: Isn't this the exception rather than the rule, Miss Freud?

Anna Freud: Not as much the exception as one would think.

Joseph Sandler: My impression was that one gets more the reactions against such wishes, or displacements.

Anna Freud: You get both. We can recall certain adolescents we treated here where we got crude and undisguised sexual fantasies which appeared at no other time. They were frightening, but at the same time we couldn't even say that they were not acceptable to the adolescent. Because they are both. They are repudiated, but at the same time they are accepted.

Joseph Sandler: Presumably this would also apply to aggressive wishes. I notice you tend to give emphasis to the libidinal wishes in this chapter, but perhaps if you were to write it now you would add the aggressive impulses equally. Or do you feel there is a distinction?

Anna Freud: The aggressive drives are less frightening, I would think. They are also less defended against.

Joseph Sandler: Like the death wishes to one or other of the parents, which are often quite openly expressed in adolescence. Perhaps we can recognize those much more readily than the incestuous wishes, because the aggressive fantasies about the parent help the process of defense as well.

Anna Freud: Yes, we see the denigration of the parents, and the whole turning around of the relationship between child and parents.

Joseph Sandler: Miss Freud, you say in this chapter "hysterics repress the genital impulses associated with the object wishes of the oedipus complex but are more or less indifferent or tolerant in their attitude toward other instinctual wishes, e.g., anal or aggressive impulses" (167,153). Similarly, you say that obsessionals defend against anal-sadistic wishes but are tolerant toward all gratification, exhibitionistic impulses, and the like, that have no connection with their neurosis. You develop this idea further, and contrast it with the tendency to a more general rejection of the drives in adolescence. I wonder whether you still hold the same view about the particular impulses that are repressed in different pathological conditions. I have the feeling that in putting it the way you did you underemphasized the role of the ego in neurotic illness, or took it for granted in a way, and emphasized more the link between particular illnesses and particular drive impulses. What would you say now about the constellation of defense mechanisms that might characterize the hysteric or the obsessional, for example? Perhaps we can look at different types of illnesses either from the side of the drives or from the side of the defense mechanisms used. Would you comment on this?

Anna Freud: What I was writing about does not refer to adolescence, of course, but to neurosis in general. I wanted to emphasize that whereas in adolescence drive activity in general is defended against, in the various neuroses it is only specific types of drive activity that are defended against.

Joseph Sandler: But to what extent can we link the specific neurosis with the specific type of drive activity, because we also link it with specific patterns of defense?

Anna Freud: Isn't it the same? I mean that the defenses belong to the specific type of neurosis, and so does the specific drive activity.

Maria Berger: I wonder what it is that makes some instinctual wishes so ego dystonic for the hysteric, and other ones—for example, anal-sadistic wishes—for the obsessional. Is there something in the ego that needs to be specified in this connection?

Joseph Sandler: I think we have to accept that a regression to anal-sadistic fixation points is not in itself enough to cause an obsessional neurosis. There must be a particular type of thinking on the side of the ego, perhaps one could say a sort of ego style, and as you put it, Miss Freud, "in periods characterized by an accession of libido general attitudes of the ego may develop into definite methods of defense" (172,158). I think it should be possible to say that general attitudes of the ego become specific patterns of defense that are correlated with particular neuroses. General characteristics in regard to thinking and perception may get blown up into defense mechanisms, and a general disposition to tidiness may turn into a reaction formation characteristic of obsessional neurosis. So personality features may become defense mechanisms.

Anna Freud: I can see what you're after. I would say that we didn't think that way at the time. What we have now is the question of whether the kind of defense we see is due to what is defended against. Does the object of the defense determine what defense mechanism is used? Or does the ego level reached determine what defense is used? Certainly at the time we were inclined to think the former, but now we are more inclined to think the latter.

Joseph Sandler: We come now to another point. You speak of the way in which the adolescent's repudiation of instinct differs from ordinary repression, and you contrast it with neurosis. Could you differentiate for us between what goes on in the asceticism of the adolescent on the one hand, and reaction formations on the other? Is it that reaction formations are specific, while the asceticism is a general attitude to any drive derivative?

Anna Freud: Absolutely yes. Reaction formations are completely specific. They are always the opposite of what is wished for and forbidden. But with asceticism this is not the case. There is a general battle against instinctual gratification as such, and it really doesn't matter much what it is. I had in mind at the time certain points which could be observed very well in the adolescents of the time. But you must remember that adolescents have changed greatly. There were whole movements among adolescents, for example, to go without overcoats in a very cold winter in order to deny themselves the comfort of being warm.

Joseph Sandler: Things have changed!

Anna Freud: Well, they have changed in both ways. They wore nothing or they wore too much. You could see the same sort of fight against food, not that they should eat what is really good for them, but only the simplest food. You could see the battle against sleep, in order not to indulge. There were the adolescents who got up at five in the morning and did exercises for two or three hours in order to train their body, but really to deny the body any comfort. Which means that whatever could come under the heading of pleasure, indulgence, or comfort was fought against. This is enormously different from reaction formation.

Joseph Sandler: We see much more now the excessive wish for comfort and self-indulgence, I think. There are adolescents who won't get up in the morning and stay late in bed.

Anna Freud: Well, they did then also, but that was another type of adolescent, certainly not the ascetic.

Hansi Kennedy: One can see the food fads still very much. There are all those that are vegetarians not because they have any oral conflicts, but because they feel that half the population overeats, while many people starve.

Anna Freud: You know, we still see a whole group of adolescents who turn against all comfort that the parents have, but now it's much more often under the heading of some religious or social principle. I think it was much less so at that time. Now the adolescent battle can get dressed up as a cultural attitude.

Joseph Sandler: Except perhaps in the youth movements of the time.

Maria Berger: But in the current youth movements, the ultraleft ones, there is a tendency to say that we must be frugal, our parents eat too much, and so on.

Anna Freud: This very often goes with sexual license, which it didn't at that time. Sexuality was included in the things that were turned against.

Joseph Sandler: I think that in spite of the sexual license which is socially permitted now, it is still the specific sexual wish which remains threatening to the adolescent. The current liberal attitudes don't seem to affect the infantile sexual wishes that get revived during adolescence, and the same essential problems remain, in spite of the fact that there is so much sexual freedom.

Anna Freud: There is much more of an earlier genital outlet, which very often means nothing in regard to getting pleasure. In the flower people, for example, we see a general denial of aggression, which then comes out again somewhere else. But it is the same sort of conflict, in spite of the sexual freedom.

Joseph Sandler: Could I clarify something? The repudiation we have been speaking of is a conscious repudiation, so it differs from repression and also from reaction formation. In the repudiating there must constantly be, of course, the fantasies, the images of what is being repudiated, so that in some displaced way there is still an instinctual expression, an expression of the wish.

Anna Freud: I would doubt it in the asceticism.

Joseph Sandler: But isn't it projected and then rejected, so there is a constant rejecting of something that is attributed to others rather than to oneself ?

Anna Freud: Much more when it is seen in others. If it is present as an unconscious fantasy, then it is an unconscious fantasy which is fought against.

Joseph Sandler: I was thinking that one could make a parallel to the point you made in the previous chapter, where you spoke of people getting vicarious gratification.

In a sense, by taking up the ascetic attitude one can get vicarious gratification through thinking about what it is that one objects to, by saying that the others are the bad ones. It is a sort of externalization. Other people do this or that which is bad, and I must guard against any tendency in myself to do it.

Anna Freud: It isn't quite the same, you know, because if you follow this asceticism to its peak, it ends up in the destruction of the body. It very often goes as far as harming the body, but it can end in suicide, because it seems to the person that the only way to get rid of the impulses is to get rid of the body. They do not kill the object by killing themselves, as other suicides do, the internalized object, but they kill the body as the source of all evil.

Joseph Sandler: Which would differentiate them as a special group. You also refer to other extreme cases, Miss Freud, when you say that the extreme repudiation of drive can result in "a paralysis of the subject's vital activities—a kind of catatonic condition, which can . . . be recognized as a psychotic affection" (170,156). You contrast this with a normal phenomenon of puberty, and I wonder what you were referring to.

Anna Freud: I was referring to the normal abnormality of puberty. For instance, the early rising that we used to see at that time, the exercises, the rejection of comfort, and the revolt against pleasure I would class as normal. But this can go far into abnormality, as I said before, with actual harm to the body, or excluding absolutely any other activity because the battle against the body and its pleasures becomes overwhelming and leaves no time for anything else.

Hansi Kennedy: What is the relation between this type of enactment or living out and the fantasies that adolescents have? The more neurotic type of adolescents have a lot of fantasies of self-castration, or castration as a punishment, which belongs somewhere in this picture. Are you saying that they are living out their fantasies in reality?

Anna Freud: I think it's a qualitative difference, that when the fear of the drive rises to a certain height, the fantasy isn't enough.

Hansi Kennedy: You mean it's a different level of dealing with the conflicts?

Anna Freud: Yes. And the dealing can go toward the psychotic.

Maria Berger: I should like to ask, Miss Freud, about the idea that alternating with instinctual excesses, the adolescent sometimes shows an antagonism toward instinct in general (167,153). Are the ascetics that you talk about people who ever permitted themselves instinctual gratification? Are they not different kinds of people and therefore different kinds of adolescents?

Anna Freud: No. You know, you find the contrasting behavior in the same adolescents, sometimes in the same period, but very often in periods which follow each other.

Take for example the adolescent on the border of pre-adolescence and adolescence, who doesn't wash, who smells, who's dirty, takes no baths, and doesn't change his clothes unless his mother makes him do it. Six months later he may buy elegant clothes and may appear like a dandy. He has suddenly changed over.

Maria Berger: Is he the same type who a few months later may become ascetic?

Anna Freud: He's the same person. I mean you get the dirt and you get the cleanliness. You also can get the same person who lives out all his wishes and gratifies them, and suddenly becomes ascetic. But he may not. There is no strict rule about it.

Joseph Sandler: There must also be an element here, Miss Freud, of identification, because the conformity of the adolescent is enormous, as you have pointed out. So when they're dirty you find that all their friends in their class at school are like that.

Anna Freud: But in each class you will also find a few who are the opposite. I remember an adolescent girl who used to be most neglectful of her appearance and said in analysis, "Oh, but until I was this or that age I was always beautifully dressed." She stopped being beautifully dressed and started to be horribly dressed.

Joseph Sandler: You've put it in terms of wishes, Miss Freud, and I can't help having the feeling that the defensive aspects of all of this, particularly as part of the adolescent revolt, play a larger part than one might assume at first sight. So much of being dirty and unkempt is a rejection of what the parents want.

Anna Freud: Sometimes that's a secondary use of it, and of course we see it. But the aggression against the parents could also be expressed by the child spending all his money on clothes he shouldn't buy. It's a choice of weapons. Just as not eating can be aggression against the mother, it can also be something quite different. It can be destruction of the body. Of course, this doesn't mean that the parents may not in all the different cases feel it is directed against them, but the parents' view is not always the analytic one.

Joseph Sandler: You say in this chapter that "the analytic study of the neuroses suggested that there is in human nature a disposition to repudiate certain instincts, in particular the sexual instincts, indiscriminately and independently of individual experience" (171,157). Do you still believe that, Miss Freud? I have to say immediately that I don't.

Anna Freud: You know, this is an old question and many people don't believe this. Many disputed it when I said it, and I still say that the ego as such is hostile rather than friendly and helpful to the instincts, because it's against its nature to be friendly. The instincts would have an easier time, in a sense, if there were no ego.

Joseph Sandler: May I clarify this, Miss Freud? Would you say that equally the ego is intrinsically hostile to the external world, becuse if what you say is correct you would have to say that any source of potentially threatening stimulation is dangerous, and that generally speaking the ego is on its guard against being overwhelmed. I, for one, would certainly find this perfectly acceptable. It seemed to me, however, that you were saying more, that there was a disposition to repudiate certain instincts, particularly the sexual ones.

Anna Freud: Well, yes. There are two sorts of things combined here. One is the idea that it's taken over from generation to generation that certain drives are not acceptable, so that there is a predisposition to repression. But then there's a second point that due to the secondary process dominating all activity, all drive activity is on strange territory, since it's on its own territory with the primary process.

Joseph Sandler: If you say that generally an organized ego is on its guard against whatever is disorganized, that I can understand, but why certain instincts in particular?

Anna Freud: Well, that goes back to the phylogenetic idea.

Joseph Sandler: From the point of view of natural selection just the opposite should happen. The sexual instincts would be the ones that would be facilitated.

Anna Freud: Our culture demands a restriction of the sexual drive. But it's not only one generation that does that. It happens over and over and over again.

Joseph Sandler: I suppose this would tie in with the whole controversy about inherited memories. I still find it very difficult to believe that there would be specific drives against which there would be a greater tendency for the ego's antagonism, as opposed to its antagonism to too much excitation in general.

Anna Freud: Well, take for example the cannibalistic drive. There is really no difficulty for the individual child nowadays to come to terms with it. We do not have to teach children in any way. But we have to teach them to be clean and not to touch or eat their excrement. Do we ever teach them not to eat parts of a human body? I don't think so.

Joseph Sandler: But do we have a cannibalistic drive, or a cannibalistic wish that develops out of an oral drive?

Anna Freud: But can you take it that cannibalism, which was after all very natural a long time ago, is still the same? Isn't it rather that human beings have increasingly become estranged from cannibalism, that with every new generation it's easily overcome?

Hansi Kennedy: Isn't that learned? Don't children, for instance, still bite other human beings and have to be taught not to bite? I suppose if we would feed them human flesh then they would have to learn not to do it if it became prohibited.

Anna Freud: It's given up more easily. Just think of the long struggle you have with children about the anal instincts. But the cannibalistic fantasy is still there, although the activity is given up.

Joseph Sandler: Look how easily our neurotics give up sexual activity and aggressive activity.

Anna Freud: Not easily, because there's a long struggle around it. It needs powerful countercathexis. But does cannibalism need such a powerful countercathexis? I would say not. It submits, it disappears.

Hansi Kennedy: But we like eating meat. Isn't that a sort of cannibalism?

Anna Freud: Cannibalism is eating human meat.

Hansi Kennedy: I think we should also look at it from the point of view of taboos. For instance, if you are brought up as an orthodox Jew you may have a revulsion against eating pork that you cannot overcome, even later on. I think we have similar cultural phenomena which are psychologically as real as that.

Anna Freud: Yes, I remember analyzing an Indian patient who would really feel sick every time he passed a butcher's shop. The idea of the meat hanging there made him immediately feel sick. It's culturally transmitted.

Joseph Sandler: You do commit yourself here to something intrinsic in human nature, I think, by speaking of phylogenetic inheritance and of human nature. I wonder whether you might be prepared to say that there is in human nature a disposition for certain drives to be more readily given up than others. If one puts it on that level, then the problem may disappear. But it's this intrinsic, independent antagonism to the instincts which seems to be causing the problem.

Anna Freud: Hansi Kennedy will remember that in the Hampstead Nursery we found that there is a difference in the drive education of children who come from different races and cultures. They have, I think I would say, a different inheritance.

Hansi Kennedy: But they still had their mothers, even if they were in the background.

Anna Freud: But some of the children from other cultures were much less inclined to submit to education than our children.

Joseph Sandler: I think we could talk a long time about this, and I'd like to go on to something which startled me a bit when I read it. In this chapter you say, Miss Freud, that to describe the "dual attitude of mankind toward the sexual life—constitutional aversion coupled with passionate desire—Bleuler coined the term *ambivalence*" (171–172,157).

Anna Freud: I think that's what Bleuler meant by ambivalence.

Joseph Sandler: But it's not what we mean now.

Anna Freud: No, not at all. But I think that what I attributed to Bleuler he really meant. I remember being surprised at the time when I was reading Bleuler. What I really meant to say was that we can want something as much as we reject it.

Joseph Sandler: I think that it's worth spelling out the difference between ambivalence and so-called mixed feelings, because the term ambivalence is often used colloquially even by analysts and therapists to describe something else.

Anna Freud: We mean opposing feelings toward a person in the context of object relations, and we don't mean opposing wishes, of course. We certainly don't mean it in the sense Bleuler used it, although he was known for his own ambivalence. In his lifetime he never had a straightforward wish without having, at the same time, the opposite feeling. Somebody once called him *seiner Ambivalenz*!

Joseph Sandler: You speak, Miss Freud, of the antagonism to the sudden accession of instinctual energy as "a specific and active defense mechanism" (172,157). Do you still hold to this?

Anna Freud: Well, it can also be something else, and be used as a defense. I wasn't adding it to the list of defense mechanisms. It is something used defensively.

Joseph Sandler: Could you explain, Miss Freud, your

point (173,159) that the storms of instinct or affect have an inverse relation to intellectual activity?

Anna Freud: On the whole we are not at our most reasonable in an emotional state. The higher the emotional pitch, the less we rely on reason and intellect. The cooler we are emotionally the more chance the intellect has to show itself. I give the example of being passionately in love, but generally any high level of emotion or drive opposes reason, intellect, and judgment.

Joseph Sandler: We will have to wait for another day to discuss the difference between the drives and the emotions, and whether it is the drives or the feelings that threaten the ego.

Session two

Joseph Sandler: Last time we became very aware of Miss Freud's description of the tremendous gap that exists in adolescence between what is aspired to on the intellectual level and what is going on at the emotional level. The attempt to deal with things by overinvesting reason and intellectual processes seems characteristic of adolescence.

Anna Freud: It's not only that the adolescent uses intellectualization in the sense of using his intellect to solve problems. What he thinks about becomes abstract rather than concrete. Perhaps I don't emphasize it enough in the book. What is so important in the adolescent's way of trying to get hold of instinctual storms by means of the intellect is that he puts it into the abstract; and the more abstract the better, the more it seems to serve its purpose.

Joseph Sandler: I have always understood that the defense mechanism of intellectualization involved considering things in the abstract, in generalities which are at a distance from oneself. The classic example was always, for me, the adolescent who is involved in homosexual conflicts, discussing with his friends such things as the incidence of homosexuality in the country. This is then a defense against the inner turmoil about homosexuality. We see the same sort of thing in relation to masturbation.

Anna Freud: Or, on a higher level, about freedom of choice. Then it goes beyond statistics, it goes into the distance, it goes into the past, it goes into the sky, away from the concrete physical facts, and that seems to me the important thing.

Joseph Sandler: Is it that the very high degree of abstraction is particularly important for the adolescent? Isn't it characteristic of all intellectualization?

Anna Freud: Well, it's of course a general feature of intellectualization, and can appear later in life and be used in various ways. The important thing seems to me to be that it does not really occur before adolescence. It comes into being then. If we find it in a latency child it's a bad sign. It might be the sign of a schizoid personality. But in adolescence it is normal that it comes into being. Of course it can be enormously overused, but then it can be integrated into the personality as a useful mechanism. With the scientist who uses intellectualization, the difference is that it has an outcome, and in the adolescent it has no real outcome. It's a thing in itself, which means its purpose is to hold the impulses in check. It hasn't got the purpose of problem solving, but of course it can be in the service of problem solving when the pressure from the side of the drives is not as strong as it is in adolescence.

Joseph Sandler: In adolescence the problem it solves is not the problem it purports to solve.

Anna Freud: No. It solves the personal problem. With the scientist it's displaced and solves the real problem.

Joseph Sandler: While perhaps solving a personal problem as well.

Anna Freud: I think I described somewhere else what I'd seen in a patient once. This was someone who lived with a very high level of anxiety which could from time to time cause a panic attack. But in that state of anxiety he became extremely clever. He was a very intellectual man, but it was not the adolescent kind of abstract cleverness. He was really driven by anxiety to become able to solve real problems. And that isn't quite the same as what I meant in the book.

Joseph Sandler: It touches on the whole area of sublimation, and on our classical way of seeing sublimation as involving a change of aim and object in regard to an instinctual drive. Lots of things we would call sublimation really seem to be ways of dealing with anxiety, and this is not at all the same as the smooth channeling of an instinctual wish or impulse into another direction. Many very creative scientists are, I think, really anxiety-driven as much as instinct-driven.

Anna Freud: But there the displacement comes first, or rather the avoidance of the real problem. They don't deal directly with their anxiety. They use the displacement to prevent the arousal of anxiety.

Joseph Sandler: I was thinking of the scientist who did very good work searching for a magical substance. One might quite easily call this a sublimation, but it was very anxiety-driven.

Anna Freud: What I am wondering about is whether the attraction of young people nowadays to Indian meditation is really the same as what I call intellectualization here. I'm not quite sure what they meditate on, but it seems to me that it is on a very abstract level, from what I've heard.

Joseph Sandler: One characteristic is that it's an attempt to get away from the body.

Anna Freud: Yes, and that's why I think it is the same—it is a way to free the mind from the body and from all bodily concerns.

Hansi Kennedy: And the seeking of peace is an important aspect of it.

Maria Berger: I wonder if we can bring under the heading of intellectualization what might be called the sublimated studying of adolescents. Very often it has to do with their not understanding themselves. They read psychology and philosophy, and I remember many adolescents beginning to read Freud in later adolescence.

Hansi Kennedy: Isn't it also like that when we talk about intellectualization as a defense, as distinct from a generalized intellectual approach? Isn't there something very obsessive about these intellectualizations? They're very circumscribed, they seem to go around in circles, and have a sort of obsessive quality about them. So that the adolescent is constantly dealing with anxiety, probably in a rather ineffective way, because as the anxiety comes up they go through the same kind of circular argument.

Anna Freud: Well, they can of course become ruminations, only the rumination is concerned with more abstract matters than in obsessional ruminations, which can be quite down-to-earth. You know how often the adolescent begins with the question: "Who am I?" "Where is the world going?"

Joseph Sandler: There is a paragraph I should like you to comment on, Miss Freud. The first part of it goes like this: "Hitherto the decline in the intelligence of little children at the beginning of the latency period has been explained in another way. In early childhood their brilliant intellectual achievements are closely connected with their inquiries into the mysteries of sex and, when this subject becomes taboo, the prohibition and inhibition extend to other fields of thought" (179,164). I wonder what you had in mind at the time when you spoke of the decline in intelligence. Were you thinking of children with inhibitions?

Anna Freud: It was something that was talked about a great deal at that time, about how stupid schoolchildren really were, in comparison with the way they had seemed to be in their preschool years. I remember I used to have an uncle who would say, "Why are all little children clever and beautiful, and adults stupid and ugly?" And he said, "We know where they become stupid—in school. But where do they become ugly?" I don't know whether latency children have become cleverer or whether little children have become stupider, but you may remember how we always used to say how highly intelligent the little ones are in their search for knowledge, in the freshness of their intellect, and how they become later much less interested, much duller. But we mustn't forget that school was really very different at that time. I think it dulled the intellect.

Ilse Hellman: I was going to raise the same point. I was always struck by your reference to the decline in intelligence of the latency child. It must certainly be connected with the passivity that is suddenly enforced on the child. The whole active-passive change used to be so very marked at the time when the child had to go to school. He had to verbalize in certain ways, and could no longer be as free as before. Nowadays I think that we wouldn't see this at all.

Anna Freud: Nor is there so much the restriction of curiosity in early childhood, so that has changed.

Ilse Hellman: And the search for things—children are now quite free to go on searching. I don't think anybody could say there's a marked change in the expression of their intelligence, but at the time I think it was certainly very marked.

Anna Freud: It may have been these two reasons—the nonprohibition of sexual curiosity on the one hand, and the stimulation and activity in school on the other—which have brought about the change. There is much less filling of the mind with dull material that isn't really taken in by the child.

Joseph Sandler: I think that certain children, who appear not to maintain their intelligence, may often be children who have failed to enter latency. They still instinctualize their activities to a greater degree than normal. It's true that some children can use this for intellectual achievement, when the achievement represents something very phallic, for example. But others will show conflict over it, and may appear to fail intellectually.

Anna Freud: There are, of course, more possibilities. What I wrote about was, so to say, the common overall view at the time, but certainly there are also many children who merely displace their curiosity and don't repress it. Sexual investigation may be forbidden, but all other investigation is permitted and they become very clever. That's another possibility.

Joseph Sandler: How do you fit that in with your remark, Miss Freud, that it "may be that in the latency period children not only *dare* not indulge in abstract thought: they may have no need to do so" (180,164)? There is certainly a limitation in the capacity of children to think in abstract terms, depending on their age, but it doesn't ring any bells.

Anna Freud: What I meant was that we don't find in latency the kind of abstract thinking we find in the adolescent. And my idea here was that this is because the pressure from the instincts, and the defense against the drives, is not there in the same way. So I wouldn't say that there is abstract thinking in early childhood, before latency, but it's what one can call wide-open thinking, according, of course, to the developmental level. That's all I say. The small children may not have the need to defend themselves in the same way because the same danger is not present.

Joseph Sandler: And, of course, the capacity for that sort of thinking only properly develops gradually after the oedipal phase.

Anna Freud: Yes, that's what I meant. But if you find an eight-year-old, as we do sometimes in the Clinic, who begins to muse about the world as a whole and his own place in it, and what he is there for, you should be very worried about it. You don't find this sort of thinking with a normal child. His thinking is concrete, physical and practical, linked with action. I would also say with bodies, with machinery, with performance—with adventure, with discovery, with emotion.

Joseph Sandler: More pragmatic in a sense.

Anna Freud: Yes.

Joseph Sandler: Although the romantic element also comes in during latency to some degree, I think.

Anna Freud: In the sense of adventure.

Joseph Sandler: I suppose also in the feminine version of adventure stories.

Anna Freud: Schoolgirls' books, you mean. I don't think they're very romantic.

Joseph Sandler: Perhaps we can move to the question of the idealization of the so-called teenage idol, which occurs also in late latency, even perhaps before prepuberty, although prepuberty may be earlier nowadays.

Anna Freud: Much earlier.

Joseph Sandler: You describe, Miss Freud, the way the adolescent lives with the members of his family as though with strangers, and I wonder whether this has changed to some extent with changing cultural conditions.

Anna Freud: Has it changed? Don't mothers still say, "He treats the home like a restaurant"?

Hansi Kennedy: Like a hotel. That hasn't changed.

Anna Freud: They ask, "Why doesn't he sit down at table with us and tell us what he's done?" I don't think that has changed. He still treats the members of the family like strangers.

Ilse Hellman: Perhaps "stranger" isn't the right word. It is more a very well-known person whom one tries things out on. I would agree with the idea of the home being used like a hotel, but I think it is necessary to have the parents there in order to attack them, to test out how much they can take. Isn't it very much that?

Joseph Sandler: It has been said recently that the human being is the only species in which the parents do not throw the adolescent out at puberty. In every other species it's the other way around, and it's the adolescent who wants to stay. Perhaps humans are not very wise in this regard.

Majorie Sprince: In a good hotel you don't invade the hotelier's privacy, and I think that adolescents have to be invasive and intrusive, while at the same time trying to insure that the parents aren't intrusive and invasive.

Anna Freud: I tried to isolate the factors. Adolescence is a very different phase, somehow, and you hear so often from parents that the adolescent isn't like their son anymore, he's like a stranger, he comes and goes, he hardly sees them. This is another phase, I would say, of the attack against the parents. It's a pure withdrawal. But he returns then, and the withdrawal is not enough. There follows the hostility and hate which he uses to try to cut the bond with the parents. So that eventually withdrawal won't be necessary anymore because the parents are no good anyway.

Joseph Sandler: It's the hate which really reveals the involvement with the parents, because the parents become hostile antagonists, and then are not simply strangers. I was very much taken with the point you make later on in the page, Miss Freud, where you use the term "repression of the superego" (182,166). Probably you wouldn't want to use that term nowadays, although I can understand your use of it then.

Anna Freud: I would say that the ego alienates itself from the superego.

Joseph Sandler: That is a little different from repression, but I think we have to take into account the fact that you were speaking more or less loosely. What you point out is that the superego is treated as a suspicious and intrusive incestuous object, and it is interesting that the internalized parents, in the form of the superego introjects, are also reacted against. You go on to say, Miss Freud, that "the principal effect of the rupture of the relation between ego and superego is to increase the danger which threatens from the instincts" (182,166). I thought this was extremely interesting, because only relatively recently have we begun to put emphasis on the role of the superego as a protector as well as an attacker. And yet, implicit in what you say is the assumption that the superego has a protective function. Of course it has always been said that there is a danger if one alienates the superego, but it's not just the danger of greater retaliation but the danger of loss of protection.

Anna Freud: Yes. You know, there are parallels to this during the whole of the latency period, when children get estranged from their parents, not for developmental reasons as in adolescence, but because they are let down by the parents, for example by death, separation, or sudden insight into the parents' imperfections. I mean those cases where the parent goes to prison or to a mental hospital, and suddenly his role in superego formation is attacked by the event. This affects not only the object relationship, but also the relationship with the superego, and is in some cases the reason for delinquency. This can happen with the seven-year-old, the eight-year-old, the nine-year-old, long before adolescence. It just means that the superego is not wholly independent of the existing object relationship.

Joseph Sandler: This is a fascinating area, one in which we need to do further research. You say in your text, Miss Freud, that "we now have the following situation: asceticism, itself due to an increase in instinctual danger, actually leads to the rupture of the relation with the superego and so renders inoperative the defensive measures prompted by superego anxiety, with the result that the ego is still more violently thrown back to the level of pure instinctual anxiety and the primitive protective mechanisms characteristic of that level" (183,167). Could you comment on this? How does the process render inoperative the defensive measures prompted by super-ego anxiety? Do you mean the ways in which the person would deal with guilt? What is the link with asceticism?

Anna Freud: What it means is that in regard to the person's relationship to the superego, he feels unprotected in the face of the drives.

Joseph Sandler: This would tie in with something we discussed years ago when we were talking about the superego, and considered situations in which people can ignore their superegos. We didn't use the specific example of asceticism, but were thinking of group phenomena, and situations in which alternative sources of narcissistic supply, other than from the superego, were gained. One of these could be drugs, for instance, or identification with a hero, with the result that people could ignore the superego completely at times. I think you say here that asceticism (and presumably this holds for meditation, if that is its modern equivalent) can provide a source of well-being which decreases the dependence on the superego, and enables the person to turn away from the superego introjects. Or do I have it wrong?

Anna Freud: What I say is if the intactness of the superego goes, the feeling of guilt goes, and the feeling of guilt is, after all, a protection against wrongdoing. Now if there is no fear of the external world and no fear of the superego, we still have the fear of the drives, which is the most primitive fear of all and is linked with the most primitive defense mechanisms. That's really the thought that I tried to express. As I meant it in what I wrote here, it's the asceticism that attacks the object relationships; that is, it brings about a withdrawal from the oedipal fantasies. These again are connected with the superego, and the superego becomes weakened. So the asceticism, instead of protecting the individual against instinctual danger, against danger from the id, does exactly the opposite. It exposes him more because of the absence of guilt.

Marjorie Sprince: On the basis of fear of incest?

Anna Freud: Incest fear, yes.

Joseph Sandler: Both positive and negative oedipal tendencies are, I think, problems for the adolescent. Perhaps here we see the negative oedipus complex more than we see it during the oedipal phase.

Anna Freud: In the present perhaps the revolt doesn't go so much against the parents, but against the so-called Establishment, which is the whole parental world. The Establishment symbolizes all the forces that the battle is against.

Joseph Sandler: You describe in this chapter the tendency of the adolescent to identify with many others, when you say there is "another peculiarity of the object relations at puberty. The adolescent does not aim so much at possessing himself of the object in the ordinary physical sense of the term as at assimilating himself as much as possible to the person who at the moment occupies the central place in his affection" (184,168). Is this the only identification that you are speaking of in regard to the adolescent at this point?

Anna Freud: Yes, that is the identification. But it goes a step further. It's really an appropriation of many of the qualities of the person. I remember one adolescent of whom her parents used to say, "One always knows to whom she has talked last in school," or, "We know whom she has fallen for in school, because she talks exactly like that person. She assumes the same voice, the same handwriting." You know, many adolescents actually copy and learn to act like the people they admire. In a way they really assume the body and the mind of the other person. This is more than the usual identification.

Joseph Sandler: You go on then to talk about the "as if " types described by Helene Deutsch. I always thought that the "as if " children do not only identify with the object of the moment, but rather identify with the role that they believe the object expects them to take.

Anna Freud: That's different again. That's distorting the whole person to please, or to be in union with, the object. It's different from being the object.

Joseph Sandler: I always understood "as if " to be that particular distorting of the role, and I don't get that in your description. Perhaps Helene Deutsch meant both aspects, but I know that many people think of the "as if " child as the characteristic institutional child, who changes himself to be the good child for whoever is around. Of course this can be in part the identification with some adult characteristic. People say of others that they are "as if" persons, and what they mean is that the person is, in a sense, many-faced, and becomes the pleasing person to whomever he meets. I may be wrong in this, and have never thought to question it until now. Perhaps Helene Deutsch was thinking in terms of identification with the object.

Anna Freud: I think it's nearer to what Winnicott meant by the "false self." Only he puts the false self very early in life, but this is the false self of the adolescent.

Joseph Sandler: Winnicott speaks of a relatively permanent false self personality, whereas here the characteristic thing is that the person can change from one moment to another.

Anna Freud: According to the object. It only means it's not the person. It's not the "I." It's not the real self, but it's modeled by these external influences, or by the object relationship. It reflects what Erikson means by the identity crisis.

Joseph Sandler: What you describe here, Miss Freud, is very characteristic of adolescence. I mean the fluid identifications. The other, the "as if" is, in a way, uncharacteristic of adolescence. Being the person the other person wants him to be is atypical in the adolescent who is in revolt. The easy identifications that you describe are very appropriate and correct for the adolescent, but

I don't think the "as if" character that one sees in institutional children is characteristic.

Anna Freud: If what you mean is compliance, this is not it. But I make the comparison with the "as if" only because the process may in some way be the same.

Marie Berger: The fleeting identifications we see in the adolescent don't necessarily distort the personality. He might well be able to form ordinary relationships afterward.

Joseph Sandler: We should note that what Winnicott talks about in regard to the false self is not the same as the "as if" personality. There can be a false self which has been built up and is very stable, and consistent irrespective of the object, as a consequence of the person's development and particularly his defenses. I think that what Miss Freud is pointing to here is precisely the fleetingness of identifications. Now, if we like, all these identifications are false pictures, and in that sense there is a connection with the false self and the "as if," but I think they are very different.

Anna Freud: Yes. You know there is another characteristic of adolescence. I remember especially one adolescent who used to make lists of his friends and love objects on paper, writing the names down, and to me this meant quite clearly that the relationships were tenuous. There was a fear of losing himself and therefore he tied himself to the name. This means it can also be that the apparently violent relationships of the adolescent can be very shallow at the same time. Dangerously shallow, and what the adolescent defends against is the regression to his own narcissism. I don't know whether I've got it down in the book.

Joseph Sandler: No, I don't think you have it in that way here. You speak of identifications of the most primitive kind and I wonder whether you can elaborate on what you had in mind there. Clearly you don't mean the most primitive identification in which there is a fusion with the object. Did you mean fairly gross identifications, unsubtle identifications? You say, "The psychic situation in this and similar phases of puberty may be described very simply. These passionate and evanescent love fixations are not object relations at all, in the sense in which we use the term in speaking of adults. They are identifications of the most primitive kind . . ." (185,169).

Anna Freud: I say in German *Es sind Identifizierungen der primitivsten Art*. What I mean is the primary identification of the child with the parent: we are one.

Joseph Sandler: But presumably not primary identification in the sense of confusion with loss of boundaries. The adolescent knows his own boundaries. What you have described is a sort of quick copying.

Anna Freud: Well, it goes over into a loss of the boundaries between the self and the nonself. I mean identification that is not the result of object relationship, that comes before it.

Joseph Sandler: What distinguishes this from the psychotic primary identification?

Anna Freud: If as an adult you develop a process that belongs in the first year of life, then you are a psychotic.

Joseph Sandler: But not every adolescent is completely psychotic.

Anna Freud: But the adolescent has the right to near-psychotic processes. I mean we would say he is mad were it not for the fact that he is only adolescent.

Joseph Sandler: Yes, but we say that about our colleagues. I heard it said about a whole committee the other night.

Anna Freud: Primary identification you find only in adolescents or in severely ill people.

Joseph Sandler: I think that what we would have to say is that the capacity to *dis*identify, to impose boundaries, is not lost in the adolescent, whereas in the schizophrenic it can be.

Anna Freud: It's temporarily lifted in the adolescent, but it's not lost.

Joseph Sandler: I think, Miss Freud, that when you speak of the near-psychotic state of the adolescent you refer in particular to the love fixations, the falling in love with someone without really knowing them, and then identifying with them. The turmoil that accompanies this can be very distressing, but I think that the adolescent is still capable of saying, "This is me, and that is the other person." He might say, "I get all confused," but I think this is very different from the psychotic.

Anna Freud: The feeling the adolescent has is, "You and I are really one." Of course, it's not in the sense that he does not know who he is, and who the other is, whereas the psychotic wouldn't know. I refer to the feeling he has. It's not a change in the ego that you find in the psychotic. What I am referring to is a change in the quality of the love relationship from object relationship to a primitive form of identification.

Joseph Sandler: In order to finish this chapter, I should like to look briefly at the following passage: "The rupture of former relations, antagonism to the instincts, and asceticism all have the effect of delibidinizing the external world. The adolescent is in danger of withdrawing his object libido from those around him and concentrating it upon himself; just as he is regressed within the ego, so he may regress in his libidinal life from object love to narcissism" (187–188,171). Of course, he may do the opposite as well, mayn't he, Miss Freud, in the sense that he hypercathects certain objects. But perhaps your point would be that he does this in a very shallow and superficial way.

Anna Freud: Yes. As I say here, the passionate object relations of adolescents are very often attempts at returning to the object world.

Joseph Sandler: We will have one more meeting, and that will bring our discussions of the book to an end.

Conclusion

In her final, short Conclusion Anna Freud summarizes her attempt to classify defense mechanisms according to the particular anxiety situations that evoke them. The connection between individual experiences and particular modes of defense is still unclear, but it seems that denial tends to be used in relation to threats connected with fears of castration and the loss of love objects. Altruistic surrender seems "to be a specific means of overcoming narcissistic mortification" (190,173). The parallels between defenses against external and internal dangers are more clearly visible. Thus repression of drive derivatives is paralleled by denial. Reaction formation has its counterpart in fantasies in which the real situation is reversed. Inhibition shows a correspondence to ego restrictions that avoid unpleasure from outside. Intellectualization matches the alertness of the ego to external danger. All defensive measures against the drives have their counterpart "in the ego's attempts to deal with the external danger by actively intervening to change the conditions of the world around it" (191,174). Anna Freud continues with the suggestion that the various defense mechanisms against threats from inside and from outside have their origin in various aspects of the instinct's function. The defenses draw on "the essential nature of instinctual processes" (192,175). One cannot fail to be impressed by the achievement of the ego in developing its mechanisms of defense, and every neurotic symptom shows that the ego's "plan for defense has miscarried" (193,175–176). But "the ego is victorious when its defensive measures effect their purpose," and anxiety and unpleasure can be restricted and the drives transformed so that "some measure of gratification is secured, thereby establishing the most harmonious relations possible between the id, the superego, and the forces of the outside world" (193,176).

The Discussion

Joseph Sandler: This is the last meeting of the group discussing Miss Freud's *The Ego and the Mechanisms of Defense*. The book has been an important part in the psychoanalytic education of all of us, but many of the things we have discussed have been revelations to us. At the time of writing, the book was thought to be a very daring one, and Miss Freud said at one point that when she wrote it she was told by a very distinguished analyst that she would find herself outside the psychoanalytic movement because of the book. It was so revolutionary at the time. This sounds strange to us now, but it can give us an idea of the tremendous step that was taken in 1936 with the publication of this work. Perhaps you'd like to amplify what the situation was when you first brought the book out, Miss Freud.

Anna Freud: In talking to Dr. Greenson before the meeting I was interested to hear how very strong the reaction of older analysts was at the time, when the value of an analyst was thought by many people to be measured by the distance from the surface of the area he was exploring. So the idea that I advocated at the time, that the analyst's position should be equidistant from the id and the ego, from the surface and the depth, was not a popular attitude at all, at a time when the whole tendency was to go deeper and deeper into the unconscious. From the beginning I felt that this was maligning analysis, because analysis was always the exploration of conflict, the examination of the defense neurosis. This, after all, was seen from the very beginning of analysis as reflecting conflict between the surface and the depths, and later between the id and the ego. It was a misunderstanding that we had to explore the depths alone, and to see that as analysis. By the way, the depths alone could never produce a neurosis. This can only happen in interaction with the surface.

Joseph Sandler: We've seen something of a swing in the other direction in certain quarters, where the emphasis has tended to be on the surface alone.

Anna Freud: I don't know whether I should say that is just as bad, or worse. It's just as wrong.

Joseph Sandler: What we left for today's discussion was the last three or four pages of the book. It's a very happy situation that we couldn't quite finish it, and we have the chance to do so today. Some very general points are raised in the Conclusion, many of which merit detailed discussion. You begin by telling us, Miss Freud, that you tried to classify the different defenses by reference to the particular anxiety situations that evoke them, and you have suggested that a more precise classification might become possible later. We are still hoping to get that precise classification, but perhaps we are not yet ready for it. You go on to say that there is "still considerable obscurity about the historical connection between typical experiences in individual development and the production of particular modes of defense" (190,173). You suggest that the "typical situations" in which denial is used are those connected with ideas of castration and with the loss of love objects. In contrast, altruistic surrender seems "to be a specific means of overcoming narcissistic mortification" (190,173). I'd like to ask here, in reference to the classification of the various defense mechanisms according to the specific anxiety situation, whether you would now say that the emphasis should be as much on the content of the anxiety as it was when you wrote the book, or whether you would now think more in terms of the defenses against particular *sources* of anxiety. For example, defenses against anxiety arising as a result of a threat from the drives, or of the threat of superego retaliation, or danger from the outside world—I mean the real fear of punishment from the parents, and so on.

Anna Freud: I would certainly say this, but I would also say that it was exactly what I meant there. What I had in mind were not situations really, but sources. It was just as you put it now. But I want to add another point here. I was very much concerned at the time with the possibility of a chronology of the defenses, which was also debated then—the question of what comes first, of what is a primitive defense and what a sophisticated defense—and I tried at one point in the book to give a vague outline as we had it then, in the hope that in the future we would learn more about this, especially as our knowledge of ego development advanced. This hope has not really been fulfilled up to the present day, at least so far as the written word is concerned. But I have recently had an idea which I hope to work out further, that we can learn more about the chronology of the defenses by tracing what I have called the developmental lines. What I mean is that we need not take ego development and its interaction with the id in the global sense in which we always take it, including four or five years of development under one heading. If we rather take it piecemeal and consider the actual steps taken toward every human achievement—which is always an interaction, in a sense, between id and ego development—then we can see and determine which modes of defense are made possible according to the positions on the developmental lines. I think that in time we will arrive at the chronology of the defenses. So, perhaps in a year or two or three—I don't know how much time is given to me—I may attempt to put that down in greater detail.

Joseph Sandler: I think that the idea inherent in the

concept of the developmental lines, in which the apparatus functioning as a whole is taken, is particularly useful, in regard to both our theory and our clinical material.
If I recall our previous discussions correctly, Miss Freud,
what was put down at the time you wrote this book as
conflict between ego and id, and what was theoretically
dissected out in this way, was very often what we would
see now as conflict between the ego wanting to participate with the id in one way, then something making this
combined tendency dystonic—guilt feelings, for example—and then defensive activities being initiated by the
ego, which turns against the drive-ego combination. The
major structures are reference points for us, giving different qualities to what is going on, but in all the discussions about defense, although we see it as a function
of the ego, we do not speak of the drive alone, but of
the derivative of the drive. We found ourselves speaking
much more of the instinctual wish as including those
aspects of the infantile ego which would implement that
instinctual wish, and then perhaps thinking of the defense against that particular drive representative, when
we discussed defenses against the drives.

May I ask about your suggestion that the typical situations in which denial is used are those connected with
the idea of castration and with the loss of the love object?
I think we can see the historical roots of this in terms
of the child's sexual theories, in relation to the denial of
sexual differences, and the way in which children try to
push aside the impending or actual loss of a love object.
But I have the thought that you may be making too
specific a link here between the use of this particular
mechanism and the situations you mention. They cer-

tainly occur in clinical situations in which we see denial operating, but I wonder whether there isn't a danger that what you say might be misunderstood as linking the mechanism very specifically with those particular danger situations. Could we clarify this for the record? The word "typically" may be misleading.

Anna Freud: Perhaps I could put it in another way. You can ask what is most effective when you are faced with any of these anxiety situations or sources mentioned here. There is the situation of loss, whether it's body loss, as expressed in castration fear or whether it's loss of the love object as it's expressed in mourning, and so on. But whatever sort of loss it is, the most effective method of dealing with this in childhood, and later in severe illness, especially in the psychoses, seems to be to deny. What would you say?

Ralph Greenson: I want to bring up the point about calling denial a mechanism instead of a result. If I remember correctly, you said in the book that denial is a pre-stage of defense. Right?

Anna Freud: Yes.

Ralph Greenson: And you can deny by means of projection, and can deny by means of negation. Now take losses—body losses or loss of objects. They are negated and therefore denied.

Anna Freud: You know this comes from the translation. In German denial is *Leugnung*, which means "it has not

happened," and that is the negation. But I quite agree
with you that denial means the happening is undone.
And this seems very effective, but of course, as we know,
for the psychotic it means turning away from reality, and
for the child it means not facing reality, and that's really
the meaning here. Now why I called it at the time a pre-
stage was because this negation is directed against the
outside world and external happenings, and not against
the drives. Something that has actually happened in the
external world is declared not to have happened.

Joseph Sandler: The differentiation between the mechanism of denial and the effect which we call denial is an
important one. In a sense every defense mechanism
brings about a denial, a removal of something unpleasant.
As far as denial being a pre-stage of defense is concerned,
this is something we have discussed, and I think it comes
into our considerations as a pretending that something
isn't there. But this sort of simple denial is something
that can work only up to a certain point, and it works
more easily in regard to the external world than in relation to insistent pressures from within. It can't stop
those pressures, so it doesn't work very well directed
against the inside. But I don't think that we can say that
we must define it by tying it to the external world only.
Of course, the small child can turn his head away much
more successfully if he doesn't want to see unpleasant
things coming from the outside than he can in regard to
unpleasant things coming from the inside, which are
going to come regardless of which way he turns his head.
And although I think we might have to say that something
akin to denial might be a pre-stage of repression, this is

something which would last only for a fraction of a second, because the wish has a force behind it and the denial that can work for the outside world cannot work for the inside world. What I am trying to say is that while we cannot define denial in relation to the outside world, we can say that it works well for the outside world and not at all well for pressures coming from the inside. This is an important point, because the infant doesn't know what is inside and what is outside, and the representations it experiences are only gradually differentiated into belonging to inside or outside, and perhaps the gradual awareness of whether or not denial is effective plays a part here. Miss Freud has stressed that essentially the same mechanisms operate in regard to threats from all sorts of different sources. And although there may be, as Miss Freud has pointed out, some mechanisms that are more useful than others in regard to particular threats, again we are considering a question of usefulness rather than of specific ties between particular defenses and particular danger situations. It's probably worth adding that we have throughout had to deal with the additional problem that denial means a number of different things.

Anna Freud: Yes, that's quite right.

Joseph Sandler: What I found enormously impressive is that we see in 1936 the notion of defense against narcissistic mortification, and although we have all read the book many times, I don't think it has really registered well that the idea of defense against narcissistic hurt was in Miss Freud's book. It is, of course, touched on at several places in the book, as part of the idea of the motive for defense being the avoidance of unpleasure. A particular motive is the avoidance of upset to one's well-being, one's self-esteem, one's regard for oneself, and so on. The fact that defense mechanisms are used in that way is important for us to take note of, because for so long many people have tended to speak of defenses against the drives, and to say that what Miss Freud added in this book was only the idea of defense against the outside world. What has been underlined by her as well has been the notion of defenses operating to do away with unpleasure, to maintain the ego's integrity and state of well-being. The idea of motives for defense being the avoidance of painful feelings, whatever their source and whatever their painful content, deserves a more prominent place in our thinking. And very much in the center is the avoidance by the child of narcissistic hurt. This is, I think, of particular importance now that there is such an interest in patients with narcissistic disturbances. Do you want to add anything to this, Miss Freud?

Anna Freud: We seem to have known a few things in the 1930s that people discover nowadays as if they had never been there. Perhaps in certain instances we didn't use quite the same terms, but often we used simpler terms. I had a discussion with Dr. Greenson yesterday about the term "narcissistic homeostasis." Dr. Greenson asked me what it really meant, and I said it meant that the person is pleased with himself. And Dr. Greenson then said: Why don't people say that? These notions were not so strange to us.

Ralph Greenson: I remember once your saying at a Congress years and years ago that all defenses are motivated by the avoidance of unpleasure, and you got upset with somebody who was giving a paper on defenses and kept going round and round and not getting to the central point, namely that all defenses are motivated against unpleasure and pain. That's basic, that's elementary, that's simple and understandable.

Anna Freud: And unpleasure can take so many forms, as you all know. I mean there isn't one type of unpleasure. There are as many types of unpleasure as there are of pleasure, perhaps more.

Joseph Sandler: You make the point, Miss Freud, that there are great parallels between the defenses against external and against internal danger. Then you say that regression can get rid of instinctual derivatives in the same way as external stimuli can be pushed away by denial (190,174). This raises the theoretical question of whether there is a counterforce, an anticathexis if you like, applied in denial. I think we were forced to conclude that we cannot simply say that denial is a withdrawal of attention, but as we see it clinically, and use it clinically, active counterforces are in fact pitted against the perception of unpleasant things in the external world, in what we ordinarily understand by denial as a mechanism. You go on to talk about reaction formation, the use of fantasies in which the real situation is reversed, and inhibition of instinctual impulses, ego restrictions, intellectualization, and so on. All of these things are used to avoid unpleasure, and there are profound implications

here for the psychoanalytic theory of affect. The implication of what has been said here about the motives for
defenses implies that our feeling states are as much affected by happenings in the external world as by the
drives and their derivatives coming from the inside. This
would mean that the affects as feelings occupy an intermediate position within the ego, and that it is changes
in the feeling states, predominantly unpleasure in the
form of anxiety, but also, as you have said, Miss Freud,
other forms of unpleasure, which are the motivators for
defense. And we need to include as motives the search
for certain forms of pleasure, gratification, and security,
including narcissistic pleasure. I would even take it much
further and say that changes in feeling states can be
considered to be the motivators for ego development as
a whole. I am reminded here of Freud's statement that
the development of the ego consists in a departure from
primary narcissism, and represents a strenuous attempt
to regain that state. If one sees primary narcissism as a
feeling state of well-being, among other things, the development of the ego consists in forced departure from
that "good" feeling state, and the disruptions of the feeling state are prime motivators for development as a
whole.

Anna Freud: Yes. They are the motives as opposed to
the drives.

Joseph Sandler: I very much liked the point you make
when you say, "All the other defensive measures
which . . . entail an alteration in the instinctual processes themselves have their counterpart in the ego's at-

tempts to deal with the external danger by actively intervening to change the conditions of the world around it" (191,174). This reminds me, Miss Freud, of those advertisements for slimming cures which show a "before" and an "after." It is as if the ego is aware, unconsciously, of the state before, which is unpleasant, and then it employs mechanisms to change this into the "after," to modify the representation to itself either of an unconscious wish, or of something coming from the external world. As a result the feelings which now accompany the new image allow it to come to consciousness as being acceptable, nonthreatening, and so on. What we have to say is that what is defended against must be experienced by the ego at some level, unconsciously, in order to be perceived as a threat.

Anna Freud: Quite simply, in certain instances the defense is against the feeling state connected with the danger of the drives or with the danger from the outside world, or against the anxiety or other unpleasant feelings of humiliation or frustration, whatever they are. But there are also mechanisms which operate elsewhere, and in a different way, namely by defending against the source of the aroused feeling state. These mechanisms try to do something so that the feeling state will not arise. They can alter something in the drives just as actions in the external world are directed to altering the external world. So some event that would be unpleasant is prevented from coming about. I think the important point is what I raise a little later, when I ask the question of where the individual learns the defense, or what comes first? Does the defense against the dangers arising from within come first, or the defense against the unpleasantness caused from without?

Joseph Sandler: We can do much more to alter the external world than to alter the drives and their derivatives, so that we have to allow them an indirect expression using one or other of the defenses.

Anna Freud: Well, we can do something about the drives. We can turn them into the opposite, that's the reversal. Or we can alter their direction. For example, the aggression toward the outside world can be turned toward the self, so we get the change from murder to suicide, let us say. But whereas the individual may consider the one bad, he may see hurting himself as good, namely as an attempt not to be a murderer. So we can do something with the drives themselves.

Joseph Sandler: You use the phrase, Miss Freud, "inhibition of instinctual impulses" (191,174). What did you have in mind there? Did you mean repression?

Anna Freud: No, I didn't mean repression. I meant, well, inhibition as a forestage of symptom formation. Instead of a compromise formation, we get a holding back of the expression of the drive derivative entering into consciousness or into action.

Joseph Sandler: This would apply then not only to the fairly direct manifestations of the impulse, but also to the derivatives at some distance removed. In the next paragraph the question is raised of where the ego derives the form of its defense mechanisms from. Miss Freud asks, "Is the struggle with the outside forces modeled on the conflict with the instincts? Or is the converse the case: are the measures adopted in the external struggle the prototype of the various defense mechanisms?" (191,174). Then you point out, Miss Freud, that the infantile ego has to defend itself against both instinctual and external forces, and "probably adapts its weapons to the particular need, arming itself now against danger from within and now against danger from without" (191,174). I think this fits so very well with the developmental view that we take, that the child only builds up distinctions between inside and outside slowly and will use what it has as its resources to deal with whatever danger arises. Labeling the source is then something secondary. This suggests that there is not so specific a link between the particular mechanisms used and the source of the danger. And I suppose that later on we have to add to the dangers or threats those coming from the superego, although at this point it is the presuperego infant that is being referred to. We know that defenses are used to deal with guilt and anticipated internal reproaches from the superego introjects.

Anna Freud: Yes.

Joseph Sandler: You ask, Miss Freud, "How far does the ego follow its own laws in its defense against the instincts and how far is it influenced by the character of the instincts themselves?" (192,175). You make the comparison with the way latent dream thoughts are converted into manifest content, and you show that some processes, like condensation and displacement, belong to the id, so the work of distortion is not entirely the work of the ego. And then you say that the modification of instinctual processes in the course of defense can make use of the special properties of the instinct. You show convincingly how some defense mechanisms can be related to primary process functioning. I think the idea that you put forward here, that defenses grow out of the properties of the id, is one which has troubled a lot of people, because in the dream work we look not only for the primary process functioning, but also for the ego's defenses. I suppose what you say is not difficult to understand if one thinks that the total apparatus first works in a primary process way, and then secondary process grows out of what is available as the ego develops. So if reversal is already there, it's at hand for use in a more structured and organized form for defense. But perhaps some people push the analogies between the defenses and the modes of functioning of the drives a bit too far, and I wonder if you have any comment on this. I should also like you to amplify the point you make at the end of the paragraph that "a defense is proof against attack only if it is built up on this twofold basis—on the one hand, the ego and, on the other, the essential nature of instinctual processes" (192,175).

Anna Freud: To me this has always seemed very simple, and I am surprised when people find it a difficult point of view to understand, because we have these two ways of functioning in our mind, primary process functioning and secondary process functioning. But the mind is one and the same, and it seems to me quite easy to imagine that naturally they are both there at the same time, and they interact, and if we deal with the difficult matter from the side of the ego, wouldn't the most practical way of dealing with it be by making use of the processes which are at hand? It seems to me very clever, in reaction formation, for instance, for the ego to realize that in primary process the opposites are very near to each other. So the ego will say, "All right, let's make use of that; we'll change it into the opposite." Then reaction formation can secure repression, which on its own might be insufficient, and then we get a fairly secure position. To make use of something that is there on a lower level of existence, namely the primary process, is a most practical matter. We need only allow ourselves to personify the ego to see how clever it really is in its actions!

Joseph Sandler: What may have given rise to some of the difficulty is the fact that ego and id are so constantly contrasted, particularly when we think of conflict and then of defense. It's as if there is an iron curtain in terms of knowledge of one and of the other. But in fact, as you point out very consistently in your book, most of the time they work hand in hand. Although one has one type of organization, and the other has another, you emphasize that they also work as one. You have spoken of the ego lending its functions to the instinctual drive, so we could say that the processes that we allocate to the id, the primary processes, are at times processes of the joint ego-id. Perhaps this makes it easier to understand the way in which higher level processes might keep the characteristics of lower level ones—the primary processes could be looked at as, in a sense, the joint property of both institutions for much of the time. Would that be a way of putting what you are saying, Miss Freud?

Anna Freud: Yes. I don't know whether we have enough time for examples, but there is the very simple example from children, in whom it is easy to change any of their reactions into the opposite, because they are so much nearer the primary process. Let us imagine that you have a group of children—say nursery school children, or children in one of the younger classes in school—who have a handicapped child among them. The child limps. Now children very easily make fun of the weak, and they tease the child and they mock him. The teacher who doesn't understand about that would forbid it, would say, "You mustn't do that," so when the teacher is there the children won't do it. But they will do it when the teacher is absent. The clever teacher will have a talk with the children and say, "You know, we have a weak one among us, we should all really take care of him, so that he doesn't notice that he limps." And the whole class will in two minutes begin to protect that handicapped child. Now if you take that, together with what we've said about the relation between the ego and the id, we have a very good example. The ego knows that there is this possibility of reversal and makes use of it. What I wrote is meant as simply as that.

Joseph Sandler: In the very last paragraph there's a point which is, I think, a controversial one. You tell us that the study of the defense mechanisms of the ego "impresses us with the magnitude of its achievement" (193,175). And, of course, your study of these mechanisms has equally impressed us. You then go on to talk about neurotic symptoms. It has been said that the symptom is a sort of irruption, bypassing the ego. But I am convinced now that the symptom is constructed by the unconscious ego, which is a little different.

Anna Freud: It's not an irruption, it's a compromise formation.

Joseph Sandler: Well, it has bothered me that it is said to be a compromise formation on the one hand, and yet an irruption through the ego when defenses fail, on the other. Perhaps in these last minutes we could clear the matter up, because I am sure that symptoms are very carefully constructed as last-line measures when the defenses fail. You tell us that this is done in order to preserve well-being, to avoid anxiety, in order to serve the same function the defenses served, even though the individual may suffer from the pain of the symptom.

Anna Freud: You are quite right to criticize that last paragraph. I think I simply wanted a happy ending. It's not a good paragraph at all, because it doesn't give the symptom its right place. What I meant really is that symptom formation, even though it's better than nothing, is a compromise. It avoids the worst, but of course we wouldn't call it a symptom if it didn't also cause pain and loss. What I meant was that the defense activity as a whole should not lead toward symptom formation, but should create a state of equilibrium between the inner and the outer world, between inner demands and outer demands.

Joseph Sandler: Well, I think we do have a happy ending here after all. I need hardly tell you how grateful we all are for the way in which you have clarified your book and our thinking about defenses. We are all very much richer for the discussion.

Anna Freud: So am I. It has been quite an experience.

Index